PRAISE FOR AXE OF IRON SERIES

"Author J. A. Hunsinger is an expert in the mores and customs of the Northman, the Vikings, and the Norse in general. His research is beyond reproach and he provides an educational, yet attention-getting plot. The characters are believable, filled with faults and foibles, most realistic. The descriptions of ancient North American shores are vivid, and in depth. Readers can picture the landscape, the animals, and the settlement of the settlers."

Shirley Roe, Allbooks Review

"This great historical chronicles the Norse culture of 1008 AD. Six ships of Norse families, including their livestock, horses, and dogs, sail to the American continent. The details of how they lived and supported themselves are both practical and believable. The author's writing reminds me of the great Mika Waltari, who produced so many detailed historical novels and clearly defined the genre. I found this to be a fascinating read and rated it five hearts."

Bob Spear, Heartland Reviews

"We become well-acquainted with the main characters and minor characters including credible and fierce villains. I confess to re-reading pages to recall the characters, but then became more involved in their lives, interactions and thoughts. I wanted to know how their stories would play out. And play out they did in a carefully-crafted, somewhat involved but always engrossing plot. I recall the English master E. M. Forster's definition of the novel: 'Yes—oh dear yes—the novel tells a story.' And Axe of Iron tells a story, an enthralling, believable story."

Donald Hansen, Viking Trader Review

"As historical fiction, the author successfully captures a glimpse of the life of the Norsemen. It becomes quite clear that a great deal of research went into creating the story. The attention to detail is quite remarkable. That is the author's descriptions of Norse ships, Norse customs, dress, the day to day struggles to survive that include hunting techniques, food preparation, weapons, and tools. As well, Hunsinger provides a detailed historical perspective of the time period, a glossary, and a map to assist readers in following the journey. The author clearly shows his knowledge and expertise on the subject."

Tracy Roberts, Write Field Services

"This novel is extremely well researched and provides great historical detail about the daily life of the Vikings, their sources of food and methods of cooking, tool making, hunting, and sailing. I enjoyed the story and the character development; the author did a good job of portraying the social tapestry of this hearty group of people. Packed with fascinating information about this little known time period, readers of historical fiction, nautical fiction and adventure novels would all enjoy this book."

Tome Travelers Web Log

ASSIMILATION

ASSIMILATION

An Axe of Iron Novel

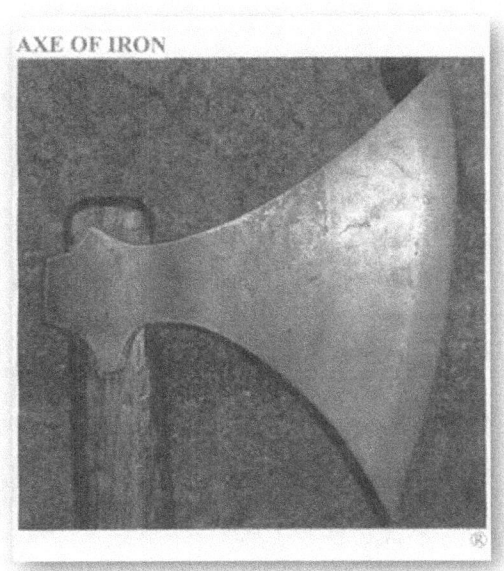

J A HUNSINGER

Disclaimer

This is a work of fiction. The characters, incidents, and dialogue, while possibly having parallels in history, are products of the author's imagination and are not to be construed as real. Any resemblance to actual persons, except those who are mentioned in an historical context, living or dead, is entirely coincidental.

Published by
Vinland Publishing
661 Tamarron Drive
Grand Junction, CO 81506

ISBN: 0988945525

ISBN 13: 9780988945524

Library of Congress Control Number: 2016908954

Printed in the United States of America.

AUTHOR'S NOTE

This novel is the last book in the Axe of Iron series. As always, before reading *Assimilation,* I encourage you to read or reread the *Historical Perspective* that is included in the first volume of the series, *The Settlers*, to provide you with a historical sense of what this work of fiction is all about.

You will have trouble with the names of the characters, all of us do, especially the pre-historical Indian names. They are authentic, or a diminutive of an authentic name or term. How are they pronounced? I do not know. I have my way of pronouncing them and so will you. I implore you not to allow the names and terms to detract from what I have tried to fashion for you, the story of a people.

Each book of the series is a stand-alone tale; however, in keeping with the first two novels of the series, *Assimilation* begins where *Confrontation* ended.

J. A. Hunsinger
2016

DEDICATION

This book is dedicated to my brother, Tom Hunsinger, who passed away unexpectedly November 15, 2011. It is always difficult to lose a sibling, especially when that sibling is younger. I would have finished this work several years ago had it not been for his loss. I put my writing aside for quite some time, because my brother did my Indian research and I could not see a reason to continue without his input. I have no other excuse for taking 5-years to complete this novel.

Thanks to all of my fans that gave me a nudge, too, asking, "When will Assimilation be finished?" Here it is, Ya'll!

My thanks also must go to Debi DeSantis, Wild Orchid Design, for creating and formatting the beautiful cover of the book that you hold in your hand.

As always I thank my wife, Phyllis. She kept me on the straight and narrow insofar as the English language is concerned and provided her editing expertise to tighten up the many mistakes I made in my prose. Were it not for her frequent nudges — I will characterize them in that way - I never would have completed this three book series. And, this final tale is for them, the Norse Greenlanders that came to this continent so long ago, finally disappearing into the mists of time in the process. They are still out there somewhere, and I will feel them in my soul to the end of my days.

J. A. Hunsinger

2016

FOREWORD

O ver the course of 1000-years, about 50-generations as such things are reckoned by us humans, the great expanse of the Canadian north, specifically Quebec province where this story takes place, undergoes enormous changes both to its landmass and to its native peoples.

Between approximately 800-1300AD, the exact time span depending on what political view you are pushing, the Medieval Warm Period freed the people of the northern hemisphere from the severity of winter that had previously held sway. As often happens in nature, well, naturally, that benevolent period was followed by the Maunder Minimum, or as it is more commonly called, the Mini-Ice Age.

The Mini-Ice Age was a fact of life for much of the Northern Hemisphere between approximately 1300-1800AD when truly savage winter weather in the form of cold temperatures, snow, and ice gripped the affected regions of the planet.

To digress, the Medieval Warm period may have fostered the rise of the people we call Vikings, as it freed those folks from their icebound harbors much sooner than normal and allowed them to explore further afield before the onset of another winter again trapped them in their home fjords. The benign weather and their advances in shipbuilding certainly played major parts in this momentous 400-year period that we now call the Viking Age.

A recent discovery by Dr. Sarah Parcak, a renowned space archaeologist who has previously used space imagery to make important discoveries here on Earth, was made at Point Rosee on the southwestern coast of Newfoundland, Canada, using the same type of imagery. Based on preliminary findings on site Point Rosee promises to be Norse in origin. Her team will be excavating up there this summer, and perhaps we will have corroborating data that the site is definitely of Norse origin by this fall.

Dr. Parcak is looking for the Vinland of the Norse sagas. That's fine, but the Norse did not call North America, Vinland. Nobody knows what they called it because they wrote nothing down. Certainly they told tales of their exploits, but none were written at the time they occurred. If Vinland exists at all, it is an area, not a specific place. The sagas that people use for guidance nowadays were not written by the Norse in question, but by scholars and others 200-300-years after the facts that they portend to be reporting. The German clergyman, Adam of Bremen is singularly responsible for much, or perhaps all, of the myth of Vinland, its grapes, and self-sown wheat. The sagas are useful fiction, not facts as some people pretend they are.

If one believes the sagas, then this site of Dr. Parcak's could be either *Hop* or *Straumfjord*. Both were mentioned in the *Groenlendinga Saga* with *Leifsbudir* (old Norse-Leif's Booths), the settlement of Leif Eriksson, which was found on the northeastern tip of Newfoundland in 1960 by the Ingstads of Norway. The other two settlements have never been found.

So, perhaps Dr. Parcak has found either Hop (old Norse – tide pools) or Straumfjord (old Norse – stream fjord). If you have an interest in the whole concept of the Norse sagas, I go into them in some detail in my *Historical Perspective*, in the first book of the *Axe of Iron* series, *The Settlers*.

Like the first two books of the *Axe of Iron* series, *Assimilation* features a Table of Contents and a Glossary of Norse and Indian terms that many readers may be unfamiliar with. Toward the end of this tale, the reader will also encounter an occasional footnote to identify a geographical feature in contemporary terms.

Happy reading...
J. A. Hunsinger
Colorado, USA

N

Kitchi Gami

100 Leagues

CONTENTS

Chapter 1

NEAR A HAUDENOSAUNEE VILLAGE, EARLY WINTER

One hundred seventy-five leagues southeast of the Naskapi village of Sachem, two Naskapi warriors lay concealed in the thick brush near the top of a knoll overlooking a lake and heavily forested river valley. Travel to this place at night by canoe had minimized the chance of detection. During the fourth night of travel they concealed their canoe well back from the river and crept overland through the familiar countryside to their destination. They carefully checked their immediate area for security before selecting a spot in the thickest forest that offered concealment from all directions. Satisfied, they covered themselves with leaves and fell into exhausted sleep.

A drizzly mist had cloaked the river valley for much of the night. The leaden skies promised more of the same. At first light a slight breeze rose out of the valley, stirring the damp air. The light of the rising sun filtering through the cloud cover elongated the shadows of each tree in the thick forest as the darkness receded west. A perception of weak warmth came with the sun.

A smell of smoke borne on the morning breeze awakened one of the sleeping warriors. He unfolded silently from the deep bed of leaves and crawled slowly forward to get a better view of the village below. The other man joined him a moment later. In the increasing light of dawn they watched the sprawl-ing village of their arch enemies. The light of day began to bring definition to the shadows that cloaked the village. Familiar details remembered from previous raids, for both had been here before, began to sharpen.

"We must get closer, Manshipit," Atkaa whispered. "We will not be able to see him from here."

"It is too risky. If their sentries see us we are dead." Manshipit beckoned toward the two guards they had identified. "The boy's hair is the same color as Ingerd's hair and his skin is pale. He should be easy to see if he is in this village. We will wait here to see what happens."

His companion did not comment.

In the silence, Manshipit's mind wandered to the recent past, to the canoe journey back home from the village of Chisasi with the Northmen, Ingerd and Lothar. Sachem, the supreme chieftain of all the Naskapi bands had decreed that the two be brought to visit Nipishish, their former prisoner and Ingerd's husband, during the Time of Falling Leaves. On the final day of the journey, Manshipit and his three companions had talked over the capture of Ivar and what they could do to find out what happened to him. Ingerd and Lothar had been able to follow much of the conversation as the day wore on. Kejo, the man in nominal command of the party, felt that a war party of Haudeno warriors under the infamous war chief, Sakohkea, had probably been the ones to capture Ivar given that his was the closest Haudeno band to Sachem's village. It had been decided by mutual consent that Manshipit and Atkaa would trek overland to a lake where canoes were kept hidden and then journey south to scout the Haudenosaunee village for the presence of the boy, as Kejo had promised Ingerd. Kejo, Ingerd, Lothar, and Miknap would continue to the village of Sachem. The boy Lothar had made his mother understand what the men planned to do and Ingerd's effusive appreciation had made the four Naskapi warriors uncomfort-able. They muttered among themselves good-naturedly, taking her reaction as typical of what they understood about the Northmen, who seemed more prone to expressions of their feelings than the Naskapi, where stoicism was more the norm. Manshipit smiled to himself over how complicated the story had become.

I was there for all of it and I cannot keep the details straight in my mind, he thought, shaking his head at the twists of life.

His companion looked at him quizzically. Manshipit shook his head at his friend's questioning look.

They continued to watch the village in silence. Smoke rose lazily into the still, damp air from the longhouse smoke holes as overnight embers were stirred to life and the fires rekindled.

Both men were soaked to the skin and although they wore leggings and hip length pullovers, they were chilled. Their pullovers became a shapeless, sodden mass as water penetrated the oily leather. In spite of that, their clothing afforded insulation from the creeping cold. The misery that came with being cold had little effect on them. Lethargy from inactivity accompanied their discomfort in differing degrees, causing them to doze off occasionally only to jerk awake a moment later as their innate situational awareness came to the fore, for their lives depended on it.

The upslope breeze carried the curling wisps of smoke toward their place of concealment. Soon, a whiff of cooking came to them as the Haudenosaunee village awakened and the people began their day's activities.

The smell of food borne on the heavy air made the two men salivate. They ignored their grumbling stomachs for a time, but the smell gradually overcame self-control. Manshipit rolled onto his back to gain access to the contents of the pouch at his belt. He tore a chunk of pemmican in two and passed a piece to his companion. Atkaa supplied two strips of jerky from his pouch. They chewed slowly, savoring the rich taste that flooded their mouths as the pemmican and tough jerky mixed with their saliva.

Below their vantage point there was little to observe. A trickle of people moved back and forth between the wigwams, but most had not ventured outside in the intermittent drizzle.

Midday came and went; the drizzle finally stopped and the skies opened. The warmth of the sun started the droplets of water clinging to every surface to begin to evaporate; a mist swirled out over the valley, periodically cloaking the village from the two watchers.

Shadows lengthened as the day wore on. The mist finally cleared in a freshening breeze, bringing the village back into sharp focus. The men took turns napping. The village guards were changed.

Later, two women carrying baskets walked from one of the wigwams and out the gate, turning up the slope. They followed a well-worn path in the general direction of the men's hiding place. The Haudeno women, one young and the other somewhat older, walked slowly through the tall grass and low-growing bushes, obviously looking for something in the mast of the forest floor.

Fully alert now, the men remained still as the women passed out of sight under the brow of the hill. The only way they could have kept them in sight would be to stand and they could not do that. The men made eye contact, but nothing was said as they waited for the women to reappear.

A moment later the sound of voices and occasional laughter came to the men as the women topped the knoll and continued into the forest. They alternately appeared and disappeared through the dense brush as their position shifted relative to the watcher's place of concealment.

Manshipit whispered urgently to his companion. "They will tell us if the boy is in the village."

Atkaa grunted in agreement. The two rose from the ground, and quickly secured their bows in quiver scabbards. For this task they preferred to use the belt axe that each wore. They stole silently after their oblivious quarry. Separating slightly, each man focused on one of the women as they crept rapidly forward in a crouch.

Conditions could not have been better for stealth as the two warriors closed the distance to their prey. The forest floor and its thick mat of dry leaves were still wet from the recent drizzle. The men's buckskin clothing was also damp, making the scrape of a twig or branch soundless.

Manshipit signed suddenly to Atkaa that the older of the two had a knife in her right hand as she stooped to cut something loose at her feet.

A single bob of Atkaa's chin indicated his understanding.

The women's low-voiced conversation served to cloak any slight sound coming from the approach and simultaneous attack of the Naskapi warriors.

The older of the two women, hearing or sensing the attack, wheeled on Atkaa at the moment before contact, snarling like a cornered animal as recognition dawned. As quick as the beat of a humming bird's wing, her knife hand swept forward in a vicious backhand slice.

Atkaa tried to leap back. He almost made it, narrowly avoiding being disemboweled. She struck so quickly that her keen knifepoint opened the leather of his pullover like a grinning mouth and scribed a red line across his stomach. The knife entangled in the wet buckskin as he grabbed her wrist. At the same moment, the flat of his belt axe thudded into her forehead and she collapsed unconscious at his feet.

Manshipit had clubbed the younger of the two unconscious before she could even turn to face him. He grinned at Atkaa.

The man stood over his target, examining his pullover and the shallow cut across his stomach. "That was close. She almost got me," Atkaa looked down at his erstwhile attacker. He stooped to remove the knife clutched in her hand.

"It looks like she did get you." Manshipit bent forward to poke a finger at the long cut. Atkaa pushed his hand away. Manshipit chuckled. "I think you will live." He poked the inert form at their feet with the toe of his moccasin. "She is something. If her arm or knife blade were a little longer, you would be trying to keep your guts from falling on the ground right now. How would you like to live with a woman like that?"

"I would not want to live with her." He stooped and picked her head up by the hair. "Her forehead is split open. I may have hit her too hard."

"No matter, we will kill them anyway."

"Of course we will." He looked up at his companion. "Now she needs to be alive. She cannot answer questions if she is dead." Atkaa dropped her head back on the ground.

"I do not think this one will tell us anything anyway," Manshipit looked down at her. "She is a tough woman." He looked around. "Find a pole to carry her. Dead or alive we cannot leave her to spread the alarm. I will tie the young one up before she awakens. We must get out of here before someone comes looking for these two."

Atkaa quickly cut and limbed a pole long enough to carry the woman between them. The two men trussed her hands and feet securely over the pole. Atkaa pulled the now conscious young woman to her feet. He gripped her chin in his hand. "Do not make a sound. Do not try to escape or we will cut your throat. Do you understand?"

She turned frightened eyes on him and bobbed her head.

"Good, we go now." He tied a tether around her neck and looped the other end through his belt. "Follow right behind me." He pointed to his companion. "He will be watching you." She nodded again. He stooped and picked up one end of the pole, while Manshipit picked up the other.

The men moved off at a trot, with Atkaa in the lead and the girl following behind him. The unconscious woman hung from the pole, swinging back and forth as they made the best possible time overland toward the river and their hidden canoe.

Just after sundown, they came to the place where they had hidden the canoe. Dropping the unconscious prisoner on the ground at the river's edge they launched the canoe. Intent only on putting as much distance as possible between themselves and the Haudeno village, they quickly boarded with their prisoners and set off upriver, staying in midstream to avoid the rocks and snags along the shore.

Visibility on the river was terrible, a matter a few canoe lengths. Low clouds rolled in with the darkness, and the drizzle returned. The rattle and sigh of the droplets against the canoe and river's surface were almost hypnotic.

"Paddle!" Manshipit handed the prisoner the extra paddle.

She complied without comment.

Atkaa turned and tossed the bark scoop used to bail accumulated water out of the canoe's bilge in her lap. His intent needed no explanation. He rode in front, guiding the canoe by instinct and the low sound of the slow-moving river. The girl rode in the middle with her still unconscious companion, and Manshipit had the stern position. There was no conversation, the grueling pace saw to that. They stopped for nothing.

This stretch of river was deep and slow. There would be no portages to slow them down. Later that first night, they stopped at a mid-river island to take a short rest and question the girl. Atkaa tied her securely to a tree. He and Manshipit dumped the unconscious woman out of the canoe on the ground and then carried the canoe back in the brush a ways so it could not be seen from the river.

Manshipit crouched down to examine the other prisoner as best he could in the darkness. "She is barely breathing. You hit her too hard. I do not think she is going to awaken."

"She is of no use to us, then. Pick her up, we will give her to the river." Without further comment, they picked up the woman and threw her in the river.

Manshipit chuckled. "Maybe she can swim."

"Not with her hands and feet tied." Atkaa showed his white teeth. "They will never find her body. It will catch under a snag and the fish and other creatures of the water will eat the flesh."

The other prisoner had watched the men, her expression a mixture of disbelief and terror, as they threw her friend in the river and then turned toward her.

"Now it is your turn to tell us what we want to know." Atkaa untied her from the tree and jerked her to her feet. "We will ask you only once. If you do not answer truthfully you will join the other one in the river after we have finished with you."

Manshipit leered at her; a knowing smile curved the corners of his cruel mouth.

She looked from one to the other, knowing these men would show her no mercy. The grinning one looked especially cruel. It was he who asked the first question.

Manshipit pulled her close to his face. "We came to your village to find a pale-skin boy with hair the color of ripe corn. Have you seen such a one?" His sour breath assaulted her.

She nodded quickly.

The two men made eye contact, a look of satisfaction passed between them.

"Tell us about him," Manshipit said, releasing his grip on her shift.

She gathered herself, steeling her mind for the end she felt would follow. "A war party captured him. He is adopted into our band to replace the lost son of Odatshedeh."

"So, the boy is well?" Atkaa watched her closely.

She nodded again.

"How is this boy called?" Manshipit asked.

"Ivar, he is called Ivar."

The men again made eye contact at this final confirmation. They said nothing.

The girl watched the silent exchange. Glancing from man-to-man she averted her eyes, waiting for one of them to strike.

Manshipit grinned at his companion. "She waits to die. We will not kill you. A good slave is always welcome in our village. You have saved your life by answering our questions." He pulled her forward and untied her bonds and tether. "Do not try to escape, you would fail."

Atkaa laughed aloud at the look on the girl's face. "If you try to escape you will be caught. We will not kill you, then. Both ankle tendons will be cut and we will leave you for the wolves." He watched the effect of his words on her. "We go now."

As the trio paddled away from the island the young prisoner fought to still her trembling body. She gripped the paddle tightly to suppress the terror that threatened to boil to the surface of her mind. With an effort of will she calmed her thudding heart. As calm settled over her, she grappled with thoughts of her dead friend, her family, her village, and her people. For the moment she felt alive, regardless of what the future had in store for her. She resolved to face captivity with her head held high, proud of what and who she was. Her people would expect no less of her.

<hr />

Chapter 2

NASKAPI VILLAGE OF SACHEM

Nipishish, formerly the Northman, Gudbjartur Einarsson, had done his best to appear stoic and unconcerned, but he fooled nobody. They all knew what occupied his thoughts. He had tried to keep busy, to maintain some control over his raging emotions. Although Glooscap had told him that he need not help the village women any longer, given his earned status as a warrior of the people, he had insisted that he wanted to help them finish the new wigwam and harvest their gardens.

In time, the wigwam was finished, the families moved into it, and the framework of the old became firewood. While waiting for the remaining garden produce to mature he spent his days hunting and fishing with the men. Their canoes plied the shorelines of lake and river at dawn and dusk to harvest the moose, caribou, deer, and bear stealing from the dense forest to drink.

The bear, fattened on the bounty of summer, was especially sought after. Time was short for they would soon seek their winter dens, sleeping securely through the time of twilight and cold, not to be seen again until the solitary males and females with their cubs ventured out in early spring

For night hunts, jack-lights in birch bark containers of sand, rigged from two small poles lashed along each side of the canoe and extended forward from the bow, lit the shoreline, almost guaranteeing close-in killing shots on the game animals revealed by the flickering light. He thought this hunting method especially clever, given that the white birch bark reflector, a part of the container of sand, reflected the relatively bright light of the burning pitch-pine faggot forward and away from the hunters and into the eyes of any game animals at the water's edge. Much of their hunting successes came in this way.

Large fish rolling on the surface were also regularly harvested with a barbed fish spear when they broached in the illumination of the jack-light to seize the small fish gathered to eat the insects attracted by the light. The well-aimed blow of a club dispatched them before serious damage to the canoe resulted from the fight to subdue these powerful predators, oftentimes the length of a man.

Although the company of the men, after his long association with the women, was particularly favored, the necessity for stealth ensured that hunting and fishing were endeavors that did not contribute much to the further-ance of his conversational abilities. Most of the men had little to say anyway. Not that they were unfriendly--he had been readily accepted by every man after the battle with the Haudenosaunee raiding party--rather, most were tac-iturn by nature. Finding humor in the everyday tedium of hunting and butch-ering, the men were especially keen to joke with each other over the slightest mishap or mistake, especially if the occasion allowed them to transfer the brunt of attention to a companion and away from themselves. Except for obvi-ous differences in appearance and language he thought the Naskapi men to be remarkably similar to his own people in their interrelations. Perhaps all tribes were like that.

Late in the afternoon, the dozen or so hunters of the party were scattered about a small clearing just inland from the shoreline of a large lake, resting as they waited for darkness. Five canoes lay scattered about at the water's edge, drawn far enough up the bank to keep them from floating away. Some of the men were snoozing while others repaired equipment or conversed in low tones. They planned to use the late afternoon hours and the dark of night, when the game animals they sought came from their bed grounds to wa-ter before beginning to forage, to hunt them when they were at their most vulnerable – thirsty and hungry.

Nipishish lounged against the trunk of an uprooted tree. Nearby, his friend Glooscap lay stretched out in the grass of the clearing. To a casual observer he would appear to be asleep, but Nipishish knew better. The man had the senses of a fox, alert for the slightest danger; he seemed to sleep with one eye open. It felt good to be among these men. Like the Norsemen, these Naskapi men were hunters and warriors. He admired their abilities. As he had grown to know all of them on a personal basis he saw how like his many friends at Halfdansfjord they were. He unconsciously sorted them out in his mind as the hunt progressed or languished through midday into early evening while they rested, taking note of each man's defining contribution to the whole -- humor, honesty, bluster, insincerity, leadership, dependability – all the human traits of which he was aware were present. It satisfied him to realize that his companions possessed many of the foibles common to any similar group that he had encountered in his travels, regardless of the culture. *It is why I am comfortable with them. They have become like my own people; I am one with them.* His low chuckle at this revelation brought a questioning glance from Glooscap.

"It is nothing, my friend. I find humor in how much smarter I am with the passage of each day," Nipishish said, grinning at Glooscap.

The war chief snorted. "Not everyone is that lucky. Some people never learn anything new," Glooscap said, watching his companion with amusement.

Before either man could continue, a low hiss from the water side of the clearing drew instant attention to the frantic gestures of Kejo, who mimed the swinging gait of a bear.

Every hunter in the clearing melted into the grass or froze in various attitudes of alertness as they strained to see the bear through the thick underbrush and trees between them and the lake.

A light breeze blowing onshore from the lake effectively masked the presence of the bear's mortal enemies so close at hand. The slight lapping of small wavelets against the shore also masked any sound that might have come from the surprised group of hunters.

Nipishish uncoiled from his place against the tree trunk. Using the bole of the downed tree as concealment and standing on tiptoe he caught sight of movement through the brush. The biggest brown bear he had ever seen ambled unconcernedly in the water along the shoreline. Certain the bear was a solitary male, he watched the animal stop occasionally to turn over a rock or piece of driftwood. Nipishish ducked down behind the tree bole again, certain the bear's poor eyesight had not detected any movement from him or his companions. His glance went to Glooscap, who had just ducked down after he caught sight of the bear. Glooscap grinned and gave a single shake of his head; an indication to Nipishish that he, too, thought this was a big one.

Glooscap did not need to attract the attention of his men; all watched him attentively, waiting for him to decide their course of action. Pointing to Nipishish he mimed shooting an arrow.

Every man knew the powerful bow of the Northman was the best weapon at their disposal to place the first, vital shot into the bear. The longbow in the hands of Nipishish was capable of shooting a heavy hunting arrow a great distance with an accuracy and force unmatchable with any Naskapi bow and arrow.

Nipishish nodded in understanding, quickly selected one of his new arrows with the flint points made especially for him by the tribe's best flint knapper and began crawling toward his target, intent on finding a spot to make a clear shot.

The others fanned out, following behind him as they all stole toward the bear.

Nipishish gained the cover of the low brush at the forest verge, slowly came to his feet behind the brush and waited for the bear's position to present a good shot.

Meanwhile, the bear had straddled a large piece of driftwood grounded at the shoreline, picked up one end in his jaws and waddled up on the beach with it. He sat down and began to tear chunks off the rotten wood to get at the grubs and worms that had taken up residence within.

Nipishish glanced toward Glooscap and shook his head slightly, indicating to his waiting companions that he did not have a shot yet.

After a time, the bear lost interest in the driftwood and resumed his quest along the shoreline. The loud splash of a fish close to shore caused him to turn toward the sound. At that moment, a sharp pain in his right side caused him to grunt loudly and wheel away from the arrow that cut into his vitals. Confused, he wheeled about on the beach, biting at the feathered shaft protruding from his side. The flexing muscles of his great body caused the arrowhead at the end of the shaft to whip from side-to-side, cutting his vitals to pieces in the process.

Nipishish quickly followed his first arrow with another that sliced into the bear's back, disappearing from view as it plunged into his vitals. Mortally wounded, the animal's movements slowed.

Glooscap chose this moment to burst screaming from hiding with his men. They fanned out in a semi-circle at the shoreline around their prey, cutting off all avenues of escape. The men shouted and feinted to taunt the bear, jabbing him with spears and shooting arrows into him at every opportunity.

With loud roars of rage the animal spent his energy rushing first one man and then another, only to absorb more punishment from behind as each attack was foiled. Each rush pumped more blood from his many wounds, rapidly weakening him. Bloody froth poured from nostrils and mouth, covering his head and chest. Suddenly, he sat down, no longer able to respond to his tormenters. Slowly, his head sank. His front legs, no longer capable of supporting his upper body, folded under him. His purple tongue lolled to the side of his jaws and the great head came to rest on the ground as the life force left the king of the forest.

As one, the men drew back, watching silently as the great animal died. As they gathered around him, each in his turn touched the carcass with a weapon in tribute to the spirit of the great bear. Some dipped a finger in his blood to mark their faces or bodies in the belief that his bravery would be conveyed to them in that way. All gave thanks to his spirit, for the meat he provided was vital to the survival of the people.

Later, gathered around the cooking fires in two groups, the men roasted liver, tongue and heart, gorging on the spoils of the kill.

Increasingly cooler nights put a finish to the garden crops. His need to help the women harvest the last of the squash and pumpkins from the scattered gardens called him away from the hunt. From a period of relative quiet and calm with the men, his plunge back into the daily world of the women and his work on the harvest had just the opposite effect insofar as his growing facility with the Naskapi language. Their constant chatter provided him a growing level of expertise with the language that would not have been possible otherwise. He smiled at the thought. *Why, their gossip alone ensured that I have had to gain facility with the hand signs and speech in order to spend any time at all with them. Much of their gossip is at my expense.* He glanced up in time to catch Meshika's eye as she twisted a pumpkin loose from the tough vine.

Her mouth twisted in a smile. She dropped her eyes back to her work.

He had found that pulling the vines and cornstalks from the ground as he searched for pumpkins and squash hiding in the debris from the growing season simplified this end of harvest work. The vines and stalks accumulated in piles that would later be burned to ash to enrich the soil while the produce went into the baskets scattered about. After a time the garden plots looked like a rampaging bear or a whirlwind had done the harvest.

The women watched him in amazement as he tore through the garden. He smiled at their chatter, adding comments here and there.

Thoughts of Ingerd, his sons, and Halfdan returned to mind. Since Glooscap had told him about Kejo's journey to Halfdansfjord at Sachem's behest, he had thought of little else. Sachem had decreed that Ingerd and his sons could visit the village during the Time of Falling Leaves. That time was about over. As was his daily habit concerning the weather, just this morning he had noted a surge of cold winter air from the north that carried the promise of an early winter. *If they do not arrive soon, they may be trapped somewhere by a snowstorm.* He straightened from his crouched position among the pumpkin and squash vines and rubbed his lower back as he looked out over the gardens and his busy companions.

"Nipishish." Meshika called softly.

He glanced at her. She responded with a lift of her chin back toward the village. Turning around he saw a smiling Ingerd and Lothar standing together with Kejo. His heart seemed to jump into his throat and a chill coursed through his body. He stood rooted for a heartbeat, thinking it all a dream, an hallucination.

Ingerd, unable to contain herself another moment, shrieked his name and ran toward him. They came together about midway.

"Oh Gudbj, my love, my life!" She leaped into his arms. Her eyes brimmed, but the tears were belied by the radiant smile she beamed at him as her eyes searched his face.

A low moan escaped this man who could be hard and violent, now overcome by a wave of emotion he seldom felt as he clasped her to his chest and drank in her smell. Their mouths hungrily explored. Breathless, he held her at arms-length, a mist seemed to dim his vision as he looked at her. "You were never out of my thoughts, Ingerd, even through the worst days after I was captured. Memories of you sustained me when I despaired. You are my love, my woman." He kissed her again.

"It was the same for me. I never gave up, nor did Halfdan. He swore to me that he thought the gods had chosen you for a special task for our people." She turned slightly and indicated Kejo with a lift of her chin. "When Kejo came with Chisasi and told us that Sachem's band had captured you, I felt as though I had been reborn. Much has happened since you and your men left Halfdansfjord."

He threw his head back and laughed happily. "Much has happened here, too. I cannot wait to tell you everything."

Ingerd looked him up and down. "You look different, Gudbj."

"It must be my new clothes." He held his arms out and turned back and forth.

She fingered the buckskin pullover. "No, I have seen their clothing before and I like it. That is not what I mean. You seem different to me. You act differently."

"I **am** different, Ingerd. This experience and my association with these fine people have made me different. I regard myself as one with them and I think you will feel the same after a time."

"I already have friends among Chisasi's band, so I doubt this band will be any different."

"Good! As you say, there is much to talk about." He held out an arm to Lothar, who still stood beside Kejo. "Come here, son!"

Lothar grinned at Kejo, who lifted his chin toward Gudbjartur. The deep lines around his mouth softened as the boy ran to his father and mother.

Still having difficulty with the mist restricting his vision, Gudbjartur wrapped his arms around the two of them. The three were without words for a moment, overcome by emotion and oblivious to their surroundings, until he realized that a crowd had quietly gathered. He looked about him at these people he had come to love; from the village, the women he had been working with, and Kejo, who had remained nearby. He suddenly realized what he had missed at the joyous reunion with Ingerd. "Where is Ivar?" His eyes searched the crowd for sight of his other son. Coldness gripped his heart as his eyes settled on Ingerd's face.

Ingerd glanced toward Kejo then looked back into her husband's eyes. Her eyes slowly filled and her face twisted in the anguish that seized her mind and heart once again. "He has been captured by a Haudeno raiding party."

Gudbjartur's face reflected disbelief for a heartbeat and then the rage for which he was famous overwhelmed him. He glanced quickly around the garden clearing while he grappled with self-control. He glanced wildly from Ingerd to Lothar. Without conscious thought he seized Ingerd by the upper arms. "How did this happen?"

She squirmed in discomfort. "You are hurting me, Gudbj!" The pain was apparent in her voice.

A look of concern crossed his face; he turned her loose. "I am sorry, Ingerd," he said, contrite and uncomfortable. His eyes beseeched her to answer.

She made eye contact with Lothar.

"Ivar was captured on the hunting trip with Gudrod." Lothar looked unflinchingly into his father's eyes.

Gudbjartur was visibly surprised that Ingerd expected Lothar to do the talking. He looked the boy up and down. A slight lift of his chin bade his son to continue.

Lothar took a breath. "Ivar was alone on the riverbank after a canoe upset. They captured him then. We went right after them, but the men who had Ivar got away. There were two of them."

"Why did you not catch them?" Gudbjartur asked.

"A war party ambushed us. We fought them for a time and then they disappeared into the forest. Skeggi tracked the two men until they got in a canoe with Ivar."

"What did Gudrod do then?"

"Gudrod was killed in the ambush, and so were Ofeiger and Sturla. Bjarni was wounded by an arrow and Bersi drowned in the river." Lothar literally blurted the details. Breathless, he paused, closely watching the play of emotion across his father's face.

Silent for a moment while he grappled with what Lothar had told him, Gudbjartur glanced from one to the other. "Gudrod is dead?" His friend's death was hard to accept. All the men had been his friends, but none like Gudrod.

"Aye, he died fighting, with sword in hand," the boy said.

Gudbjartur nodded slowly. He sighed and looked out over the silent people watching the three of them and then back to Ingerd and Lothar.

Ingerd had not said a word to interrupt Lothar; rather she seemed content to let him tell his father what had happened. Her quiet bearing, amidst the anguish reflected on her face, bespoke a pride in her remaining son.

Gudbjartur squeezed her shoulder in understanding. He studied Lothar, as if looking at his son for the first time. *He has grown in mind and body since I last saw him. The boy is no more. He has the mind of a man now.*

Ingerd indicated Kejo with a lift of her chin. "Kejo sent two men to find Ivar; they left us at midday yesterday."

"Come, let us talk to him," Gudbjartur said. He took Ingerd's hand and the three of them walked toward Kejo.

Gudbjartur greeted Kejo with a nod. "Thank you for bringing my family here, Kejo."

The man smiled at Gudbjartur. "I heard you mention Ivar, Nipishish. I sent Manshipit and Atkaa to find him," he said.

Gudbjartur nodded slightly in acknowledgement. "When will they return?"

Kejo shrugged. "A few days, perhaps by the new moon, I do not know."

Ingerd looked at her husband, a slight frown on her face. "I forgot that you have a new name. And, I am surprised how well you speak the Naskapi language."

Gudbjartur chuckled. "Aye, it is the only language I have heard and Sachem has decreed that I will learn it. I am called Nipishish here, but all of the people know that I am also Gudbj. To you I will always be Gudbj, though. Kejo understands much of what you are saying and so do others. We have all learned together. You must meet them, they are a great people and we are lucky to be friends with them." Gudbjartur turned and motioned to the others scattered through the garden that had borne silent witness to the reunion. "Meshika, Ekuanit, all of you, come meet my other family."

Ingerd's eyes fastened on a smiling woman who carried a basket of squash as she walked toward them. The two made eye contact and Ingerd knew immediately that they were kindred spirits.

Meshika stopped next to Gudbjartur and set her basket down. He put his arm around her. She did the same. "Ingerd, this is Meshika. She is the woman of our war chief, Glooscap. I lived in the longhouse of Glooscap when I came here. She helped me learn many things about her people. She is my friend."

Ingerd took Meshika's hands in hers. They smiled into each other's eyes.

"Nipishish has told us of you, Ingerd. You are welcome in our village." Meshika said, smiling her greeting as she examined the mate of Nipishish. She liked what she saw in the other woman.

Kejo made eye contact with Nipishish. "A council of the men has been called, they are assembling." He glanced at Lothar, the boy who was fast becoming a man in mind and body. His words acknowledged that fact to all within earshot. "You come, too."

Lothar smiled and inclined his head in assent.

Nipishish watched the exchange with interest. *Yes, many things have changed.* He and his son made eye contact. A slight smile drew the corners of his mouth as he regarded his son. He clapped him on the shoulder and turned to the group of women.

"Ingerd, go with Meshika until the council is finished. There will be a feast and Meshika will have much to share with you. Speak slowly to her, you will find that she knows much of our language." He laughed as he looked at his wife and the other smiling women. "There will be plenty of time to catch up later; the rest of our lives, I think."

———

Several days passed. At the council meeting Sachem had queried Nipishish and Kejo closely on what was known about the Haudeno war party that captured Ivar. The fact that the enemy warriors passed close by the Naskapi village on their way north, without detection, had the council visibly upset, with each member having his say. As always Sachem was the grounding force, saying nothing as the others vented, giving each man all the time he wanted. After all had their say, Sachem told the assembly that he would think on this problem and wait until Manshipit and Atkaa returned before deciding on a course of action.

Nipishish had come away from the council relieved that Kejo had taken it upon himself to send two of his men to reconnoiter the Haudeno village for the presence of Ivar. He felt that a course of action was still possible to free his son before the onset of winter. His pride in his other son was evident to all who attended the council. Lothar had understood much of what was being said. Though obviously awed to be in close proximity to the supreme chief of all the Naskapi, the boy came forward when called, stood tall, answered questions, and relayed the story of Ivar's capture in a mix of both languages. Many of those present offered him helpful assistance where necessary when he faltered or hesitated in the telling.

The feast that followed the council meeting spanned the better part of two days as the people welcomed the new arrivals to the village with dancing, storytelling, and visiting. A kind of collective sigh of contentment, occasioned by respite from the normal daily toil, and lethargy brought about by the gluttony of the feast, gripped the revelers. Vast amounts of fresh garden produce, and the fish and game of river, lake, and forest were consumed.

When it was all over and the daily issues of life had assumed a normalcy once again, a kind of frenzy gripped everyone as supplies of foodstuffs for the Time of Whiteness that ensured survival continued to accumulate. The men went out in groups each day to hunt and fish. The smoke filled air of the village and the sagging racks of smoking and drying strips of meat and fish were a testament to their success. Bears were especially sought after. Their delicious flesh, with its thick layer of fat accumulated from foraging over the late summer and fall before they denned up for hibernation was a valuable food source.

Ingerd had quickly adapted to the life of the village and was readily accepted by all the women as the mate of Nipishish. The tedious, repetitious tasks associated with converting the fresh meat and fish to a dried state that would keep almost indefinitely provided ample opportunities for Ingerd to become acquainted with all the village's women and girls, for they did all the work. As quantities of dried meat accumulated, it was pulverized and then mixed with dried berries in bowl-like green hides suspended in supporting frameworks throughout the village, where melted bear, deer, and moose fat was mixed in to the desired consistency. When the pemmican mixture cooled, the loose ends of the hide were gathered together and securely tied. This staple lasted for many moons suspended from the inside framework of each longhouse until finally consumed over the long winter.

Ingerd was enchanted by the variety and overall quantity the gardens added to the Naskapi diet, soon looking forward to the strange and delicious tastes of these previously unknown foods. Meshika had assured her that this plenty only came during the Time of Falling Leaves and after a successful harvest.

The principle crops of corn, squash, beans, sunflower, and rice, surplus to the tribe's daily needs were stored by the women under the floor of each longhouse in large stone-lined storage pits, kept sealed to exclude mice and other varmints.

Until the autumn harvest the people subsisted almost entirely on the meat of large game animals and the fish of stream and lake brought in daily by hunting parties. In addition to other duties the woman and children foraged daily along the lakeshores and woodland verges in ever-widening circles for edible roots, mushrooms and greens. All manner of birds and small game were harvested by the arrows and snares of the older boys and girls; their efforts added variety, but little quantity to the diet.

Late one morning, Manshipit and Atkaa returned with their prisoner; several women took her away. Her treatment and survival as a slave would depend entirely on her attitude and how hard she worked.

Glooscap called another council for later in the day, after the hunting and forage parties returned.

This time the council house bulged at the seams and overflowed at the entry. Everybody wanted to hear what the two men had learned.

Nipishish, Ingerd, and Lothar sat in the front row, right in front of the council, patiently waiting for the storytelling to begin. He had explained the process in a low voice to Ingerd and Lothar, emphasizing that this part could not be hurried.

Lothar said nothing. Ingerd nodded her understanding; her demeanor conveyed her depth of feeling and barely checked impatience to know the fate of her other son. She watched the two warriors closely as they stood in front of the council with their heads together in conversation.

Conversation died away in the council chamber as Sachem signed for the men to speak.

By mutual agreement it was Manshipit who would tell their tale. He caught the eyes of Nipishish; something unspoken passed between them. He turned away. Still not saying a word, allowing the tension to build, he paced back and forth in the small cleared area in front of the council his eyes alternately traveled over the council members and the people crowded together in various postures of expectancy, ready to be entertained.

In a low voice, intended to make his listeners strain to catch each word, he began with mention of the uneventful four night journey by canoe, concentrating on their arrival overland on foot, and detailing the shared misery of lying in the cold and wet waiting for sight of Ivar. The other warriors present were all familiar with the terrain near the Haudeno village of Sakohkea; Manshipit's detailed descriptions served to transport all his listeners to the knoll above the village of their mortal enemies.

"It was difficult to see the people in the village clearly through the occasional mist. Few people came outside the longhouses at all because of the wet. Nobody we saw that day had hair the color of a ripe ear of corn. The light of the forest was fast being swallowed by the long shadows that give way to the night when two women walked from the village gate and turned up the hill toward our hiding place. They both carried baskets for foraging. We decided to capture them. They would tell us if the boy we sought was in the village. The women passed our hiding place without seeing us. We attacked them from behind." He paused a moment to let his listeners hang on his last statement.

Beyond an occasional grunt to enforce some detail of Manshipit's tale, Atkaa seemed content to stand idly by.

"They couldn't hear us because they were talking and the leaves underfoot did not rustle because of the rain," Manshipit continued. "Atkaa's prey had a knife in her hand that she had been using to cut mushrooms. She was warned by a slight sound or something; she turned quickly and cut at him at the same time. He jumped back and hit her in the head with the flat of his axe. But, she almost gutted him."

He lifted his chin toward Atkaa, who pulled up his recently repaired jumper, turning for all to see. The cut had scabbed over, making it look worse than it was, no doubt the reason for the enthusiastic reaction of the onlookers.

Manshipit grinned at Atkaa at the people's reaction before he turned to continue his tale. "We tied them both up. The younger of the two woke up then and we questioned her. It was she who told us about Ivar." He glanced toward Nipishish, Ingerd, and Lothar. "Ivar is there."

Glooscap spoke for the first time. "Bring the prisoner before the council."

Meshika entered the council house prodding the young Haudeno woman before her. The prisoner, her eyes downcast, stood before the council and the packed humanity, trembling like a leaf in the wind.

Without preamble, Glooscap spoke to her. "Look at me, woman. Tell us about Ivar, the white boy held captive in your village."

With considerable prodding and help from Meshika and Miknap with the differences in the spoken languages, the prisoner relayed what she knew.

Nipishish and Ingerd sat with their heads together while he translated or clarified the meaning of the copious hand signs and facial expressions used by the Haudeno woman to relate her tale. The woman concluded with the revelation that Ivar was not a prisoner, but rather an adopted member of the Cokanuk band of the Haudenosaunee people.

Exclamations and expressions of surprise briefly swept through the onlookers.

Ingerd glanced at Nipishish, noting his open-mouthed reaction to the final statement of the prisoner and the look of surprise on his face.

"What is wrong, I did not understand her words." Ingerd anxiously grabbed her husband's arm, her tone conveying confusion.

Nipishish shook his head in disbelief. "Wrong? Nothing is wrong. Ivar fought with a Haudeno boy right after arriving at their village. It turns out this boy is the son of Sakohkea, their war chief. The fight was staged to test Ivar's mettle. He fought well and has been adopted into the band."

Ingerd stammered in confusion. "But, what does that mean?"

"It means that they will not kill him. He is one with their people. It is their way, Ingerd, to replace the dead son of a warrior called Odatshedeh. As a reward for his bravery, they have given Ivar a new life."

Ingerd's eyes darted back and forth between her husband and the Haudeno woman. A look of confusion twisted her face. "But, how will we get Ivar back, Gudbj?"

Gudbj raised his hand to silence her as all eyes fastened on Sachem. "Watch and listen, Ingerd, I will explain what Sachem tells us," Gudbj whispered.

Glooscap sat down next to Sachem, a move recognized as significant by the people.

Sachem spoke from his place among the council. "At dawn, Glooscap will lead a large party to the village of Deganawida to try to recover Ivar.

As a token of peaceful intent, Glooscap will return this Haudeno girl to her people." He gestured toward the prisoner.

When the prisoner realized what Sachem had said, her eyes filled. She strained to hear and understand as he continued.

"Glooscap will have at least fifty warriors with him. Deganawida has about the same number of warriors in his village, so he will be inclined to talk rather than fight." The old man's eyes settled on Nipishish; he directed his words to him. "You and your other son, Lothar, will want to go with Glooscap. I think this is important for the success of the expedition. Sakohkea, the Haudeno war chief, will not listen to why you have come, he will want to fight. The fact that you come for your lost son will be valuable and I think Deganawida will honor you for the courage it has taken to come among them. It is he that you must impress for he is a strong man, a leader of his people. His words carry weight, his wishes will prevail. Your son has been adopted into their band; it will be difficult to change that. Deganawida may leave it up to Ivar, I do not know." Sachem got slowly to his feet. "This council is finished. Glooscap will make preparations for a dawn departure. These are my words. It will be as I say." Sachem and the council filed from the council house.

Shortly after sundown, after most of the people had sought the peace of their sleeping robes, Nipishish and Ingerd lay in each other's arms in whispered conversation.

"Tell me about Halfdan, about our people. I want to hear everything," he said.

Over the course of the next hour or so, Ingerd filled him in on the momentous events that had consumed their settlement at Halfdansfjord since he left on his expedition. Beginning with Halfdan's chance visit to Yggdrasil, the World Tree, and the vision of Gudbj's capture, Ingerd skillfully wove a tale of her heartbreak, the pride and confidence Halfdan had for his close friend, the second and third visits of Chisasi's Naskapi band, and the friendship that developed after Halfdan's canoe trip to Chisasi's village. Ingerd told of Chisasi's return to Halfdansfjord with four strangers, Naskapi warriors of another band, and their message from Sachem. The event was so emotional for her that tears glistened in her eyes, reflecting the final tongues of flame from the dying hearth fire.

Nipishish held her tightly; his hand absently stroked her hair. "Glooscap told me that Sachem had sent them and that Chisasi took them to meet with Halfdan." Nipishish watched the painful memories and anguish disappear from Ingerd's face at his words.

She nodded, brushing her tears away. "Yes, Chisasi brought Kejo, Atkaa, Miknap, and Manshipit to Halfdansfjord one day. Chisasi holds you in high regard as Halfdan's war chief. You impressed him and his men. People still talk about the way Halfdan and you reacted to the rape of those young Naskapi women by two of our men. It was a good thing." She turned to look into the shadows of his face, trying to gauge his reaction.

Nipishish said nothing, waiting for her to continue.

"It all seems like so long ago, but it is only a moment in time. It was Kejo who told me that you were well, one with the people after fighting to protect them from Haudeno raiders. When he said that, and Deskaheh made us understand his words, Halfdan and I were almost overcome with relief. I have never seen Halfdan display such emotion."

Nipishish nodded, his mind filled briefly with thoughts of his chieftain and friend. He signed for Ingerd to continue.

"Kejo then told us that he and his men would bring Lothar and me here. The next morning we began our journey. You should have seen Lothar, Gudbj, you would have been proud of your son. By journey's end he had gained the respect of Kejo and his men. He is no longer a boy, you know?"

"I noticed that right after you arrived here. Ivar was always the strong one. Perhaps his capture has made Lothar mature faster than normal."

"The change in him has occurred since Ivar's capture, so you are probably right. He is very protective of me and gradually I have let him do our talking. He does it well and I am proud of him."

Both were silent for a time, seemingly mesmerized by the flickering tongues of flame from the hearth as they reflected on the recent past.

Ingerd sighed and stretched. "The day before we arrived at Sachem's village, Kejo sent Atkaa and Manshipit on to the Haudeno village to see if Ivar was there. The rest you know. Their prisoner confirmed that Ivar was in that village." She got up on one elbow and strained to see Gudbj's face in the dim illumination. "I am worried about your journey to the village of Deganawida. Sakohkea scares me, he is known as a very violent man."

Nipishish chuckled. "Of course he is. He is the war chief of his people and as such he is responsible for their success in war. He is also a man, with at least one son, and I will try to appeal to that part of him if it comes to that. If not, I will fight him for my son, which is my right."

"Sachem has said they may not give Ivar up. What will we do then? I cannot lose my only blood son."

"Sachem also said that Deganawida may leave the decision up to Ivar."

"Ivar will not choose them over us," Ingerd blurted out angrily. "We are his mother and father."

"Settle down, Ingerd, before you wake up everybody in here."

"She already has," said a disembodied voice from the gloom.

Nipishish laughed aloud.

Ingerd hit him in the chest. "I find no humor in this, Gudbj," she hissed. "They cannot keep my son."

"Listen Ingerd, they will do what they want. It will not be up to us. The decision will either be Deganawida's or Ivar's. Either way we will have no say in it."

"Ivar will never choose to stay with them."

"You do not know what he will do, or what has happened in his life over these many moons since his capture. He has always been headstrong. Now he is a young man and will do as he wishes, what he deems is best for him given the circumstances. I know what he will be thinking. I have been a prisoner, too, and it changes everything you have ever thought. The experience mixes up all your values."

"I am not going to stay here while you and the other men go off on this quest to get my son back. I am going; it is my right as his mother."

"I will decide what you do, Ingerd," he said forcefully. "This is a war party that goes to Deganawida's village. It will be up to him whether the outcome of our invasion of his lands is peace or war. I cannot risk the safety of my wife on such a venture."

"You forget, Gudbj, I am a Viking woman. I can fight. You and Lothar are the only family I have left. I must go with you. If we are to die, we will be together in death as we have been in life. That is as it should be."

Realizing that she had won, again, he looked at her and shook his head. "Go to sleep, we shall decide tomorrow."

"Yes, go to sleep," said the same disembodied voice from the gloom of the longhouse.

—⊷—

In the chill, grey, half-light of predawn, 56 warriors set out from the village shoreline in a flotilla of 15-canoes, beginning the four day journey to the Haudenosaunee village. Except for the calls of awakening birds and the occasional swish of a paddle no sound from the contingent intruded on the morning as they bent to their task. A casual observer might have noted that the large, heavily armed force was not adorned for war; rather, although certainly armed for conflict, their appearance and demeanor bespoke of another mission entirely.

—⊷—

A MEETING WITH DESTINY

Glooscap had cut the journey to three days by utilizing the light of the full moon for half of the first two nights before halting for the night. Now, he and four men, including Manshipit and Atkaa, lay concealed atop the very ridge above the Haudeno village that his men had used previously. The main body of his warriors rested within an area of dense forest well back from the village and away from the numerous trails used for the comings and goings of the Haudeno villagers.

Late that same day, as Glooscap lay studying the village and the activities of its residents, his thoughts kept returning to the only part of his mission that he could not control. The unknown that could doom their mission of peaceful intent, had to do with small bands of men that were afield hunting. If hunters stumbled into the main body or happened across his place of concealment as they returned to the village, there would be no option for a peaceful resolution. Just like his people, small groups of Haudeno hunters fanned out in all directions this time of year to stockpile all the fresh meat possible before winter intruded. The chance that the main body would be discovered in the dense forest where they were concealed was slight, but his scouting party was vulnerable in their exposed position. He quickly made his decision.

"Manshipit, make haste and get the others, we cannot wait until tomorrow." He watched the man rise without a word and steal off in a crouch until he entered the forest verge where he broke into a trot and disappeared.

Chapter 3

HALFDANSFJORD

The face of the sun had just slipped below the western horizon when the peace that normally holds sway at day's end was shattered by the guard's horn wailing from the south tower, soon replicated by the guard's horn from the north tower. Both combined to set up a frightful din. People came running from every quarter, to pour from the south gate onto the landing beach in response to the guards' gestures and shouts, "A ship rounds the headland! It is Steed of the Sea."

Halfdan and Frida, in the forefront of the crowd swelling out along the beach caught sight of the ship in the distance. Her mast top and sail swam into view through the ever-present haze as she beat close-hauled around the headland.

Frida grabbed Halfdan's arm, excitement flushed her beautiful face as she shouted above the din of the crowd. "Just look at her! She is a sight to behold!"

Halfdan's arm encircled her shoulder and he pulled her close, his eyes drinking in the sight of his ship as Bjorn brought her about and she charged downwind on a broad reach for the landing beach. A flush coursed through his body at sight of the bow wave creaming out, the graceful prow slicing the water's surface asunder as her speed rapidly increased on the downwind tack.

"She has the bone in her teeth, just look at the white foam of the bow wave. Gorm has her hard on the wind."

Before Steed of the Sea reached the shoreline the people of Halfdansfjord had poured through the settlement's south gate and spread out onto the landing beach. Except for the guards themselves and groups of hunters and fishermen still afield everyone not busy with something they could not leave gathered to witness the return of one of the ships that had been away most of the summer. The excitement of not knowing what Bjorn had brought home dominated the many conversations. Several wagers developed over the substance of the ship's cargo. After all, what better way to put a finish to the day than with some spirited wagering? Trading was the lifeblood of Norse society and the sturdy ships and their crews made most of it possible.

Beyond the normal chatter of such a gathering, an undercurrent of anticipation ran through the people; they knew that their presence alone put pressure on the captain of the approaching ship. As one would expect of a captain that Halfdan personally selected to command his ship, Bjorn would want to handle his charge perfectly while under the gaze of his chieftain.

The midday wind blew directly onshore, making wind conditions favorable to sail all the way in rather than use the sweeps to beach the ship. So, Bjorn would have to get this approach exactly right. To have to row ashore because he dropped the sail too soon or worse yet to come ashore under full sail would not be good choices for ways to end an otherwise successful voyage.

Most of the bystanders would view the performance as a friend would, happy for the safe return of ship and crew. While others, out of petty jealousy or a past slight that left a simmering anger for captain or crew, would observe the performance differently. One such person, Thorgill, Bjorn's second-in-command was aboard the ship. His problem had nothing to do with Bjorn; rather it was left over from when Halfdan gave Gudrod's ship to Tostig instead of him. Like any perceived slight, the passage of time made it worse. Now that the object of his anger, Halfdan, would be seen daily, the situation could only worsen. At that moment, Thorgill stood in the bow, one hand on the forestay and the other resting atop the rail, intent on the crowd coming into view on the beach. *I must get control of myself. I cannot win against my chieftain,* he thought.

Halfdan and Frida waited with some of the others atop the highest point of the sloping beach, talking and watching the ship's approach. Halfdan watched closely, knowing what Bjorn would be thinking. *Right now, he is watching the masthead weathervane, gauging the wind and the thrust of the sail. If he waits too long to loose the sheets and lower the sail, he will drive the ship ashore; the keel could be damaged. If he acts too soon, or the wind dies as it is dampened by the island just offshore, he will lose control and the ship may broach to on the beach instead of beaching bow to as he desires.*

Frida glanced at Halfdan in time to see his eyes narrow and his lips compress. He tightened his jaw in anticipation. She chuckled at her husband's discomfort and pulled him aside, slightly apart from the others. "No matter how many times Bjorn, or anybody else for that matter, commands your ship, you will always feel this way. I know you trust him or he would not be in command of Steed of the Sea."

He looked down at her fondly. "Aye, I do trust him, but only you know that I still feel discomfort at such times. No one else can know of this. The people must never know that I experience the same feelings and doubts as they do."

"And, why is that?" she asked, hooking an arm through his, her eyes on his face. Her lips drew up in a slight smile as she watched his face while he considered her question.

He leaned toward her, making certain his words would only be heard by her. "I am their chieftain. I cannot be like other people." The twinkle in his eyes belied the words that he would have shared with no other.

She hugged his muscular arm without comment and looked back offshore at the approaching ship.

Aboard Steed of the Sea, Bjorn stood near Gorm, his helmsman, on the starboard aft side of the ship. Both men swayed easily to the motion of the deck underfoot. Both also kept a sharp eye on the set of the sail, the weathervane atop the mast, and the ship's course toward the distant beach.

Gorm held the tiller bar hard against the force of the wind pressing on the tightly sheeted sail, making good their course downwind. He loved feeling the heartbeat of the great ship through the steerboard to which the tiller bar was attached. A kind of resonance, a hum of constant vibration coursed through his hands and feet as the big steerboard sliced through the water well below the deepest fore and aft part of the ship's keel. The ship talked to him in this way and he handled her with an expertise gained from the many ocean crossings that they had made together. He knew the onshore wind would hold steady until influenced by the islands close inshore - that they must leave to port in order to fetch the landing beach on this tack - where he expected the wind to decrease in velocity and slightly change direction.

The ship's passengers lined both rails; anticipation ran through them as they pointed and chattered about what they saw ahead. The details of the settlement and its surrounding countryside swimming through the mist were their first sight of their new home. It had been a long voyage from their homeland in Hortafjord. With the stops in Iceland and Greenland their journey took most of the short, northern summer.

Ingunn Hákonsdattur, standing with the others along the rail, stole an occasional glance aft, in the direction of Bjorn. He paid her no mind, but she did not expect him to at this time. He had told her earlier that Halfdan would be among the people on the beach and he would be watching the performance of his ship for which he, Bjorn, was responsible. She watched him nonetheless, a heat rising in her loins at the thought of his hard body pressed against hers. Sighing with happiness and anticipation at the future together that they had discussed, she returned her attention shoreward. Her strong young body swayed easily to the motion of the ship; a wide smile spread over her beautiful face as details on the beach and the countryside inland swam into clear view through the dissipating sea mist. *The gods are smiling on us this day, for it is here that life will truly begin. I can feel it.*

The crowd began to move toward the point where the ship would beach, Halfdan and Frida among them.

"I am anxious to meet Thorgeirr's kinsmen, especially the tall blonde woman that he told us has captivated Bjorn," Thora said, stepping up beside Frida.

"Aye, some new gossip will be welcome, I think," Frida answered, smiling at her friend.

Halfdan snorted and shook his head. At Frida's raised eyebrow, he chuckled. "Since when do any of you need new subjects for your gossip?"

Frida and Thora ignored him, strolling slowly toward the water's edge with their heads together in animated conversation. Halfdan followed, speaking with those around him, stealing glances toward his ship as her details became more defined.

Back aboard Steed of the Sea, the two inshore islands passed to port and Gorm altered course slightly to port, aiming for a landing on the beach in front of the large crowd of people now clearly visible. Without orders, Thorgill, Bjorn's capable second-in-command, and his mates at the sheets retrimmed the sail to the new heading.

As they drew nearer to the landing beach the need to begin a slow reduction in the ship's speed became necessary and Bjorn issued the first of the expected orders for landing. "Ease the steerboard, Gorm, let her luff a bit." The outer edges of the big sail begin to flap slightly as Gorm let off the tiller pressure that he normally held into the hard bellied sail; the flapping sail edges acted as a brake against the thrust of the wind, gradually slowing the ship.

A shout from Thorgill drew the attention of all aboard, "Look at the burned out ship and boats near the landing beach. They have had a battle here recently." He gestured in animation as people gathered in the forward part of the ship, jostling for position along the port rail, all talking at once as the full extent of damage ashore became clear as the ship slowing closed the landing beach. Almost to himself, Thorgill continued. "That must have been Gudrod's ship. Sweyn and Athils have still not returned and Brodir's and Thorgeirr's ships' are drawn up on the beach." A slight smile of satisfaction curved his lips at the thought that Tostig might now be without a ship, too.

"The south palisade has been burned, too," Gorm spoke over his shoulder, an edge to his voice.

"I see it," said Bjorn through gritted teeth. "By the gods! Where is my ship, she is not here?" His voice trailed off after the affirmation as the enormity of the damage to their settlement became apparent. "All right, enough!" He shouted to the people clustered in the bow. "All hands stand to your duty! The rest of you scatter through the ship as before or we will be so bow heavy the ship will ground before we get to the beach."

Passengers and crew hastily returned to their places, all knowing the importance of maintaining the trim of the ship, especially fore and aft, otherwise steering control could be compromised. Without proper weight distribution the ship did not always react as expected to the forces at play.

A period of silence gripped the ship's company, until Gorm, in an attempt to change the grim set to his captain's jaw called attention to a new subject, even though he knew Bjorn had seen them too.

"Brodir and Thorgeirr have beaten us home," observed Gorm, with a lift of his chin toward two ships beam-to further up the landing beach from their intended point of landing.

Bjorn chuckled at his friend's words. The two men made eye contact, each knowing the other's reasoning at the abrupt change of subject. "Aye, I see their ships. That leaves Sweyn and Athils. They better come soon before we have a bad storm."

"I will bet you one shiny silver coin that they are right behind us."

Bjorn glanced at the man, not taking the bait.

"They will land today or tomorrow."

"Which? Pick one and I will bet you."

"Tomorrow, they will land tomorrow."

"Done! I say they will not land for two days."

Gorm grinned at him. "I will want only a shiny silver coin."

Bjorn snorted. "Let her fall off the wind a bit more," he said, glancing aloft at the set of the sail.

"Aye," Gorm responded, easing the tiller slightly, his lips spread in a satisfied grin.

People began waving from ship and shore alike. At one with travel by sea and the dictates of that environment, they did so without the shouting one would think normal in such circumstance, so as not to interfere with the handling of the ship during this critical final stage of the voyage, the landing at their destination.

A short distance out from the beach; Bjorn cupped his hands and called to Thorgill and his waiting crew, "Loose the sheets!"

Two men pulled the sheet lines, one on each side of the loose-footed sail, out of their cleats and turned them loose, spilling the wind from the sail. The ship immediately slowed as the sail lost its purchase on the wind.

"Lower the sail!"

Hearing this final order from Bjorn, Thorgill gestured to his two crewmen standing by the halyard and they pulled the thick line loose from its cleat and lowered the sail by paying out line through the double blocks, one each at the masthead and atop the yard, bracing themselves against the weight of sail and yard. With the yard and sail down and guided into the yard supports fore and aft of the mast they joined their fellows who had fisted the heavy wadmal sail into folds as it came down the mast. Reefing point lines, evenly spaced across the sail's height and width, were used to lash the folds of sail securely to the yard.

While this was going on, the ship, deprived of the sail's thrust, lost way rapidly. Momentum continued to carry her forward until the keel rode up the shelving bottom and the ship came to rest with her high, pointed bow hanging out over dry land. Just before the keel touched bottom, Gorm jerked the strap loose that secured the steerboard in its downward position, allowing it to swing up out of the way so it would not be damaged as they came ashore. It was no longer needed, the journey was done; Steed of the Sea had brought them back home again.

Bjorn called to his men as he wound his way forward through the crowd along the port rail, "Secure the ship!" Willing hands aboard and ashore accomplished this task with practiced efficiency.

As Bjorn moved forward, he paused to give Ingunn a squeeze. "Welcome home," he said, a big grin on his face. "I will be back to get you, wait for me. I must go to Halfdan first." Without pausing for her reply he vaulted the rail onto the beach and walked to his chieftain, responding to the many shouted greetings along the way.

Halfdan stood at the forefront of a group of men. Bjorn enthusiastically shook hands with him and greeted the others.

"It was a good voyage," he said, speaking directly to Halfdan. "We have more of the same goods brought by Brodir and Thorgeirr," he nodded toward the two men standing just behind Halfdan, "plus many useful things traded from the Thalmiut."

"We heard the dogs barking," Halfdan said, a twinkle in his eyes.

"Aye. I traded Essipit out of two pairs. One of the females will whelp soon. Essipit acted reluctant to trade the dogs, especially the pregnant female, like you told me he would, but in the end he could not pass up the knives, cooking kettles, and hatchets I offered." He cupped his hands and called to one of his men looking over the ship's rail. "Turn the dogs loose!" Turning back to Halfdan, he said, "We traded for much else, too. But, first I have something else to show you. I will be right back." He grinned, turning away to make his way back to the ship.

"We know what that will be, I think," Halfdan said to those around him, getting the expected grins and nods. Looking out over the crowd, he spied Frida, called to her and waved her over.

As she threaded her way through the crowd to him, all four of the ship bound dogs jumped onto the beach, creating pandemonium for a time as they ran here, there, and everywhere, barking happily as they inspected their new surroundings and the settlement's dogs that converged on them from all directions. Further discussion among the men ceased momentarily while they watched the process with everyone else.

Halfdan looked down at Fang, sitting beside him, tongue hanging out the side of his mouth. The animal gazed back at his master, aloof and unconcerned about the antics of those of his kind. Halfdan grinned and scratched the big dog's ears.

At that moment, one of the new male dogs chanced by, coming to a stop a short distance from Fang. The new arrival's tail pulsated slightly – not really wagging from its curled position over his back – as he inspected Fang from a safe distance. The new dog continued his inspection, one front foot raised off the ground.

Fang, for his part, turned baleful eyes on him, not even bothering to close his mouth or get up on all fours. The new dog, no doubt sensing a course reversal might be his best option, suddenly turned away and trotted off.

The men laughed appreciatively at the abrupt loss of interest by the new dog. "Good decision," Halfdan said, as he made eye contact with Fang.

At Halfdan's words, the animal got to his feet, retracted his dripping tongue, his jaws snapped shut, and what looked suspiciously like a grin drew up the corners of his mouth as he looked at his master.

Halfdan laughed aloud again and took hold of the big dog's snout, gently swinging the great head from side to side. "I think so too. You are a joker, but that dog will never know that about you." The moment of communion between man and animal ended abruptly with the arrival of Frida.

"I think I see who has captivated your ship's captain," Frida said with a lift of her chin toward a striking blond woman leaning over the ship's rail.

"Aye," offered Thorgeirr from among the men with Halfdan. "That is her, Ingunn Hákonsdattur."

Frida watched the young woman closely. Her lips compressed as she studied the new arrival. She pulled Halfdan aside a bit, wishing her words to be for him alone. "She certainly is pretty enough. We shall see what else she is."

"Do I detect an undercurrent of concern, or is it jealousy from you?"

"No, not really, she may not be a good worker. She may not blend in with the other women. Beauty does not always make one a good companion or a good worker."

"Really," chided Halfdan, openly smiling now. "You are beautiful. You were the biggest troublemaker in the settlement and look how you turned out."

She stabbed him with one of her intense looks, complete with the raised eyebrow.

Halfdan snorted. "I know you dislike it when I have the final word. I predict you will be fast friends with Ingunn, especially if she is as troublesome and wild as you were."

"What do you mean, 'were'?" She punched him playfully in the arm.

He wrapped her in a one-armed bear hug, momentarily crushing the air from her lungs, leaving her breathless.

She broke away from his embrace and took a deep breath. "Now we will see. Here they come," she said with a lift of her chin.

Previously, Ingunn had been watching the activity ashore, trying unsuccessfully to keep Bjorn in sight as he wound his way through the crowd. The other passengers stopped milling about on the ship, gathering their belongings and suchlike and began climbing over the bow to drop onto the beach. Impatient with the waiting, she decided to join them when she saw Bjorn winding his way through the crowd toward the ship. Leaning over the rail, she grinned down at him. "I would have come in another minute."

"I know. Jump!" he cried, grinning up at her as he held out his arms.

She grabbed the forestay and leaped atop the rail. Without pause then, she jumped out and fell into his arms.

Her arms went around his neck as he lowered her to the ground. They hugged and kissed to swelling applause.

Smiling happily, they looked adoringly into each other's eyes, in complete communion and oblivious to the boisterous crowd. Bjorn finally broke the spell. "Come, greet your chieftain." He took her hand and they walked quickly up the beach toward a smiling Halfdan and Frida. As the distance between them closed, Bjorn's eyes travelled over those clustered around Halfdan. Something was missing. He put the thought momentarily aside.

"Halfdan and Frida, this is Ingunn," Bjorn said proudly, one arm at her waist. Halfdan just smiled and nodded, not so Frida.

"Ingunn, we are pleased to meet you, welcome to Halfdansfjord."

The hands of both women met in greeting. Both had smiles in place while they took the others measure. Apparently, both liked what they saw.

"Come, I will show you around and introduce you to people. You will like your new life here," Frida said.

As the two moved away from Halfdan and Bjorn, Ingunn made eye contact with Bjorn in time to catch his wink and smile. It made her heart swell; she knew they had come home.

Bjorn turned back to Halfdan. "Where is Gudbj? I have not seen Ingerd either, where is she."

"You don't miss much, Bjorn. They are with the Naskapi." Halfdan raised a hand to stop Bjorn's next question, which formed on his lips while Halfdan spoke. "They are both well. It is a very long story and I will not relate it now. Much has happened over this summer." He waved a hand vaguely in the direction of the burned out ship, boats, and the scorched palisade wall.

Bjorn nodded, fixing his chieftain with a direct look. "I do not see my ship, where is she?"

Halfdan gestured toward the east. "I sent Hrafen in your ship with a six man crew to catch sturgeon spawning in the rivers that flow into this bay. He is Thorgeirr's kinsman."

"Aye, I met him on Greenland. How come my ship was not burned with Gudrod's?"

"It did get burned, Bjorn, but not badly. It took fire during the attack, too, but the fire went out by itself, while Gudrod's ship burned to the keel. Hrafen and his men repaired what damage there was, so I put him in charge of your ship. Thorgeirr told me that Hrafen is an able shipwright, and he is."

'Good, another shipwright will be welcome," Bjorn said with enthusiasm. He paused a moment, looking at the wreckage of Gudrod's ship. "I have many questions, Halfdan, but first, tell me about the attack."

Halfdan held up his hand. "Not now. You only just arrived home and there are many details to attend to. I expect Sweyn and Athils soon. They will have many questions, too. All will be answered when I call a council after you and they have settled back into life back home. Be patient, my friend, you just came ashore."

"Alright, I will wait for the council, but I will wager that a few small bits of news slip out in the meantime."

"I would not be surprised. Let us go see what you have brought to us," Halfdan said, slapping Bjorn on the back as he and his men walked down the beach to the ship.

Things gradually settled down. The new arrivals scattered out into the settlement, their numbers absorbed by the population as they were welcomed into the groups and longhouses where they were to live. The majority were men, without wife or mate, so they gravitated toward others of their kind. This process of joining became an altogether satisfying time for everyone, especially the settlement's womenfolk, who took the newly arrived women and children in hand with an infectious enthusiasm, proud to show them their new home and help them settle into their respective longhouses.

The children mixed readily. The six newly arrived children, two boys and four girls, ranging in age from six to twelve, were so happy to get off the ship and onto solid ground once again, that they ran off with their new found friends to inspect the village and all its mysteries, content to leave the details of their arrival and accommodations to others. As it happened, the two boys, the oldest of the new arrivals at eleven and twelve, were about the same age as the settlement's oldest boys, Atli and Haki, now that Ivar and Lothar were away. Atli and Haki had previously gained recognition by discovering the first bee hives in the forest near Halfdansfjord, a discovery that produced two buckets of fresh honey and many bee stings for them. Eager to share their expertise with their new friends, Od and Egnar, the two ran off toward the north gate to take their new friends exploring. As they ran from the walk through gate, a shout from the tower guard brought them to an abrupt halt.

"Where are you boys going?"

"We are going to show these new boys the bee tree we found," Atli answered through his cupped hands.

"You cannot leave the settlement without a guard and your own weapons, you know that."

"It is not far. We will not be gone long," Haki answered hopefully.

"Get back in here. Go tell Tostig or Helge what you want to do. One of them will decide whether you can leave the settlement or not."

"Ahhh!" Atli said, kicking at a handy dirt clod in disgust.

Since he had assumed the lead in their minds the new boys watched him hopefully.

"That is too much trouble. They probably will not let us go," he added for their benefit.

"Atli, we knew we could not leave the settlement alone anymore. Halfdan has decreed that for the safety of all of us here," Haki said. "We should go get our bows and arrows and then ask Tostig or Helge if we can go, like we should have done to start with."

"Who is Halfdan?" Od asked.

"Aye, and who are Helge and Tostig?" Egnar added.

Both Atli and Haki found humor in their questions.

"Who are they? Here, I will show you," Haki gestured back into the settlement commons as his eyes searched the sea of faces until he spotted Halfdan with a group of men walking toward the council house.

"There," he said, grabbing a handful of Od's tunic and pointing. "See that big man walking with those other men, heading up this way? They are coming to this big longhouse beside us, it is the council house. He is our chieftain, Halfdan. Tostig and Helge are with him. They are two of his right hand men."

"Well, let us go and ask Halfdan if we can go exploring," Od said.

His new friends both laughed. Atli seemed to especially consider the question outrageous. "I do not think Halfdan talks to little boys," Atli said.

"We are almost as old as you, Atli. We are not little boys," Od said defiantly.

"In that case, you go ask him," Atli sneered, looking at Haki for support and getting none.

"Okay, I will," Od flung over his shoulder as he walked away.

A laugh of derision came from Atli.

"Leave him alone, Atli. He is right. Halfdan will talk to us," Haki said. Without waiting for an answer, he called, "Od, wait, we must get our bows and arrows, so we will be ready to go if he says we can go exploring. Go get them and we will meet back here at the council house. Meet you outside at the entry door."

Shortly afterwards the four boys entered the council house together and made their way through the ever present groups of adults engaged in various tasks to where Halfdan sat talking with a group of men around a long table.

As the nominal leader of this foray, Od was the nearest to Halfdan when his men noticed the boys and conversation ebbed at the table. Halfdan turned toward them. His glance took in the bows and arrows.

"What is it?" he said. The crow's feet deepened at the corners of his eyes as he looked at each boy in turn before his attention settled on Od.

To his credit, the boy stood his ground before the overpowering presence of the men sitting around the table, finding his voice in response to Halfdan's direct question.

"We want to go exploring," the boy said. He tried to look at Halfdan without flinching, but given the man's fearsome appearance, he did blink several times before audibly exhaling as a smile spread across the face of his chieftain.

Halfdan turned and winked at his companions, then riveted the boy in place with his full attention. "Exploring you say. That seems like a worthwhile thing for four boys to do on this fine day. What is your name, boy?"

"I am called Od." He found himself relaxed now before this man who obviously bore him no malice.

"Well, Od, it seems that you are the leader of this little band." Halfdan glanced pointedly from boy to boy before continuing. "Your new friends have told you of our rule about being armed at all times and in the company of a guard while outside the palisade. That is good."

"Aye, they did." Od spoke in what he hoped was his best and strongest tone of voice.

"Good, we will see what we can come up with for you boys." He turned a questioning look on his men.

Helge spoke from across the table. "Halfdan, we were talking about Grimr and Thorkell and their association with the Naskapi girls just before these boys showed up. Both of them have been hunting geese with the other hunters as the geese migrate through here on their way south for the winter. They will be checking their snares and nets for geese late this afternoon; the boys could go with them."

Halfdan nodded in agreement. "Good idea, make it so."

Directing his attention back to the boys, Halfdan made them aware of the importance of what they were about to do. "Running the fen with the hunters for trapped geese will be a valuable lesson for you. You will learn how to set the traps, how to harvest the wing flight feathers to fletch our arrows, the down for robes, and the meat and fat to eat. Go with Helge now. He will tell you what is expected of you."

"Thank you, Halfdan," Od blurted.

Halfdan waved a hand in dismissal. He grinned with his men as they watched the four excited boys follow closely behind Helge as he walked from the council house. "We all remember what it was like to learn to be men. My memories of that time are good for the most part. I hope theirs are as well."

His men nodded in agreement, their thoughts momentarily on another time, another place.

The arrival of several more men brought the period of introspection to an abrupt end. Among them were Thorgeirr, his kinsman, Hrafen Ormersson, and several of their fellows that Halfdan and his men had not met. All found a place around the long table.

Halfdan acknowledged the new arrivals. "With time, we will get to know one another. I am happy to have you with us. We were discussing the ongoing hunting and fishing expeditions. Tostig will tell you where you are needed the most." He jerked a thumb in Tostig's direction. "As you may know by now, I am waiting until Sweyn and Athils return before we hold council. I want the full council of six ships' captains in attendance, so that all of our people are represented. Then we can decide which tasks to accomplish over this winter and assign those men best able to get the work done. Both ships should come in before the new moon."

After a time, men came and went from the informal gathering as their needs dictated. Those that remained hunkered down over a bowl of hot fish chowder, a horn of mead with their fellows, or both, while they watched the women bustling about the chamber. An air of expectation, hung over the activity, for a celebration was on for the evening. Music, dancing, storytelling, and lots of food and mead would be consumed to ensure that Bjorn and Ingunn had a proper jumping across ceremony and all the new arrivals felt welcome in Halfdansfjord.

With the promise of a clear night to follow the day of boundless clear blue skies that they had enjoyed, the women decided it would be easier to serve the food outside rather than in the council house. As usual in such circumstance, food in all its forms drove the preparations. Men far outnumbered the women and children and they wanted food and drink, most having little or no interest in dancing and music.

Earlier, the large pile of firewood that had accumulated over time in the settlement's outdoor fire pit was set alight. While the leaping flames added warmth to the coolness of the lengthening shadows in the commons area it also provided a primal focal point. As the raging flames consumed the long pile of firewood in the pit, people paused briefly in their work to stand for a moment mesmerized by man's ages old fascination with fire, to just stare into the leaping flames, lost briefly in their own little worlds.

But, preparations continued nonetheless. Thrall women carried large trenchers of uncooked raw meat, fish, and marrow bones, to accumulate on the stone hearths at each end of the pit. They also put pots of water on to boil crabs and chunks of fish around the edge of the pit, later to be hung on hooks over the coals.

Nearby, Thora, Frida, and their new friend, Ingunn, worked among a group of chattering women cutting quarters of bear and seal, recently brought in by the hunters, into manageable sizes for grilling.

Today the hunters had been especially lucky. Several boat crews corralled a large number of porpoises in a small estuary, managing to kill 26 of the animals before the others escaped back into the bay. Four of the boatmen came from the landing beach into the settlement commons where the women were butchering. Each carried one quarter of a dismembered carcass to announce their success.

"We have 26 porpoises like this, Frida. How many do you want for the celebration?" asked Arni, the first of the hunters to arrive.

"By the gods, Arni, we have a lot of meat here already." She called to Thora. "They have 26 porpoises. Do you think we can get them butchered before the celebration begins?"

"Not without lots more help. I will go round up everybody I can find. It will not take long to finish this." Thora marched purposefully away into the milling crowd in the commons.

The skinned carcasses had already been chopped into quarters by the hunters. The women finished the job of dismembering each carcass by cutting the large muscle groups into steaks and chopping the ribcages and marrow bones into sections to be roasted over the coals.

Thora laughed as she swung her axe, the final blow separating the ribcage of the bear along the spine. "How satisfying this work is," she said enthusiastically. "By the time I finish butchering any meat I am drooling in anticipation."

"Me too!" Ingunn spoke around a bite-sized piece of seal blubber that she had just stuffed in her mouth. "I am tired of the dried meat and fish diet aboard ship. It is good to have fresh, bloody meat to chew on once again."

The others agreed.

"We will all enjoy it while we can," Frida said from a pile of leg bones that she was chopping into manageable lengths. "At most we have another moon before all of us will be on dried food until next spring. Except for a few seals and fish caught through the ice this winter, it will be an endless cycle of stew and chowder."

"Nothing tastes better on a cold day than a big bowl of stew or fish chowder, with a hunk of bread to hem it all up and push it into your spoon," Ingunn said enthusiastically, not to be deterred by Frida's words. "From what I have seen of the stores laid up for winter, nobody will go hungry. It has not always been like that for us. Towards spring, many times in my life, we barely had enough to make it to ice break up."

Thora grounded the head of her meat axe, holding it in one hand while the other rubbed her sore back. "We do have much food for winter. Next year we will have even more with a good crop from our new barley field. With all the barley Thorgeirr brought and that which Bjorn and Brodir traded for on Greenland, we also have more than enough this year for bread and thickening for stew and chowder, but in spite of that, we all have known those lean times. We have many mouths to feed. We do have more than enough right now. But, what you may not know, Ingunn, is that the Naskapi in Chisasi's band may not have enough. If they do not, Halfdan will most assuredly share our food with them, they are our friends. If that happens, this winter will be like all the others we have known. Spring will come and the ice in the bay will break up just in time."

Most of the woman stopped working for a time while they watched the principle players and listened to the conversation. Besides Ingunn, the group had only one other woman new to Halfdansfjord; all the others had been there from the beginning and they wanted to know the mettle of the new residents.

"I did not know about the Naskapi. How many are there?" Ingunn asked.

"Five lodges, about 150-people," Thora answered.

"That would be a real challenge to feed all of us." Ingunn glanced at her friend, Jodis, a short solidly build redhead, with glowing coppery skin covered in freckles, who had been working nearby. A lift of her chin brought the redhead into the conversation.

Jodis looked from woman to woman before she spoke. "I do not have anything to suggest, I have not been here long enough to know the situation. But, judging from what I have seen here, Halfdan, and all of you together," she swept her bloody butcher knife out to encompass all of them, "have everything well in hand."

"I agree," Ingunn added. "We are happy to be a part of this and we are sure that we can all work together to ensure everybody has enough food through the winter, no matter what happens." She grinned at the others and dropped to her knees to continue cutting steaks from a bear's haunch. "But, right now we must finish cutting up all this meat for my wedding celebration." She laughed happily as she threw another thick steak on the long trencher.

Frida purposely had not entered the conversation, preferring to watch and listen to what Ingunn and Jodis had to say. Because of her position in the settlement's hierarchy anything she said always guided the conversation and she did not want that this time. She wanted to know what the new women thought, on their own. She returned to her own work, stealing glances at Ingunn while the young woman sliced straight through the large haunch to the leg bone, freeing another steak to add to pile. Her eyes played over the others, all of whom had returned to work, before meeting Thora's eyes.

Thora nodded slightly, a slight smile curled her mouth. Frida inclined her head slightly and winked at her friend. It was done. Ingunn and Jodis had stood the test and were accepted by the chieftain's mate and one of her closest friends.

Genevra and Halla, two of the thralls working on the pile of meat, picked up one of the long trenchers to carry the steaks to the hearth. As she bent over to grasp the handle at the end of the trencher, Genevra spoke in a low voice that only Frida could hear. "I think they will do."

Frida made brief eye contact with the woman, but did not respond directly to her statement. "Have somebody else carry that trencher, or you will have your baby before it is due," indicating Genevra's swollen belly with a lift of her chin.

"I am fine, Frida. I can do my work," Genevra said. She and Halla struggled toward the fire pit with the heavy trencher of meat swinging to and fro between them. She smiled to herself. She knew the fiery Frida well enough to know that the concern she had just voiced was the same as spoken agreement. Frida liked the two new women, too.

The intense heat from the fire pit kept everyone at bay for a time, but finally the flames subsided, leaving a deep bed of hot coals. Much of the heat rose into the still air, but some also took the edge off the air of the commons as the chill of early evening began to creep over the land. The cold seemed to wait for the moment, for it closely followed the fading light of day. Out in the bay the Fog Giant spread his cloak over the water and the dampness of the night crept out over Halfdansfjord.

Many people milled about in the commons. The artisans and craftsmen of Halfdansfjord plied their trades and traded back and forth in the sheds and lean-to's of the village commons, where they worked every day. The impending feast added to the normal activity as others were drawn by rumbling bellies or attracted by the hubbub as their day's activities drew to a close.

The fare included the meat of whale, porpoise, seal, walrus, bear, and boiled crabs, fish chowder, firkin's of whale oil, larger casks of mead, and a large pile of roasted marrow bones, with more of everything available. All of it was testament to the bounty of their new home.

The long fire pit afforded plenty of room for people to select meat from that piled on the hearths at each end, pick up a long handled fork or grilling iron, and thrust it out over the rising heat of the coals for a quick sear. The mouthwatering smell of cooking meat and the strong odor of the sea rising from kettles of crabs in boiling seawater was irresistible.

After making their selection people scattered throughout the commons with family or close friends, to straddle a bench, sit at a table, or any available handy place to rest their tired backs against while they ate.

Later, the sun set on festivities in full swing. Oil lamps were scattered about the commons, hanging from any handy elevated pole or lean-to cross-piece. They provided enough light for people to find their way once they ventured away from the fire pit. Most had already eaten all they could stuff down, but people continued to come and go nonetheless. A huge bed of grey-ing coals was all that remained of the pile of wood the cooks had fired earlier. The dull glow of the coals provided weak illumination, a complement to the warmth and comfort afforded by just being close to the heat source.

A rising level of noise arose from the mass of people in the commons as the time came for the jumping across ceremony of Ingunn and Bjorn. Without prodding or any discernible direction the women and girls formed a line on either side of Ingunn and across a space facing them the men formed their own line to either side of Bjorn. No set ceremony existed; the participants did what felt good to them. To the accompaniment of much whistling, the twit-tering of flutes and the boom of a drum or two, the two lines began to sway to and fro. Ingunn and Bjorn had their eyes fixed on each other, both sported smiles of invitation and acceptance of what they were about. As the two lines swayed forward, both leapt across the open space into each other's arms. The two lines dissolved and the people crowded around the couple. It was done; they were one according to the customs of their people.

Mid-morning of the following day, as most of the real intense revelers began showing signs of life, stirring from their lethargy to get out of the intense sunshine if for no more important reason, Thora and the thrall, Genevra, lounging comfortably on one of the many benches scattered about the com-mons, watched their friends with amusement. That the feast and celebration of welcome and marriage had been a resounding success was evidenced by the chaotic appearance of virtually every corner of the settlement proper. The dogs took care of all the bones and the leftovers were thrown to the pigs, so it was not food waste making the clutter, it was the participants scattered about trying to sleep off their gluttony. Of course the consumption of prodigious amounts of mead did not help the outcome, either.

Genevra glanced at her companion. "Your tales are always the best part of our celebrations, Thora. Now I will be looking over my shoulder at night, waiting for Death Wind to pounce on me from the darkness." Thora turned her eyes on Genevra, the beginnings of a smile evidenced by the crowsfeet forming at the corners. "Why, do you believe in this Haudenosaunee legend?"

"Aye, I do! Your tale brought out my natural fear of the dark. I think most people are afraid of the dark, especially now that you have told us of this demon that lurks in the forest. Even during the day heavy forest is dark and foreboding. Now that I know the Haudeno's Death Wind and the Naskapi's Night Wind is a belief in the same demon of darkness, I think it is true, there is such a demon. You describe the demon's appearance as always heralded by the wind moaning through the trees. I have heard this wind many times. Now, I am convinced that the demon waits for victims whenever the wind moans through the forest."

Thora chuckled appreciatively. "Good! My tales are to entertain all of us. If my tale of Death Wind touched some people that listened last night, then I have been successful."

"Touched us, you scared many of us to death!"

Thora laughed aloud, bending over and hugging her knees, her mirth infectious to Genevra to the point that both women dissolved in a paroxysm of laughter until they were left breathless, bent forward on the bench. They looked at one another, wiping their eyes. Both had smoke from cooking and grime from a day of hard work on their faces. The tears of their mirth had caused the grime to appear as mud or wet ashes.

"You look terrible. You are so dirty and the tears have ruined your pretty face," said Thora, wetting a corner of her smock with spit to wipe at the other woman's face.

"So do you. I know I must look just like you." Genevra impulsively threw her arm over Thora's shoulder, and immediately realized what she had done, removing it quickly. "I am sorry Thora, I forgot my place, please forgive me."

"There is nothing to forgive. We worked side by side all day and we are exhausted. It is alright to enjoy each other's company, we are friends after all."

Genevra was contrite. She unconsciously twisted her smock in her hands, her eyes downcast.

"Genevra, look at me. It is alright. No harm was done."

"I am a thrall, Thora. I can be killed for touching you or any other free-man. I am truly sorry. I forgot myself in the moment. It will not happen again." Her eyes brimmed with tears as she looked at Thora.

"Aye, you are a thrall and we both know our laws. We have known each other most of our lives. We played together as girls." She took her friend's hands in hers. "It is alright. Now let this be an end to it." She put her arms around her. Genevra was shocked to feel her touch, but she unconsciously followed suit.

They pulled back, their hands still on each other's arms and each studied the other a moment.

"You really are a mess," Thora said, rising to her feet, the spell broken. "I think that is it for today. I am ready for a quick steam and a dip in the bay before going to bed." She looked at the other woman and nodded. "I will see you tomorrow." She turned away. "Now where is that man of mine?"

Genevra watched her make her way back into the commons. She shook her head at the way of things, took a deep shuddering breath, and headed into the commons herself. *I will not get a steam bath, but a thorough wash is going to feel good*, she thought.

—⚬⚬⚬—

Later that night a line of violent thunderstorms woke almost everyone and ensured that restful slumber would not return until passage of the storms. Incandescent lightning of an intensity to be visible through closed eyelids penetrated the roof smoke holes and bathed the longhouse interiors with an unworldly illumination that was difficult to ignore.

Unconsciously counting the intervals between the lightning flash and the crash of thunder that followed, to determine whether the storm was coming or going, Halfdan reclined comfortably on the sleeping platform on his back, both hands clasped behind his head and his feet crossed at the ankles. He stared into space waiting for the next flash, knowing from his count that the storm was coming toward the settlement. It had not started to rain yet, beyond an occasional large drop. That was about to change dramatically.

Suddenly blue white light suffused the longhouse interior, leaving all those with their eyes open, momentarily blinded. Halfdan had just begun his count when a tremendous crash of thunder shook the longhouse to its foundation. *Njord brings the storm; he and Thor are busy tonight.*

The first few large drops of rain mixed with slush gradually increased in intensity until reaching a roar of fury as the gust front preceding the line of thunderstorms smashed into Halfdansfjord. Bands of wind-driven hail added to the cacophony. Wind gusts tore at the fabric of each longhouse, toppled benches and tables, sweeping everything left loose in the settlement commons from the celebration before the onslaught of the gods of wind and weather. Fragile lean-to roofs were shredded to nothing, to be carried away on the breast of the wind while their supporting sidewalls were sundered and scattered about.

The wind sucked the warmth from the longhouses. Cold settled over the land as the leading edge of the storm charged southeast, out across the bay. Frida finally rolled out of her warm bed to join Halfdan and their thralls as they struggled to get the east windows crossbars in place to secure the shutters before the wind gusts sucked them open.

"I wondered how you could sleep through this, Frida. The gods are spending their fury on us this night," Halfdan said, as he turned from helping his two thralls secure the shutters.

"I could not sleep through this either, I..."

Before she could utter another word a rain cap on one of the three rooftop smoke holes carried away and wind-driven rain invaded the security and comfort of the longhouse, drenching everything and everyone nearby. Fortunately, an inner hinged door was a part of the smoke hole design and the thralls Finnbar and Ewyn quickly got it closed. Although it was not water-tight, the constant drip was preferred to the torrent of water that had come in before it was closed.

Halfdan and Frida sat dejectedly on their sleeping platform, surveying the mess made of their comfortable accommodations, their sleep over for the night. Both were aware that the other four longhouses would have suffered similar or worse problems for the storm still spent its fury just outside.

Halfdan turned to look around their sleeping platform. "Where is Fang?" he asked. He crouched down to look under the sleeping platform, catching sight of a pair of glowing, slanted eyes reflecting the dim light cast by the oil lamps as the dog watched him. "That is a good place to hide. If this keeps up I may crawl in there with you." He shook his head and rose to sit back on the platform with Frida. "At the first clap of thunder he is gone. That dog fears nothing but the deep voice of Thor when he hurls his lightning bolts."

"Smart dog," Frida said. She paused a moment before sharing her thoughts. "By the time this storm passes almost everyone's clothing, furs, and sleeping robes will be sodden or damp," Frida said. "Nobody will be sleeping anymore, so I was thinking that you might want to have a meeting of the leaders of each longhouse, so you will know the damage situation."

Halfdan looked at her; a slight smile twisted the corners of his mouth. "So, you thought I would want to do that?" He chuckled and hugged her close. "Well, I do. We can make them think it was my idea." He grinned while studying her face appreciatively. "You are really something, woman. You often know my thoughts before I do. You might even make a good chieftain."

The famous eyebrows arched to their maximum. "Might, you say? Aye, I would, but I am not. You are our chieftain and none of us would have it any other way. We complement each other, I think. Do you agree?"

"Aye, I do. You are the only one, with Gudbj away, that I can turn to with the doubts that I have on occasion. You never fail me and that is why I have come to depend on your counsel. I may not do as you wish, but I will listen."

"I would have it no other way, my love, you are a chieftain like no other and all the people, me included, know this." They made eye contact. Halfdan nodded at her and gave her hand a squeeze as he got to his feet. "Finnbar, Ewyn," he called.

The two men turned toward him at his summons.

"When this storm passes and after the rain stops, I want you to go to each longhouse and tell the leaders to report their situations and damage to me in the council chamber. In the meantime come with me and we will see what damage has been done in the council chamber." He walked purposely toward the doorway separating his living quarters from the council chamber, his thralls following behind.

Chapter 4

HALFDAN CALLS A COUNCIL

A t first light on the morning after the storm, a sodden countryside basked in the light and warmth of clear skies. A new day had begun. A gentle breeze blew out of the southwest as the rising sun heated the earth. The morning mist swirled and slowly burned off. Steam rose from every surface into the soggy atmosphere as the brassy sun, filtered by the haze of water vapor present in the atmosphere, slowly overcame the pervading wetness.

The fabric of Norse society at the north end of the big bay, at Halfdansfjord, began to dry out. The residents of the settlement moved about outside, checking on the longhouses, livestock, and to get a general idea of what the deluge had wrought. Piles and windrows of hail were everywhere about, floating in the puddles of water and stuffed into every nook and cranny. Minor wind damage was apparent everywhere one looked. The debris and wreckage scattered about, most recently parts of the structures within the commons, seemed to be piled against every immovable object. Tree limbs ripped loose from the many trees within the palisade had been cast, as if by giants, before the wind like barley straws. The worst of the damage came when the driving rain found a weak spot in the wattle and daub back wall of one of the animal sheds, melting away the daub and turning the interior into a quagmire, leaving only the wattle framework. The sheep within were found huddled in a corner for warmth, their wet, wool coats hanging like rags, none the worse for wear from the soaking they had received. The shed gate was opened wide and the flock finally ventured out into the open air by themselves, where it was at least warming up somewhat.

The gods of weather, Njord and Thor, had combined forces to remove every lean-to thatched roof in the commons, stacking most of the wreckage against the south palisade wall. More substantial livestock loafing-shed and lean-to roofs, constructed of sapling splits and sod, survived the onslaught unscathed for the most part.

Horses and cattle had been corralled when the storm struck, without shelter. Like all their kind they turned tail to the wind and stood head down in stoic acceptance. The colts and calves, born during the spring and early summer, were all weaned now, but corralled separately from the breeding stock – making room for the next generation - until just before their second year when they would join the herd. Grass hay forked into their feed bunks soon had all of them munching contentedly, seemingly unconcerned by the deep mud they stood in and the steam rising into the air from their drying backs.

The chicken flock habitually roosted in the rafters of the settlement's largest sod roofed, loafing shed each night. The shed was more like a small barn with solid walls, sloping sod roof, small window openings to the east and west, and a wide doorway to the south. With the good protection from the elements afforded by this shed, the flock's feathers were not even damp. Most of the hens and young pullets laid their eggs in old hay that sifted through the wall mounted hay racks of the loafing shed, but not all of them. Gathering eggs each day was the job of the youngsters of the settlement. Finding where the hens had hidden them was a daily challenge. The chicks of summer, fully grown now, were indistinguishable from the adult birds except for their small combs and high energy levels. The flock had more than doubled in size over the summer, to the point that a young rooster could be harvested from time-to-time without compromising the flock's integrity. Always the protectors of the flock, the several roosters that had been allowed to mature, stood guard atop the fence rails crowing to the morning sun while they watched their charges. The hens and young chickens, pullets and cockerels, followed the rooting pigs through the mess created by the rain, dashing here and there as morsels of manure and other treats came to the surface in the wake of the pigs.

Beyond a few minor irritants that would need repair – smoke hole covers, shutters, the melted daub and wattle shed wall, and so forth, the storm had not caused any extensive damage to the settlement. Thank the gods, the long-house structures were unscathed. Although the open ground to either side of the log walkways throughout the settlement was a sea of mud, little rain-water had accumulated, as the knoll on which the main buildings had been sited usually drained quickly via the scattered drain ditches. A single large drain ditch funneled the several smaller ditches to the south, to exit under the palisade and drain into the bay. To keep the wandering pigs and chickens from escaping the confines of the settlement proper, a weir, built of stakes the diameter of a man's arm and driven into the bottom of the main drain ditch where it went under the palisade wall, closed off this egress to small livestock and denied access to nocturnal predators on the prowl for a meal.

During the storm, several empty containers – baskets, piggins, small boxes, buckets, and firkens – and benches, stools, and odd bits of wood and split lumber utilized for various projects, that littered the commons area on any given day, floated or blew away, to eventually wind up piled against the drain ditch weir as they floated to the lowest spot in the ditch system. After every storm it became the job of the youngsters to gather all these containers up, take them back where they came from, and ensure that the drain weir was cleared for the next storm. As often happens with youngsters, they made a game of it as each vied with the others to retrieve the most containers. There was seldom a clear winner, but the effort made the participants happy.

—⊗⊗⊗—

The smoke of cook fires rose from each longhouse, to be whipped away by the freshening breeze. Kettles of the ever-present stew, both fish and various meats, along with loaves of barley bread and the leftovers from the previous day were the fare for the most part. Sounds of conversation and laughter float-ed out of every open window and open doorway as the people enjoyed the be-ginning of another day. With the need to have a look at what the storm did to the settlement satisfied for the time being, those gathered in their longhouses with kith and kin ate a leisurely breakfast, giving the sun and wind time to do their work outside.

That was not to be. A cry went up throughout the settlement when it was discovered that the ships drawn up on the landing beach were dangerously full of rainwater and the tide was going out; this combination made the con-dition especially hazardous. Breakfast forgotten, every able-bodied man and boy made for the landing beach on the run.

Although the ships were capable of transporting huge loads, the thin hull strakes could not withstand the weight of accumulated rainwater as the tide receded, leaving the vessels lying on their sides, high and dry on the beach, without the normal support of seawater. The massive daily fluctuation from high to low tide was well along as people congregated on the beach; the scene quickly became one of frenzied activity.

Tostig cupped his hands and yelled at a group of men running from the south gate. "Bring those timber balks with you." He pointed at several piles of heavy timbers used to prop the ships upright. He knew it was not necessary for him to direct every task, but the need for haste drove him from ship-to-ship as the assembled men quickly placed the timber balks. Each man knew exactly what had to be done and with the direction and assistance of each ship's captain the initial hectic efforts became more organized.

Bjorn hammered a wedge between Halfdan's ship's hull and the top of a timber balk with a large wooden mallet. He repeated this process as each balk was placed against the side of the ship, securely jamming the balks in place. Another man on the other side did the same, to keep the strain on the hull as even as possible. The balks were of differing lengths to accommodate the width amidships and the hull's upsweep at stem and stern.

A breathless Halfdan arrived and pitched in without comment to help two men lifting a balk into position.

"Thank the gods; the ships' keels are on the bottom and there is enough water around them to keep them upright on their keels in the shallows. A little later, with the tide streaming from the bay, the ships could not have been propped upright in time," he said, grinning at Bjorn as he hammered home a wedge.

Bjorn paused for a moment while two men muscled a timber into place. "It is my fault, Halfdan. Ingjaldr, one of Thorgeirr's men, raised the alarm that the ships were almost filled with water. I should have checked them myself, but I did not," said Bjorn. "Thorgeirr and Brodir got here just before I did, but we were all taken by surprise by the amount of water that had accumulated in the ships. If Ingjaldr had not seen one of the boats on the beach leaning over at an unnatural angle and checked all the boats and ships..." His thoughts hung in the air. 'Well, I do not wish to think of what might have happened to our ships."

"It is alright this time, Bjorn," Halfdan said, trying to make light of the situation. "All of us were surprised by this storm. It is the worst we have had since we built our settlement."

His words did little to mollify Bjorn. His facial expression told the story as the work continued; he still felt a responsibility for Halfdan's ship, even though the voyage was over.

Every man there knew that if the balks were not in place before the supporting water receded, the ships would lie over on their sides slightly, concentrating the tremendous weight of water within the hull to one side of the ship, surely springing the hull strakes or loosening the rivets that held the fabric of the ship together, destroying the hull's symmetry and ultimately destroying the hull.

Norse ship hulls did not have a sharp entry below the waterline down to the keel – the entry was gradual, almost flat across the ship's bottom, so the ship did not lay completely over when out of the water. This hull cross section was a two-edged sword. The ships could be transported overland – rolled on logs – because of the relatively flat bottom, which was the intent; however, the water would not drain from the interior hull by itself because of the bottom shape; it must be bailed out before the ship lay over.

While crews worked with the balks, other men and boys – boys were not yet strong enough to manhandle the balks into place – bailed water from the hulls using bailing scoops and buckets. No below water level, through-hull, stoppered drain holes were in Norse ships at the time, to drain the water from the hull, so the water had to be laboriously removed by hand and thrown out over the ship's side.

With the balks in place and mindful of the cold water being thrown out over the ship's side Halfdan and Bjorn withdrew to a safe distance. The four ships were all propped safely up and the last of the water was being removed.

Tostig joined Halfdan and Bjorn. "We are lucky the landing beach is sloped. If it was flatter the water would not have drained into the stern while we bailed it out and we would have had to remove all the ballast stones before we could get the water out." He said, shaking his head. "The tide would have won the race. It almost did anyway, even with all of us working."

Both of his companions nodded without comment, all three men thinking about the time and labor involved to remove the tremendous weight of ballast stones from four ships. The ballast stones covered the lowest portion of the interior ship's hull, unless cargo was aboard, to balance the hull against the thrust of the sail when the ship was under way. They were large, heavy stones, wedged in place, so as not to shift position in heavy seas. The men had to pry them loose before they could be picked up and dropped over the side.

"Aye, we were lucky. The gods smiled on us this morning. Otherwise..." Halfdan looked at his two companions, leaving the obvious unsaid.

Halfdan happened to be looking out over the bay when the dim outline of a ship swam into view through the mist, as she rounded the headland. "Look there, here comes either Sweyn or Athils," he said. Turning toward the south tower, he was about to yell at the guard stationed there, when he too saw the ship. His horn sounded the alarm.

"I think it is Sweyn's ship," said Tostig.

"Perhaps, it is hard to tell with the mist. Whoever it is the ship is heavily laden; she rides low in the water," said Bjorn.

The ship changed course to head straight into the landing beach, exposing the forward surface of the sail, which had been hidden while she weathered the headland. All three men saw the hammer amulet design woven into the big sail at the same time, agreeing that the ship was definitely Sweyn's, Hammer of Thor.

Shortly thereafter, Sweyn and his small crew waded ashore from their ship that had grounded two ship's lengths from the water's edge. Two men carried the coils of spring lines to moor the ship and control its surge ashore when the flood tide began.

A smiling Halfdan and the men on the beach met the ship's crew, spreading out around them.

"Welcome home, Sweyn, and all the rest of you," Halfdan swept his arm toward the settlement palisade. "No more tents. The people named it Halfdansfjord."

"And well they should." Sweyn nodded and smiled to the others as he shook Halfdan's hand. "It all looks good from here. We are happy to be back."

With a lift of his chin, Halfdan indicated the ship, Hammer of Thor. "You have a heavy cargo."

"Aye, we do. She is crammed with walrus hides and frozen meat." "After your long voyage, do you think it is still frozen?" Tostig asked.

"Aye, winter cold and snow chased us all the way. Layers of meat are between the hides, so it is still frozen."

Halfdan had previously held back, enjoying watching the byplay develop among his men. "You got back just in time then," he said. "It has been cold here, too, and yesterday and last night we had the worst storm since we finished building the settlement. Winter comes soon."

Sweyn nodded in agreement. "Aye, we got into that storm too. The weather was looking bad and we could see the storm coming, so we spent the night in a small cove. The anchor kept dragging in the wind, and somebody had to bail almost all the time, so we did not sleep much, but eventually it passed."

"With all that heavy cargo it is a wonder your ship did not fill with water and sink," Bjorn said, entering the conversation.

Sweyn just grinned at him, knowing that his friend already had the answer to that baited statement. "Speaking of ships full of water," he indicated the three ships propped upright on the beach with a lift of his chin. "Is that what happened here?"

"Aye, we just barely got the balks in place before the outgoing tide would have let the ships roll onto their sides," Bjorn said.

The helmsman, Einar, answered Bjorn's previous question for Sweyn. "When we were loading the ship, Sweyn had us leave a well amidships, all the way down to the keel, so water could be bailed out."

"Did he now?" Bjorn punched Sweyn in the arm. "That is plenty smart, Sweyn."

Sweyn laughed aloud and so did the others at what all knew to be standard practice when loading a ship with cargo.

"When did you get back?" Sweyn asked Bjorn, the merriment still on his face.

"Two days ago. That reminds me; I bet with Gorm when you and Athils would arrive." He looked toward the headland. "Where is Athils?"

Sweyn and the others also looked out into the big bay.

"I have not seen him since yesterday morning," Sweyn told them. "The sea was rough and the wind ahead of last night's storm was so bad we had reefed the sail by more than half. He had to seek a safe anchorage or a cove to beach the ship in before the storm hit. He will be along soon."

"If he beached his ship in a cove he is aground. High tide will be about midday. If he does not get here by nightfall, in the morning we will go look for him," Halfdan told his men, who nodded in agreement.

Finished with their ships, Brodir and Thorgeirr joined the group with Halfdan. "Good to see you made it back before winter sets in, Sweyn." Brodir shook hands with him. He gestured toward his companion. "This is Thorgeirr the Hortalander."

"Hortalander," exclaimed Sweyn as he shook the man's hand! "That is far from here."

"Aye, it is. When we left Hortafjord, there was still much ice about. The voyage was broken up by stops in Iceland and Greenland. We all like Halfdansfjord better."

The group swelled with others as the immediate work with the beached ships wound down. The men talked back and forth for time, catching up with newly arrived friends.

Then Sweyn glanced at Halfdan, thoughts of what he could see on his mind. "You have had some problems here I see." He gestured at the burned out hulk of a ship and the blackened palisade. Then his eyes swept out over those still milling about on the beach. "I do not see Gudbj or Gudrod." He turned questioning eyes to his chieftain.

Halfdan nodded and beckoned the large group of men to gather around. He had expected the questions. He had ordered his response while the others enjoyed the moment of reunion. Speaking loud enough for all to hear he focused on Sweyn and his men.

"Aye, you will have many questions about what you see and what you hear from others. After Athils gets here I will call a council." His glance took in all those grouped around him. Every man hung on his words. "We have much to discuss, but I want the council to be held with all of our leaders together. Afterwards, there will be a *Thing* for the people. Every man, woman, and child, freeman and thrall alike, must attend. I have waited for you and Athils' return for this council. It is that important to our future, the future of our people. Now, to your other questions; Gudbj is away, doing the work of our people. Gudrod was killed on a hunting trip with three others. Many are missing from our ranks; you will notice this and we will talk of it, but save other questions for the council and *Thing*. I expect them to take all day, perhaps into the night."

Sweyn and his men said nothing, all shocked to hear of Gudrod's death and the deaths of so many others of the people. It was a sobering moment.

"Tostig went to get a couple horse carts to haul your cargo inside the palisade. There are many people to get your cargo unloaded. Then it will be up to all of us to care for the meat and hides. It will be a busy time around here until your cargo is taken care of."

Sweyn made no comment. His mind grappled with a flood of emotion and deep-seated anger at what he had been told. He looked back at Halfdan as he got control of himself once again. "Athils has the same amount of meat and hides, maybe more, his ship is a little bigger."

"I know; we will get it all taken care of." Halfdan turned as the carts and horses arrived. He glanced back to Sweyn. "Others will unload the ship. You and your men go with Bjorn. He will show you where to get some hot food."

"I can wait to eat until the flood tide." He turned to look at the water of the bay as it began its daily rapid rise to high tide. "My crew can take care of the ship until she is safely grounded beside the others."

"Let my crew do it, Sweyn." Bjorn's steady gaze held Sweyn's attention. "I know how you feel about your ship, but others can moor it for you. You and your men have done enough today, just getting here. So, gather them up and come with me into the settlement, sit down at a table, and have some hot food."

Sweyn sighed in resignation and spoke to his helmsman. "Get the others Einar. We will go see this Halfdansfjord, and get some hot food.

TWENTY LEAGUES NORTH OF HALFDANSFJORD

Earlier that same morning, in a cove to the north of Halfdansfjord, Athils and the five men of his crew lolled about the ship, some sleeping, while others sat doing anything to pass the time.

They had spent the night aboard, huddled under makeshift tents of walrus hides draped over the sail boom. The hide tents allowed them to spend a relatively comfortable night out of the incessant rain, secure in the knowledge that the ship was not going anywhere, for she was hard aground. Now, they waited for the flood tide to float the ship free from the muddy bottom, so they could be on their way once again. The flood tide had only just begun and could not be hurried.

The day before, Athils had told them that they would shelter for the night in one of the many coves gouged out of the shoreline, providing the depth of water close to shore could accommodate the heavily laden ship. He admitted that he almost waited too long; the gods of storm, wind, thunder, and lightning were almost upon them.

Just before sundown of that same day, the ship was rolling and plunging in steep seas as the storm's leading edge tore at them. The big sail was reefed to its last two panels, the sail yard almost all the way down the mast. The ship's downwind course angled slightly inshore as the helmsman watched for a break in the coastal tree line, indicating a cove or small bay entrance.

The rest of the ship's crew huddled nearby in the stern, seeking what little protection the upthrust stern offered from the howling wind. Their clothing had become soaked over time, but it still captured body heat. In spite of the conditions the men were not uncomfortable. The food bags and a need to get out of the wind had drawn them together. Beards streaming with water, and eyes squinted in the wind, the men sat silently, contentedly eating their final meal of the day - dried meat and fish dipped in the new supply of walrus oil. The same fare as the day before, and the day before that.

When he finished eating, Athils took the tiller, so the helmsman could eat. His eyes scanned the coast looking for a break in the tree-lined shore. A short time later he saw what he sought, and made a course change direct for the entrance of a likely cove.

"Brattr, cast the plummet line on the way in." Athils gave the order over his shoulder to his men, still huddled in the stern.

Brattr made his way forward without comment. The ship's two plummet lines hung on pegs hammered into the stem and stern posts. When in position in the bow, Brattr swung the line in an arc. When he released the line, the stone plummet on the end carried it out near the full extent of its thirty odd feet of length, and ahead of the ship. As the ship moved forward, he hauled in the slack, accurately measuring the water depth as the ship passed over the plummet hanging straight down into the water. If the plummet was not on the bottom when the ship passed over it, the water was deeper than the length of the plummet line, which was the case with his first cast of the line.

"No, bottom on the line," Brattr hollered over his shoulder. He rapidly re-coiled the line for another cast. This would continue until Athils told him to stop.

Athils glanced again at the line of low gray black clouds to the northwest, and the pennant atop the mast. It stood straight out in the moaning wind, like an iron bar. He knew that they were in for a long night.

"Take another reef in the sail," he shouted through cupped hands. The ship slowed to steerage way. A boom pole held the sail foot to port and the sheet line cleated the sail foot tightly in; only the last panel of the sail powered the ship now.

Falki, still chewing the last mouthful of oil soaked, dried fish, stepped up beside Athils to take over the tiller. Small rivulets of oil ran unchecked from the corners of his mouth.

Athils looked at his thrall, took in the oil running into the beard covering his chin, and the look of sappy contentedness on his face. He grinned in spite of himself.

Shaking his head at the ability of all of them to see humor in most circumstances, he directed his attention to the sea ahead of the ship. His thoughts dwelled for a moment on his crew. *They are all like Falki, accepting of whatever the gods throw at them. They do the hard, dangerous work of handling the ship every day without complaint. I handpicked each of them, and I value the work they do for me and this ship.*

Athils gave the tiller over to Falki, and looked again at the man. Although he was his thrall, he was also his trusted helmsman. "I am going forward to guide our approach. Keep her just off the wind; let the sail luff a little. I want steerageway, no more. Watch for my hand signals." He turned away to make his way forward.

"Aye, I will." Falki watched Athils make his way forward through the piles of walrus hides and ivory. He glanced aloft at the rigid pennant, its length vibrating in the fierce wind and moved the tiller bar slightly, feeling the lack of normal water pressure against the big steerboard. He threw a leg over the tiller bar, cupped his hands, and shouted at Athils. "When we sail through the entrance I may need that last reef shaken out. The land will dampen the wind and I will not be able to steer this close to the wind's eye."

Athils waved an acknowledgement.

The wind had the surface of the small cove they chose for sanctuary covered in whitecaps. Relatively calm water, close to the north shoreline offered the best choice and Falki responded with a turn to port as Athils pointed in that direction. Athils sent two men aft to shake one reef out of the sail and retrim the boom and sail foot.

The ship's speed increased quickly. The wind moaned in the rigging like a demented troll, the sound pervasive and disquieting. Falki tried not to listen to the sound. He told himself that he did not believe in the little people or giants either, but... He unconsciously dampened the effect of the additional thrust by allowing the sail to luff, trying to put the moaning from his mind. Certain tones of the storm always left him tight as a bow string. He knew the gods were watching, trying to invade his conscious mind. He shook himself, willing them to leave him be. The pitch of the moaning suddenly changed, as if the gods knew what he tried to do. He saw Athils suddenly pointing to port. The need to comply snuffed the uncomfortable thoughts from his mind. He moved the tiller bar for a turn to port.

"Stand by to loose the sheets!" Athils shouted to his waiting men.

"Six feet on the line; mud bottom!" Brattr bounced the plummet line up and down, feeling the soft bottom mud.

Athils raised both arms as a signal to the helmsman and the two men at the sheets. He felt the mud suck at the keel of his ship as she passed over. He dropped both arms to his sides.

Falki jerked the steerboard keeper strap loose, so the big steering oar could swing up and not be damaged when the ship grounded on the bottom.

Released from the restriction of the sheet lines the reefed sail boomed in the wind, flapping without purpose, effectively braking the ship's forward momentum as the keel grounded in the soft mud of the cove bottom.

Two men wrestled the anchor over the side; tying it off with sufficient slack in the anchor rode to gain a purchase on the bottom in the unlikely event the flood tide refloated the ship while the crew slept.

Athils helped the rest of his crew throw a few heavy hides over the sail boom to create shelter for all of them. The outside edges of the big sail closed both ends of the makeshift shelter. Without further delay the crew climbed inside with their sleeping bags and soon fell into an exhausted sleep while the storm raged outside.

HALFDANSFJORD

Before full light pushed the gloom of night from the land, the daily work of the people began in earnest. While they worked, word spread rapidly through the populace that this council was to be of particular import to all of them, and that a *Thing* would follow. Two *Things* in one year was unusual; anticipation and a certain amount of anxiety invaded the normal demeanor of most of the free adults; little changed for the thralls. The commons quickly became a beehive of activity as every available man, woman, and child began working to finish that which had been begun the day before with Sweyn's cargo. The arrival of Athils' ship would more than double the amount of meat and hides needing processing. This fact alone added a sense of urgency to the work. Frida and Thora had earlier estimated for Halfdan that two full days would be required to finish processing, because of the curing time alone, and providing the good weather held.

Walrus hides, spread on the ground hair side down had been employed to keep the meat free of dirt, or mostly so. Fat and blubber went in one pile and strips of lean meat went in another. Drying racks sagged with meat curing in the smoky air above the smoldering fires that had been kept burning throughout the night. Space on the racks held up the whole process. As a consequence, the meat had to be dried in batches. When dried and smoked the leathery meat strips kept until consumed, packed as they were in large leather bags, and stored in each longhouse for the coming winter.

Chunks of fat and blubber piled on a walrus hide beside the fire pit were added to four kettles suspended over the fire to be rendered into the nutritious oil so important in the diet of the people. The settlement's four oldest boys, Atli, Haki, Od, and Egnar took turns with the tedious task of constantly stirring the liquid to keep it from burning. As the connective tissue in the fat and blubber crisped in the hot oil and floated to the top, one of the boys skimmed it off with a long-handled wooden skimmer. The cooks would make future use of these cracklings in soups and stews, adding both body and taste to these staple foods – nothing was wasted. After the chunks of fat and blubber rendered to oil, and the cracklings were skimmed, the oil was dipped from the kettles and poured in firkins for storage.

⸺

Thorvard the Tanner, and his crew, had hauled off all but the few walrus hides in use by those involved with processing the meat. His men used teams of horses to drag the heavy hides from the beach to the tanning pits. Because of the smell, the pits were located just west of the barley field and downwind of the settlement proper.

Over time the tanning area assumed a permanency and character of its own as needs dictated how Thorvard and his men transformed it to facilitate their work. Hides usually arrived in the same condition as the walrus hides - partially dried and salted - or freshly stripped from the animal in the case of those harvested or killed close to the settlement. In any case, salting and drying while spread out flat was the first care a hide received that was to be cured into useful leather. Typically this process took several days, depending on weather conditions – the walrus hides were partially dried stiff when received, so they went directly to the next phase, soaking. The pit for this purpose contained a gruel of wood ashes and water; the combination of these produced a weak lye solution that caused the hair to slip. Soaking for a few days softened the hide and allowed the tanners to scrape off the loosened hair. After the hair was scraped off, the hides were staked to the ground around their periphery for the final scraping to remove any remaining fat and flesh. Stretched as much as possible in an oft repeated process, the hides became both thinner and larger. The softened and cleaned hides then went into the tanning pit for the final soak.

For these purposes two pits had been dug. The water necessary to fill both pits came from a nearby rivulet, via a ditch. A fortunate happenstance was the presence of a hot spring. The foul smelling hot water issued from the base of the cliff out of a hole stained yellow from the mineral content. The hot water flowed away in a rill that emptied into the rivulet that fed the two ponds before finally flowing into the bay. So, the water that fed the two pits kept the water in the pits warm, assisting in the process of slipping the hair and softening the hides left to soak there. The first of the pits was used to soak hides long enough to slip the hair, and the second contained the tanbark, its water almost black with a rich stew of tannin leached from crushed oak bark.

The cleaned hides were left to soak in the second pit until Thorvard was satisfied the tannin had done its work. The tanbark solution imparted a rich dark brown color to the hide.

The last of the heavy work involved at least two men pulling the hides back and forth over a horizontal beam to finish breaking down the fibers. Not unlike a washer woman, the final handling for most of the hides involved wringing out as much of the water as possible and then hanging them over the drying racks where they would dry in the wind and heat of the smoky smudge fires beneath. Although Thorvard did not know why, he knew from long experience that the smoke did something to the leather that allowed clothing made from it to remain pliable after it dried from a thorough soaking in a rain shower or river crossing. For that reason all the clothing leather received this important processing step. From the smoked leather, Thorvard selected the finest pieces that would be finished in a stew of animal brains to a tanned softness and pliability suitable for clothing.

Leather from around the thinner edges of the hide was destined to become shoes or boots, winter hats, mittens, arm and wrist guards, thongs, or any of the other myriad uses for leather in Norse society. Pieces of thick rawhide that had received minimal tanning were always set aside for boot soles and warrior's armor jerkins of overlapping, heavy leather tabs,

Walrus hide leather made the best rope, so most of this batch would be cut into strips and twisted into rope. This essential and highly regarded trade commodity was utilized in daily life and traded abroad. The tightly twisted strands, heavily oiled with the same whale, walrus, or seal oil consumed by the people on a daily basis, produced a stranded rope that was both strong and almost impervious to moisture and rot. To this end, many of the hides from the bounty of the hunt brought home by Sweyn and Athils were destined.

THE COUNCIL MEETS

Later that day Halfdan, his constant companion, the dog Fang, and Tostig stood on the landing beach watching the flood tide. Halfdan found he was confiding more and more in Tostig. The man was a rock. He was no Gudbj – there was only one Gudbj - but he was dependable and intelligent. Best of all he felt a duty to his people and his chieftain - attributes held in high regard by Halfdan. "The flood is about to the halfway point. Athils is somewhere north of here, so the tide where he is will be ahead of us. He will be here soon, I think." Halfdan glanced at his companion. "Pass the word to the others, we will gather down here on the beach when the lookouts spot Athils' ship and sounds the alarm. Tell them to bring every man not busy with something else and we will get the ship unloaded."

"I will also have horse carts ready. That worked well with all the meat and hides from Sweyn's cargo."

"Good, so be it then." Halfdan turned away and headed toward the tanning pits. *Even upwind with this light breeze I can smell the pits. I don't know how Thorvard has stood the smell all these years.* He glanced at Fang walking beside him. The dog's nose wrinkled as he sniffed the air. Halfdan chuckled, drawing the dog's attention. "It does stink. It will soon be a lot worse." The tip of Fang's tail moved back and forth slightly, as if he understood.

Thorvard, always proud to have Halfdan show an interest in the important work provided by him and his crew of hard-working men, had brought his chieftain up to date while the two men walked through the tanning area. Halfdan nodded or spoke to individual workmen while he examined leather in various stages of completion. At the moment they were stopped beside four large casks that stunk like death itself. Halfdan recoiled when Thorvard reached in the slimy looking liquid and drew out a piece of thin, dark brown leather.

Thorvard and the workers nearby laughed at Halfdan's reaction.

"Whew, that smells rotten!" Halfdan backed away a safe distance. "What is that liquid?"

"A stew of brains. It smells rotten because the leather soaking in there is rotting. We soak the thin leather in casks until it is as soft as we can make it. This piece I have here is almost ready." He demonstrated by easily manipulating the softened leather. "It will be washed in saltwater, dried, and oiled. The women will make some of our clothing out of it. Your vest is this kind of leather," added Thorvard.

At that moment, the wail of the guard's horns stopped the conversation about leather. Everyone's attention focused on the ship rounding the headland. She turned to port and steered a direct course for the landing beach.

Halfdan turned back to Thorvard with a big grin on his face. "Good, they have all come home." He gestured toward the landing beach. "I want to get Athils' ship unloaded as quickly as possible. Tostig will have horse carts on the beach to haul the meat and hides. You and your men handle the hides. It will save time." With that, he turned away and made his way toward the landing beach, Fang trotting along behind.

Thorvard gathered his crew together from their various tasks, and told them what Halfdan had said. Then he and his men headed toward the beach to join the throng of greeters, and collect the walrus hides from Athils' cargo.

Athils dropped the sail as his ship passed the two beach islands. Soon after the watchers onshore saw the long sweeps poke from the sides of the ship. The tide was in full flood and everyone knew that Athils intended to ride the surge into the beach. His men stood by with sweeps at the ready in the event they would be needed. The tidal surge had the ship's speed above steerageway, so Falki had no difficulty steering for a spot by the large crowd gathering for their arrival. Judging from the exuberant shouts back and forth from ship to shore, the exhilarating surf ride into the beach was the perfect end to the voyage.

The heavily laden ship grounded on the gravel bottom more than a ship's length from the beach. The sweeps rattled inboard and were stowed with the others. Two lines were thrown from each side of the stern to men waiting ashore, who tied them to stakes driven into the beach above the high water mark. As the tide continued to surge in, refloating the ship, slack would be taken up in the mooring lines to keep the bow pointed in as desired. Athils vaulted over the side into the shallows, reached up to get something one of his men handed to him, and waded ashore. His crew followed behind, all shouting and laughing with the throng gathered on the beach.

Athils headed straight toward Halfdan, who waited on the beach at the forefront of a large group of men, including the other ships' captains.

"The tooth of a bull narwhal!" Halfdan exclaimed, as he saw what Athils carried ashore. Athils grounded the heavy tooth. The two men shook hands while the others crowded around to look at the prize.

The darkly mottled, spiral tooth was longer than Athils was tall. He picked it up in both hands and held it aloft for all to see. From its base to the sharp point of its tip, the tusk, as most people called it - really the left tooth of the male narwhal - was a beautiful example of arctic animal ivory. As such it was valuable in any society.

"Inuktuk wanted me to give this to you, Halfdan. It is from him and his people." He handed the tusk to Halfdan.

Turning it over in his hands, Halfdan rubbed the spiral surface. His eyes travelled over its length. He looked up at Athils. "I am impressed by his gift. I have never held one before."

Many of the men nearby added that they never even seen one before.

Athils chuckled. He was enjoying the reaction the tusk engendered in his friends. "I think such a heavy piece of ivory is usually reserved for chieftains and Kings, which is why most of us have never before seen one. It will make many hafts, combs, and broaches, Halfdan."

"Not this one. I will display this great tooth on the wall in the council chamber for all to see, so that all will know that we have friends in the far north."

"Inuktuk would be pleased. He wanted to send you something the equal of the parka you gave him. I think he has done so," Athils added with big grin.

Halfdan sat the base of the heavy tusk on the ground. Again, his eyes travelled up its full length. "I think I got the best of the bargain, all Inuktuk got was a colorful parka."

"He does not look at it that way, Halfdan. That parka is his most prized possession. I do not think he ever takes it off."

"He did not take it off while we were there," Sweyn added from the press of men. "He smells a little gamey, or the parka smells, I could not tell which."

Everybody laughed; this was a long speech for Sweyn.

Halfdan's eyes swept the crowd of men. "Tostig, find Finnbar or Ewyn and tell them what I want done with this tooth." He handed the man the tusk.

He looked at the clear skies. "We all know that these warm days cannot last. That last storm began the weather change." He looked pensive for a moment. His next statement told all his men why. 'If Gudbj were here, he might tell us that it will snow tomorrow." He swept his arm to encompass the western sky. "I know there is not a cloud to be seen, but that is what he would say."

Knowing his feelings on the subject of Gudbj, nobody offered comment.

Halfdan's eyes played over his men. He indicated the activity around Athils' ship with a lift of his chin. "Now, let us help get this ship emptied of her cargo. The weather will break soon. When we finish, I want the council to meet. We are all here. The women will have food and drink for us in the council chamber."

The six ships' captains and the principle lieutenants of Halfdansfjord - Tostig, Helge, Thorgill, and Hrafen — gathered around the long trestle table near the center of the council chamber for the long-awaited event. Most were silent as they stared into the flames spreading through the fuel in the nearby fire pit. Others conversed in low tones.

The fire had only recently been kindled in the long pit; the big room was cold. The flickering light of the fire pit and soapstone whale oil lamps suspended from roof support timbers pushed back the cave-like gloom. A haze of smoke hung in the still air as if it, too, awaited the council.

Three thrall women entered the chamber. Two carried a kettle and net bag of either barley loaves or wooden bowls and spoons. The third carried a trencher piled with meat joints. Steam rose from the food as the women carefully sat them down on the stone hearth across the end of the fire pit.

The wood and charcoal mix was spreading through the long pit from the hearth end where it had been set alight. The mass of stone and tamped earth of the hearth was already warm to the touch.

The men gathered around the hearth to investigate the midday fare, making their choices before returning to the table. Beyond a word or two, conversation was unnecessary. The men were hungry, food was on their minds. Talking would not change that fact.

In due course, most finished eating. Those that had, sat hunched over the table picking their teeth, or pensively pulling their fingers through their beards, waiting for Halfdan to begin. All had given considerable thought to the topics likely to be discussed with the others that were of particular import to each of them. Their minds dwelt on those thoughts now.

Thorgill had been consumed of late by thoughts of Halfdan's decision to give Gudrod's ship to Tostig instead of him, and his reaction to that decision. While realizing that the topic was a moot point since the ship had been destroyed in the Anishinabeg raid, the sting of what he considered to be a slight persisted in his mind. He stole a glance at Tostig, who sat on the opposite side of the table near the other end, smoothing the edges of his beard around his mouth. *He does not seem concerned by anything. Why should he be concerned? What is the matter with me? For that matter, why have I let this bother me, I must be crazy?* He closed his eyes for a moment, to order his thoughts.

Deskaheh and Thora entered the chamber at that moment.

"Close the doors." Halfdan called as they walked in.

Deskaheh did so; the pair made their food selection, and joined the others at the table.

Fresh from the business of processing meat, Thora looked the part, a condition that gained her a couple ribald comments, which she ignored, as they knew she would.

Beyond those comments, there were a few nods of greeting, but none questioned their attendance, knowing that Halfdan wanted them there for a reason.

While Halfdan waited for all to finish eating, he watched the group as a whole, not focusing on anyone in particular. Since Bjorn's return, he had noted that Thorgill seemed different somehow. He could not quite put his finger on the problem, but he knew the man well enough to know that something troubled him. *Perhaps, whatever it is will come out today.* He sighed, and stretched. Getting to his feet he stepped over to the hearth to get another cup of hot broth. The heat of the fire drew his attention and he basked in its warmth while he drank the hot liquid slowly. His eyes played over the group of men. Conversation died as he returned to his high seat at the head of the table.

Halfdan began without preamble. "I know you have all discussed what has occurred here since we completed construction of our settlement, but I will tell you everything anyway, mostly for the benefit of those of you that were away all summer. We can discuss whatever you want when I have finished."

Over a portion of the next hour Halfdan related the high notes of life in their new home. He was a good storyteller and missed nothing. Even those who had witnessed the events firsthand listened attentively.

As expected, he spent the most time on Gudbjartur, noting that had Deskaheh not witnessed him being a prisoner of the Naskapi, none of them would have known the fate of the expedition. He also noted that the three men still unaccounted for were presumed to be dead, because none of the Naskapi bands were known to have them. His views on the importance of their friendship with the Naskapi bands of Glooscap and Chisasi he covered in detail, glossing over the deaths of the two rapists that began those friendships.

To Gudbj he gave full credit for the excellent relationship they now enjoyed with all the Naskapi.

When he followed with the visit of Chisasi with Kejo and his men to the settlement with details of Gudbj's capture it brought forth a few rumblings from his listeners until he told them how Gudbj had managed to turn his captivity into a boon for his people. He quieted them with a raised hand.

"Be patient, I am almost finished."

He told them briefly about Gudrod's hunting expedition, the death of Gudrod and three of his men, the capture of Ivar by the Haudenosaunee war party, and the current expedition to retrieve him.

"Deskaheh is best suited to answer questions about this expedition. Thora will help him with translation if need be." He indicated them with a lift of his chin.

"Helge was with Gudrod. He is the one you should question about what happened when the war party attacked them."

"There was much else that occurred in your absence. I suspect you already know most of it. The rest you can ask now, or find out with the passage of time." He got to feet to get another cup of broth.

"Brodir and Thorgeirr arrived here in time to take part in the end of the battle with the Anishinabeg. Shortly before that attack, six Anishinabeg warriors came in the night, killing two of our guards and entering the palisade, before the dogs scared them off. One man was captured. I released him in the hopes he would tell his people of our justice. My plan did not work, as the later attack by several hundred of them confirms. This tribe is the gravest threat to our continued existence that we face as a people, and why Deskaheh is here today. Most of you already know about this threat. Deskaheh will tell us the whole story concerning them and what should be done to survive the threat these people pose. When he is finished, and has answered your questions, we will move on with other business." He waved a hand to Deskaheh.

Deskaheh and Thora arose from their places. Deskaheh's briefing was similar in content to the one he gave after the attack, and most had heard it, but that did not lessen the impact of what he told them. As before, Thora helped him when he needed help with specifics.

He finished with what he felt the Anishinabeg would do in the spring. His final comments got both Athils and Sweyn to their feet.

The two men looked at each other. Sweyn raised his chin at Athils, who nodded and turned back to Deskaheh.

"Are you certain that we cannot defend ourselves against these men?"

"I am certain, Athils. There are too many of them."

"We have all winter to prepare. They cannot attack us in winter, can they?"

"They can attack in winter, but they will wait until they can come in canoes rather than on snowshoes. The journey from their homeland will be easier and faster."

Athils looked from Deskaheh to the others, coming to rest on Halfdan. His angst apparent, he blurted out what many of them had already thought of but none had vocalized. "Then, I think we should consider loading everybody up in the ships and going somewhere else."

"That question I will not answer, Athils," Halfdan said evenly. "We have worked hard on this settlement, it is our home. We have made many friends in this land. I will ask our people this question at the Thing that follows this council. I want a majority to decide such an important issue for all of us."

Satisfied, Athils and Sweyn sat down. Halfdan signed for Deskaheh to continue.

"Naskapi and Anishinabeg are kinsmen. They have many disagreements, but the chieftain of all the Naskapi, Sachem, might be able to keep the Anishinabeg from attacking us. I do not know that he will do this, but if he will not, you cannot survive in this land. The next time they attack, they will keep coming at you until all of the men are dead and Halfdansfjord is destroyed. The few women and children that survive will be taken away into slavery. It is their way." He gave the cutting sign.

Surprisingly, not a sound came from the other men; Deskaheh's words were that sobering.

Halfdan nodded his thanks to Thora and Deskaheh. The two left the council chambers.

"Alright, now you all know our situation. There is nothing more to say about the Anishinabeg. The Naskapi are fully aware of our problem and we must be patient for them to respond. Nothing happens quickly in this land. Chisasi has told me that they are discussing what they will do in the spring." He looked around the table. "Are there questions about anything I have covered?"

"I want to hear more about Gudrod and Gudbj," Athils said. He glanced at Helge, then back to Halfdan. "Sweyn and I will talk to Helge later about how Gudrod died, but perhaps you can give us the latest about Gudbj."

"It is a long tale; I can only relate the part I know." He paused a moment to get to his feet, so all could see him. "Ingerd and Lothar went with Kejo and his men to the village where Gudbj is living. He is not a prisoner, but he must remain until their time of green grass - spring. The Naskapi captured him alright, but Sachem spared his life so that he could learn their language and they in turn could learn about us. He later fought a Haudeno war party that attacked the village. He was instrumental in defeating them and saving many of the Naskapi women from certain death. He is now one of the people. They call him Nipishish. It means Axeman. What he does for our people by being there with the principle band of the Naskapi tribe cannot be over emphasized. We all miss him, but we are alive today only because of the relationship he has forged with Sachem and his people. It is a miracle ordained by the gods!" Halfdan finished passionately.

His men sat silently for the most part, for most had already heard the tale. After a moment, Sweyn asked the only question to come from the table.

"I heard that they are trying to get Ivar back from the Haudeno?"

"Aye, we heard that from Chisasi. He told me that his band might not know what happened until spring. He was not certain. That is all I know."

Halfdan looked around the table waiting for another question. When none came, he moved to another topic.

"There are six ships here once again, since Thorgeirr and his people arrived. Thorgeirr's ship is the largest after mine, so it should be used for our long distance trading voyages. Bjorn's is the smallest of the remaining ships." He looked at Bjorn. "If you agree, I want you to be my partner in Steed of the Sea, with equal shares. She is our largest ship and half her cargo is the equal to what your ship can haul. Your ship can be used here for local trading and fishing. I recommend you pick the man you want to captain your ship on shares from these three." He indicated Tostig, Thorgill, and Hrafen.

Bjorn got to his feet and approached Halfdan. "I agree with your proposal." The two men shook on it. He turned to face the three men in question. "Thorgill is my pick for captain. We will discuss the shares later." He grinned at the man.

Thorgill's surprise at being selected was all over his face. His expression slipped to one of unease as his past anger at being previously passed over by Halfdan to command Gudrod's ship came to the fore. In a few heartbeats thoughts about the perceived slight raced through his mind. He glanced from Halfdan to the still grinning Bjorn. A grin slowly spread over his face as awareness returned as quickly as it had been lost a moment ago. He got to his feet and reached across the table to shake Bjorn's hand.

"I was surprised. I do not know what to say." His voice conveyed sincerity. He glanced from Bjorn to Halfdan, noticing the intent look on Halfdan's face, the slight narrowing of his eyes.

"Do you feel better now?" Halfdan asked.

"Aye, I do. I will do a good job." *He cannot know what I have been thinking, but still...I should never have doubted him. Instead of holding a grudge I should have talked to him.*

Halfdan nodded slightly, his expression did not change.

Bjorn glanced from Halfdan to Thorgill. *There is something going on here. Something is amiss with these two.* He went on like he was unaware, clapping Thorgill on the shoulder. "And, that is why I picked you; I know you will do a good job."

The others dutifully laughed, but Halfdan saw no humor in the exchange. He waited a moment for the banter to trail off. "Alright, two ships are taken care of. As we have discussed, two ships are needed for local trade and fishing. Bjorn's ship and Thorgill fills part of that need. The shipwrights have been gathering oak and birch. Suitable lengths of oak and birch for planking is hard to find here. Thicker than normal, straight-grain pine and fir will be used instead. They have enough frames cut and finished for two ships. Both will be about the same length as Bjorn's ship. These ships will go to Tostig and Hrafen." He glanced at both men. "The two of you will want to work with the shipwrights. They will be your ships and you will want to be familiar with them." The two men nodded in agreement, knowing that his statement was more than a mere suggestion.

Halfdan paused a moment before continuing to voice his requests and thoughts to the three new captains. "Local trading and relations with the people of this land are vital to our continued success. You must establish friendly relations with those we do not know about, continue our friendly relations with Essipit and his people, and all the Naskapi bands you might contact. You three men will be responsible for this work. I want one ship in the home waters all the time, as a mother ship for the fishermen; that arrangement has worked well since Gudbj started it right after we arrived here. The other two will engage in trade and exploration on both coasts all the way south to Leifsbudir. I suggest you trade off staying in the home waters, so that each of you gets a chance to explore and trade. You work that out yourselves."

Bjorn stood. "I will be right back."

Halfdan nodded to him. "Anybody else need to step outside? No? Well I do." He paused midway to the door, turning back toward the table. "You men stay for the remainder of the council," he said, indicating Tostig, Thorgill, and Hrafen. "You are captains now, some without ships, but captains nonetheless." Appreciative comments and laughter followed him out the door, as he knew it would.

The others stretched or revisited the hearth while Bjorn and Halfdan were away. None wanted more food, but the hot broth beckoned.

Halfdan returned and joined the men around the hearth. They talked about the prospect of the new ships and the hard work to follow that would make them a reality. It was hoped that the winter conditions would allow the building to proceed without too many storm related interruptions.

Bjorn entered a moment later, a huge smile on his face. His return caused an abrupt change of topic when the others caught sight of what he had brought. On his right forearm perched a large white falcon with black-barred back and wings. The hooded bird of prey's long talons were firmly clamped onto Bjorn's thick leather armguard. In his left hand he carried an ornately carved, chest high, T-bar perch, which he sat down on the floor at one end of the table. He coaxed the falcon onto the T-bar while the other men, including Halfdan, milled about admiring the magnificent bird.

Bjorn beamed at his friends. He subdued their exuberance, and put off their questions with a raised hand. In the other hand he held the end of the leather jess that was attached to the falcon's leg. He extended the jess to Halfdan, who took hold of it. The two men coaxed the bird to Halfdan's armguard.

"Halfdan, Essipit sent this gyrfalcon to you in the name of the friendship that the two of you share." Bjorn threw his head back and laughed at the expression on Halfdan's face.

For the first time in recent memory, Halfdan seemed at a loss for words, a condition that was not to last long. He just stared at the bird for a moment, and then he removed the bird's hood.

The animal shook his head and ruffled his feathers, in apparent joy at having the hood removed, and then the cruel black eyes swept the room, examining the men clustered around him. That he was accustomed to human presence was apparent by his relaxed attitude. Although Halfdan held the jess firmly, no attempt was made to take flight.

Halfdan had not taken his eyes from the falcon; now the falcon met his stare. The unblinking eyes of the bird of prey sent a chill through the man. "By the gods, this is a beautiful bird. I have never seen a gyrfalcon this closely before. He is big and heavy. Just look at those talons and that cruel beak." He laughed, his eyes playing over his men. "Doubtless, the last thing a goose or duck sees in its life."

Bjorn laughed with the others. "Essipit took him from the nest this spring, just before he took flight. He trained him and hunted with him, so he will return to you when you take him on the hunt."

"As soon as our business is complete here, I think we all should go out into the fen and see how he hunts." Halfdan returned the falcon to its perch. He stood back, examining the ornately carved perch for the first time. He turned to Bjorn, a question in his eyes.

"Aye, it is Jorundr the Carver's work. He just finished it in time for this council," Bjorn added.

"I thought so. There are few his equal." Halfdan glanced at those around him and returned to his seat, a signal that he wanted to return to the business at hand. He waited a moment while the others took their seats.

"I think matters concerning our ships have been covered for now. Are there any questions?" There were none.

He made eye contact with Sweyn and Athils. "Do either of you have anything you wish to discuss?"

The two men looked at each other. An unspoken thought passed between them. Athils nodded to his friend.

"I freed, Rolf," Sweyn said, looking at Halfdan. He ignored the explosive comments from some of the other leaders.

Halfdan's eyes swept the table, silencing his men. "I heard that. Why?"

"Rolf told me that he might want to stay with the Tornit, if he was free."

"That does not tell us why you freed him, Sweyn. We want to know."

Sweyn sighed and shrugged. "I just wanted to free him. In all these years his freedom never was discussed. When he told me he would stay if he was free, I suddenly wanted to give him that chance, one he had never asked for before." His simple explanation had the others thinking, as evidenced by their expressions and silence.

"Why did he come back with you, then?"

Sweyn chuckled at the thought. "He told me that he wanted to stay with me, it is what he knew. We all went back to work and that was the end of it."

"The end of it!" Brodir exploded, unable to contain himself any longer. "No, it is only the beginning. By the gods, Sweyn, what were you thinking?" The big man was on his feet, waving his arms in anger.

Halfdan stayed out of the heated conversation that followed. Brodir owned the most thralls and was far and away the most vocal. Every man in the council owned thralls, except Thorgill, and all had an opinion to voice on what Sweyn's action had done to cause problems. Halfdan allowed discussion of the volatile issue until the words shouted back and forth left the issue at hand and moved into the volatile area.

The only thing keeping Brodir, Thorgeirr, and Hrafen apart was the big, wide trestle table. That obstacle to close combat was in danger of being surmounted by the heated argument at any moment. The situation was getting out of hand when Halfdan got to his feet.

"Enough!" He shouted to be heard, his arms extended overhead. He was aware that Tostig suddenly appeared near him, much as Gudbj would have done.

This fact was not lost on the assembly. The men slumped onto the benches. Brodir stalked off, still fuming, walking off his rage.

"Brodir, we cannot settle anything like this. You know that."

The man stopped pacing and faced his chieftain from near the doorway. He shook his head in agitation, but returned. He could not deny Halfdan's wishes in a time of tension. None of them could.

All eyes were on Halfdan. He stood from his high seat at the head of the table, his eyes played over his men. With the exception of the new arrivals, Thorgeirr and Hrafen, he knew them well. A threatening undercurrent hung in the air.

"This stops here, now. Thralls are the property of their owners. I make no demands on our ancient customs regarding them. Sweyn freed the one thrall he had. That is his right as it your right to keep your thralls. Freeing any of them has never been discussed before. To do so is your business, and only your business. I am certain that all of us will be thinking on this as time goes by. What each of us does, if we do anything, is for each man to decide alone. Are we agreed?"

Each in his turn, the men voiced their agreement, save Brodir.

Halfdan knew it would be this way with Brodir. It would take time for him to settle down, but Halfdan gave him no time.

"And you, Brodir?" Halfdan's flat tone of voice always indicated when he would broach no further disagreement on the matter at hand.

Brodir glanced around the table and locked eyes with Halfdan. "Aye, Halfdan, I agree. The matter is closed."

"Good, so be it." Halfdan's manner abruptly changed as he changed the subject.

"Sweyn, I heard that Ormiga decided to stay with the Tornit."

"Aye, he did." To Sweyn that was sufficient explanation.

Athils looked at his friend quizzically and continued for him when it was obvious he was finished. "Ormiga fancied one of their young women. He also liked and admired the people and wanted to stay with them. The woman was agreeable. Everyone in Inuktuk's band wanted Ormiga to stay. They are very friendly people." Athils paused a moment. "Ormiga is his own man. He knew what he wanted." He bobbed his chin at Sweyn, silently telling him to say something.

"I will miss him, he was a good crewman," Sweyn said, grinning at the others.

Brodir just watched Sweyn without any display of his true feelings. His anger simmered just below the surface.

As for the other men, a few smiled with Sweyn, the others remained taciturn. The argument regarding their thralls still grated. Although none had any wish to alienate Halfdan, or anger him, the issue was far from over. It would eat at them for some time to come.

Chapter 5

TIME OF WHITENESS

Snow grains rattled through the trees and against the buildings of Halfdansfjord as the Frost Giants left their lair in Jotenheim to assault the northland. The mighty god, Thor, in concert with the Frost Giants, hurled the first snowstorm of the season at the land. The onslaught pummeled every living thing into submission; the cold crept into every haven sought.

Halfdan sat staring unfocused into space from the partial shelter of one of the common's sheds where he often sought seclusion to commune with his thoughts. Dressed for the occasion, he wore the heavy bearskin parka that Frida had just this morning presented to him. The parka extended to his knees and included a hood fringed with wolverine fur – a custom Frida had borrowed from the Naskapi women – and thick mittens from the same animal. She had told him that frost from the moisture in his breath would not freeze on contact with the fur. Although dubious about such a claim, he knew he would soon know one way or the other.

With his back to the thrust of the storm, his mind sorted through the myriad thoughts and reflections that consumed him at such times. Predominate were thoughts of Gudbj. He missed his friend; it was more than that. They shared everything. Gudbj could read his mind, knew intuitively what he wanted, how he would react to any situation. Most of all, the man's loyalty, honor, and integrity were dependable and unquestioned, as it should be. He realized early on that he had never had such a man at his side, one to carry out his orders unto death. Even knowing what Gudbj had accomplished with the Naskapi for his people, for him as their chieftain, did not lessen his need to sit and talk with his friend and lieutenant. It was the only way he had to put his thoughts to rest; to share them with the only man he felt a oneness with.

He shook his shoulders, shrugging deeper into the warmth and protection of his parka. *There seems less wind.* Squinting into the opaqueness from the open-ended shed, he realized how hard it was snowing. Snow grains had been gradually replaced by snowflakes that accumulated on and against every surface.

As far as he knew he was the only person outside. He saw smoke pouring from the smoke hole of the smithy, so he knew that Asgrim and his mates, Haakon and Sigmund were hard at it in the smoky warmth of their little world. Their work never stopped. The three men made every tool, weapon, and cooking utensil vital to Norse society, including smelting their steel and iron supply from the abundant bog iron of the fens around Halfdansfjord. He knew they would be making buckets of iron rivets and washers with which the ship builders fastened the long, thin hull planks of the ships together.

In preparation for building the two ships, the men erected a windbreak on the beach with a shed roof, a handy place to keep tools and the assorted paraphernalia of their trade, but little shelter from this kind of storm. Earlier, he had been with them when it had just begun to snow. He had been shown the stem and stern members for each ship, internal framing knees, as well as a considerable pile of sheathing planks accumulated for the time when assembly would begin. The men told him that the ships would be virtually identical, a little longer and deeper than Gudrod's ship had been at about forty feet. He had left them to it, for they knew what he expected and they had all winter to finish the job. As the storm increased in intensity slamming into Halfdansfjord with a fury seldom witnessed this early in the winter, the ship builders had given it up for another day.

After the shipbuilders left for the security and warmth of the longhouses, he had the tower guards recalled – conditions being too dangerous in the howling wind to do otherwise -- in favor of a periodic four man roving patrol after the wind died down a bit. He felt that nobody in their right minds would attack in a storm of this magnitude; the natives of this land would be hunkered down in their lodges, just as his people were. "Besides," he muttered aloud, "the dogs would set up a din if any intruders tried to climb the palisade to get into the settlement. They could not open any of the gates with all this snow piled against them."

At the sound of his voice, the great head of Fang rose from the pile of drifted snow at his feet. He smiled at the dog and leaned over to scratch his ears. "Do not let me interrupt your slumber."

The animal stood, shook the snow from his body, and watched the man expectantly. His tail wagged slowly.

Halfdan looked back at the dog. "I would not want to be an uninvited stranger within our village with you on the prowl." He stroked the dog absentmindedly, his mind returned to thoughts of the council and the Thing that followed.

The dog watched the man until he saw that no more attention would be forthcoming. His slanted eyes played over his surroundings without noting anything of significance. Lassitude overcame him once again; he took a couple turns around in place, checking for exactly the right spot, before stretching out on his side at Halfdan's feet.

Halfdan's mind had already taken him to another place. He felt satisfied with the council except for the thorny issue of the thralls. He had always avoided discussion of them because he knew it could only end in trouble. What, if anything, ever came of the heated discussion would be entirely up to the individual. As for himself, he was acutely aware that violence could still ensue.

He had decided that the matter of Ormiga staying with Inuktuk's band of Tornit was a good thing for both peoples. He hoped in this way that a gradual joining would occur between his people and the friendly tribes of this land. The men needed mates and he felt the native women would solve the situation on their own, given time. With Gudbj, and those of his expedition still alive, living among the Naskapi, and Grimr and Thorkell taking mates in Chisasi's band of Naskapi, things were looking up. Not knowing how Ivar had fared among the Haudeno bothered him considerably. The boy might not even be alive. Gudbj would seek revenge if his son had been killed, of that he was certain. Time would tell, but he felt no optimism regarding relations with the Haudenosaunee, especially since relations with their enemies, the Naskapi were good.

He had called the Thing immediately after the council finished. Being the first Thing held in Halfdansfjord, no site existed, such as a knoll to seat the leaders in full view of the people gathered below, so he had chosen the parapet above the south gate as the best spot within the settlement's palisade. He and other leaders gathered on the parapet, facing the people gathered below. Traditionally, a site for the Thing was carefully chosen, affording the leaders an unobstructed view of the various speakers, and the people the same unobstructed view of their leaders. Later, perhaps a suitable site would become the permanent location for the Thing, such as Thingvallir on Iceland.

He had known that normal gossip would have already provided his people with the main topics of the council, so he began by asking them if anybody had questions about what was already common knowledge. A grin spread on his face when he recalled the laughter that rippled through the crowd at his opening statement.

There were questions, of course, because there are always those in any gathering that seem compelled to ask questions that either have obvious answers, or for which there are no answers, given the particular circumstance. He always allowed them the latitude to ask questions, regardless of merit. Some always took advantage of what he considered the only loosening of the stern demeanor with which he governed his people.

Over a period of about an hour, people had asked him and their other leaders questions about the two ships that would be built, the plans for trapping fur bearers to bolster trade goods for next summer, and various reports on the bulging larders of each longhouse were made public. Askhold told of his schooling of small groups of youngsters in the art of the runes, and the various trades — smithies, bowyers, basket and pottery makers, and wood carvers, to name a few - of their society, and reported on the availability of their wares.

He had braced for the inevitable broaching of the topic of thralls. It had come as no surprise to him when Sigmund opened the discussion with a statement and question. The young man's voice still rang in his ears. "Sweyn freed Rolf. Will any other thralls be freed?" Sigmund had said, glancing pointedly at Brodir, who owned the woman he hoped would be freed.

Halfdan recalled meeting the question with silence while his eyes swept the upturned faces to gauge the reaction of his people and their thralls to Sigmund's question. He saw that the thrall, Genevra stood beside Sigmund, her belly swollen with his child. Not a sound came from the multitude as they awaited the will of their chieftain.

He remembered choosing his words carefully; the answer had been harshly delivered, purposely cutting off further discussion. "I will say this only once. Do not ever mention it to me again. Thralls are the property of their owners, you all know that. I will not intercede on the behalf of a thrall with their owner, nor will I change our customs and laws regarding thralls." He liked Sigmund and the young smithy stood his ground for a couple heartbeats, his eyes locked on those of his chieftain, before he nodded and looked away. Sigmund and Genevra had put their heads together for some time afterwards. The woman was noticeably distraught, and neither Sigmund nor any other man could help her with that. Halfdan had given their problems no further thought. He felt that he had left no doubt in anyone's mind; the matter of the thralls was closed with him.

He had purposely saved the question of the danger that would be faced by all of them come spring, and what they wanted to do about it, for last. Gossip alone ensured that few points of discussion remained; he had been glad about that. The only question regarding the Anishinabeg that he had asked, did they want to leave Halfdansfjord in the early spring, or remain and fight? He recalled with pride that when he called for a vote on the points of the brief discussion the sea of raised hands told him that they were not leaving.

After the vote, he shared his thoughts with them on the defense they must mount. The discussion he encouraged revolved around how the palisade could be improved and strengthened. They all knew that the only reason their settlement's stockade had not burned to the ground was because the upright logs used to build it were still green. He told them that a wide moat around the settlement must be dug as soon as the frost left the ground the spring. A barrier of outward pointing sharpened stakes around the entire outer perimeter of the moat, to slow the Anishinabeg assault, would be an added defense. Surprisingly, nobody commented about the prodigious effort necessary to build such a defensive complex. Every man, woman, and child would contribute as necessary.

Herjolf the Bowyer had told them that he and his mates had a supply of arrows sufficient to repel any siege, and with an adequate supply of extra bows. Asgrim had reported that his smiths had extra men helping them produce spearheads, knives, and hatchet and axe heads, to the point that the carpenters had been kept busy over the winter providing hafts for all of them.

He smiled as he recalled that every craftsman, not wishing to be outdone, had taken the opportunity to report the available supply of their wares.

His people were as ready as he could make them. They knew what would be coming at them with the spring thaw. Their collective minds would rise to the occasion, as they always had in the past.

Sometime later, he had sat long enough that his limbs had grown stiff from disuse. Arching his back to relieve sore muscles, he arose and stretched, swinging his arms to and fro, he swiveled at the waist to speed up his heart and get his blood to flowing.

The dog arose too, shaking the snow from his coat. His sensitive noise tested the wind as he turned his eyes on the man. All seemed well in his world.

Halfdan noted that considerable snow has piled up against where he had sat as the howling wind blew it through the open ended shed; he realized that he did not feel the slightest chill in spite of the conditions in which he had sat. Ice encrusted his beard from his breath. He brushed it away. A wide smile split his face as he examined the outer edge of the wolverine fur around his hood. *Not a sign of frost. Frida will be pleased.*

Thoughts of Gudbj filled his mind as he and the dog trudged through the snow toward the warmth and security of his longhouse. *I wonder what he is doing; how he is faring in this storm.*

GLOOSCAP AND SAKOHKEA

The snowstorm had not yet reached far enough south to affect the drama unfolding on the knoll above the Haudeno village. The slate gray clouds of the lowering skies, gathering in the north, would soon change that.

Nipishish, always mindful of the weather, sniffed the north wind. He made eye contact with Glooscap, standing at the forefront of his men as they gathered around.

"Snow comes," he said simply.

Glooscap inclined his head in assent. He glanced at the sky briefly.

"We must make contact with the Haudeno before they are all holed up from the storm," Glooscap said. His eyes travelled over his silent men.

Glooscap quickly laid out his plan. "Kejo, you will be in charge while I am away. Nipishish, Ingerd, Lothar, and the Haudeno woman will come with me to the village." His eyes fastened on the Haudeno woman.

"Listen carefully to what I say, woman. I am not trading you for Ivar; I am releasing you to your people."

Momentarily overcome, the young woman cast her eyes downward at his words, before recovering to give him her full attention.

Glooscap continued slowly, emphasizing his words with copious hand signs. "In return I need your help to avoid bloodshed. You are to tell Deganawida and Sakohkea, that I, Glooscap, the war chief of my people and the representative of Sachem, come in peace for a parley about Ivar, the son of this man and woman, as you know." He indicated Nipishish and Ingerd. "When your guards see us walking toward their village and raise the alarm, we will stop. You will continue forward when I tell you, when I am certain they have seen you. Be quick about it. You must make them understand that I want a peaceful parley before Sakohkea has time to gather his warriors. They must give us a chance to talk; otherwise many will die this day, including you. Do you understand my words?"

"Yes, Glooscap, I understand. I will do my best for you because you have returned me to my people."

Glooscap paused a moment before continuing his instructions to the captive. "Tell them what happened with the woman that was killed when you were captured. They will want to know this. Tell them she fought and cut one of the men that attacked the two of you. Tell them why you were captured, that the two men wanted to know if Ivar was in your village."

"I will do my best, Glooscap." She averted her eyes from his face. The intensity of his expression scared her.

Glooscap studied her for a heartbeat, before he continued laying out his plan to the others. "Kejo, scatter the men along the knoll, out of sight of the guards. When the alarm is raised I will hold out the wampum belt for the Haudeno to see. When you hear me calling our intentions to them, stand in plain sight, so they know how many we are. If it is to be a parley, stay put. Sit down or gather in groups along the knoll to talk. Remain alert, but do nothing threatening unless I call you to the attack. If they do not parley, attack the village when you hear my war cry. I do not want to fight them, but if we must fight the advantage will be ours because of our sudden appearance in force."

His eyes locked on Kejo's for a brief moment before he looked over his men, coming to rest on the three Northmen.

"If we get a chance to talk, you three will play the most important role. Deganawida is a hard man, but known to be fair. The presence of Ingerd and Lothar may have the biggest influence on him. Show no fear. If you see Ivar, do nothing. I will be calling out our peaceful intentions; I will let them make the first move. The unknown is Sakohkea; he will not listen to anyone but Deganawida. If Deganawida does not intervene there will be no parley. We have faced one another many times; he is a brave man, and the ruthless war chief of his people, as he should be." His eyes played over the group as he paused for comment. There were none. A wordless lift of his chin bade his watching warriors to scatter out along the ridge line.

"Ingerd, loose your yellow hair, I want them to see it," Glooscap said.

Ingerd looked up at Nipishish questioningly.

"Unbind your hair, he wants them to see it," he said.

Ingerd unwound the leather binding and shook out her long hair.

Glooscap looked at her yellow hair blowing out in the slight breeze. "Good; we go now."

The well-worn path they followed single file down off the knoll toward the village palisade was out of the sight of the village guards for a short time, but the five of them, Nipishish, Ingerd, Lothar, the Haudeno maiden, and Glooscap in the lead, knew the alarm would sound the moment they stepped into sight. All were armed, save the captive, including Ingerd, who had her bow and a quiver of arrows slung over her shoulder. In addition to a bow and arrows, Lothar also carried the ceremonial calumet of the Naskapi, given into his hand by Sachem himself. The boy had basked in the attention paid to him by his parents and many of those present. The calumet was Sachem's personal gesture to Deganawida. He had chosen the young brother of Ivar to convey the pipe to the parley, if there was to be a parley. To say that Lothar was overwhelmed by the trust placed in him by the chieftain of all the Naskapi would be an understatement. It was much more than that. It was chilling for him to feel the weight of the calumet in its leather sheath that hung over his shoulder, moving against his back with each step. He knew the importance the pipe played in the ceremony of the smoke, especially between habitual enemies like the Naskapi and Haudenosaunee. If Deganawida accepted the gift, and began the ritual ceremony practiced by all the tribes, the boy realized that everyone at the parley would draw smoke through the pipe, even him.

As they walked into view, in the time it takes a dry leaf to flutter to the ground, the alarm was shouted by one of the palisade guards, to be instantly taken up by the others.

Pandemonium gripped the village at the guards' shouts, people ran hither and yon. This apparent disorder soon coalesced into order as the women and children disappeared like smoke in the wind, and armed men converged on the gate from every quarter.

Glooscap stopped his advance. He turned to his captive. "You are free to go. Life and death go with you. Choose which it will be this day."

The young woman nodded without comment, squared her shoulders and hurried along the path, down toward her village.

Glooscap held the wampum belt up and exhorted the Haudeno warriors flooding from the village gate to listen to his words.

Sakohkea ran through his warriors to the forefront of the throng. The young woman that Glooscap had just freed approached him; her hands signed as she talked to the war chief. He stopped her with a raised hand as his men became agitated, gesturing up the slope of the knoll. His head turned slowly as he looked at what his men had seen. The sight of it filled him with rage.

Glooscap did not need to turn around to know that his warriors were spread along the crest of the knoll, in plain sight. He knew that it was their presence near his village that had enraged Sakohkea. Glooscap continued to hold the wampum belt aloft and his voice continued to carry a message of peaceful intent. He saw a swirl in the press of men behind Sakohkea as an old man came forward. He knew this man to be the Haudeno chieftain, Deganawida. Glooscap stopped his message delivery and lowered the wampum belt. The fate of many people now rested with the old chieftain.

Glooscap keenly watched the conference that developed between Deganawida and his war chief. That Sakohkea was angry was obvious. The sound of his raised voice carried up the hill. The violent gestures of his hands were plain to see as he tried to force his will on his chieftain. Deganawida's raised hand stopped the tirade in mid-sentence. Glooscap saw him turn his attention to the young maiden; he placed a calming hand on her shoulder. The young woman talked to him, using copious hand signs and gestures toward the knoll. He asked her many questions and then he paused and looked up the slope at Glooscap and his companions. He turned to the throng of warriors and a few moments later, two men ran back into the village to do something at Deganawida's behest. Sakohkea vehemently opposed whatever it was judging from his display of emotion and agitated pacing.

The two men returned quickly, one carried an armload of firewood and the other a piece of bark containing hot coals to kindle a fire.

Glooscap spoke over his shoulder. "They kindle a fire to parley. Deganawida wants to talk to us." Glooscap fastened his eyes on the chieftain. Deganawida gestured to his warriors and they fell back toward the gate, assuming an unthreatening stance and distance from the impromptu fire. A moment later, with just him and his war chief standing by the fire, he looked up the slope and gestured to Glooscap.

Glooscap glanced at the warriors arrayed along the crest of the knoll, raised his arm and swept it aside, the signal to disperse. Within a few heartbeats the threatening phalanx of armed men became a group of men resting in place. Glooscap made eye contact with Nipishish. An unspoken message passed between the men. Glooscap noted that the fearsome battle axe was slung over his friend's shoulder. Except for his imposing size, short beard, and light brown, neatly clubbed hair, he looked like the rest of his men. He nodded slightly, and turned to Ingerd and Lothar. "Show no fear. Come, we parley." He then turned away and walked down the path, his back arrow straight, the wampum belt held out in front in a show of peaceful intent.

Ivar, his new friend, Otetiani, and three other boys watched the drama unfold through cracks in the palisade from their secret hiding place. When the alarm sounded the women and old men had herded the children, regardless of age, to safety within the longhouses of the village. Nobody knew the cause of the alarm, but the safety of the women and children was always paramount, regardless of the cause. The old men, many of the younger women, and the older boys all armed themselves, and prepared to protect the longhouse from the enemy. As each longhouse settled down to await developments the five boys slipped away undetected. None wanted to hide with the women, children, and old men when something was unfolding outside. An adventure like this did not happen every day and they must know what was happening.

As soon as the boys crawled into their secret place between the palisade and one of the longhouses, Ivar saw his family as they walked down the hill. He wanted to run out and greet them, but Otetiani stopped him.

"You cannot, Ivar. Sakohkea would be angry. That man in the lead is Naskapi. They are our enemies. Look at the Naskapi warriors on the knoll, something important is happening." We must wait." He held Ivar's arm firmly, their faces close, as he hissed the warning.

Reluctantly, Ivar gave in. He watched as best he could through the chink between the upright palisade logs, but his field of vision was so restricted that he found it necessary to constantly shift position to see what was happening. He watched his father more than his mother and brother, knowing that his father had come to retrieve him. Stealing a quick glance at Otetiani and his other friends, he realized that he was uncertain how he felt about this effort to return him to his former life. Truth be told, he liked these people; they treated him well and he rather liked his new life with them. Actually, he had not thought that anyone would ever come for him, and as a consequence he put his old life aside and completely embraced the new.

Except for his blonde hair he was identical in appearance to any young Haudeno male. The responsibilities associated with his relatively new status he had found to be not much different than what was expected in Norse society, with the exception that here among the Haudeno, hunting and trapping small game, and spearing fish were regarded with greater importance than previously. Boys began their hunting and fishing at an early age under the tutelage of old warriors, both for the vast knowledge of woodcraft that the old men possessed, and also to provide security for the daily forays into the forests and along the lakes and streams close by. Ivar knew that the training with the short bows and arrows they used, as well as the fishing spears, was important to the survival of the people, for all these little boys would grow up to be warriors one day, he included. Fish and small game brought down by the arrows and throwing sticks of the boys provided an important part of the people's diet, not to mention the fun they had.

He liked the food, as long as there was enough of it, but he was unaccustomed to the garden produce they ate during summer. His preference remained lots of meat and fish, which they ate sparely because most it was being dried for pemmican, their winter staple. Hunters brought in deer, bear, and moose almost every day, but the animal's big muscle groups were cut into strips and air dried for making into pemmican. Pemmican was okay, he recalled that Deskaheh had made it for the Norse people, but it took getting used to, and he was still working on that. The rest of the animal, organs, marrow bones, fat and meat scraps were either seared in the cook fires before being eaten half raw, or used in the daily pots of soup or stew. He missed eating the big, bloody chunks of meat regularly consumed by his people, which just did not happen here. It made his mouth water to think of a chunk of meat snapping and popping over the flames until the outside was seared, leaving the inside red and bloody. He could taste it.

His reverie was interrupted by Odatshedeh calling his name. He and Otetiani were the first to squirm out of their secret place. Odatshedeh waited impatiently for them.

"Deganawida wants both of you boys at the parley," he said. He looked directly at Otetiani. "Your father sent me for the two of you."

"Why does he want us?" Otetiani asked.

"He did not tell me," Odatshedeh said, his voice tinged with an edge of exasperation at the question. His eyes went from boy to boy. "Both of you say nothing until you are spoken to. You especially Ivar, must be quiet and patient. Do you both understand what I say?"

The boys nodded without comment. Odatshedeh's meaning was plain.

Odatshedeh gave the cutting sign. "Good, now come. They are waiting."

Otetiani glanced at his friend, shrugging his shoulders, the frown on his face belying the gesture of dismissal that his shrug would indicate. Both boys manner changed when each realized that they were to play a part in what was happening at the parley.

Ivar did not understand everything that was said, but he knew from Odatshedeh's tense demeanor and clipped speech that something important was afoot, and with his Norse mother and father here, he was certainly part of it. His level of concern became elevated even further when Nahcomis joined them as the trio made for the village gate. She smiled at him, and he returned the silent greeting, but the carefree manner of the boy that had existed but a moment ago dropped away as the crowd of warriors around the gate parted to let them pass.

Glooscap halted just before the fire that had been kindled for the parley. His eyes flicked to his old enemy. Sakohkea's cruel face was contorted in hatred, barely held in check by Deganawida's presence and calm demeanor as the old chieftain stood in silent regard of his traditional enemy.

Glooscap held out the wampum belt to Deganawida. "Sachem sends you this wampum. He has sent me to talk. I welcome this chance to talk to you and Sakohkea."

Deganawida inclined his chin somewhat in assent, his eyes never leaving Glooscap's face.

Glooscap stepped around the small fire and held out the gift to the chieftain. He took it without comment.

Glooscap waited. Nobody else had uttered a sound save he. The tension was palpable.

Deganawida signed for them to sit.

At that moment a Haudeno warrior, a woman, and two boys came through the throng of warriors by the village gate. One of the boys was Ivar.

Ingerd gave a sharp intake of breath at sight of him, but no other outward sign of recognition came from her.

Nipishish glanced at his wife. A sense of pride in her swelled his heart, for he knew of the inner turmoil she felt. He glanced at Ivar. The boy gave no outward sign either. *He acts as he should in these circumstances,* thought Nipishish. He studied the other Haudeno's present for the parley. The two groups had formed two half circles around the small fire, not close to one another, but within arm's length. He noted that Ivar sat between the warrior and a woman, people that he was obviously familiar with. His innate sense told him that these two people were important to Ivar. He glanced at Ingerd again. *I hope she has her emotions firmly under control. This parley may not turn out as she wants.*

Beside him, Glooscap had similar thoughts. He knew why Ivar was alive and what this couple meant to his being alive. He waited patiently, his natural stoicism masking his thoughts from the others.

"Tell me why you have come among us, Glooscap?" He gestured up the hill toward the warriors he knew to be there. "You come prepared for war, yet you tell me that you wish to parley."

Deganawida spoke without preamble, as Glooscap knew he would.

"It is for you to decide whether there is to be peace or war. I came prepared for either, as you or Sakohkea would do if you were in my place."

Glooscap indicated the three people with him. "I bring these people to you, for they have lost their son and this boy has lost his brother. I come to seek your wisdom and your justice in this matter."

Deganawida said nothing; instead he studied Nipishish and Ingerd. He glanced briefly at Lothar. Sakohkea had told him of these people. Except for the boy Ivar, he had never seen a pale skin before. "The hairy one wears the clothing of Naskapi." He glanced at Glooscap for his answer.

"We captured him. He fought for us against a Haudeno raiding party. Now he is one with us."

Ivar understood enough of what Glooscap said to quickly react to his statement. Until this moment he did not know that his father had been captured, too. "How did this happen, father?" His question came in the Norse language.

Sakohkea's head snapped toward the boy like a striking snake. "Silence, you will be told when to speak."

Nipishish said nothing at the war chief's vehement outburst, but the two men locked eyes. The only thing keeping them apart was the fact that Deganawida controlled the parley.

Deganawida's glance at Ivar carried sufficient message to the boy that he dropped his head. He then turned his eyes on Sakohkea. The man clenched his jaws, but deferred to his chieftain.

"I can forgive the outburst of a boy." Deganawida left the obvious unsaid as his penetrating eyes studied those seated across from him. His eyes stopped on Glooscap.

"Why would a prisoner fight for you?"

Glooscap made eye contact with Nipishish; a bob of his chin bade his friend to answer.

Nipishish spoke for the first time. His ability to communicate continued to improve and he answered Deganawida directly, both verbally and with copious hand signs. "Sachem wanted to learn about my people, Deganawida. He decreed that I was to remain with them until the Time of Green Grass, to learn the language of his people. They treated me well; I lived among them, and worked for them. I liked the people and they grew to like me. When a war party attacked the village I fought to protect the women that I worked with." He gave the cutting sign. He chanced to glance at Ivar, who watched his father in open mouthed amazement.

Not a shred of emotion crossed the face of the old chieftain as he sat in silent regard of the hairy man who sat across from him. "How are you called?"

"I am called Nipishish."

Deganawida glanced at Glooscap when he heard the name that they had given their former prisoner. He spoke to Nipishish.

"Your name carries honor."

He turned back to Glooscap. "Our people have similar customs. Sakohkea's warriors captured Ivar. The boy sits between Odatshedeh, the man who captured him, and his mate, Nahcomis. Ivar is one with them. He has replaced Odatshedeh's dead son. He is now one with our people."

Glooscap said nothing. He looked at Nipishish, his face expressionless.

Nipishish held the war chief's eyes a moment -- both knew how this was to be -- and then he faced Ingerd, to explain what Deganawida had just said.

When the full import of his words became known to her, she turned in anguish toward her son. "Is this what you want, Ivar? Why ..." She choked on her own words, her voice trailed off. She twisted her smock in her hands as the intense emotion overcame her.

Not knowing what else to do at the moment, Nipishish laid a consoling hand on her knee.

Ivar's face reflected acceptance. His mother's public display of emotion cut deeply, but he knew that she was unaccepting of that which he regarded as his fate. He glanced at his brother, Lothar. The two held the contact a moment before Lothar looked away. Their bond was broken; their childhood together a thing of collective memory, as it must be in the circumstance.

Ingerd suddenly exploded, her emotions having run the gambit from despair to anger.

"Do something, Gudbj! This cannot be. Ivar is our son. I will not allow him to stay here."

Nipishish glanced quickly at Deganawida.

With the exception of Ivar, not a word of her outburst was understood on the other side of the fire. The old chief remained impassive, well accustomed to the explosive nature of the human female, and their seeming inability to separate emotion and reality. His eyes travelled over his companions, assessing their reactions. He knew that Sakohkea would continue stoking his anger — an attribute for his war chief -- Ivar and Nahcomis remained as before, but he noticed that Odatshedeh had something to say. He shook his head slightly, his focus on Nipishish.

"Ingerd, I can do nothing. We have come in peace. Deganawida granted this peaceful parley, so that all will know what is to be. I am honor bound. He is their chief; he has spoken."

Glooscap understood enough Norse that he got the gist. He made eye contact with Nipishish; a brief flash of approval crossed the stern visage. He turned to Deganawida.

"Nipishish has told his mate that he can do nothing about their son. It is done, that you have spoken." Glooscap watched Deganawida and Sakohkea carefully as he spoke, observing a slight easing in the rigid set of Sakohkea's shoulders, and no change in the impassive expression on the chieftain's face. He turned to Lothar.

"Give Deganawida the calumet."

Lothar got to his feet, stepped around the fire, and handed the wrapped bundle to the chieftain, holding the black eyes for a moment before retaking his seat.

"Sachem sends this ceremonial calumet to you in peace, for allowing this parley to take place." Glooscap gave the cutting sign, indicating that he was finished.

"I want to talk to Nipishish. Ivar should talk, too," Odatshedeh said to Deganawida.

The chieftain waved his hand in assent as he busied himself removing the ornate calumet from its case. He held it out for all to see.

Odatshedeh got to his feet. He motioned for Ivar to stand beside him. In deference to the Naskapi war chief, he addressed him first.

"Glooscap, I am the man that captured Ivar. I will tell his father and mother of this thing, so that they will know my heart. Ivar will let them know his heart."

Glooscap held the other man's eyes, his face expressionless. A lift of his chin toward Nipishish and Ingerd was the only sign of assent from him.

"Nipishish, I do not need to explain to you, but I will do this thing, so you will know. I saw Ivar resting on a riverbank. I captured him and brought him to my village to replace my dead son. I knew how brave he was because he fought me and the man that was with me. Sakohkea tested Ivar with his own son, so that all the people would know if Ivar was worthy of life." He gestured to Otetiani to stand with him and Ivar. "Ivar and Otetiani fought; they fought bravely to a draw. Now these two are friends. They both learn the way of the hunter and warrior together." As if on cue, Ivar and Otetiani grinned at one another.

Odatshedeh continued his tale. "Deganawida and the council accepted him into the Cokanuk band of the Haudenosaunee Nation and granted my wish that he be my son. My mate Nahcomis," he beckoned to her to stand beside him, "welcomed Ivar to our fire. He cannot replace our dead son, but he brings warmth to our hearts." The cutting sign told his listeners that he was finished. The four people stood silently while Nipishish finished translating for Ingerd and Lothar.

At a sign from Nipishish, the three got to their feet. The two groups stood across the dying fire from one another, a few feet separating them. Each took the measure of the other.

Ivar took the period of silence as an opportunity to speak to his parents and his brother for the first time since their arrival.

He spoke directly to his mother, knowing that his father and brother would be more accepting of his new reality.

"Mother, I know how hard this is for you. I am alive only because these people have taken me into their tribe. Odatshedeh and Nahcomis treat me like their son. I like them and all these people. Otetiani cannot replace my brother, Lothar, but he has become like a brother; he is my brother." He paused to let his mother speak.

Her blue eyes brimming with tears, Ingerd looked from Ivar to Nahcomis. A look of tragedy and despair twisted her beautiful face as she fought with the deep feelings that threatened to consume her. She had had enough of men in this tragedy. None of them, including her husband, knew what a woman feels for her offspring. How could they? She could see that the other woman knew her feelings, her face reflected that, but she also had seen the affection that the woman held for Ivar.

Deganawida, Sakohkea, and Odatshedeh watched the drama cautiously. Glooscap, Nipishish, and Lothar did the same. This had come down to the two mothers to accept that which could not be changed, as far as the men were concerned, and they would not interfere.

"Mother," Ivar said beseechingly.

Ingerd turned her attention back to her son. "I cannot do this, Ivar. You must come back with us."

A great gust of a sigh escaped unbidden from Ivar. He had known this would be difficult, but his own emotion surprised him, because he thought himself too mature for such nonsense. The look on his mother's face cut to his soul.

He struggled to begin, but when he did, the wisdom and understanding of his words would have done justice to anyone of more maturity.

"My life was spared to become what I am. Odatshedeh and Nahcomis lost their only son, their only child to sickness. It left a hole in their hearts. The gods saved me from certain death at the hands of a raiding party, and I was brought here to fill that hole. You still have one son, they had nobody, and the fire in their wigwam was a lonely place for them. In the short time I have been here, I have come to love this couple, and the people of this village. My best friend is Otetiani. We share everyday life, he teaches me the language of the people, and both of us are being trained with all the other boys of this village in the way of the hunter and warrior. If I still lived with you and father in Halfdansfjord, you would have me for only a short time before I moved off to seek my destiny. Being captured by Odatshedeh is my destiny; it is what the gods have ordained for me, and what I accept. You and father must also accept it, because it is, what is. I will hold you, father, Lothar, and our people in my heart forever. But, now I have these people to spend life with, they are my family. This cannot be changed." The cutting sign indicated he was finished.

Ingerd had hung on every word, and watched her son's face carefully while he spoke. She saw a transformation come to his face; his expression no longer conveyed a sense of the same depth of sorrow that she felt. The sound coming from his mouth began to sound foreign to her, unlike her son, when she realized that his words meant that he embraced what had changed in his life. Something gave way inside her; a detached feeling came to the fore. She knew at that moment that her son, the young boy that she had known and cared for all his life, was no more. In his place was a young man that, except for his blond hair, lighter skin tone, and blue eyes, had the same appearance and manner as his friend, Otetiani. She felt the buckskin leather clothing -- leggings, vest, and moccasins fostered this impression. But, it was more than that; before her stood a budding Haudeno warrior who would occupy a place in her heart for the remainder of her days, but the memory of him would be all that remained. She glanced at Nahcomis, but observed no succor there. The dark eyes watched her, but conveyed no feeling, because the woman understood nothing that had been said. Without conscious thought she glanced at Lothar, and then her eyes settled on Gudbjartur. Both watched her closely. It came to her that she had been alone in this; her men already knew how this would end. She shuddered and sat back down without a word, purposely not looking at Ivar.

Those left standing also took their seats, knowing the drama was over. None looked at Ingerd. Her stony face invited no words.

Deganawida finished loading the calumet with kinnikinnick from the small pouch that had come with the pipe. He had not understood what Ivar said to his mother, nor did it matter to him what he had said. The facial expressions told him all that he needed to know. He leaned forward and picked a stick with a glowing end from the bed of coals that remained from the fire and lit the calumet. After puffing it to life he passed it to Sakohkea who did the same before passing it on. Only the males smoked the pipe, it was not offered to Ingerd or Nahcomis.

The calumet made its round and returned to Deganawida, who got to his feet. The others followed suit. It was finished, the parley was over.

Deganawida and Glooscap locked eyes. Those in attendance were silent, waiting for the chieftain to speak.

Sakohkea took the opportunity to put the parley behind him. He was the first to turn away, walking rapidly through his warriors and back to the village, his eyes downcast and his face set in a mask of hate and anger at having to endure such a thing.

"Go in peace." The old chieftain held the eyes of his Naskapi enemy for a heartbeat before he turned away and walked back toward the village entrance, followed by those with him. None looked back.

Glooscap's eyes travelled over the tableau presented by the file of people walking back into the village, the crowd of warriors that parted before them, the women and children watching from every vantage point, the smoke of cook fires rising into the air, and the peaceful forest beyond. It occurred to him that he had never before been this close to so many of his enemies without fighting with them. He glanced at Nipishish, who with the others had watched the same scene unfold. The two made eye contact. Glooscap read nothing on the man's face. He shook his head once to his friend, knowing the man would have some of the same thoughts.

Glooscap looked up at the leaden sky. It smelled like snow. Like Nipishish had said earlier, snow would come soon. It could be a long journey home. If it was a bad storm they might have to hole up until it passed.

"Come, we go."

He turned away and headed up the path, followed by his companions. As he wound up the hill to the crest of the knoll, his warriors stood waiting.

Glooscap walked through his men without comment, none being needed, and the long trek overland back to their canoes began.

Nipishish, Ingerd, and Lothar paused before the village disappeared under the brow of the knoll as they walked into the forest, and looked back. People moved about below, indistinct in the distance, but they saw nobody with blonde hair. Not a word passed between them. Her men turned away first, but Ingerd lingered a moment, her eyes searched in vain for sight of Ivar. Her throat constricted as a spasm of emotion coursed through her body. She turned and followed the others, knowing she would never see her son again.

———

Deganawida's people were in a high state of agitation over the parley with the tribe's enemies, and every person in the village clustered around the old chieftain and Sakohkea, who met him as he walked through the gate.

"I must go after them," said Sakohkea, his manner brusque.

"You will do nothing. We can do nothing. They came in peace, offering wampum and the calumet to parley. I accepted their gifts. It is done." Deganawida's manner was equally brusque, the hard warrior that he had been coming to the fore, but tempered by the wisdom that had made him a chieftain.

Sakohkea angrily walked off a few paces as he struggled to quell the beast within. Few made eye contact with him as his smoldering gaze swept the sea of faces. His eyes stopped on his son and Ivar. He pointed at Ivar, motioning him forward.

He noted that the boy stood before him without fear, his gaze steady.

"What did you say to your mother?"

Ivar understood enough of the clipped question to respond, but he paused as Deganawida joined his war chief. Although uncomfortable under the scrutiny of the two men, Ivar did not appear intimidated.

"Wait," said Odatshedeh, from the crowd as he wound through the press to stand beside his adopted son.

Ivar glanced at Odatshedeh. A slight nod and softening of the man's eyes made him feel more secure.

Ivar glanced at each of the three men before his eyes settled on Sakohkea. Speaking directly to him, and fumbling with the still unfamiliar words and hand signs, he relayed what he had told Ingerd to the best of his ability. He finished with the cutting sign.

The three men stood in silent contemplation of Ivar. Not a sound came from the throng.

Sakohkea looked the boy up and down. He wanted to hate him for what he represented; invaders in his land, but found that he could not hate him. Instead, what he felt was a grudging admiration at his courage and conviction. The boy had told him that this was his destiny, that he was one with Odatshedeh and Nahcomis, and one with the people. He glanced at Odatshedeh, seeing the look of pride on the man's face, and then he made eye contact with his chieftain, who watched him impassively. The flame of the anger that had threatened to consume him flickered out as he once again regarded Ivar. The cruel face softened somewhat, almost like it did when he looked at his own son. He gave a short nod to the boy, glanced at Deganawida and Odatshedeh and walked away without a word.

Ivar and Odatshedeh stood silently waiting for Deganawida to say something.

A smile suddenly split the chief's weathered face.

"All of this talk has made me hungry." He turned away, walking slowly toward his wigwam as laughter rippled through the crowd.

Odatshedeh grinned at his son. His eyes searched the boy's face for a moment with obvious approval and affection. "Come, some food would be good."

As they walked away, Ivar would later recall the sea of smiling faces and the words of acceptance that had come from many of his people.

Chapter 6

IVAR OF THE HAUDENOSAUNEE

Many moons of the Time of Whiteness had come and gone since Ivar's capture by the Haudenosaunee war party led by the war chief Sakohkea.

Held firmly in the grip of winter, the land was lashed by storm after storm until snow blanketed forest and fen to depths not seen in living memory. Huge drifts piled up against each wigwam, making the interior snug and warm, but coming at a price as each flake of snow added more weight to the already strained fabric of the dwellings. In appearance, the village came to be a scattering of white mounds, from which tendrils of wood smoke rose lazily into the chill air from the smoke holes, or was whisked away on the wind, as the case may be; as yet another storm bore down on the village. Waist deep footpaths, beaten into the snow by frequent use, connected the wigwams, for the business of life continued in spite of the ceaseless snowstorms.

As the winter wore on it became necessary to periodically remove snow from the sagging structures. To this end baskets were used by men and women alike in an attempt to at least lessen the weight at the top of each rounded roof. In spite of such efforts, older longhouses occasionally collapsed from the unaccustomed weight, inevitably leading to overcrowding as the others absorbed new residents.

It always seemed that the roofs collapsed in the dark of night. Those that died usually died quickly in their sleep, crushed under the weight of snow and debris. Others, not so lucky, suffocated alone in the cold and dark, in some cases an arm's length from the frantic rescue efforts of the survivors. Many of those that survived did so with broken bones and torn flesh. Few escaped a collapse unscathed.

—

In spite of the adverse winter conditions, a number of groups consisting of two men and five or six boys undergoing transition training between youth and early maturity spent much of their time afield, scattering out over the countryside to hunt and trap. Every activity became training for the boys, for the time when they would assume their places as the hunters and warriors of the people. Forays typically lasted five to seven days while the deadfalls and snares of a particular trap line were run in the heavily forested areas of the hunting grounds.

The men taught the art of the snare and deadfall by example and demonstration, pointing out to their charges that a large part of the tribe's success in trade and survival as a people came from winter trapping. Trapping also taught the boys how to live and survive in adverse conditions with minimal food and shelter.

The physical effort expended daily working the trap line was an important part of their training during the long winters. The process toughened their bodies for the demands that would be placed on them as warriors, and taught them to be the hunter/gatherers that sustained their people.

The tribe's numerous trap lines were scattered throughout a dense mix of hardwood and evergreen forest that covered the rolling hills. Interspersed with lakes and watercourses these forests surrounded the village, and made up the general lay of the hunting grounds of the Haudenosaunee Nation.

The forest was the home of mink, fox, lynx, squirrel, rabbit, bobcat, otter, beaver, marten, fisher, puma, wolverine, and wolf, furbearers, and the deer, moose, and forest caribou that provided the major portion of the meat for the tribe. The hibernating bear was the only large animal unlikely to be encountered during the Time of Whiteness. Turkeys, grouse, and partridge meat was considered to be some of the most succulent available. A host of small animals inhabited the forest as well, providing both meat and fur during the winter when all the fur pelts were in prime condition.

No part of these animals was wasted; either the flesh was eaten, or used for trap bait. Pelts were stretched and dried at day's end for later use as trade goods, or for raw materials for the women and girls to make clothing.

Rounded brush huts, covered with interwoven pine boughs, were interspersed along the trap line to shelter the trappers at night and during storms. They had been built during a previous season and like the longhouses of the village, they would be repaired and utilized until it became necessary to build anew. As the trappers worked a section of the trap line they moved to the next shelter, working in both directions from it until day's end, setting and resetting the traps and deadfalls as they went.

The traps had to be checked daily in the section being worked. An animal that is not killed by the trap will free itself by wringing or chewing its foot or leg off if left in the trap for any long period of time. Few trapped animals were lost in this way because most were killed by the trap, or found and killed by the trapper before they could escape.

The trap lines being tended wound through the countryside, taking advantage of watercourses and lakeshores, windfalls of downed timber, and rock outcroppings and sheer cliff faces frequented by the prey animals. Animal tracks and scats were abundant, making it easy to identify the areas frequented by the animals and devise methods to trap them as they followed the trails that they themselves made through the deep snow as they travelled the forest in their constant quest for food.

Many of the prey animals moved about only at night, and had secretive habits, making trapping the only way to catch them. Snares were set, insofar as loop size and distance off the ground, to trap a particular animal. Twisted sinew snares were used for all small animals. Braided multi-stranded sinew, or braided rawhide rope was used for large animal snares. Some were just a simple loop suspended over a rabbit trail, a hand's breadth above the trail, while others were attached to a bent over spring sapling and trigger sprung by the prey animal's movement along the game trail. In all cases, the trap included twigs or limbs to restrict the animal's direction of movement, thereby directing it into the snare.

The boys were taught that the snare killed by choking the prey animal to death. What appeared to be a simple loop and slipknot was actually more complex than that. The animal could conceivably escape from a simple loop once it stopped struggling – the loop would loosen. The men had the boys practice fashioning the snare loop over and over until they had it down. A small eye, about a finger joint in length, was tied in the sinew end, elongated slightly and then the end twisted to create two eyes, one larger than the other. The smaller of the two eyes was bent over the larger eye and the end of the sinew was fed through, creating the snare's loop end. When the animal's head got caught in the snare loop, it invariably struggled to free itself. Once the snare loop tightened down on the animal's neck, the double eyes locked, and would not slip or release, strangling the animal until it died.

Many deer were also caught with a snare, but the much larger moose and caribou were trapped exclusively with a deadfall – the sheer weight of the log or rock used in the deadfall crushed or choked them to death. A deadfall could be set to trip by the passage of an animal by or over the trigger assembly. Most often a carnivore tripped the deadfall when it tried to eat the fresh carcass that had been left as bait to attract a specific predator, such as a wolf or puma. The bladder sacks of both male and female furbearers were carefully removed from the offal and the urine saved as an attractant. This pungent liquid was especially effective in attracting animals in close to the trigger of both snares and deadfalls. The smell of the urine from the opposite sex of a particular species caused the prey to abandon its usual caution, making it easier to catch.

Toward the end of a particularly grueling day of travelling by snowshoes along one of the trap lines that they tended, one of the several groups of trappers had gathered at their camp for the night.

Two men and five Haudenosaunee boys, sat around a fire in front of a brush hut skinning the partially frozen carcasses of their catch and stretching the pelts on bowed willow frames to freeze-dry. The fire felt good after a day of hard work. The leather winter clothing, although warm and comfortable when dry, invariably soaked through as the day wore on, especially the knee length moccasins. Inured to the cold and discomfort of having wet feet, the work went on until every trap had been emptied and reset.

One of the boys, busily skinning a large male lynx, was Ivar. The others were the same boys of the village that had become his close friends, Otetiani, Ganeodiyo, Igoo, and Gyantwaka.

To an observer Ivar's hair and skin color set him apart as being different. As for clothing and mannerisms, he was indistinguishable from his four friends. His fluency with the language approached the level of a native speaker. It was obvious from the banter around the fire at day's end that he was liked and accepted by the other boys and the two warriors, Odatshedeh and Seawi, that they accompanied.

It had taken Seawi some time to accept Ivar. His initial dislike of the boy went back to the day that he and Odatshedeh had captured him. His pride as a warrior had been wounded by the boy's resistance and the whole affair had almost cost him a valuable friendship. The man had been forced to confront the problem by the fact that he was Odatshedeh's companion in almost every activity that the two undertook, not to mention the fact that they were life-long friends. His outright dislike and distrust of Ivar had been begrudgingly replaced by stoicism in the face of warnings from Odatshedeh to a final acceptance of the boy as a useful member of his tribal band. Thinking back on it now as they all set around their campfire at day's end he realized that the transformation in his feelings toward Ivar had changed because of the boy himself, not anything that anyone else did or said. Ivar was hard to dislike. He threw himself into everything he was involved in, worked hard, and seemed to fear nothing. That was enough.

Odatshedeh stood up, stepped on the hind legs of the red fox he had been working on, and pulled the hide over the animal's head in a long tube, carefully cutting loose parts of the hide that still adhered to the carcass. All the small animal pelts were stripped in this manner; large animal pelts had to be split along the back or belly for removal. As he stretched the inverted hide over a bowed willow frame to freeze-dry, he glanced at Seawi, who seemed to be in deep thought.

"What are you thinking about?"

"I was thinking that I am happy we are almost finished skinning for the day. I am hungry and the stew smells good."

Looking doubtful, Odatshedeh played along, but gave his friend a searching glance before crouching at the fire to warm his hands. *He is thinking of something, but not food.*

"I noticed that myself. What did you boys put in the pot?" Odatshedeh looked into the clay pot sitting in a bed of coals at the edge of the campfire.

"Rabbit, fox, and squirrel," Otetiani said.

"Not rabbit and squirrel again," complained Igoo. "I am tired of both."

"You complain about everything, Igoo. Fox is one of my favorites. Rabbit and squirrel meat is better than not having any fresh meat to eat with our pemmican," said Ivar.

"Not much better," said Igoo in apparent disgust.

"Bring something else for the pot, then. You have not brought in any meat for us to eat," chided Ganeodiyo from the other side of the fire.

"I will. Tomorrow I will trap or shoot a deer. I might even give you some."

Ganeodiyo snorted. "I will bring rabbit and squirrel just in case you do not see a deer. I agree with Ivar, rabbit and squirrel is better than nothing. We might starve waiting for your deer meat."

Otetiani and Gyantwaka jumped into the good-natured exchange.

"Otetiani and I will hunt for deer too. We doubt that you will make a kill in time to cook meat for tomorrow." Gyantwaka elbowed Otetiani for support.

"Let us all try for a deer tomorrow. I do not care who wins. The winner must have the meat cooked for the camp meal at day's end tomorrow," said Otetiani. His announcement got a nod from his four friends.

The men watched the exchange with amusement. This banter and baiting between their charges went on every night around the campfire while the catch of the day was skinned and stretched on the willow frames. The work was always finished before the contents of the cook pot were consumed.

The banter continued as the boys joined the men to help put the finishing touches on the day's catch. Freeze dried pelts accumulated in a pile in the snow as they were pulled off the willow frames to make the frames available for the day's catch.

Ivar and Igoo, the subject of meat forgotten for the time being, gathered frozen pelts and piled them on a rope that they had stretched out atop the packed snow. The others were similarly engaged.

"That is enough," Ivar called to Igoo as he returned with an armload of pelts.

Igoo dropped to his knees atop the pile of pelts, compressing them while Ivar looped the rope from end-to-end and across the bundle as they had been taught.

Ivar securely knotted the bundle and got to his feet. Igoo coiled the remaining length of rope, chose a stout tree limb overhead and threw the coil over it. The two boys then hoisted the bundle to the limb and tied the rope's tag end to the tree trunk, to join others, each representing a day at this campsite, hanging from other tree limbs. The suspended bundles would remain high in the air, secure from marauding animals, until the trappers returned to the village.

This process was repeated each day while the trapping party remained in the forest. It was the only method available to keep their hard won pelts safe while they worked the long trap line each day.

Finished for the day, they all gathered around the fire to scrub the blood from their hands with snow, and enjoy the flush of warmth radiating from the flames. Seawi added an armload of wood and the others stepped back momentarily to avoid the shower of sparks that rose into the chill air.

Igoo, the first to crouch down and poke around in the stew pot with a sharpened willow stick, came up with a stewed squirrel's hind leg. He leered at the others and sat back on the packed snow to tear into it with abandon.

"I thought I heard you say you were tired of squirrel," said Odatshedeh.

"It was a joke, I am very fond of squirrel, but rabbit is my favorite. I left the fox, and the best pieces of the rabbit and squirrel for the rest of you."

The other boys howled and kicked snow on him. Everybody laughed. He continued eating, seemingly unaffected by the reaction to his joke.

Every chunk of meat was quickly consumed, along with the daily ration of pemmican. There would be no more cooked meat until the same time tomorrow.

Bark cups were produced and dipped into the steaming broth to wash down the meat and course pemmican. Later, with the broth consumed to the last drop, and the fire reduced to a bed of coals, full bellies and fatigue had them straggling into the brush hut and into the comfort of their sleeping robes.

Ivar awoke with a start at first light. Intermittent scrapping sounds and the crunch of footsteps came from outside the brush hut. He sat up in the dim illumination of the shelter, quickly realizing that Odatshedeh was also setting up next to him. The man put a hand on his arm, hissing a low warning. The others began awakening, and each sat up, listening to the sounds that now seemed to come from all around the shelter.

Otetiani had slept nearest the entry. He carefully pulled a corner of the deer hide flap aside and looked through the slit. There was just enough light to see the dark shapes against the backdrop of snow. He quickly dropped the flap back into place and turning to the others he gave the hand sign for wolf, sweeping his hand in a circle at the same time. A pack of wolves were all around their brush hut.

On hands and knees, Seawi came up beside Odatshedeh, spear in hand. Odatshedeh motioned Otetiani and Ivar back with the other boys, all of whom had weapons in hand. Odatshedeh gave the hand signs to watch him and follow his lead. He locked eyes with Seawi, nodded to him, and the two men arose to a low crouch in the confines of the hut and burst through the entry, closely followed by the four boys, all screaming their war cries in the hopes of scaring the pack away.

It worked for a moment; the screams spooked the animals into the cloaking forest. Their hunger brought them back to warily circle the trappers that faced them in a tightknit circle.

Seawi and Odatshedeh had heavy hunting spears at the ready. The boys, arrows nocked on bow strings, faced the circling wolves. Ivar and Otetiani, the best archers, held arrows nocked and ready to draw and shoot.

"Ivar, gut-shoot one of them." Odatshedeh spoke softly without turning.

The words had not left his mouth before the boy drew his arrow to its head and loosed it into the paunch of a wolf to his front. The arrow zipped into the animal dead center between its short ribs and hip, driving the shaft out of sight in his guts.

The wolf jumped in the air when the arrow bit into its body. Setting up a frightful din with its yelps of pain it ran in circles into the trees. All the wolves close by chased after the wounded animal. They caught it just out of sight of the trappers and the pack quickly silenced its pitiless yelps and cries as they tore their comrade to pieces.

"Good shot!" Odatshedeh glanced at his son. "They will eat him and then they will come for us."

He glanced at Seawi, on his knees at the fire pit looking for a live coal among the ashes of last night's fire.

Without prompting the boys scattered around the campsite gathering wood.

Odatshedeh knelt down by his friend, his eyes searching the forest fringe for sight of the pack. He could hear them, but so far they remained out of sight in the clocking forest.

"When the sun is up I fear that we are going to have fog. This morning mist seems thicker to me."

"I agree," said Seawi, as he worked on the fire. "If fog comes, this fire will be the only safety we have. We cannot fight them if we cannot see them until they are on us."

Tendrils of smoke rose from a single live coal that Seawi had carefully enfolded in a handful of tinder from his belt pouch. A moment later tongues of flame crawled through the sticks and bark he fed to the tiny fire. He erected a pyramid of dry wood over his fire and a moment later flames began leaping into the air as the pile caught.

"Everybody form a tight circle. Keep the fire at your back if you can, here they come," said Odatshedeh, his voice tinged with apprehension. If they only come from one side, everyone face them together. Keep the fire at your back."

No immediate attack materialized. They came straggling from the forest and underbrush muzzles and faces red with blood. The ghosts of the forest moved in a loose semi-circle, as they weaved through the brush, their prey centered before their advance. Cruel, slanted eyes fastened unblinking on their next victims, as they licked blood slathered jaws in anticipation.

The men had seen it all before. To the five boys it was unnerving to watch them glide soundlessly forward. The animals seemed to be guided by commands, their advance purposeful, directed by something unseen.

For the benefit of the boys continuing training, Odatshedeh provided a short lesson in wolf etiquette.

"Watch the big, black male that just moved out in front, the one looking at us through the brush."

The black wolf began to weave through the underbrush, using it as cover from his adversaries. He disappeared from view into the forest.

"The others will not move before he does. If you get a shot at him, shoot him. He is the most dangerous. We have to stop him or they will win this fight. The female following him is his mate. She is the lead female wolf and she is almost as dangerous as he is. Kill her if you can." He glanced back at the fire. "When they come, keep the fire going. Use burning brands to fend them off when they get close. No matter what, do not run. They will all come after you. Nobody can outrun the pack."

"The mist thickens, I cannot see very far," Ivar observed.

"I thought it was getting thicker," agreed Ganeodiyo from Ivar's side.

"Fog is coming," said Odatshedeh. Just stay in a tight group. It makes us seem big to the wolves. The fire is our protection, stay close."

"Great, it is beginning to snow a little," said Otetiani.

"Things are getting worse," Ivar said through clenched teeth. He looked at his adopted father. "I want to attack them rather than wait for them to make the first move. I am tired of waiting."

Odatshedeh chuckled. "Attack them. We cannot even see them anymore. The only chance we have is to stay alert and stay next to the fire."

At that moment a lone wolf materialized from the mist and snow running at the small cluster of trappers.

Ivar saw him first, but he could not swing his bow quickly enough for a shot.

"Watch out," Ivar screamed.

Seawi just had time to drop to his knees, lower the tip of his spear, and ground the butt end before the wolf was on him.

The forward momentum caused the animal to impale itself on the grounded spear. The obsidian point entered at mid-chest, angling upward to exit between the shoulders, severing the spine. The animal yelped once and died. Before death claimed him the snapping jaws opened a long gash in Seawi's right forearm, the one that held the spear.

Seawi held the gash closed, trying to staunch the blood flow.

Ivar pulled a thong from his pouch. "Here, I will bind it."

The thong was long enough for three wraps, which closed the gash. The blood continued to seep.

Seawi met Ivar's eyes. He nodded his thanks. The hard eyes softened somewhat as he looked at the boy.

Ivar leaned forward and pushed the spear all the way through the wolf's chest and pulled it free. He handed it to Seawi and returned to his place without comment.

Nobody said anything for a time as their eyes swept their front. The underbrush at the forest verge was only dimly visible now. The mist and fog continued to thicken.

"Did anybody count the wolves," asked Odatshedeh?

"I think I saw six or eight, I am not sure." Igoo spoke without turning. "We have killed two, maybe the others will leave."

"That leaves four to six, maybe more. We do not know for certain. They will not leave. They are hungry and we are their prey. The only thing that will drive them away is if we can kill the leader. He will stay out of sight; the others will come at us before he does. Killing his mate will get him to come at us." Odatshedeh shook his head. "No, they will not leave until they have fed on our bodies or we kill the leader."

"We cannot kill any of them if we cannot see them." Ivar's words echoed the thoughts of all of them.

The trappers had the fire at their backs, thinking the wolf pack was to their front. That was not the case.

Without warning, the sound of his movement muffled by the snow underfoot, a wolf suddenly materialized from the mist at a dead run. He jumped the fire pit before anybody saw him and crashed into Gyantwaka's back, knocking him sprawling.

The animal grabbed one of the screaming boy's flailing arms and began to drag him away. Two more wolves came from the rear, coming around the fire to attack the helpless boy.

Ivar shot an arrow into one of them and Otetiani shot the other. Both mortally wounded animals yelped in pain, ran a short distance, and collapsed.

Odatshedeh threw his spear at the wolf dragging Gyantwaka away. The spear transfixed the wolf, the point sticking in the packed snow for a moment while the animal struggled and cried in pain. The spear point pulled out of the snow, and the wolf disappeared into the mist, taking the spear with him.

Left with a knife and belt axe, Odatshedeh ran the short distance to the still prostrate Gyantwaka, and dragged him back with the others.

Not a word had passed; there was not time to talk, as the group, now back-to-back in a crouch, waited for the next attack.

The black wolf and his mate soundlessly came from the side directly at Igoo. The boy did not have time to holler a warning. With time only to pull the bow string to half draw, he snap shot from the hip; the arrow hit the black wolf in mid-chest with minimal penetration.

Seemingly unaffected by the arrow the animal bowled into Igoo, knocking him down. The black wolf went for the boy's head and throat. His power, wounded as he was, completely overcame the boy's defense. The wolf strad-dled his victim, his jaws viciously slashed and snapped together, seeking his victim's vitals.

Igoo grunted with effort as he fought back, kneeing and kicking at the heavy body crushing him against the snow covered ground. He locked his arms over his head as he tried to protect himself. The heavy pullover parka saved his life. The wolf could not get to his neck, but his bare hands were bit-ten and slashed repeatedly as the animal tried for his face. The arrow shaft protruding from the wolf's chest stabbed painfully into Igoo's face. Grabbing the blood slick wooden shaft in both hands he shoved with all his strength, pushing the shaft to the feathers in the wolf's chest. The animal shuddered but pressed his attack.

Ivar jumped on the black wolf's back, wrapped both legs around his mid-section and got an arm around the animal's neck.

The wolf went crazy. Twisting and trying to bite Ivar, he jumped and twisted, trying to dislodge his attacker.

The boy hung on for his life. As the wolf bucked and lunged in circles around the campsite, Ivar plunged his knife into the base of the animal's neck over and over again, twisting and working the blade as he sought the jugular. The long, slender chert knife blade snapped off at the handle, deep in the neck of the black wolf. Slippery with blood, Ivar fell off the wolf's back in a heap. Rolling over, he turned to face the wolf as the animal turned back to him. On hands and knees, almost eye-to-eye with the animal, Ivar saw that the fight was over, his adversary was finished.

Blood ran from the animal's nose and mouth. He stood still, legs splayed, too weak from loss of blood to move, the cruel slanted eyes watched his erst-while prey.

Seawi ran past Ivar and buried his tomahawk between the wolf's erect ears, severing the great neck joint at the head. The wolf collapsed on its chest.

Ivar watched the light fade from the animal's eyes. He thought the wolf watched him until he died. The boy collapsed on his stomach, spent.

Seawi came up and bent down. "Are you hurt?"

"No, I do not think so. This is not my blood." He wiped bloody hands in the snow and scrubbed the wolf's blood from his face and neck with hands full of snow.

Seawi helped him to his feet. He looked Ivar over. A slight smile crossed his face as he examined the disheveled, blood smeared face of the boy. He bobbed his head at the sight.

"You fought the good fight." Seawi turned away to check on the others, leaving Ivar to watch him go.

The others stood silently watching Ivar. The body of the female wolf lay close by, an arrow protruded from an eye socket.

Ivar walked up to them, his face twisted in a tired grin. "I hope the rest of this pack ran away."

Odatshedeh smiled at him. He looked his son up and down, his expression spoke of the pride he felt. "I think you killed the last one. The pack is all dead."

"I did not kill him by myself. Igoo and Seawi helped."

"My arrow did not go deep in his chest until I pushed it in. He was not hurt badly. If you had not jumped on his back he would have killed me. Your knife killed him." Igoo spoke from next to the fire where he sat - teeth clenched in pain - while Otetiani cleaned his torn hands with snow, smeared on a mixture of warmed pine pitch and fat, and bound them with leather strips.

Nobody had anything else to say on the matter, it was over and there was much to do. Ganeodiyo and Gyantwaka walked into the forest for firewood.

Odatshedeh looked around the campsite at the bodies of the pack. Brushing accumulated snow from his parka he glanced at the others, his eyes came to rest on his son.

"Ivar, do you have another knife in your pack?"

"No, this is my spare knife." He held the knife up to examine the short blade protruding from the haft. "I unwound the rawhide and pulled the blade out far enough to skin with it. It is short, but it will work." He looked at his father.

Odatshedeh shrugged out of his pack's shoulder straps and taking out his spare knife, he handed it to his son.

"You can have this knife. You earned a new knife today."

The two held each other's eyes a moment. Ivar nodded his thanks.

Odatshedeh turned away, and speaking over his shoulder he began following the erratic trail of the wounded wolf. "I am going to find the wolf that carried my spear away. We could use some hot stew before we break camp."

Ivar watched him disappear into the mist and lightly falling snow. He looked again at the beautifully made knife that Odatshedeh had given him, testing the keen blade with his thumb. Comparing it with the stub that remained of his knife blade, he swapped the two in his belt scabbard and put the old knife in his backpack. The others were watching him. He shook his head, sighed, and went over to the body of the black wolf. He stood looking at it a moment. Stooping down he grabbed the hind legs and dragged it nearer the warmth of the fire to skin.

Odatshedeh returned later with his spear, a fresh wolf hide draped over his shoulders. His companions lolled around the fire on freshly skinned wolf hides, eating chunks of steaming meat. He glanced into the cook pot bubbling on the coals.

"Wolf meat," Seawi said, in answer to the questioning expression on Odatshedeh's face. "We saved the back straps and boned out the hind quarters from the fattest wolves."

"Good, dog and wolf meat are my favorite. I smelled the cook fire long before I got here. I, too, am tired of rabbit and squirrel," he said, glancing pointedly at Igoo, who laughed dutifully with the others. "Remember, that some of you promised a deer today."

He knelt down to examine Igoo's hands. Looking at the boy's scratched face, he continued. "You were lucky. I do not think you can pull your bow to shoot a deer.

"Maybe not, but I will try if I see one," Igoo answered.

"With all this fresh meat from our fight with the wolf people, getting a deer is not as important now." Odatshedeh spread the wolf hide he had brought out atop the snow near the fire. Then he speared a piece of meat from the cook pot with his knife and sat down on it to eat.

"If you want a deer, Igoo, one of us will shoot it. You had best let your hands heal." Otetiani said.

The others agreed.

Odatshedeh spoke between mouthfuls. "Okay, but only shoot a small deer and bone out the meat. We cannot eat it before we start back, so it will have to be carried." He paused in thought, his jaws working on the tough meat. "At nightfall today we will have finished the last section of trap line and moved our camp to the last shelter. Take one toboggan and leave the other here; we will pick it up on the way back. Tomorrow morning we will check the traps we set today, take them up, and start back to the village, picking up our pelts as we go. It takes almost two days, pulling our toboggans, to reach the village. "

Later, with full bellies and the resulting lethargy put behind them, the trappers busied themselves bundling pelts to hoist into a tree. A short time later they broke camp and paired up to work the last section of trap line.

⌘

Ivar contrived to be by himself for the first part of the morning, so he could put a plan he had hatched into play. As he and his partner, Ganeodiyo, set the deadfalls and snares in likely places along the last portion of the trap line, they typically leapfrogged one another – as one worked on a set the other went ahead to the next spot, and so on.

Finished with the deadfall set he had been working on it was easy for him to double back toward the camp they had just vacated. He ran easily on his snowshoes, employing the swinging gate peculiar to rapid movement when wearing snowshoes.

Almost everything was in readiness back at camp; he just needed to put it all together. He had the two forked sticks of the spring pole trigger in his backpack, both cut to length and scrapped smooth, so the trigger would slip easily when disturbed by someone, or something, passing by, and spring the trap.

Previously he had selected a likely sapling to use as a spring pole for his trap. It was positioned beside the trail that they all used as they returned to this particular camp site. The trail wound through the forest, conveniently passing between and under two tall spruce tree with snow laden boughs. The trap he envisioned was actually to play a joke on his companions; one of them would surely trip the trap. When the trap was tripped, whoever was passing under the trees would be buried in snow when the spring pole snapped upright and hit the snow laden boughs. No snare would be attached to the spring pole line, so nobody could be hurt.

He whistled happily as he worked, unable to keep the grin from his face.

While previously encamped in the area he had positioned the bottom end – the ground half - of the longer of the two forked trigger sticks at the edge of the trail. In preparation for setting the trap he had laboriously bored a hole in the frozen ground to accommodate the bottom forked stick into which he had poured water. The water had quickly frozen around the trigger stick securing it in place. He had then concealed the trigger stick from prying eyes with a fallen bough.

Now that the time had come to set the trap, he bent the spring pole over, and securely tied a braided sinew line to the top end. While holding the bent over sapling under his arm, he tied the other forked trigger stick to the bottom end, along with a trip line. Then he carefully hooked the two halves of the trigger together. Slowly he released the sapling, allowing the strain on the trigger to increase gradually while taking care not to allow it to slip loose. Satisfied, he stepped back to admire his handiwork with a big grin on his face. He laughed aloud. *This will be a very big surprise to someone.*

To finish up, he brushed the trampled snow with a spruce bough, and secured the trip line across the trail. Any pressure against the trip line would cause the trigger forks to slip off one another immediately springing the trap. Against the whiteness of the snow the trip line was all but invisible.

By the time they all returned here tomorrow the intermittent falling snow would completely mask his trap's presence from his friends.

He hurried away along his back trail to continue with his part of the trapping effort, satisfied that one of his friends would trip the spring pole tomorrow, providing a wandering animal did not trip it beforehand. That thought bothered him somewhat as he rapidly moved through the forest.

⸺ ∞ ⸺

Several hours after dawn the following day, Ivar, Ganeodiyo, and Otetiani were the first to arrive at the camp site from the previous day. They retrieved the bundles of pelts from high in the trees around the hut, and were dividing them between the two toboggans when Odatshedeh and Igoo came snowshoeing into camp. Both carried pelts tied to their backpacks – it had been a good day.

With just Seawi and Gyantwaka still out, Ivar felt a rising panic that nobody would trip his spring pole surprise. *After all my planning somebody has to come back that way. The trap cannot be missed if somebody takes that trail, and it is not possible to step over the trip line wearing snowshoes, they are too long.* His reverie was interrupted by Odatshedeh.

"Seawi and Gyantwaka will be here soon, so we can begin the journey home. Ivar, you and Otetiani pull the toboggans first. One of us will follow behind and the others will break trail. It will be hard going; the last leg of our trek will be the worst, we will have all the pelts on the toboggans then. If we get going from here soon, we should get back to the village before dark tomorrow, unless there is trouble on the trail."

The moment he finished talking, Gyantwaka staggered into camp, pointing to his rear and laughing so hard he could not tell them what was so funny.

Ivar already knew; Seawi had sprung the trap.

Gyantwaka pointed at Ivar, finally getting his mirth under control. "That is why you disappeared yesterday. You came back here and set a spring pole trap under two snow covered spruce trees."

Ivar said nothing. The grin that spread over his face told it all for the others.

There was still no sign of Seawi. Odatshedeh looked in the direction Gyantwaka had come from, then back at the boy. "Tell us what happened." He tried to sound stern, concerned, as a leader should be in such circumstance. The deepening crowsfeet at the corners of his eyes belied that attempt.

"I followed Seawi on the trail. I was close behind him when I heard a snap and the swishing sound made by a spring pole. The spring pole hit one of the snow covered spruce trees, most of the snow fell from the boughs, and the bouncing boughs caused the other spruce to lose its snow. Seawi was almost buried under all the snow that fell on him. I tried to help him get out of the snow, and I began laughing so hard at his angry cursing and threats that I came back here instead. He is okay, but he knows who set the trap." He glanced at Ivar. "Your name was mentioned several times."

By that time everybody had joined in the laughter, including Odatshedeh. They were so engaged when a snow covered apparition, carrying his snowshoes, came out of the forest.

What could be seen of his face was set in a scowl that slipped, to be replaced by a slight smile as his companions clustered before him, enjoying the joke at his expense.

Seawi fastened his eyes on a grinning Ivar, while nodding his head repeatedly. "When I heard the spring pole it was already too late. I knew it could only be you that would set such a trap. I admit you got me good. One day I will get even."

Everybody laughed.

"I did not know who would spring the trap, Seawi. I meant it as a joke. You are not hurt, are you? You are not angry with me?" A touch of seriousness tinged Ivar's voice.

All knew his air of concern was feigned; their laughter proved it.

Seawi's arm shot out around Ivar's head. He pulled the boy close. "No, I am not mad. I am not hurt. Someday I will get even." He released Ivar.

Always the joker, Ivar brushed snow off his parka. "You have gotten snow all over me."

The other boys laughed again, while helping Seawi brush the snow off his clothing.

Seawi waved them away. He shook his head at the whole affair, making eye contact with Odatshedeh; he smiled at his friend, and nodded slightly.

Odatshedeh had watched the boys while they enjoyed the joke played on Seawi. The two men played similar jokes while growing up, it was all part of the process. Soon enough the harshness of life would change these boys into men, as had always happened among the people. He watched his son. The way the boy handled himself, his quick wit, courage, ambition, and personality, set him apart from his friends. Otetiani and Ivar were close in all things, including their friendship, but Ivar excelled in every physical aspect of their lives. Otetiani seemed accepting of Ivar's slight edge over him, and his tendency to lead. Odatshedeh glanced again at each member of the group as they began to finish up around the camp in preparation for heading home. The flush of pride in his son brought a smile to the normally hard face.

Ivar had been impressed before with the load carrying ability of the toboggan. He had not paid much attention when Odatshedeh had schooled him in the finer points of its construction and the many uses of the sled, but now, after almost two days of taking his turn in pulling one loaded with pelts and camping gear through the deep snow, he had a new appreciation for its utility.

He recalled the words of Odatshedeh back in the village while they made necessary repairs to the two toboggans they would take on the trapping trip during mid-winter. He had been shown every part of the sled and told how to build one.

On the second day of travel, as he pulled the toboggan along the freshly packed snow behind those ahead breaking trail, he had his head down, leaning into the leather harness. He had to think of something, so his mind wandered back to what Odatshedeh had told him.

The toboggan is made of two to four narrow — about the width of a man's hand, he had said - thin birch planks, and three or four birch stiffeners sewn across the planks from side-to-side with rawhide. The planks, longer than a standing man, and as thick as his little finger, are split from green wood and scraped smooth on the side that will be on the snow. While still green, the planks are weighted down under water and left to soak until they are pliable. When pliable, one end of each plank is put into the back side of, and between two horizontal log sections, one atop the other with a space between, secured in place, and gradually bent back over the top log until it is almost doubled back on itself. Then it is tied in that position and allowed to air dry thoroughly. Each is then toughened over a fire to set the wood in its rounded shape. The planks are then joined with the stiffeners. Rawhide rope is tied between the ends of each stiffener along both sides, and secured to the rounded nose, stiffening it further. They not only provide more strength, they make a handy place to tie the load down securely. When completed the sled has an upthrust, rounded nose, almost circular, that will not dig into the snow. A narrow full length fin or cleat, sewn to the center plank's bottom side keeps the toboggan from slipping sideways or fishtailing – it tracks straight and true because of this cleat.

Two to four dogs in harness normally provided the motive power for the sleds, especially around the village. They were also taken with the trappers – animal carcasses provided the meat source to feed them - but not normally when young men were being trained. The two warriors in charge of each party wanted the work to be as hard as possible; it was a vital part of the training the young men were to receive.

Thoughts on toboggans ended abruptly when the trail breakers disappeared from view as they made their way over the brow of a hill. Ivar stopped a moment to catch his breath, before starting down the hill.

Otetiani pulled the other toboggan up beside him. "I like going down the hills, it is easy."

Ivar nodded as he looked down the long slope. "We can ride down this one; no trees are in the way." He jumped on his toboggan and was away before Otetiani could answer.

Otetiani grinned at the cloud of powdered snow churned up as his friend flew down the hill. Gyantwaka and Seawi, who had brought up the rear, helped Otetiani push his toboggan to the brow of the hill. All three then straddled the load and pushed off to enjoy the exhilarating plummet down the slope.

When the downslope was forested a quick run downhill was too dangerous. In such a circumstance the two trappers following the toboggans took ropes that were attached to the sleds and provided braking down the hill. A toboggan running downhill could not be guided well, rather it was aimed at a desired point and the rider hung on for the ride.

The toboggan with its three riders came to rest a short distance away from where Ivar had stopped. The three trail breakers had joined him and they were all sprawled out, resting, their snowshoes stuck upright in the snow like little people.

"We smelled smoke awhile back. There is one more hill before the river valley and the village. We are almost home," said Odatshedeh. "The best part is coming. It is downhill to the village."

"Good, I am ready to be home. It has been a good trip. The trapping is some of the best I have seen, but it will be good to be warm and filled with hot food," said Seawi. "My arm throbs and is a little swollen." He bobbed his chin toward Igoo. "Both of us need the potions of the medicine man to heal."

"Wolf bites are bad. Your wounds will heal with the care they will be given." Odatshedeh glanced at each of the four young men in turn. In truth he no longer thought of them as boys. "You have all done well. I am proud of you. Seawi is proud of you. We have both enjoyed teaching you the ways of the trap line."

They rested and talked for a time, and ate a little pemmican. A lump of compressed snow to suck on afterwards slaked the thirst that followed the pemmican.

Anxious to get home, they began to get up from where they had rested without prodding. Positions were changed to give everyone a break, and they set out trudging toward the tree covered hill that overlooked their village.

Each toboggan required two in harness to pull the load up the hill, with two ahead breaking trail, and one bringing up the rear.

Sometime later, having worked up a sweat getting the toboggans up the forested slope in the deep snow, the trappers stood at the crest, their village visible below.

Steam rose into the still air from their overheated bodies and breaths as they looked at the scene below. Two other groups of trappers, recently arrived from other directions could be seen below, with villagers milling about as the toboggans were unloaded and the people visited.

A virtually treeless slope flattened out into the valley floor, before the river, with the village on the other side of the river. They could sled down the hill almost all the way to the palisade of the village.

There had been three groups of trappers in the field similar to the one led by Odatshedeh; all were now back in the village. Days of comparative lassitude passed for the groups of trappers while they rested and worked on equipment in the comfort of the wigwams.

One such group consisted of the four young men that had accompanied Seawi and Odatshedeh. Two were asleep. Ivar, Otetiani, and Ganeodiyo were conversing in low tones while they fletched arrow shafts, when Odatshedeh and Seawi entered the wigwam and walked up to them.

"Sakohkea and the council want the five of you in the council house," Odatshedeh said, without preamble.

Ivar looked up at him. "When?"

"Now, they are waiting."

The young men put their projects aside and got to their feet. Igoo and Gyantwaka, rudely awakened by Seawi's foot, also got to their feet.

"Come," Odatshedeh said. Turning away, he led the group toward the council house.

Deganawida, the council of elders, and Sakohkea sat in a semi-circle on large, thick bear robes. They all turned to look when Odatshedeh walked through the entrance, followed by Seawi and the five young men.

Deganawida signed for them to sit with the council.

After greetings had been exchanged, and the shuffling of the new arrivals had subsided, Ivar became aware that he was the focus of the council. Ivar sat between Odatshedeh and Otetiani. Judging from the elbow he got from his friend, he, too, was aware that Otetiani knew that Ivar was the focus.

"It is the custom of our people to bestow a different name on a male when he goes from boyhood into manhood," Deganawida said, his eyes on Ivar's face. "This name is to recognize an act or deed that is deserving of the name he receives."

Although humbled to be addressed by the chieftain before the council, Ivar was excited at the same time. He stole a quick glance at Sakohkea, a man he held in awe, reading nothing but acceptance in his expression, before returning his attention to the words of Deganawida.

"The council has met for this naming ceremony after hearing the words of Odatshedeh and Seawi. We are unanimous in bestowing the name Okwáho on you for bravery in the fight with the wolf pack, without regard for your own life."

An intense heat coursed through Ivar's body when he realized what the name he now had implied. *Wolf, I am to be called Wolf.*

Otetiani grabbed his friend's head in an arm lock and pulled him face-to-face. "Okwáho, it is a good name for you," he said enthusiastically.

"Hold," Sakohkea said. The command was not loud, but it got everyone's attention. His chin indicated that Deganawida was not finished.

"We can excuse a lapse of manners in the circumstance," he smiled at Okwáho and Otetiani, both of whom seemed suddenly contrite.

"I am sorry for interrupting, Deganawida," Otetiani said.

Deganawida accepted the apology with a short nod. "We are well pleased with how you have become one with the people, Okwáho. This name you have received is one that comes with honor. Living up to such a name will not be easy for you. We all think you will bring great honor to your name and this band of our people." The cutting sign indicated that he was finished.

Okwáho knew that he should say something. He looked around the circle of leaders, his friends, and his father. All watched him attentively.

"I am happy to be one with the people. I regard this village as my home, where my mother and father live, and where my friends are. You have given me a great name that I cherish."

His gaze shifted to Sakohkea, the powerful war chief of the people. They held each other's eyes. "I will work hard to learn the ways of the warrior and hunter. One day, when you decide I am ready, I will be honored to stand by your side."

Sakohkea nodded slightly. Never one to say much, he surprised his audience. "I have no doubt, Okwáho that you will stand at my side. All five of you will one day join my warriors." His eyes sought his son's eyes. "Otetiani has become your friend, Okwáho, this is a good thing. He has kept me informed. One day all of us will go into battle together. It is the way of things. Our success in battle is achieved because we fight for our brother, the man beside us." He waved a hand in emphasis. "All of you young men will stand at my side one day. That is your destiny. You will be welcome." His hand gave the cutting sign.

The council was finished. The participants milled about for a time before returning to their various endeavors.

Life in the village assumed a purpose in keeping with the season. The men and boys worked on their equipment, made new weapons, and repaired the old. The women and girls repaired old clothing, made new clothing, cooked the food, and gossiped about everybody else. It was a good time for the people and they made the most of it.

Storms swept the land with regularity, confining most to the warmth and comfort of the wigwam. Regardless of the weather, the trapping groups continued their work unabated. Fur provided warm clothing and items for barter, and winter was the only time the pelts were in prime condition.

Within a very short time every man, woman, and child knew the name that had been given to the tall, likeable son of Odatshedeh and Nahcomis. The proud parents displayed the happiness that the young man had brought to their lives. Nahcomis had become positively doting, a condition enthusiastically welcomed and supported by Odatshedeh.

As for the young man, he continued to blossom. He and his constant companion, Otetiani, son of Sakohkea, soaked up the rigorous training of the trap line, while learning to use the disciplines and weapons of the warrior and hunter.

While in the village, Sakohkea and his select warriors, including Odatshedeh and Seawi, trained all the young men in the fine art of war. In any group of ardent novices there are always a few standouts. Some of these are exceptional. Sakohkea recognized early on that one of his young men was of this select group. The war chief knew from long experience that the young man that bore the name, Okwáho, Wolf, would one day be feared all over this land.

—✺—

Chapter 7

NIPISHISH MAKES A DECISION

Midwinter held sway over the land and the tribal bands of Naskapi throughout Nitassinan. Storms came in regular succession like ripples across a pond. Within each village, food was plentiful, the people performed their tasks in the comfort of their longhouses; life was good.

In the village of Sachem, many moons had come and gone since Ingerd had last seen her son, Ivar, and still the memory of that meeting was like a raw wound to her. She had grown to love the Naskapi people, but in spite of all the support and sympathy they gave her she could not forget Ivar's words, nor could she accept that she would never see him again. She knew that young males often left to pursue their destiny, just as Ivar told her that he was doing, and at about the same age. Somehow that fact made no difference to her in this case. She often found herself staring south, knowing that Ivar was out there somewhere, doing something that she was not a part of.

Nipishish and Lothar had done their best to bring Ingerd out of her funk, to no avail. They too felt the sense of loss, but from a different perspective. The decision to remain with the Haudenosaunee had been Ivar's. Nipishish had talked at length with Lothar, and both felt that Ivar had done the only thing possible to avert bloodshed. As Lothar had pointed out, Ivar genuinely wanted to remain. He also told his father that he doubted that Ivar's going back with them was an option. Ivar was no longer a prisoner, but he was not free to leave either. But, none of this helped with Ingerd.

Nipishish decided that Ingerd must be taken back to Halfdansfjord. Only there did she have lifelong friends that could possibly help her deal with her broken heart. To that end he and Lothar went to look for Glooscap and Kejo. He felt that only Sachem could give him permission to take Ingerd back before the Time of Green Grass, but he also knew that to be successful with his request he must start with the two powerful Naskapi warriors that had become his close friends. Nobody just walked up to Sachem and started talking, there was a certain protocol involved in communicating with the chieftain of all the Naskapi, and he wanted to do this right.

He and Lothar found Glooscap and Kejo, with several other men, and many of the village's older boys, in the council house working on their weapons and personal equipment.

A savory smell of food rose from a soapstone kettle of venison and vegetable stew warming on the hearth as they entered. Two women had just brought in the kettle with a basket of wooden bowls. The men would eat when the mood suited.

Like all such gatherings among the males of any culture, the Naskapi men spent their time together discussing topics of mutual interest: hunting, fishing, the best weapons, the strongest bow, the best wood for arrows, where to find the best material for flint knapping, women, sex, and so forth. The boys and young men were usually included as these gatherings were an important part of their training to be men.

Interspersed in any of the animated discussions were the inevitable jokes that brought forth loud boisterous comments as one or another of the men became the brunt of a jest or the central character of a joke. Gales of laughter usually followed the telling, especially when the victim good-naturedly joined in in an attempt to parry the thrust.

Nipishish and Lothar happened to enter the council house in the midst of a joke, judging from the laughter and disparaging comments. They sat down not knowing what the joke was about, but smiling nonetheless, to join in as best they could in the circumstance.

Laughter died away and the general conversation resumed as though it had not been interrupted.

Lothar had already proven his mettle to these men. He was older than the other young men and boys in attendance. Although he had not received all the training of some of the young men, this fact was not regarded by the warrior culture as a detriment. Glooscap and Kejo had told him that the training would come as he joined the activities of the other young men of the band.

Naturally drawn to the man by a deep respect that had developed over time, Lothar sat down next to Kejo, and watched him work at replacing the binding of a snowshoe. A moment later he picked up its mate and began replacing its binding with new rawhide thong. The thongs were wet, soaked through in a bark container filled with water, to make them pliable and easier to work. When smoked over a slow fire later, and dried in place, the rawhide webs and binding of the snowshoes were hard and durable.

As the work progressed, Lothar made eye contact with Kejo in time to see a smile cross the man's face. He returned it. Glancing around at the group, a feeling of belonging came to him. He felt happy to be with these men.

Nipishish sat down near Glooscap, but unlike Lothar, he did not become a part of any activity. His mind was obviously elsewhere.

The very perceptive Glooscap knew that something was amiss with his friend. His direct question brought it out.

"What is the matter, Nipishish?"

Conversation abruptly ceased among the other men as they listened for the answer to the war chief's abrupt question.

Nipishish looked up at his friend. "It is Ingerd. Her heart is broken, and I cannot fix it."

In answer to the quizzical look on Glooscap's face, Nipishish continued. "I want to speak to Sachem, to ask him if I can take Ingerd back to Halfdansfjord."

A flurry of hushed comments swept through the other men, until Glooscap raised his hand. He seemed to consider the request a moment. His decision came abruptly. Glooscap got to his feet.

"Kejo and I will talk to Sachem about this. He will want to talk to you and Ingerd before he makes his decision. I do not know if Sachem will come here, or we will meet him in his longhouse."

"Regardless, Lothar should be there, too," said Kejo. "Sachem may want to know what he thinks."

Glooscap nodded in agreement. "We will not take long. Go get Ingerd."

Nipishish followed Glooscap and Kejo from the council house, going to Glooscap's longhouse to fetch Ingerd. Lothar stayed behind, helping the men work on their equipment and enjoying their company.

THE GYRFALCON

The falcon disappeared from view in the sun. He saw the group of humans from whence he came, but they could not see him. The men below had scattered out, to flush prey for him. He was on his stoop above them, gliding in circles. With his powerful eyesight, no movement below would escape his notice as he scanned the ground and sky for prey.

A flicker of movement in front of the walking men drew his attention as a hare darted away from the intruders who had flushed it from its cover.

The gyrfalcon fastened his attention on the darting hare; he folded his wings and plummeted from his stoop at the unsuspecting target. At the bottom of his stoop his wings opened, the plunge from the sky slowed just above the ground, and he flashed in for the kill. The powerful talons crunched into the soft back of the hare. A cloud of fur marked the point of impact. The hare died instantly, back broken, and its vitals pierced by the talons of the gyrfalcon. The falcon turned completely over in a cloud of disturbed snow from the abrupt change of speed from the stoop, the hare's body clutched in his talons. He came up atop the hare, covering his kill with his wings, and looked around for possible intruders. His eyes riveted on his prey a moment before he tore into the limp body and began to feed.

"I lost him in the sun," said Halfdan, shielding his eyes as he searched the sky for the bird. "I hope he comes back."

The bird's keening cries could be heard from above.

"He will. You have spent every day with him. He knows that you are the source of his meat," said Bjorn.

Bjorn, Helge, and Tostig accompanied Halfdan on the hunt. The men, on skis atop the deep snow, had fanned out in the brush of the fen, hoping to flush game for the gyrfalcon.

"He has come to the fist many times. I just hope he remembers. I would hate to lose such a valuable bird," said Halfdan. He chuckled at a recollection. "The first time he came to fist, I was amazed at his weight, and the power of his talons. Without the heavy gauntlet for him to perch on, my hand and arm would have been torn to the bone."

"I felt the same when Essipit handed him to me. I had never before felt such a powerful grip," said Bjorn.

At that moment a hare jumped up in front of Helge and ran off. "A hare," he shouted, "that may bring him down."

The men scanned the sky for the gyrfalcon, but the bright sun hid him from view.

Suddenly a dark object flashed into their field of vision as the falcon stooped its prey. His wings were partially folded in the stoop, making him difficult to see against the bright sun.

"Here he comes," shouted Tostig, the first to catch sight of the gyrfalcon.

Although all the men had seen hunting birds before, none were prepared for the accuracy and speed of gyrfalcon. The bird opened his wings, flattened his descent, and crashed into his prey almost at the same instant, turning completely over in a cloud of snow and flurry of wings as he righted himself. Scattered fur marked the spot. The hare was still, killed by the force of the impact.

"By the gods!" exclaimed Halfdan.

The bird glanced toward the men, then dropped its head to feed on its kill.

Halfdan raised his hand to the others. "Wait for him to eat his fill before we approach him."

Tostig laughed out loud. "I have never seen anything like that. I think he could kill anything up to and including a deer fawn."

Halfdan shook his head in awe of what he had just witnessed. "Now I know why hunting with hawks and falcons is so popular in the homeland. This is just plain fun." He grinned at his companions.

The falcon had folded his wings now that his possession of the kill was established. The men could better see what he was doing.

"Look how he holds his kill down with one foot while he tears chunks off," said Bjorn.

"Aye, I do not think there will be much left for the pot tonight," said Helge.

The men watched the falcon eat for time. The bird pulled out gobs of fur, shaking his head and spitting most of it out while it consumed almost everything else it tore from the carcass, including much of the fur it pulled out, small bones, and meat. After feeding on a kill, a bird of prey later vomited up a casting, consisting of small pieces of bone, feathers, or fur, as well as everything else that it could not digest. The casting is often mistaken for scat by those that do not know about the digestive habits of raptors. The men knew all of this about their hawks and falcons, having gained the knowledge through close association with the birds.

The bird paused in his destruction of the hare carcass, and looked back at the men and then out over the fen. Seeing nothing of consequence during his inspection of the surroundings, he sedately stepped off what remained of the hare and began to preen.

Halfdan laughed. "I think he is finished." He approached the falcon slowly, talking to him in a low, soothing tone.

The falcon stopped preening, regarding the intrusion with a baleful, unblinking stare.

As Halfdan drew close, the bird appeared ready, but not tense or agitated. Halfdan extended his gauntleted arm out to the side, signaling the bird to fist.

The gyrfalcon shook his head, leaving the cape of his head and neck feathers ruffled. The black eyes never left Halfdan's face. Without further prompting the bird hopped onto the gauntlet, and Halfdan took hold of the jess attached to one leg of the falcon with his free hand, securing the bird.

Halfdan continued his soothing discourse as he stood slowly erect. The falcon glanced down at the scattered remains of his erstwhile prey, again ruffled his plumage, and glanced out over his surroundings, completely unconcerned.

The men gathered around, to admire the bird. The falcon watched them without apparent distress for a moment before returning to his examination of the countryside.

"He is really something, Bjorn," said Halfdan. "I am happy that you brought him home with you. I wish I could thank Essipit personally. Perhaps one day I will."

"I thanked him for you, and I think he bested me in our trading, so he is a happy man."

Halfdan nodded, looking at his falcon. "Look at his eyes. Have you ever seen such a cruel look on a face before? I love the way he looks at us. We do not scare him at all."

The men skied slowly back to the settlement, in animated conversation about the hunt. Halfdan was well satisfied with his gyrfalcon.

WINTER TREK

Word spread quickly that something was afoot when people saw Sachem accompany Glooscap and Kejo to the council house. They also knew that the general public was not invited; this was a private matter, for now. Curiosity peaked when council members and certain warriors were summoned to the council house.

"Such a journey in the midst of the worst winter we have ever known will be dangerous, Nipishish." Sachem spoke from the informal circle of men near the hearth.

"I know, Sachem, but with your permission I must go. I want your wisdom on this request, and I seek the ideas and advice of all here."

"You do not need my permission, you are one with us, and your loyalty to me and the people is without question. Such a journey has been done before, but not in these conditions. You and Ingerd cannot go alone; three or four men should go with you. I want the ideas of everyone here."

"I will go with Nipishish; I know the way," said Kejo. Laughter swept through the men. Even Sachem smiled. "There will be safety in numbers; the wolves will be hungry."

Nipishish smiled at the man, knowing he would be one of the first to volunteer.

Miknap, Manshipit, and Atkaa also volunteered.

"We know the way, too," said Miknap, speaking for both men.

Laughter again swept through the group.

Nipishish nodded his thanks to the men.

"I do not know the way, but I will go with Nipishish."

Eskanan's statement surprised all of them. As the man that would wear the kiss of the axe of Nipishish for the rest of his life, Eskanan, had maintained his distance from the man who had given him the terrible wound in battle. Until now, the two men had not spoken directly, about the battle in which Nipishish was captured, or the long scar that ran diagonally from below Eskanan's left shoulder, and down across his chest.

Taken aback, Nipishish made eye contact with Eskanan. "I welcome your help on this journey, Eskanan."

The man nodded in silence, his face without expression. Perhaps the passage of time had healed the wound, both physically and mentally for him.

Perhaps this journey with his former enemy would finally close the matter in his mind.

There were no comments to the exchange. Although Eskanan's participation was certainly unexpected, the men seemed to accept it as the way of things.

Into this period of introspection, stepped the youngest member of the assembly, with an even more surprising announcement.

"I do not wish to go this time, father," said Lothar. The young man spoke haltingly in the Naskapi language, so that all would understand. "Unless mother needs me I will stay here. I have made friends with other young men. They teach me their language and I am learning about their people. With Ivar gone there would be only sadness for me at home. I belong in this place for now."

When Lothar finished, every eye in the gallery turned toward Nipishish.

Visibly surprised at Lothar's announcement, the man studied his son while his mind sorted the flood of feelings that came to the fore. *He has his own mind, now. He has grown up since our days at Halfdansfjord.* He liked what he saw in the young man. *He speaks to me with conviction, without fear. That is good.*

"Ingerd has been through a great deal lately, Lothar, are you certain that is the right thing to do?"

"It is right for me to stay here, Father. But, if Mother wants me to go with you, I will go."

The byplay between the serious young man on the one hand, and his dubious father on the other hand, had the gallery of Naskapi males, including Sachem, enthralled. Heads turned back and forth as they tried to follow the dialogue from each speaker, which was being delivered in a mix of Naskapi and Norse. The hand signs being used helped with their understanding, even when some of the words were not understood.

Earlier, Glooscap had slipped out at Sachems request, and he returned with Ingerd at that moment in the developing conversation.

Everybody had gotten to their feet at this point, eager to be part of drama, rather than remaining seated as spectators.

Ingerd greeted Sachem with a perfunctory nod, certainly out of character for her given the man's status. Considering the circumstances of the recent past, all of her actions were out of character – she was angry, disillusioned, sad, vengeful, and she did not care who knew it. Her feelings came to the fore unbidden, and none her actions had been rational. She knew that about herself, but her son had been taken from her before she was ready. How could a mother ever be ready for such a shock? It was a question that simmered just below the surface at all times.

"Glooscap has told me of this journey we are to take. I will miss Meshika and the other women, but I do want to be with Frida and Thora. To see Halfdan and all the others and to know what has happened with all my friends will be good for me, especially now that I have lost Ivar. You may stay if you wish, Lothar. I do not care anymore. Thank you for offering to return with me, but this is the beginning of your passage to manhood, so do whatever you want."

Nipishish held up a hand. "Take a breath every so often, so I can tell them what you are saying."

Ingerd snorted, anger flashed across her face, but she kept her tongue.

He translated for the apt gallery. Every eye shifted to Ingerd.

She made eye contact with all the men in the council house. Their open, interested facial expressions mollified her somewhat.

"You men decide what is to be done. I will be prepared for the journey whenever you say it time to go." Her eyes sought out Sachem. She approached him.

"Sachem, before I leave your village, I wanted to thank you for sparing the life of my husband, and sending Glooscap and his men to retrieve my son if possible. I love your people. I have made many friends here, and I wanted you to know my heart. My heart is sick with sadness." She paused while Nipishish translated.

She looked at Glooscap. "You saved Gudbj, Nipishish, from certain death, Glooscap. We have not spoken of this before, but I want to now. I am forever in your debt. Your wife, Meshika, and your mother Ekuanit have become my dear friends. They have taught me many things about your people. I will thank them for this before I go."

Nipishish translated. A slight softening of Glooscap's hard face, followed by a bob of his chin indicated his understanding.

Her eyes looked at the group of warriors that watched her every move, the sound and inflection of her every word. "As I have told you all, I love the Naskapi people. I believe that my people and your people will always be friends. The gods have ordained this. I will return during the time of Green Grass, and I will bring my other friends with me. Perhaps, Chisasi will bring us here." The cutting sign indicated that she was finished.

While Nipishish translated, Ingerd approached Sachem, a smile on her face. She held out her hands to him; they clasped hands.

"Sachem, I hope you will allow me to return here to my friends in the Time of Green Grass."

"You are welcome among the people, Ingerd." He spoke before Nipishish translated her words.

Ingerd's eyes filled. She nodded her thanks, not trusting her voice. She released Sachem's hands, and turned away, walking from the council house without a backward glance.

Every eye followed her; not a word was spoken for a moment.

Glooscap looked at Nipishish. "When will you go?"

"We will go with the dawn."

"So be it, then," said Sachem. "I will leave you to make your preparations."

"Thank you, Sachem," said Nipishish, as the chieftain and his retinue made for the doorway. "I will return here with the others, to complete my task for you and the people."

Sachem paused, turning toward Nipishish. "I knew you would come back with Kejo. You are one with us, Nipishish. You will do as you think best. I will see you whenever you return."

"Aye, you will see me again."

Sachem turned away, leaving the council house.

Nipishish watched him go, and then turned back to Kejo, Miknap, Atkaa, Manshipit, and Eskanan. "Ingerd and I will meet you all at the palisade gate at dawn tomorrow."

"Good, we will be ready," said Kejo.

With that said, the men left the council house to gather the gear they would carry, and spend the final evening with their families. Nipishish walked toward Glooscap's wigwam, where he knew Ingerd and Meshika would be gathering food and the simple gear necessary for the journey.

As for the others, the activities resumed while the men talked over the fine points of such an ambitious journey in the dead of winter.

———

It had taken Ingerd the better part of three days to grow accustomed to the widespread, swinging leg motion necessary to walk on snowshoes. It was not difficult to master, but the constant use of muscles unaccustomed to such a range of motion made the activity a study in mental discipline for her. The muscles of her inner thighs still burned from the effort. The first two days had been sheer torment; her upper legs and lower back suffered the most. The men set a grueling pace, giving her no quarter, and she expected none. When she found out that they would be on the trail for seven to ten days, she resolved to toughen her mind in concert with her body, otherwise her current pain would continue to the end. That prospect was unacceptable to her.

From a distance the party of seven looked like a single file of Naskapi. All were attired in similar fashion in fur-lined leather clothing, mittens, and fur hats. Each carried cased bows and arrows over a shoulder, and a small backpack containing jerky and pemmican. Rolled sleeping robes were tied to the sides and looped over the top of each backpack.

Their luck had been good so far, there had been no snowstorm, and each day had been uniformly cold. They travelled under clear skies ablaze with brilliant sunshine that finally made it necessary to don the snow goggles that each carried in their kit. The narrow slits cut into the eyepieces filtered the glare and protected their eyes.

The long trail snowshoes – longer than the distance between the ground and a man's shoulder - ensured that they stayed on top of the crusted surface, otherwise travel across country in winter would have been impossible.

The only reason to stop at dark each day was to eat their single daily meal and sleep. Kejo did not want to attract unnecessary attention with the smoke of a fire during overnight camps; so long as the pleasant conditions continued there was no need of a fire. They ate their rations for the day, made a body-sized hole in the snow, lined it with pine boughs, and lay down to sleep, wrapped in their warm sleeping robes.

The entire journey had been atop the snow covered ice along the river and lakes that would ultimately take them to Halfdansfjord. The snow was so deep atop the river's ice layer, and the small connecting lakes fed by the river, that the surface was almost entirely smooth. While the journey had certainly not been easy, the ability to travel in this manner was to be preferred to passage through the dense surrounding forest.

They were not the only ones to select this route.

Nipishish had recently taken over breaking trail from Eskanan. The narrow river valley that they followed north curved away to the right and out of sight, so he set a straight course for a forested point of land that represented the shortest distance from where they were around the point, rather than following the meandering river bottom. Just short of the point, a line of eight people on snowshoes suddenly came into his sight.

"Kejo," he called over his shoulder as he came to a halt.

His companions spread out to either side, watching the other party, which had also halted.

"Who are they?" Ingerd shielded her eyes as she studied the other group in the distance.

Although he did not understand the question, Manshipit answered her. "Anishinabeg!"

The Anishinabeg had gathered in a group, obviously talking over the surprise encounter.

Kejo held up his hand, palm forward in the universal sign of greeting, and began to walk toward them. "Come, we will show them who we are, and that we come in peace."

One of the Anishinabeg raised his hand as Kejo and the others came toward them.

"I thought they were kinsmen of the Naskapi," said Ingerd.

"They are, Ingerd, most of the time," said Nipishish.

"I hope this is one of those times," she said.

"They do not have weapons in sight, except that one man who has a spear," said Eskanan.

HAUDENOSAUNEE BOY'S SHAM WAR

All the native peoples of the land enjoyed the playing of many games, to both pass the time and instruct the young. By necessity, some games were played by only men while others were a mix of men and women. Children too had games, either invented on the spot, as children are wont to do, or they played favorite games passed from generation to generation.

Women and girls had games that were intended to lift the tedium of their work, for they performed all the heavy work required by the tribe's way of life. They built and repaired the wigwams, cooked all the food, tended the gardens of summer, tanned hides, sewed leather and tanned pelts into clothing, butchered and dried the meat, and a host of other necessary things. They did all this without complaint, for it was their lot; however, making games of the work while gossiping continually made it all more bearable.

On this particular day, most of the village population had turned out to watch a particularly favored event, a mock war game to the finish between ranks of boys. Spectators surrounded the field of combat, clustered on hillsides, and stood atop any rises in the ground level offering a vantage point.

Groups of young women and young girls clustered together. Gales of laughter could be heard from them as they offered comparisons of the physical attributes of the participants. Many a behind the hand whisper could be seen between the older women as well – it was all part of the game.

Arrayed along the bluff between the village and the river, two ranks of seventy nude Haudenosaunee boys and budding young men faced each other across the snow covered ground. Their very nudity made this game a favorite among females of all ages.

The crowd began to grow silent for the most part as they strained to listen to the instructions of the four men in charge of this session.

Four warriors conducted the training. They had just finished dividing the participants up according to age and size, making both ranks about even. The fully clothed men walked up and down the ranks offering encouragement and advice where needed, making certain everybody was ready for the fight to come. The men were not there to oversee the play. Their active roll ended when they finished briefing the participants and the game began, unless a fight broke out, in which case they would intervene in the case of an uneven match-up. If the combatants were evenly matched, they were encouraged to fight until one was victorious. Fighting was a part of life; spectators wanted fights to break out. This was a blood sport; the purpose of the games was to learn to fight.

Besides instilling confidence, the sham war game taught the young the perennial art of warfare. As a consequence the training was deadly serious. Sessions continued year around. In spite of this inherent seriousness, laughter could be heard as the game progressed because it was fun to play at war. Hard feelings from injury or defeat were also to be expected. It was all part of the training, and every warrior in the village had been through the same thing at one time.

Most of the boys were from five to ten years of age. Five of them were older. Except for the youngest among them, all had gone through this training many times before. Each rank wore different headbands, making identification easier in the coming melee. Each participant was armed with a simple willow bow, and a quiver of twelve blunt, unfledged arrows. A small circular frame, rawhide covered shield was strapped on their bow arms. This shield offered little protection from arrows, but it made the wearer feel better about his chances of surviving the flights of enemy missiles.

Many of the smaller boys shivered uncontrollably. However, in spite of their shared misery, not a complaint was to be heard; certainly commendable given that some of them were only 5 -years old.

A slight breeze added to their discomfort. Winter moccasins were sodden by this time, guaranteeing that every foot was painfully cold through and through. Winter sessions were especially desirable for this training. The cold, often wet, and always miserable conditions toughened the young warriors both physically and mentally. It required tough mental discipline to remain outwardly calm and apparently aloof to the increasingly severe discomfort of being naked in the snow and wind. The game could only be personally won by a suitable exhibition of stoicism, and a demonstrated ability to endure, because no score was kept of how many enemies an individual vanquished in mock combat.

The rules were few. Participants were killed and out of the game when struck with an arrow or hit over the head, or anywhere on the body, with a bow, at any time while combat was joined. Unfledged willow arrows seldom flew to the mark, for accuracy was not as important as participation. The game called for each rank to attack the other as a team, but the serious endeavor rapidly gave way to mayhem and the confusion of single combat as the shouted suggestions between participants went unheard for the most part. The arrow supply of each participant dwindled rapidly in the early moments of play. When out of arrows, it was permitted to pick up spent missiles to shoot back at their adversaries – the snow underfoot would make this difficult or impossible. The arrows of a weaker enemy could also be taken from them, making the little boys obvious targets. They were expected to fight to retain their supply of arrows, which they did with enthusiasm.

When out of options players could run down any adversary and strike them with their bow, ending their participation. At this point the few rules of the game were abandoned, play reached a fever pitch, and it was every boy for himself, with enthusiastic support from the spectators.

———⊰⊱———

Okwáho stood hipshot near the center of one rank. His wet feet felt like a block of wood, without feeling from the cold, but nobody would know of his pain and discomfort to look at him. Certain that his face reflected his indifference to the situation, he had assumed the stance and attitude of the warrior he desperately wanted to be, or at least he hoped that was the case. Sakohkea was somewhere in the crowd that surrounded the game, he had seen the great man only a moment before. Feeling that the war chief had come to watch his son and the other young men, Okwáho fantasized that it was he that Sakohkea had come to size up. That thought alone governed his demeanor, prompting him to vow that his performance would be that of a warrior and not that of a young man.

Glancing to his right, Okwáho made eye contact with Gyantwaka, the only one of his friends that would be fighting on his side. The two had held themselves rigidly aloof from the younger boys nearby. Both felt the responsibility of their status as the oldest present.

Gyantwaka pointed his chin toward the opposing line. Otetiani, Igoo, and Ganeodiyo had been placed evenly through the line.

Okwáho looked toward them. Otetiani pointed his bow directly at him as they made eye contact. Okwáho did the same. Challenge had been made and accepted. The two friends, famous for their adversarial relationship, would focus on each other, as they had before, when the game began. They would have it no other way.

⸙

Finished with the preliminaries the four men moved in pairs to opposite ends of the two ranks. One of them raised a turkey leg bone war whistle, which he carried on a rawhide thong around his neck, to his lips and blew into the end that produced the shrill whistling signal for the attack. Later, the man would blow in the other end of the whistle, sounding the deeper whistling signal to retreat, which ended the game.

The attack sound of the war whistle brought forth war cries from the two ranks of participants and a roar of encouragement from the spectators – the game was on.

At first, the flights of arrows seemed coordinated as both ranks slowly closed the distance, shooting as rapidly as possible as they advanced.

The willow arrows were weighted forward, the intent being that shooting the arrow with the thicker, heavier end forward gave it some chance at flying to the mark, the target in other words. This worked some of the time, so long as the shot was not hurried. From experience, the older participants knew that the arrow must be launched rather than shot. Pushing the bow forward to release the limber arrow worked better than pulling the arrow back to its full length and suddenly releasing it. This latter method, used by the novices, guaranteed the arrow would flex around the bow and fly to the side of the intended target. This knowledge, gained through experience was closely guarded by those that knew about it. And, none of the younger boys knew about it, yet.

Okwáho naturally assumed the stance of the archer – left arm extended, bow toward the target - presenting the side of his body toward his adversaries, making himself a smaller target in the process. In this position the small shield on his bow arm gave him a little protection as he shot his supply of arrows as rapidly as they could be nocked and loosed. From experience he knew that most of the participants would be hit and out of the game in the first few flights of arrows, as had often happened to him. This time he hoped to get Otetiani before he himself was eliminated. It was not possible to dodge the arrows. He could move around, and he did, making himself a more difficult target, but he was a target nonetheless.

Otetiani was doing much the same thing from the opposing side. He launched his missiles directly at Okwáho, knowing it would be a fluke if one hit his friend. He gritted his teeth in frustration as he loosed an arrow at his target, only to see it veer off course and plunge into the snow. Like all the other players, he advanced slowly toward the opposing line, shooting as he walked.

Howls of pain at every quarter mixed with the general chaos as the two lines drew together. Arrows thudded into naked bodies. One little boy, hit near dead-center of his forehead lost a strip of skin from the point of impact all the way to his hairline. Blood flowed freely from the scrape into his eyes blinding him. He was not seriously hurt, but he howled nonetheless. He dropped his all-important bow – not that it mattered, he was killed – and began running in circles trying to see through the blood. The unused arrows in his quiver quickly became the spoils of war as an older boy pounced on him. Finally one of the men grabbed him as he ran by, scrubbed the blood from his eyes with snow, and sent him from the field.

More confusion came to the game as those hit by arrows, being honor bound to leave the field, tried to leave without being hit again. As this sorted itself out, everyone became aware that only seven players remained unscathed. All were out of arrows, leaving the remainder of the game hand-to-hand. Two of them were Otetiani and Okwáho.

Running in the snow was difficult at best, so the seven remaining players approached one another cautiously, each knowing they had an equal opportunity to emerge as the victor. Chance played a part in hand-to-hand combat; the object was to make your adversary make a mistake, to miss a thrust or strike with his bow, the only weapon remaining. A slip on the snow spelled instant doom.

The odds were heavily in favor of Otetiani's team. Okwáho had but one teammate remaining against five on the other side, one of whom was Igoo, his friend from the trap line.

Without waiting for his teammates, one of the smallest boys, a real scrapper too young to have earned an adult name, screamed his shrill war cry and attacked.

The boy with Okwáho laughed aloud at the smaller boy's pluck and swung his bow at the other's head.

The little boy easily ducked under the swing and thrust his own bow into the midriff of his adversary, eliminating him. Without pause he went after Okwáho, while his teammates watched in amusement.

Cheers and calls of support rose from his teammates and the crowd; everyone appreciated a scrapper.

Okwáho easily parried the boy's first thrust, thrusting his own bow at his small attacker, who deflected it aside with his shield. The two circled each other.

Okwáho laughed aloud. "You think you can beat me?"

The boy said nothing. With a fierce look on his thin face, his shrill voice screamed his war cry as he came in low, swinging his bow at Okwáho's bare legs. Okwáho jumped straight up to avoid the arc of the bow, bringing his own bow down hard across the top of his adversary's unprotected head. The blow knocked the little boy into a dazed heap on the snow.

The instant his feet touched the snow, Okwáho attacked his four adversaries before they came after him. A flurry of thrusts, parries, and feints eliminated two boys who reacted too slowly to his sudden attack, leaving Otetiani and Igoo for him to eliminate on his road to victory.

They circled each other, probing for openings while the crowd went wild. Otetiani and Igoo separated, dividing Okwáho's attention and making it difficult for him to avoid their thrusts.

Okwáho went after Igoo, making him turn his back on Otetiani enough so that he could keep both in sight while he concentrated on dispatching Igoo. In his haste he slipped on the snow, going down on one knee, almost ending his participation as Igoo jumped in to attack.

Okwáho rolled frantically to the side, sweeping his bow in an arc at Igoo he was rewarded with a solid thump as it hit his friend in the neck.

Otetiani's bow cracked into the shield arm of Okwáho, at the moment Okwáho's bow cracked into his shield. The two circled each other; Okwáho's breath fogged the air as his breathing came under control again.

"It is my turn to win," Otetiani joked with his friend.

"That is what you must do, win! I stand in your way."

Otetiani answered with a vicious overhand swing at Okwáho's head that would have knocked him senseless had he not blocked it with his bow held overhead in both hands.

Okwáho tried to trap Otetiani's bow by swinging his bow in a circle from the overhead position, while bringing his bow in a downward arc aimed at his adversaries head. The bow connected with a solid thump at the same instant Otetiani's bow completed a sideswipe that ended against the side of Okwáho's head. Both combatants fell stunned into the snow. Blood dripped from the scalp cuts into the snow. The blue eyes of Okwáho and the black eyes of Otetiani examined each other while the young men lay within arm's reach, gasping for air. They were unaware of the hollering spectators, or were they aware that the shrill war whistle sounded retreat. The game was over.

The spectators crowded around them. Sakohkea and Odatshedeh helped them to their feet; each gave the young men looks of pride for the game they had played. To be sure, the proud fathers would later share private thoughts with their sons.

People pressed elk robes on them; they offered no resistance. Warmth surged through their cold bodies, as people crowded in to slap them on the back.

Okwáho made eye contact with Otetiani. They held the contact, each nodding slightly to the other in tribute. Words were unnecessary between them. They would always be adversaries, for both were born fighters about to take their places among the warriors of their people. Unknown to all but them, they had also shared their blood, thereby cementing a sacred bond.

As they walked back to the village among the crowd of people, beside their fathers, Okwáho caught sight of the young boy that he had knocked senseless in the final moments of the game.

He held up his hand. "Wait, I must speak to this boy." Otetiani came with him. Their fathers stopped to watch.

The boy and his father saw Okwáho and Otetiani turn toward them.

"How is your head?" Okwáho looked from son to father.

"I am well. I have a knot on my head, but it does not hurt," said the boy, standing up straight and proud before the two older boys.

Okwáho laughed. "You fought with cunning and bravery. I will be proud to take the war trail with you one day."

'I, too, will welcome you beside me," said Otetiani.

"How are you called?" asked Okwáho.

"I am called Sparrow."

"Well, Sparrow, you are a hawk among boys. I will not forget this." Okwáho placed a hand on the boy's shoulder in tribute. He then looked at the father, whom he knew. "You have a son to be proud of, Hadawáko.

The man smiled without comment, his eyes sought those of his son.

Okwáho swept his hand down in the cutting sign. He and Otetiani returned to where their fathers stood watching.

Odatshedeh just grinned at his son.

Sakohkea looked at both the young men. He had their full attention. "You both did the right thing, recognizing the bravery of that boy." His eyes fastened on Okwáho's face. "Although you vanquished a smaller opponent, you did it as a warrior should. You gave him credit for a good fight. You left him with his honor. It is something he will never forget. It is something none of us should ever forget. Our honor is what sets us apart. You will feel hatred for your enemies, but you honor them nonetheless. It is as it should be." He and Odatshedeh walked toward the village gate.

The two young men watched them a moment before looking at one another. Okwáho threw an arm over his friend's shoulder. Otetiani did the same, as they followed the others back to the village.

They had fought the good fight. They bloodied each other and fought to a draw. In their minds, that was as it should be between brothers.

CLOSE CALL

Many leagues to the north, members of two marginally friendly tribes were about to come together as Kejo led his group toward the Anishinabeg.

"Just follow in single file, as we have been. They are not a threat to us; our numbers are almost the same." Kejo spoke over his shoulder and he headed straight for the eight Anishinabeg warriors. He focused on the man who had raised his hand in greeting, thinking he was the leader. As it turned out, he was not.

The Anishinabeg spread out a little as Kejo and his party drew nearer. None had unlimbered their cased bows.

"Spread out like they did," said Kejo.

One of the Anishinabeg reached for his bow. A guttural order from his rear stopped the man.

Kejo fastened his attention on a short man that stood slightly to the rear of the others. He was not the man that had raised a hand in greeting, but the order came from him. Kejo and the others came to a halt. Not close, but certainly close enough to converse.

"We did not expect to see Shinabeg this far from your home lands during the Time of Whiteness." Kejo spoke directly to the short man that he had determined to be the leader.

"We share this land with Naskapi. Like you, we come and go as we please." He had closely examined each member of the Naskapi group as he talked. Ingerd and Nipishish were not Naskapi and the man's facial expression altered somewhat when he realized that they were different than what he had expected.

"You come from the north; we go to Halfdansfjord, the abode of the Northmen. Have you seen this place?"

"We know of it." The man's entire demeanor changed; his clipped response telling Kejo that he was not open to discussion. Kejo glanced at the other Anishinabeg. *He and his men know that Nipishish and Ingerd are Northmen. The only reason for a party of Anishinabeg to be this far from home in midwinter is a scouting expedition – they have been watching Halfdansfjord. He wished they had not approached the scouting party; this could turn out badly.*

Kejo addressed the other leader. "I wish you well on your journey." He glanced at his party. "Come, we have far to go." He nodded to the Anishinabeg leader and resumed the journey.

The Anishinabeg warriors watched them go. One started to say something; he was obviously angry.

Before the words left his mouth a single harsh word from the leader stopped him.

"Enough! Let them go. We are too evenly matched; there would be no clear victory. Too many of us would die. Our time will come during the Time of Green Grass. Our chiefs will need what we have learned about the Northmen to plan for war with them." Without further explanation he resumed their interrupted journey to the south.

His men watched the Naskapi column continue on its way for a time without comment, and then they followed their leader.

Kejo waited until they rounded the point they had been headed for before they saw the Anishinabeg, before he stopped, knowing the others would want to talk about their encounter.

"Okay, they will no longer be able to see us. Eskanan, make sure they all kept going."

At his bidding, Eskanan walked into the forest verge covering the point to check their back trail. A few moments later he returned. "All eight of them are still together, headed south."

"Good," said Kejo. "We have seen the last of them." He looked at Ingerd. "Do you understand what happened here?"

"Aye, I think so. Two evenly matched groups of warriors decided to part company before trouble started and at least half of them were killed."

The Naskapi all looked at Nipishish for clarification. Kejo was the only one that understood enough Norse to glean the general meaning of Ingerd's statement.

"She knows what happened." Nipishish glanced at his wife, chuckling in appreciation. "She figured out that it was not worth our getting killed over."

The men laughed.

"You are right, Ingerd. Some things may be worth getting killed over, but not this," said Kejo.

Nipishish spoke to the group in general. "What were they doing?"

"Scouting Halfdansfjord," said Miknap.

Nipishish and Ingerd exchanged looks. "Why do they scout Halfdansfjord in midwinter," Nipishish asked the man.

"They are watching what the people do. They will attack the village in the spring or summer."

"The Anishinabeg have watched your village since you arrived in Nitassinan. There have been many of their scouting parties. Naskapi would do the same if we were not friendly with you. Their chiefs will need the information these scouts provide to plan the attack," said Kejo.

"Halfdan will want this information, Gudbj. It is good that you are taking me back now," said Ingerd.

Nipishish, deep in thought over the implications posed by an Anishinabeg attack, just nodded at her statement.

"Your chieftain will know of their visits, Ingerd. Winter makes it difficult to stay out of sight against the snow. The scouts pose no immediate threat to your village, so I am certain your people watched the Anishinabeg at the same time that they themselves were being watched," said Kejo.

"How much farther is Halfdansfjord," asked Nipishish.

"We should be there in two days, unless a storm comes, then we will have to build a shelter and wait it out."

Nipishish glanced at the sky. "I think a storm will come before we get there. We have been lucky, but two more days of luck cannot be. Thor stirs in his lair."

Of course, the Naskapi did not know who Thor was, but they got the meaning anyway. All agreed the signs pointed to a storm brewing in the north.

Manshipit then took the lead. "We better get as far as possible then. Tomorrow we may be holed up waiting for the snow to stop."

HALFDANSFJORD

As it happened, two days snowshoe trek north of the where the Naskapi and Anishinabeg had met it was already snowing heavily in the country that surrounded Halfdansfjord. The north wind tore at the very fabric of the settlement. Wind-driven snow piled up against every obstacle. And, it was a mind-numbing cold; the kind of cold that crept into your bones, the kind of cold that killed.

The people of Halfdansfjord worked at various crafts, snug within the longhouses, the daily business of life scarcely interrupted. The shipbuilders and guards had already sought shelter. Security for the settlement fell to the dogs to warn of intruders foolish enough to brave the intensity of the gathering storm.

A council meeting was in session to discuss the most recent sighting of hostile natives. The men lounged at their usual long, trestle table. A fire burned in the long hearth beside them, and a kettle of cod chowder warmed at the hearth. Whale oil lamps pushed back the gloom, their long, flickering yellow flames formed tendrils of smoke that rose into the still air to join the pall of ever-present smoke already spread along the ceiling of the imposing room, reflecting the light downward over the room below, not unlike light reflections from the bases of a bank of low clouds.

Halfdan sat in his high seat at one end of the table, a leg draped over one of the chair's arms. He had listened to and occasionally joined the general conversation about a host of topics of general interest to the group of leaders. Deciding it was time to move from banality to the business at hand, he gave his interpretation of the snowstorm.

"Listen to that wind. Thor is in rare form. This storm promises to be our most severe of this winter."

"Aye, it does," agreed Bjorn from the other end of the table. "It may catch that Anishinabeg scouting party before they get back to their village. They will have to seek shelter. Nobody could live out there in that wind and cold."

"The Anishinabeg are watching us to plan their attack when winter is over," said Athils.

"Aye, they are," said Brodir. "I do not want to sit idly by while they plan their attack. We know they will come. Why not attack them first, in the midst of winter?" He made eye contact with Halfdan.

The others held their tongues, waiting for their chieftain.

"I think you are right, Brodir, but nobody is going out in this storm. The Anishinabeg scouts were here two days ago, so it is too late to go after them. This storm is certain to catch them and drive them into cover until it passes. We will wait for the next scouting party. To ensure numerical superiority we can ready about fifteen men to go after them when they leave here. If we kill all the men in their scouting parties they might not be so anxious to spy on us. "

General agreement followed the men's appreciative laughter.

"It might be more effective if we leave one survivor to carry our message back to his village, like you did the first time they attacked us," said Tostig.

"That did not work out too well, Tostig; he came back with many of his friends.' Halfdan grinned at the man to blunt what might have been deemed a rebuke.

The others quickly entered into the spirit of Halfdan's statement, chiding Tostig good naturedly.

Halfdan always enjoyed these humorous interludes. He wanted these men to always have an opinion and humor often provided fresh thought for all of them. He did not want them to simply agree with everything he said. All his men knew when he would bode no further discussion on something he had said. This was not yet one of those times. After the interlude of humor ran its course, he brought them back to the topic of discussion.

"We know from fighting them, that nothing we do will impress them or give them pause. They have decided that we are their enemies and nothing we do or do not do will change that. Killing their scouts might make them mad enough to make a mistake that we can use to our advantage. With the spring they will come for us. They will do so without the scouts they send here this winter. Their scouts will feed the ravens and other eaters of the dead." He looked around the table. His eyes settled on Brodir.

"This is your idea, Brodir, so pick a group of men to go after the next scouts we see."

The man nodded, pausing in reflection before voicing his thoughts. "I will. Judging from what we have seen of their scouting parties, 12-men should do it."

"They travel on snowshoes," said Thorgeirr. "Using our skis it should be easy to get ahead of them to lay an ambush."

"Aye, they always travel along the same general route," agreed his kinsman, Hrafen. "Keeping our trail out of their sight might be difficult after we have passed them."

"The ambush could only be laid after they leave the bay, somewhere along the river where the forest offers concealment. Otherwise they will see you or your trail," said Athils.

"There are so many reindeer tracks out there that I do not think the tracks of our skis will be noticed, unless they cross our trail after we have passed them," said Brodir.

A murmur of agreement went around the table. A period of silence followed by general discussion of the details ensued. The men made use of the fish chowder while details were discussed. After a time, a plan was fleshed out that met with Halfdan's approval.

Brodir would lead the men of his choosing against the next group of Anishinabeg scouts that spied on Halfdansfjord. The scouts generally remained about three days. Groups of men coming and going from the settlement were a common sight to the scouts, making the planned ploy easy to execute.

Rather than wait for them to leave, Brodir and his men would leave the settlement in the opposite direction and then double back when they were out of sight from the scout's position. The men would be armed with bows, arrows, and axes, should close combat be joined.

If all the planned elements of the ambush came together, the next Anishinabeg scouts would be in for a nasty surprise when they left the area of Halfdansfjord to return to their village.

—∞—

Chapter 8

WINTER IN NITASSINAN

A leaden sky sagged almost to treetop level. Snow flurries came on the breast of a fierce north wind. Mind-numbing cold settled over the land, forcing the seven members of the Naskapi party led by Kejo into the forest verge to prepare shelter before the storm arrived in earnest. The expedition to return Ingerd to Halfdansfjord would have to wait on the whims of the gods. Their frenzied activity in the forest became a race with the wind and snow as they worked quickly to build a shelter that could spell the difference between life and death for all of them. '

Birch bark scoops, cut from the living trees, were used to dig the snow from a circular hole within a stand of birch saplings large enough to shelter all of them. Saplings within the circle were cleared away while saplings around the periphery of the circle were bent over, cut to length, and tied together at the apex with strips of the inner bark of the birch tree. The result was a low, domed framework over the waist deep hole in the snow. Saplings that had been previously removed from within the circle were woven through the dome's structure to give it strength and rigidity.

In the meantime, a pile of spruce and pine boughs were cut to cover the dome roof and insulate the occupants from the ice and snow of the interior's floor. Woven in overlapping layers over the framework, in courses from bottom to top, the boughs formed a tight bond to the dome itself. The loose snow dug from the hole was scooped back over the finished dome and packed into place. Entrance to the interior was gained via a simple trench in the snow down under the dome framework on the downwind south side. A block cut from crusted snow would close off the bottom end of the trench from the elements. A small smoke vent in the south side of the dome roof completed the shelter.

Ingerd stood back, hands on hips, admiring what they had created in such a short time. She shielded her face from the driving snow. Glancing to the north she saw that visibility had decreased to a short distance while she and the men had built their shelter; it was now snowing in earnest. The wind moaned through the forest. She noticed that the windborne snow had already begun to pile up against the shelter's dome, effectively obliterating the tracks they had made as they worked.

"Come Ingerd, it is time to take shelter." Nipishish's call intruded briefly on her thoughts. She waved a hand in acknowledgement. An intense gust of wind blew her hood down, packing one ear with snow. Dropping her head in the wind, she pulled her hood back in place as she trudged toward the entrance of the shelter, thanking the gods for her man and her companions. To be caught in the open in this storm would mean certain death.

Light coming through the smoke hole dimly lit the interior as she wiggled through the entrance. Her companions sat against the vertical snow walls of the shelter, watching Eskanan kindle the beginnings of a small fire of dry twigs in a shallow depression in the center of the floor.

The interior, while not warm, was comfortable. Most importantly it was out of the wind.

Eskanan used the discarded scoops of green birch bark to line the sides and bottom of his shallow fire pit to keep the snow pack of the floor from snuffing the tiny fire he had coaxed into existence.

The others lounged comfortably on the layer of pine and spruce boughs that covered the packed snow of the shelter's floor and watched the tiny flames lick at the twigs that Eskanan fed slowly into the fire. Mesmerized by the gift of fire, they stared into the flames, silent.

Body heat and the tiny flame soon made it necessary to shed the heavy parkas as the close confines of the interior warmed.

The flickering flames of the tiny fire pushed back the gloom of the interior. They settled down to wait out the storm; the men so inclined puffed on their pipes. Sporadic conversation occurred as the spirit moved them while they chewed on tough jerky or a cake of pemmican.

In a mix of Norse and Naskapi, Ingerd used the opportunity to find out more about the many bands of Naskapi scattered throughout Nitassinan. Meshika had alluded to the living conditions of many of the small bands of her people scattered over the heavily forested land that had bothered Ingerd since. She did not see how they could survive a storm such as this without permanent shelter. Meshika had done her best to explain, but the language barrier had made understanding difficult for Ingerd.

"Gudbj, Meshika tried to tell me about the small bands of Naskapi that live all through Nitassinan. I think she was telling me that they live in the old way in small extended family groups, without permanent villages such as the village of Sachem, and that they depend year around on hunting and fishing for survival. Is this true? How do they survive in winter?"

Gudbj looked at the other men before answering her. He knew that Kejo understood most of what Ingerd had said.

"I will help you answer Ingerd's question, Nipishish," said Kejo.

"Good, I need your help. You go ahead and tell her, I will fill in where necessary. Did you understand Kejo, Ingerd?"

"Aye, he will help us understand."

Kejo made eye contact with Ingerd. "The Naskapi are people of the forests. Before Sachem got many of us together in a village, such as the one you have seen, all of us lived in the old way, wandering through the forests, hunting, and fishing in the rivers and lakes of Nitassinan. The people lived in small groups, as Meshika told you, sheltering in groups of brush shelters just big enough for a few people. We followed the game that we needed to survive, so we moved often. Winters were spent trapping the forest animals for their meat and pelts. When an area became trapped out, we moved to another. We lived for the time, not planning for future needs. Food was not stored for winter to feed all of us.

In our father's time, when all of us were boys," he gestured toward his companions, "the people began to copy the farming practices of our enemies, the Haudenosaunee. The Haudeno lived in big wigwams, long-houses, in permanent villages. They lived much better than we did. We watched them prosper. Although they are our traditional enemies, we trade with them occasionally. Sachem made us see that their way was better than ours. We knew they were able to grow more food in their gardens than they needed to eat over the winter, so we traded them for some of their seeds, to start our own gardens. We started small, slowly building our village, and learning to raise the vegetables that we now have. Gradually, the small bands of wandering Naskapi heard what Sachem wanted us to do, and they came out of the northern forests to see for themselves. Many stayed, others did not; many stayed with the old ways. That is where most of our people are now, scattered throughout the northern forests. There are four villages like Sachem's. You, Ingerd, have been to the village of Antanak, where Chisasi is war chief."

Ingerd nodded in understanding, her attention riveted on Kejo as she continued her struggle to understand what he was saying without the frequent word or phrase insertions for clarification from Nipishish.

Nipishish, deciding levity was called for, added, "I could not go there."

The others laughed. He knew these men would find humor in the fact that he was not free to go where he chose when Ingerd had gone with Halfdan to Chisasi's village, at the war chief's invitation.

Ingerd shot her husband a look of impatience at the interruption. "Let Kejo continue, Gudbj, I want to hear the whole tale of his people."

Kejo smiled at her. "I think we have plenty of time for storytelling, Ingerd."

She gave him the same look, waving her hand for him to continue. This time they all laughed, except Ingerd, who did manage a smile in spite of her obvious impatience.

As if on cue, the storm manifested its presence with a tremendous gust of wind that caused a cloud of fine snow to filter down through the layers of boughs covering the dome roof, all but snuffing the flames of the tiny fire illuminating the interior, and shaking the dome's structure to its limits.

"See, even the gods are caught up in your story, Kejo," said Ingerd.

Nipishish stood to inspect the interior framework of the dome, shaking it a little to determine its strength and integrity. At every great gust, the dome shook a little, a sure indication of the storms strength. "I am relieved that we were not caught out in this."

"All we could do is burrow into the snow if we were out there. The wind kills," said Miknap, echoing all their thoughts.

"Aye, it does that," agreed Ingerd, never one to hold her tongue. She looked at Kejo, bobbing her chin for him to continue.

Kejo chuckled. "Do you have questions," he asked, looking at Ingerd.

"Aye, I do. I have spent much time in the forests around Halfdansfjord and more recently around your village, summer and winter. Often times there are not any animal tracks in the snow. What do the people of the forests find to eat then?"

"The inner bark of birch trees, the tips of shoots, grass, an occasional fish, and mice."

"Mice!" Ingerd exclaimed in disbelief. Thinking Kejo said it in jest, she looked around the circle of men; nobody laughed, and only Manshipit had a smile on his face.

"Fat mice in a stew, or roasted in the coals, taste good when you are hungry" he said.

The others got into it then, sensing a possible weakness in the woman, an opening for humorous exploitation.

"Roasted over the coals is my favorite." Atkaa offered, a big grin on his face.

"Mine too," said Miknap. "I also like to throw a handful of mice right into the coals, and wait until the heat burns off their hair and tails and they crack open. As soon as steam comes from the inside of their bodies through the cracks, they are done. You have to get them right out before they burn up."

All the men were laughing now. Ingerd looked from one to the other, the beginnings of a smile around her mouth and eyes.

"I like them threaded on a green willow stick, and passed back and forth through the flames until the hair and tails are gone. It is possible to get them roasted more evenly that way than just throwing them in the coals," said Eskanan.

"I agree," said Manshipit. "It is also easier to eat them right off the stick, rather than having to handle them hot from the coals."

"I agree that mice are delicious no matter how you cook them, but my preference is to cook them in a stew with corn, beans, or squash." Nipishish grinned at the look his wife directed at him.

"You have eaten mice," she asked him over the laughter of their companions?

"Many times, and so have you. As Manshipit said, they taste good when you are hungry."

"I have never eaten a mouse, Gudbj," she said, indignant at the suggestion that she would do such a thing.

"I have seen you eat stew many times, Ingerd. A kettle is always on the hearth for anyone that is hungry. The children catch the small animals, rabbits, squirrels, little birds, and every kind of mouse and rat. All go into the stew pot."

Ingerd studied the faces of her male companions. Nothing was to be gleaned from their expressions. Still not certain that she was not the brunt of a joke, her eyes settled on Kejo.

"Alright, so we all eat mice." A look of cunning briefly settled over her face, tempered with a slight smile. She felt certain she would now know if she had been tricked. "I can see that they would be easy to catch in summer, but how can they be caught in winter when everything is covered with snow and ice?"

"That is right; our children find their nests easily in summer. In winter the nests are seldom accessible, but the mice move around a lot looking for food. That is when they are caught."

"How do they catch them with the ground covered with snow?"

"Sometimes they come out on top of the snow; you will see their tracks. But usually they use their tunnels under the snow on the surface of the ground. They eat seeds, grass, and other plants. Summer or winter they must be on the surface of the ground to find food, so that is where they are found. Meadows are full of their tunnels. In winter, many of their tunnels end or begin at the bases of tree trunks, where the snow is melted or blown away.

When the snow is not too deep, like it is now, and when the sun is just right, you can see the tunnels under the snow, because they make a little ridge on the surface."

"I have seen those ridges," Ingerd said.

Kejo nodded, continuing his lesson on mice for her.

"The children set their little birch bark box traps, or small nets woven just to catch mice and rats, on the ground next to the tree bases." He gestured toward Atkaa with his pipe. "His 7-year old daughter is the best mouse hunter in the village. When you come back among us during the Time of Green Grass, ask her how she catches so many mice."

Ingerd looked at Atkaa. The normally quiet man nodded and grinned at her.

"I will ask her, Kejo."

"She teaches all the children how she catches small animals. She has always been very good with her traps and nets," Atkaa said.

Ingerd smiled at him. Her eyes again travelled over the faces of her companions. She felt close to these good men, whose highly developed sense of humor, fierce sense of loyalty to their people, and to each other, gave her a warm sense of belonging, for she and Gudbj were one with them.

"Alright, I thought you were all kidding me about the mouse stories. Now I know you were not, well not entirely, anyway.'

The men laughed at that. Some of the stories were retold, again bringing the warmth of laughter to the tiny shelter. Ingerd felt that to be friends and to know these men that could be so cruel and hard to an enemy yet could also be kind and helpful to one of their own was a privilege.

The tiny fire burned down, and flickered out. The wind sucked the last vestige of smoke out through the tiny vent, and Miknap closed it off with a wad of boughs to retain the warmth of the interior as long as possible.

A period of silence and introspection followed in the darkness of the shelter's interior. The tiny fire had been the only available light. A slight glow came through the thin areas of the dome, telling them that darkness had not come to the outside world yet. The roar of the wind continued unabated.

First one, and then another rolled up in their parkas and sleeping robes, an end came to the day.

For the time being they were warm and secure from the tempest. The gods would decide their fates with the dawn.

—⚬⚬⚬—

A short distance to the north of the snug shelter under the dome, and unknown to the seven members of Kejo's party, a serious fight for survival played itself out.

A group of people consisting of two men, one considerably older than the other, a mature woman, a young woman of child-bearing age, and four children, one a sharp-faced boy and three younger girls worked to dig a shelter under a huge spruce tree. The haste being made of the excavation work bespoke the extreme danger of their being without shelter in the teeth of the storm.

The little band had almost waited too long to seek cover. The fierce wind that accompanied the storm had caught them out in the open, trying to make it into the forest from the featureless, ice-covered vastness of the bay.

The people all wore snowshoes and were clothed in identical, unadorned, leather, knee-length parkas, leggings, fur-lined boots, and mittens, all sized appropriately for the individual. A single toboggan conveyed their meager possessions.

The bottom branches of the spruce tree the men had selected were buried in the snow, ensuring that a snug shelter could be had if they could manage to dig their way in to the base of the tree trunk without the deep snow caving in on them.

The men scooped the snow out from their front while the others piled it aside. Once past the crusty snow on the surface, the digging progressively got easier as the men widened the tunnel they had created into a space large enough to accommodate all of them at the base of the tree.

They had no more taken shelter than a section of the snow roof overhead caved in on them, creating a period of consternation until all had been accounted for. The older man elected to leave the overhead open; correctly assessing the effort to close the space with spruce boughs was not as important as being out of most of the wind. The snow depth itself and the entwined lower branches of the spruce overhead provided adequate shelter. They would work later to provide a more airtight shelter if necessary.

After the women and children got the toboggan unloaded, the older man used it to close off the entrance to the shelter.

While all this was going on the younger man was crouched over a hole he had hacked in the ice at the base of the tree, in which he worked to kindle a fire. The two women hurriedly rigged a piece of hide at head level above him, to deflect snow from the fire, while he worked with a small bow and drill, trying to coax a coal from a small, ice-cold piece of dry wood and tinder he had provided from his back pack. Within moments a wisp of smoke rose from the base of the drill nested in a notch in the dry piece of wood, producing a tiny glowing coal. The man carefully cupped the tinder around the coal while gently blowing into it. He thrust the tinder and its tiny blue flame under a tent of twigs in the hole at the base of the tree.

The others gathered close around him, grinning in appreciation for the tiny fire that the young man tended at their feet. Smoke rose aloft through the spruce boughs and away on the breast of the wind.

The people huddled gratefully in their robes, in a semi-circle before the fire, soaking up the life-giving warmth that coursed through their bodies.

Sometime later, after they had all thawed out from their ordeal, a soap-stone kettle of melting snow sat in the fire. After the snow water came to a boil, the last of their meat supply, the desiccated, 3-day old carcass of a snow-shoe hare, would become a stew that would keep them all alive for a time.

———

The dim light of dawn filtered through the top of the dome where the wind had worn away the snow, bringing definition to the gloom within. Sometime during the night, the wind had lessened considerably.

Nipishish awoke to the sound of running water. Rising up on an elbow he saw Miknap kneeling next to the wall, taking a wet in the hole that had been dug for that purpose in the snow packed floor of the shelter.

"I smell smoke."

"I smell it too. The wind has died down, otherwise we would not smell smoke unless the fire was close by," said Miknap, his business at the hole finished.

"Aye, the fire has to be close for us to smell the smoke." Nipishish felt like he was about to burst as he took the man's place at the hole. Sighing in relief, he finished and crawled to his place.

"I smell the smoke too." Kejo was setting up. He stretched. "Soon as everybody is awake, we will dig our way out of here, and see where the smoke comes from."

Later, the party began the task of digging out. Atkaa pulled the plug from the roof vent, revealing a complete covering of snow. Located on the lee side of the dome, the vent and entrance tunnel had drifted deep in wind-driven snow. Taking his bow, Atkaa pushed it upward through the vent. With his arm fully extended out the vent hole, the tip of his bow finally extended into clear air. He wiggled the bow back and forth to open a larger hole in the snow, so he could see out. "It is still snowing," he said. "Great big flakes; the wind is blowing a little."

Cold, fresh air filtered inside through the small opening.

"I did not realize how stuffy it had become in here," said Ingerd, inhaling deeply.

"Some air came through the wad of boughs plugging up the vent, but not much," observed Nipishish, as he helped Miknap with the large block of crusted snow blocking the entrance to their shelter. Now frozen in place because of the relative warmth of the shelter interior, it took the two men some time to pull it free and set it aside for later use.

With the block of crusted, frozen snow gone, no sign of the entrance tunnel remained – undisturbed snow choked the shelter's entrance.

"Here, I will break out," said Nipishish, pulling on his mittens. He tied the straps of his parka hood under his chin, and pushed through the entrance wall of their shelter into what had been the entrance tunnel. The snow was packed tight at the bottom of the tunnel, changing to loose and powdery toward the surface. For the most part it offered little resistance to the swimming/lunging motion he employed to break through to the open air.

The others joined him outside, crawling from the tunnel and into the gloomily opaque light of early morning. Large snowflakes, borne on the breeze, created eddies of swirling snow through the thicket, limiting visibility to a few feet. The shelter's dome was a mere hump in the featureless snow, covered completely, but still recognizable to them. To a passerby it would not elicit a second glance. Boughs protruded from the thinly packed snow on the dome's windward side, giving the interior what little natural illumination there had been. The only disturbed surface area roundabout was where they had crawled out from the entry tunnel. Their surroundings were virtually unrecognizable under many feet of new snow.

They dug their snowshoes out of the snow from where they leaned against the dome.

"The smoke is coming from out there somewhere. Fan out and we will find the source," said Kejo.

The wind guaranteed that the smoke source was close at hand. It had to be for the smoke to be recognizable as such in these windy conditions. In less than a ship's length all seven of them surrounded a large spruce, bows at the ready. Not a sign was to be seen in the snow cover, but wisps of smoke emanated from the snow covered lower branches of the tree nonetheless.

Kejo called a challenge.

A muffled male voice answered from under the spruce. The excited voices of children were briefly heard until abruptly cut short by a warning hiss from a woman.

Two days of travel to the north of the developing drama with Kejo's party, the residents of Halfdansfjord awakened to the blazing sun of a clear, new day. The reflected light off the snow's surface was an assault on unprotected eyes.

The depth of new snow made initial movement anywhere in the settlement a challenge. The split log walkways were buried out of sight. Doubtless they would remain so until the spring thaw revealed them once again. The labor to dig them out was unnecessary in most cases, given that snowshoe usage eventually produced a packed trail between the longhouses anyway.

Penned livestock seemed unaffected, taking the storm in stride while sheltering in the various sheds. Fodder and scraps for the pigs were provided, and there was plenty of snow to eat for water. They had not yet turned their pens into the morass they would later become through renewed activity now that the storm had passed.

All the milking livestock – cows, sheep, and goats – lived in pens at the end of each longhouse, handy for the twice daily milking and secure from storms.

With the storm's passage, outdoor work set aside for its duration resumed. Although the day was bright and sunny, the intense cold of winter persisted, ensuring that no thawing occurred to turn the outdoor work areas into gluey mud.

The largest and most important construction project currently in progress was the building of two ships and two ships' boats. It took the men involved a considerable part of the day to clear the fresh snow from their building materials. Once they had the general area cleared of most of the snow, the various tasks were laid out by the shipwrights, and the work began in earnest. Men working singly and in teams put the finishing touches to all the wooden structural members that comprised the ships' hulls.

In all, 30-odd men labored at the considerable task of turning raw timbers into ships' and boats' hulls. Their numbers included Tostig and Hrafen, the two men picked by Halfdan to captain the new ships. Halfdan had instilled in all of them the necessity of finishing the ships before spring and before the expected attack of the Anishinabeg.

The four shipwrights charged with the building were a special breed, experienced in all the woodworking skills necessary to produce seaworthy vessels that included everything from small boats to ships. Two of them, Hallsteinn and Kolbeinn had been with Halfdan from the beginning of the expedition from Greenland. Neither had mates, nor did they have an interest in acquiring one. Their lives revolved around their trade, the boats and ships they loved to build and repair, and the men that sailed them. Both were easy to be around, especially if their workmates loved the work as they did.

As it happened, Hrafen, the kinsman and lieutenant of Thorgeirr, chosen by Halfdan to captain one of the new ships, was also an accomplished shipwright in his own right. Chosen for his leadership and sailing abilities, like other men of his ilk he was more than capable of building the vessels that he had spent most of his life on. While working, he seldom talked much, being intent on the task; however, he was friendly to his workmates for the most part, rising to the frequent ribald jokes. The gossip was of particular interest to him. The topics would be of interest to any man: weapons, hunting, food, and women. Hrafen did not have a mate, because he was looking for a special type, and he had not found her yet. He knew she was out there, a handsome woman that could cook, mend his clothes, talk to him, and had the sexual appetite of a stray cat. He frequently smiled over his female requirements while he listened to the others talk about the different women out there. One day he would hear the right one mentioned, all he had to do was listen.

The fourth man, Thorleikr, in addition to possessing the general skills of a shipwright was also a stem master, a fortunate happenstance for the people of Halfdansfjord. A stem master's particular skill produced the bow and stern stems of the vessel, whether it be a boat or a ship. These upright timbers that curved gracefully outward at each end of the keel, the point at which ever plank began and ended, had to be carefully shaped and carved to produce the attachment point for the ends of every run of planking making up the boat's or ship's hull. If he was wrong in his calculations the ship was wrong. Of all the skills represented by the people, Thorleikr was the only man who could carve a perfect stem. He was finishing the last of the four stems with his new apprentice, Eilifr. An enthusiastic young man half his age, Eilifr had arrived with Thorgeirr's people. He would someday possess the same skills, but for now his function was to assist, to fetch and carry for the stem master.

Jorundr, the master carver, also an important part of the shipbuilding venture, worked indoors, warmed by the hearth in the longhouse where he lived with many of the other single men. He provided these men with patterns and direction to carve all the wooden rigging blocks and cleats necessary to secure the standing rigging on both the ships and boats. His current task was the two ships' figureheads chosen by the ship captains. The stylized figureheads he carved would be the last thing put on the finished ships, just before they were launched after the spring thaw. He had plenty of time to do his work. He had already met with both the captains to draw out how they wanted their figureheads to look, and discuss sizing to compliment the ships. Prices in trade goods were agreed upon by the three of them. Later, he selected pieces of oak that he kept soaking in tubs until a need arose. He hoarded these natural shapes for special projects. From two of them he roughed out both figures for the men's approval. Final finishing would come later, so he returned the roughed out shapes to the soaking tubs for when he could spare the time from all his other daily projects in wood to finish them.

When he finished the figureheads, he would also carve the massive mast fish to which the mast would be stepped in the four vessels. Of solid oak, the mast fish was attached across six heavy ribs in the ships, just forward of amidships, and just above the keel, but not resting on the keel. Mast fish for boats were much smaller. Pressure against the small sails and masts from the wind was much less. In both cases, the mast fish was an essential part of the vessel's sail plan, for the masts on all Norse vessels could be quickly raised and lowered. The bottom end of the mast fit in a socket carved in the bottom of a trough along the top of the fish. With the mast upright in position, a removable top piece of the fish was hammered into the trough, and wedged tightly, closing the top of the trough and securing the mast upright in position, ready for the standing rigging to secure it to withstand conditions at sea.

Tostig had specified the head of a raven to guide his ship through fog and give him the wisdom to make the right decisions as captain. Hrafen, being a somewhat simpler man, chose a dolphin. When asked why, he told the others he liked dolphins, they tasted good. His statement met with general agreement and a good deal of laughter.

Timber to build the two ships had been accumulated over the past summer, selected by all the same men that were now building the ships, and skidded to the landing beach building site with teams of horses. The same hot water rivulet that ran through Thorvard's tanning pond ran into the bay next to the shipyard. Easily dammed, the rivulet became a pond large enough to keep all the timber save the masts and yards from drying out.

All the hull pieces assembled were of green timbers – live trees – and they must be kept green until use during the winter; the pond accomplished this end. Hardwoods and even soft woods like pine and fir were easier to work while green. Oak and ash became so hard and dense when cured that they defied the sharpest blade.

Standing, live trees were picked for their natural shapes. Naturally shaped timbers were much stronger than cut timbers, and finishing them to their final shape took less effort. Straight, curved, forked, and almost every other shape likely to be required to shape the desired structural members were selected. Oak, ash, and birch hardwoods for the keel, mast fish, gunwale planks, and stems of the hull, as well as the ribs, knees, thwarts and other internal structural members had already been roughly shaped while green, before being put in the pond in the fall. The workmen retrieved them from the pond as they were needed.

Four straight-grained fir logs, two long thick ones for the ships and two short thin ones for the boats, were cradled side by side while men wielded axes and adzes to shape and smooth them. The sail yards, to which the wadmal sails would be attached, received the same treatment. Like most of the other parts for the ships these timbers had been selected and cut during the summer, skidded to the building site, and barked to facilitate curing until they could be finished later. Unlike all the other structural members, the masts and yards were allowed to cure until dry.

The ships' planking, a mix of curved or straight knot-free pine and fir logs had also been harvested over the summer, and kept green in the pond. Workmen staked the logs so they would not roll and began splitting each lengthwise along the grain into thin, wedge shaped planks. Other workers propped and wedged these planks into small tree forks that had been tamped tightly into holes during the summer and now stood solidly upright in the frozen ground. With the thin edge up, each plank was wedged into place in the fork, smoothed, and cut to the desired thickness with a short-handled, T-shaped side axe with a long thin blade designed for that purpose. The resulting shaped plank, thicker at the top than the bottom was stacked in the shallows of the steaming hot water pond to keep them pliable until their eventual use by the crews planking the two ships. Had the hot water pond not been available, each wet plank would have had to be laboriously heated over the coals of a long fire pit until the wood was hot enough to be pulled and bent into position along the sides of the ship.

The thickest of the planks were those that ran from the keel upward to the waterline. From the waterline to the gunwale plank at the top of the hull the planks were progressively thinner in each run until about half the thickness of those from the keel to the waterline. The gunwale plank, at the top of the hull, and the plank in the area of the oar locks were of ash. When dry, ash was one of the hardest and toughest woods available, fully capable of withstanding the stress and wear at those two sites of the ship's hull.

Wood scraps and chips from these efforts were fed into a fire that kept a cauldron of pine pitch suspended from a tripod bubbling. This aromatic mixture would be reduced by boiling until it became the black pine tar necessary to seal all the various hull members as they were joined together. A pile of pine pitch blocks, collected and cast while pine sap still freely flowed were handily piled nearby. They would be added to the cauldron as necessary to ensure sufficient pine pitch for the work at hand. The fire also provided a place for the men to thaw out from time-to-time.

Prior to the storm, the long keels had both been set across short log blocks and braced securely in place. Stem and stern posts carved out of properly shaped curved timbers by the stem master were now securely nailed in position at each end of the keels, and propped upright at the desired angle. Both the bow stem post and stern stem post were incised at the proper angle to accept the ends of each plank of the ship.

Beginning at the very bottom of the bow stem post, where it joins the long keel, the garboard plank, the first plank attached to the keel on both sides, was carefully nailed into position along its bottom edge. The angle established by this plank, outward from the keel on each side, determined the final shape of the ship as each succeeding run of planks were riveted in place to the preceding run. The garboard plank's placement was vital to ensure the ship's sides in cross section were identical and that she was watertight.

Equally spaced holes had been augered along the bottom edge of the thin planks before they were positioned along the keel to accept the long iron spikes that would be driven through and into the keel. In positions where the long iron spikes could not be safely driven in without splitting the keel, hardwood pegs, or treenails, slightly thicker than the hole they were driven into were used. These pegs would later swell as they soaked up water, making an even tighter bond.

When each garboard plank was in position on the keel, the graceful outward flow of the hull was established by the shape of the keel itself. In cross section the keel was cut in the shape of a T with the ends of the crosspiece at the top angled upward about thirty degrees from level. The keel shape created a shelf on which to mount the first plank. The bottom, vertical portion of the T-shaped keel, became the bearing surface of the completed hull when the ship would later be beached. The keel also facilitated the ships ability, in company with the huge steerboard, to hold the desired course without sideslip in the water from the pressure of the wind on the sail. The keel's shape created the outflowing curve of the bottom planks and relatively flat bottom of the completed ship.

Each of the several planks on each side of the ship was of differing lengths. An adjustable gauge, with an inset iron scribe point, gouged a channel an equal distance from the bottom edge of each plank. Spaced equidistant just above this channel, and marked at the same time the channel was cut and by the same gauge, holes were augered. These holes became a guide to auger holes through the top of the preceding plank run to which the new plank would be joined with iron rivets and roves. The channel would receive the tarred caulking twine. The edges of each plank were beveled so as to flow onto the plank to which it was joined. Each plank was clamped in place to the outside of the plank it was joining with long, hinged wooden clamps that were placed over the two planks being joined. Then a wedge was driven between the upper jaws of the clamp, firmly gripping the joined edges of the two planks together for riveting.

The ends, where they joined the preceding plank on the same level were carefully scarfed before mounting, creating a beveled scarf joint that was tarred, caulked, and riveted together, creating a continuous plank run from end-to-end along each side of the ship. As planks joined the preceding run along the bottom, the two bearing surfaces received liberal daubs of pine tar from the bubbling cauldron; twisted wadmal caulking twine was pressed into the channel, making the joints watertight when riveted.

After holes had been augered through the joined planks, men working in teams – one outside the hull, and one inside – riveted the edges tightly together with iron nails and roves provided by the smithies. These essential iron parts were actually a pointed square nail with a large head, tapered along its length to the point, long enough for the job at hand, and a flat washer with a center hole punched large enough to accommodate the nail. The nails were used by themselves whenever attachment of a structural member did not completely pierce through the two being joined. When the nail tip went all the way through the wood, as it did on the scarf and edge joints of the planks, a rove was added on the inside of the plank to protect the wood from the clinched nail point. The two together, nail and rove were called a rivet.

The nails were driven through the predrilled holes along the edge of the plank being mounted from the outside, and the man inside placed the rove over the nail's point and clinched it over with his hammerhead. The man on the outside of the hull held the head of his hammer against the nail head as resistance against the tendency of the clinching forces to push the nail back out of the hole. This force from both directions during the clinch pulled the plank edges tightly together against the pine tar and caulking twine, effectively sealing the joint.

The activity in the shipyard attracted bystanders from time-to-time as they had the time to spare from the constant work involved with daily life in a Norse village. It was fascinating to compare the progress made from a prior visit with others that turned up to watch.

Back at the south gate, Halfdan and Helge were on their way out the gate to view the progress being made at the shipyard, when they were interrupted by a call from the tower guard.

"Halfdan, look out to the southeast, where the bay narrows into the river canyon." The guard pointed into the distance. "See that black line? I do not think it was there just a moment ago."

Halfdan and Helge both saw object of the guard's attention. Halfdan turned a questioning look to the guard.

"I am not sure yet, but I think it is moving. It is a long way off. I should be able to tell within the hour."

"It could be caribou," said Helge.

"Maybe, but caribou usually do not follow one another in a line like that," said the guard.

"Alright, keep a watch on it. Tell us when you know what it is." Halfdan turned away. He and Helge continued down the beach toward the shipyard. Both glanced occasionally in the direction of the sighting. Nothing was to be seen in the glare off the snow.

—⋙—

Thorvard and his mates had just finished delivering the last few coils of twisted walrus hide rope to rig the two ships. They stored the rope in the council chambers to keep it away from damage or destruction by hungry wolves, foxes, and other nighttime predators that wandered the countryside in their constant quest for food. The rope coils were hung on pegs driven into the building roof support posts to keep them off the floor, and away from the legions of rats and mice that were everywhere about.

A contingent of village cats that were never fed – hungry cats are better hunters – kept the vermin population to acceptable levels in all the longhouses. Their numbers had markedly increased over the summer with the arrival of many litters of kittens. When culling occurred, as it must, cat meat stew would be in the kettle.

The cats were tame, but people paid scant attention to them as they were usually out of sight, lurking in the darkness awaiting prey, or sneaking about, alert for the slightest scurrying movement in their world. Often in the night, those who happened to be awake for one reason or another would here a scuffle as one of the cats caught a mouse or rat. A moment later, the sound of crunching bones would be heard as the cat ate its prey, signifying the success of another hunt.

When the coils of rope were brought into the council chambers for storage, they were stiff, partially frozen. As time went by and the rope thawed in the relative warmth of the large chamber, a smell of decay and rancid oil permeated the smoky air from the curing walrus hide rope, liberally greased with walrus and seal oil to keep it pliable. Few of the people working at their various tasks took notice. Odors of all kinds were a fact of life, especially in winter when little air circulation occurred and everyone spent most of their time confined indoors.

With the exception of the trappers that ran their trap lines in all weather, and were gone for days at a time, and the tower guards that rotated their duty periods, most everyone in Halfdansfjord worked at some task directly associated with the shipbuilding. Halfdan had decreed that the effort would involve every person at some point during the winter.

In addition to their daily tasks of cooking, milking, spinning skeins of yarn, making new clothing, and so forth, women and young girls in every longhouse busied themselves at the looms making wadmal panels that would be pieced together for sails. Coils of twisted wadmal twine accumulated to caulk the ships' planks. These sessions were enjoyed immensely. They offered chances to gossip, and at the same time the young girls of all ages were taught a skill they would be using for the rest of their lives. All had been made aware of the urgency and importance of their efforts. After all, men built the ships, but only the women's work at the looms made the sailcloth to propel them on their voyages.

Frida and Thora oversaw the efforts throughout the settlement, scattered as it was through all five longhouses, keeping track of production to ensure sufficient wadmal panels and twine was accumulated for the needs of the shipbuilders.

Earlier, with the beautiful sunny days they were enjoying, Halfdan had requested the men be fed their midday meal at the shipyard, rather than taking the time to eat in the council chambers. The work was the priority. Minimal wasted time eating the midday meals was the goal. They could relax later. There would be other storm that would shut down the ongoing efforts, but regardless, the two ships must be complete enough to sail away or be towed away from danger when the Anishinabeg attacked sometime during ice breakup in early spring. With all this in mind, Frida and Thora arranged that groups of women and girls take turns delivering food to the shipbuilders, so that all had a chance to see the progress being made.

At the moment, about half the women and girls were so involved. Frida and Thora, accompanied by Ingunn, Rannveig, several other women, and a host of chattering girls, arrived with kettles of stew, hot broth, and bags of bread for the men. Halla and a line of other thralls bearing kettles followed close behind. There was enough for everyone, and the food kettles were arranged around the fire or placed on live coals raked out of the fire pit to keep the food warm. The large pine tar cauldron occupied most of the space available at the fire pit, but the women managed to make do.

Frida straightened up from setting down her kettle and called to the men. "Come and eat while it is still hot."

Work ceased with the arrival of the food. The men needed no urging to leave their work and mingle around the fire. Most stood while eating, visiting at the same time. Others simply sat down on the tamped snow, having found something handy to lean against. People continued to arrive from the village to join the midday gathering, among them Halfdan and Helge.

Frida beamed a smile at her mate as he joined the group. The crow's feet at the corners of Halfdan's eyes deepened when he made eye contact with Frida. They did not speak, but the message passed between them nonetheless, as Halfdan entered into conversation with the shipwright, Hallsteinn.

"We are making good progress, Halfdan," said Hallsteinn.

"I see that."

Hallsteinn absentmindedly scratched Wolf's ears. Wherever Halfdan happened to be, the big dog was nearby. Hallsteinn knew what would happen if the dog perceived a threat to his master. He noted that the dog accepted his touch because of his acceptance by Halfdan, but the pale blue, slanted eyes remained watchful. "It is so cold that the timbers freeze almost as soon as we pull them out of the pond. We could not do this at all without the hot spring water keeping the ice off the pond."

"The gods have smiled on your efforts. I know it is harder to build under these conditions, but I wanted to try. The hot spring makes our lives easier." Halfdan's glance played over the jumble of finished and half-finished hull members resting in the shallows of the steaming pond, and the two ships' hulls. "It normally takes most of the summer to build a ship. Your work this winter will put us a season ahead."

"Aye, and all of us know it. We would rather be out here working on these ships than waiting for winter to pass while lying around looking for something to do."

Halfdan chuckled at his comment. "I have never seen you lying around." He turned his head toward the east, studying the dazzling brightness of the snow covered ice of the bay as long as his eyes could stand the glare.

Hallsteinn looked out over the bay to see what might have attracted Halfdan's attention. Seeing nothing, he turned away. "It is too bright today to look out there for very long. Did you see something earlier?"

"I have not. The guard told me he thought he saw a black line near the far eastern edge of the bay. He thought it was moving."

Hallsteinn regarded his chieftain with a quizzical expression in place.

"I do not know." He chuckled as a thought occurred to him. "It might be caribou, people, trolls, or wood nymphs. The guard will alert us when he knows something. Until then, let us join the others and find out what smells so good."

Later, towards day's end, the fire under the pine tar cauldron had been allowed to burn down, the men finished their immediate work in preparation for quitting for the day. Others put hull timber members back in the pond to keep them from freezing until work resumed. The men stole glances out over the bay to the east. All were aware of the line of people that had trudged steadily across the bay from early morning, gradually growing more distinct as the day wore on. That these people were openly coming toward Halfdansfjord there was no doubt. The columns of smoke rising into the still air from the longhouses would be visible from a great distance.

The sun was now low on the horizon, the surface glare off the snow from the brilliant midday sun, much diminished. Rather than a tiny dark line against the snow in the distance, the line was much closer, and it had segmented into a column easily identified as individual people, fifteen of them, three of which might be children. The last two people in the column pulled a loaded toboggan.

People began to drift out of the settlement's south gate as word spread, among them armed men at Halfdan's behest. They all mingled on the landing beach, their colorful clothing in sharp contrast to the drab brown clothing worn by the people out on the ice. Children ran about, oblivious to the drama unfolding before them. Women gossiped while stealing glances toward the bay, the men were focused on the approaching strangers. It was felt that they were not hostile, but their intent and identity were still unknown.

Deskaheh and the men he had been trapping with returned to Halfdansfjord in time to join the others on the landing beach. He found Thora with Halfdan, Frida, Bjorn, Ingunn, and several others. He walked up behind Thora, held a finger to his lips when Frida saw him coming, and gave his wife a bear hug from behind, mindful of her swollen stomach. She hugged his arms to her chest.

"I hope that is you, my man."

"It is I,' he said enthusiastically. "Did you miss me?"

She winked at her friends, Frida and Ingunn, who beamed at her obvious happiness. "I might have thought of you."

He turned her to face him. "I might have thought of you, too, if I had not been so busy trapping." Suddenly serious, he pointed his chin at the column of people on the lake.

"We do not know who they are yet," Thora answered.

Deskaheh made eye contact with Halfdan. "They are Naskapi."

"You are certain," asked Halfdan?

"Aye, Naskapi. From that direction they likely come from the village of Sachem."

"Perhaps they have news from Gudbj," said Bjorn.

Nobody said anything further for a time, their attention on the approach of the Naskapi party.

Suddenly, Deskaheh turned to Halfdan, his normally expressionless features conveying excitement. "Halfdan, I think one of those men pulling the toboggan is Gudbj."

Halfdan's eyes narrowed as he tried to focus on the figures pulling the toboggan. "You may be right. One of them is big enough to be Gudbj."

Frida watched her husband closely. She noted the play of emotion, and then pleasure that briefly crossed the face she alone knew so well. Her eyes misted as she shared the secret pleasure of the hard man who was their chieftain at the first sight of his friend in a long time.

He turned to her, the mask in place, and his emotions in check. "It is Gudbj, Frida. Ingerd will be there, too."

They smiled happily at one another, sharing the moment, each knowing what the other felt.

Until Halfdan mentioned it to her, Frida had not thought about Ingerd. But of course she would be with Gudbj. She sought her friend Thora, holding out her hands to her. The two hugged happily.

"I see her, she is walking with the children," shouted Thora. All the women with them ran down to the edge of the bay, shouting and waving like young girls. Without snowshoes they could not venture out on the ice, the snow atop the ice was too deep. Their enthusiasm was answered by a wave from Ingerd; now there was no doubt that it was her.

Word spread quickly through the crowd. Almost the entire population of Halfdansfjord massed at the point where the column of people on the ice would come off the ice.

Kejo, at the head of the column, came onto the beach first; his face wreathed in smiles at the reception accorded them. His eyes travelled over the smiling faces of the crowd. The cacophony of their voices gave him to know that he was welcome among them. He spotted Deskaheh close by. The man made eye contact with him. A slight smile opened the man's hawkish features. The two former enemies nodded in friendly fashion to each other.

Kejo turned his attention back to his people. All of them were obviously happy to have the journey ended, although most could not have known what was going on amidst the din of their arrival. The crowd surged back and forth to get a look at what was happening, and everybody was talking at once. It took some time for all of the party to come ashore, take off their snowshoes, and grow accustomed to walking about without them.

They all looked exhausted, especially the women and children. Their drawn faces were a certain indicator of the hardship endured by all of them. Long journeys on snowshoes in the dead of winter were not something anybody ever took in stride.

Nipishish straightened up from untying his snowshoe bindings. His eyes played over the faces of his people, most of whom were looking at him. He nodded to those close at hand, returned their smiles with his own tired grimace, and his eyes came to rest on his chieftain, who had come to a stop right in front of him.

The two men smiled, each taking the measure of the other, as men will do. Others kept their distance, letting these two have their reunion, and the thoughts that only they shared.

Halfdan suddenly clasped his friend's shoulders in a vice-like grip, instantly returned by Nipishish.

"I am glad you have returned. We have much to discuss" said Halfdan. His eyes searched the face of the only man he had ever regarded as a friend.

"Aye, we do. I think there is much we must do for these eight people that we found under a tree before we set down for our talk."

"Be about it then, we will follow your lead." Halfdan, Bjorn, and Tostig, followed along in case their help was called for. The group swelled with other men as the men and women of the crowd naturally separated in two as needs dictated.

Nipishish beckoned to Kejo, to help him talk with the forest Naskapi if need be. They sought out the leader of the little band, the younger of the two men. The man grinned at them, shaking his head at the wonder of it all.

Nipishish grinned in return, knowing how the man must feel to be suddenly immersed in such an alien culture.

"You will grow accustomed to my people; they will become your friends. We will get food and shelter for all of you," said Nipishish. "Your women and children will go with the woman here, and they will help them get you all settled."

"We are fine, Nipishish." He looked at the older man, Ipishui, who nodded in agreement.

"You have shared your food with us, Nipishish," Ipishui said, glancing from Nipishish to Kejo. "We can wait while you talk to your friends."

"Already, we have more than we are accustomed to having," said Muaku. "There is no urgency for us."

"That is good that you feel this way. Your women and children can go with these Norse women to get settled here," said Kejo. "You can join them later."

"As you say, Kejo. I will tell them," said Muaku.

Halfdan and the other observers were all struck by the same thing; Gudbj had no trouble talking to the Naskapi in their own language.

"Gudbj sounds like one of them," observed Bjorn, his statement echoing the thoughts of the other men.

They all observed that the Naskapi stayed in a group with Kejo and Gudbj. The men were not uncomfortable at all, as all of them save Eskanan had been to Halfdansfjord before. It was natural for them to stay together while their arrival sorted itself out, and their needs became known.

Halfdan closely watched the Naskapi men and his former lieutenant. That Kejo was a close friend to Gudbj was apparent. *Gudbj looks more like a Naskapi than one of us. He is leaner, harder, than he was. Except for the short beard and his size he could be easily mistaken for Naskapi.*

"I heard them call you Nipishish. What do you want us to call you?" said Halfdan, as Gudbj finished talking to the Naskapi.

The old smile spread over his drawn features. "Gudbj, Halfdan. It is my name here with you." His eyes travelled over the faces of his friends, the men with whom he had shared so much. "I know you all have many questions about me. Much has happened since I left here, but you all will see that I am the same man inside." They all were aware that his method of communication now included copious hand signs, as he tapped his chest for emphasis. "My life was spared for a purpose. The gods have ordained that I would become one with these fine people, and I have done that. They, too, are my people. If we are to live here, they will become your people as well."

He turned back to his chieftain. "Halfdan, can you call a council? I have much to tell. You will want to be aware of these things."

"Aye, we will have a council for tomorrow. I will want the council chamber filled with our people afterwards. They, too, must hear your words. For now, let us all go to the council chamber for food and drink. This day is over. It is time to eat and rest from your journey."

"You will not get an argument from any of us." He turned to the Naskapi men to translate Halfdan's words.

A similar scene unfolded with the Norse and Naskapi women. Frida and Thora, with the capable assistance of the Naskapi maiden Pishekat, whose language skills had grown considerably over the past summer while living among the Norse at Halfdansfjord, took control. The forest Naskapi leader had told the women and children of his little band to go with the Norse women for food and lodging. Pishekat translated his words for the others. Thora understood immediately what was happening and helped her friends understand where necessary.

The Naskapi's familiarity with Ingerd made the strangeness of their new surroundings and the exuberance of the Norse women easier to accept. Instead of bolting like frightened deer, as may have been their want, they gradually relaxed, going happily along through the gaping south gate of the settlement, and into an alien world.

By this time a large group of Norse women had joined the procession. When it became known to everyone what was happening they began clucking over the children like hens as they walked with them and the others into the settlement and the longhouses that would be their homes for as long as required.

⸺∘⸺

As one would expect, conversation during the proposed period of relaxation and eating led to the council meeting intended for the morrow. All council members were present, and all were consumed with curiosity.

All the council members naturally congregated together around the long trestle table used for such gatherings; everyone but Gudbj.

Gudbj felt outside the close-knit group at the council table; he had been gone a long time. Although all the men wanted him there, he did not feel like he belonged. Much had happened to him since he was Halfdan's trusted lieutenant. Since those days he had been nearly killed before being captured the preceding summer by some of the very same Naskapi warriors that sat nearby, gorging on roasted meat and fish stew. It was all harder for him than he thought it would be. He felt confused, although he had given it a lot of thought, trying to sort out in his mind how his return to Halfdansfjord would go.

"Halfdan, I want to see to the Naskapis before I join you. Most of the men Ingerd and I came with have been here before, so they are relaxed among you. Muaku and Ipishui are not relaxed at all." He glanced at the two forest Naskapi men. "I will talk with them."

At that moment, Halfdan and Gudbj knew that something had altered the relationship they had always enjoyed since leaving Greenland. They had adapted to changing circumstances, they had changed, each of them.

Halfdan, his keen awareness fully tuned, knew it first. His eyes narrowed somewhat as he nodded to his friend. He indicated the table of Naskapi men with a lift of his chin. "Go and talk to them. When you return to the council, bring Kejo with you."

"I will do that." He studied his chieftain a moment, a troubled look on his face. "I told you that I am the same inside, Halfdan, but..." His voice trailed off. "You will know what I mean before this council ends."

"Easy Gudbj; you have been through a lot. I know that. The gods made me know what had happened to you." Uncharacteristically, he clamped a hand on his friend's shoulder. "Go now, talk to the Naskapi. When you are finished, we will sort this out together, all of us."

Chapter 9

DRUMS OF WAR

Sixty leagues south of Halfdansfjord, at the north end of a long, narrow lake, columns of smoke rose into the heavy, cold air from the bark covered wigwams of a large Anishinabeg village. Thick hoarfrost covered every part of the village and countryside, encrusted every twig, tree branch, and bush, laying down a hard crust over the surface of the snow.

This village, one of several of the Kitchi sipi Anishinabeg, is the focal point of the Big River People. The people of this particular village fish the chain of connected lakes in summer, travelling by canoe from place to place, but it is the wide, slow moving river that flowed from the lake through forest and fen as it wound its way north that defines them as a people. The river waters nourish them, they cook with it, they bathed in it, and they used its meandering flow to journey north to where it eventually emptied into an enormous bay, the same bay where Halfdansfjord was located. That the two disparate cultures would meet was a virtual certainty, given their proximity to one another. The Anishinabeg viewed this vast country to the north of Kitchi Gami as their homeland. They shared it for the most part with the Naskapi, their kinsman, but anybody else, any stranger was regarded as an invader in their sacred homeland.

ASSIMILATION

Information passes slowly across the vastness of this land. The new village of the strangers had only just been completed when their big canoes were spotted by a party of Shinabeg hunters. Tribal leaders dispatched scouting parties that reported the construction of a large, fortified village on the northern shoreline of the big bay that was an integral part of Anishinabeg territory.

Many moons passed while scouts watched the pale-skins, as they came to be called. Finally, during the late summer, six warriors were dispatched from the village to make contact with these pale-skinned strangers, staging a night raid on their village to test the mettle of the pale-skins. They did their work, and all but one escaped the wrath of the Northmen who pursued them. That man, Migisi, had been freed by the chieftain of the pale-skins. He later returned by canoe to his home village.

Migisi would never forget the cold blue eyes of the chieftain, nor the hatred directed at him by the other Northmen in attendance. He had intuitively recognized that these hairy men were dangerous warriors. He later found out firsthand how dangerous when he was one of the many warriors that mounted an unsuccessful autumn offensive against the heavily fortified settlement of the pale-skins.

Now, Migisi was but one of many warriors attending a council of war in his home village. Emissaries from every band of the Kitchi sipi Anishinabeg attended the gathering by invitation.

An air of anticipation gripped the assembly as they bore witness to the unfolding drama in the heavy, stale atmosphere of the packed council house.

Migisi squirmed in discomfort while the chieftain of his Kitchi sipi band, Nesatin, harangued him for the statement he had just made.

"You think we should let them live in peace in our land," roared Nesatin angrily. "How could you think such a thing? The pale-skins are responsible for the deaths of many of our warriors." He paused, giving Migisi a chance to make his plea, for they all knew that is what it was, a plea for sanity to prevail.

"I know that, Nesatin, I was with the war party of our war chief, Shingoos. I am the only man still alive of the six warriors that raided their village that night. The others were killed when we attacked them in force. We should take a lesson from that. The pale-skins are dangerous fighters." Migisi glanced in the direction of Shingoos, who sat in the council near Nesatin.

The man returned his gaze without visible emotion or comment.

"We have talked of this before, Nesatin. I know you want to hear it all again for the benefit of our kinsmen from the other bands of our people." His eyes travelled over the group of emissaries. "I mean no disrespect. I will fight if it is your decision that we go to war. I have told all of you that I fear the pale-skins, even though we outnumber them many times over. They are fierce warriors, but they only fight when forced to fight. We all know this about them. They want to live here in peace."

Pausing for effect, he gestured at the intent crowd of men. "Many of our wigwams are missing men because we attacked the pale-skins. If we attack them again there will be many more of us that cross into the world of spirits after we die against the log palisades of their village. We cannot scale their walls before their arrows and spears find us. I am the only Shinabe to have come face-to-face with these men. I have not told you everything that happened with the pale-skins. Now is the time, so you will know why I feel as I do." He again took pause, his eyes travelled over the attentive crowd of warriors. Knowing he now had their full attention, he spoke directly to his chieftain. "I have looked into the face of their chieftain. Their dogs did this to me." He turned so all could see the deep scaring and gouges of missing flesh in his arms and legs. A shudder involuntarily shook his body at the recollection. "Their chieftain wanted to kill me on the spot. A woman with hair the color of flame stilled his hand. She placed the Talisman of Life around his neck." He gestured toward Shingoos. "You saw this talisman when we attacked them, we all did."

Shingoos nodded his agreement. The men of his band already knew the tale of the talisman. His comments were directed to his chieftain, out of respect for him, and to the emissaries from the other Kitchi sipi bands. These men from other bands did not know of the talisman. "As I told you, Nesatin, I called off our attack when I saw this Naskapi talisman. I did not know what it meant to us."

"That talisman can only have come from the Naskapi's, Sachem," said Nesatin, loudly enough for all to hear his words. "The man that gave it to the pale-skin chieftain did so with Sachem's consent. I have sent two men to talk to Sachem of this talisman. They should return soon." He signed for Migisi to continue his tale.

Migisi got to his feet before continuing. He paced back and forth in the space between the council and the assembly of warriors. "Their chieftain left it up to his men. They were split; some wanted me dead, others were unsure. One of them suggested they turn me loose and then send four men to hunt me down."

"Wait," said Anougons, one of the emissaries from a neighboring band. "How do you know their words? Do they speak our language?"

Migisi knew somebody would ask this question, and he had a ready answer. That his words would inflame his kinsmen, he also knew. He had never told the whole story of what had happened to him after his capture. He played the moment for all it was worth. "I understood every word the pale-skin chieftain spoke to me. As he told me what he had decided, his words were translated by a Haudenosaunee warrior that was one with the pale-skins."

Pandemonium swept through the assembly at the mention of their hated enemies, the Haudenosaunee. There was little sense to it. Normal conversation was not possible while Migisi's announcement was bandied about. The fabric of the council house fairly shook from the noise. One notable thing seemed to come from the waves of anger loosed into the air; hatred of the pale-skinned invaders increased, if such was possible.

Migisi noticed it right away. He felt that his sensible plea for sanity would fall on deaf ears after the men came to realize that the pale-skins harbored and consorted with the Anishinabeg's sworn enemies.

The council let the assembly vent while they conversed among themselves as well as they could in the din. A short time later, Nesatin held up a hand to quell his warrior's exuberance. In the ensuing quiet, he made eye contact with Migisi, and bade him continue with a lift of his chin.

Migisi nodded to his chieftain, and began to pace once again, his eyes on the dirt floor, polished and hardened from the passage of many feet. He stopped before the council, making eye contact with his chieftain once again.

"Tell us more of this Haudenosaunee," Nesatin ordered.

Without pause or embellishment, Migisi complied. "His name is Deskaheh. His clothing is the same as theirs, he speaks their language, and he has a pale-skin mate with child. These things I saw. He is one with them. I do not think the pale-skins are friendly with the Haudenosaunee nation though. I did not get this idea, but I do not know for certain. That is all I know about this man, Deskaheh."

He looked at each council member in turn for questions. There were none, so he took a deep breath and continued his tale.

"I was not in their council house while they made their decision, so I do not know what they said. When I was brought back in, the men there were silent. I was brought before the big chieftain. The hate was still in his eyes. His face is cruel as he looked at me. He began to speak; Deskaheh translated his words. Their chieftain told me I was to be freed. Four of his men would give me a short time to run away, and then they would hunt me. If they caught me I would be killed on the spot. If I escaped from them, he wanted me to carry word of his justice to my people, to tell them that he gave me a chance for life; more of a chance than we gave the two men we killed in the raid on his settlement. He wants to live in peace with all of us in this land. When he finished telling me these things, the Haudeno handed me my weapons and told me to go." Migisi crouched beside a birch bark bucket of water, drinking from the gourd ladle kept floating on its surface while the council digested what he had told them. The subdued buzz of many conversations filled the air.

Migisi straightened up from his drink. The room quickly became quiet. "That day was spent avoiding the hunters. I never lost them, they had a good tracker. I was better at hiding than they were at finding me. I kept circling back toward the bay as they tried to drive me into the forest. Many times they almost stepped on my hiding place. As darkness came, they gave up their hunt. The night was without a moon. It was easy to sneak back to their beach and steal a canoe for my trip home. I think they knew I would do that.

They let me escape after the hunt, as their chieftain told me. He is a man of honor; they are a people of honor. Their word is their bond." A clenched fist emphasized his final statement. The cutting sign gave all to know that his tale was finished.

There were no questions; Migisi's tale had provided all the information needed for the council and emissaries to make their decision. After a period of general conversation, men began to leave the council house, Migisi among them.

The council members remained, as did the emissaries from the other tribal bands. They took time for meat and smoked fish before continuing their discussion.

As the night wore on, it became apparent to Nesatin and his elders that no consensus would easily be reached. His own war chief, Shingoos had serious reservations because of the losses he sustained in the previous attack on the pale-skins. Shingoos lodged unnecessary assurances with his chieftain and the others that he would do as he was ordered, as always, but for his young men he was adamant about the need for caution.

Nobody doubted Shingoos in any way. The man was a fierce warrior that had led his people against their enemies for many raiding seasons.

"I have assaulted the palisades of the pale-skins village. I know what we will face if we do so again. The logs are still too green for fire to destroy them. Our losses all came when we tried to scale them. Sometimes a single arrow from their powerful bows killed two men. Many of my warriors were killed by our own arrows that they shot back at us. All of this happened before their chieftain and some of his men opened a gate and attacked us. They smashed into us and were pushing us toward the water's edge. We held our own for a time, but they have a long-handled axe wielded by crazy men that we could not stand against. Their axe men dart in from behind their front ranks screaming a strange war cry. Some of my warriors were cut in half by these axes. Their chieftain and I finally came face-to-face. He is a hard man to miss and I went after him. He is a head taller than me and very muscular, a big man. The brown hair on his face is cut by a long scar surrounded by white hair and it makes him look even worse. His eyes, the eyes of a fiend, and his hairy face are hard to look upon. Like his men, he roars out his war cry as he fights. He killed every man that confronted him, that came within reach of a long blade that he wielded with both hands. We saw each other at the same time and both of us attacked the other. It was then that I saw the Talisman of Life that he wore, and drew back. He stopped fighting too. He just stood and watched me. I sounded the retreat. I am not certain I myself would be here to talk to you today had I not retreated with the men I had left. The pale-skinned chieftain shouted to his men and their horn signaled them to stop fighting when I blew the horn to retreat. They all stopped fighting, standing at the ready while we collected our dead and wounded. Many the warriors in canoes along the shoreline were run down and crushed by two big canoes full of pale-skinned warriors that came into the beach during that time." He paused to collect himself. His eyes went from man to man. "I will fight them again, if that is your decision. I wanted you to all know what to expect if you decide to send your people back into battle with these devils." He chopped his hand down in the cutting sign; he had had his say.

Anougons, always a vocal emissary for his band, also had reservations about another attack. Some of the men lost in the first attack had been close friends of his. Although he personally had not participated, he knew that all of them would become involved if protracted warfare engulfed their homeland.

"Shingoos speaks words of wisdom," said Anougons. "My chief will decide if we are to follow the path of war. I will tell him what you decide here."

The other emissaries agreed without undue discussion. Due to the length of the council, another round of food was called for. Afterwards, a period of relaxed slumber came to some, while others walked back and forth in thought or huddled in subdued conversation. The leaders of their people struggled to make what was perhaps the most important decision of their lives.

In the early morning before daylight, the two men that Nesatin had sent to talk to the Naskapi's Sachem returned to the settlement. Having just completed a roundtrip journey of almost 100-leagues on snowshoes, the messengers were understandably exhausted. Their journey consumed the period of a quarter moon, about seven suns. They spent a day in the Naskapi village of

Sachem, meeting with him and the council of elders, and recouping before beginning their return journey.

Nesatin stood to stretch tired muscles when the men entered the council house. "We hoped you would arrive during this council. You have brought the word of Sachem, so that we may consider his words to make our decision." He gestured toward the food that had been provided earlier. "Eat, and then tell us what Sachem said."

The two men selected chunks of meat and fish, and sank thankfully onto an unoccupied pile of deer hides, to eat, and rest their tired legs. A prodigious amount of meat and fish disappeared from the wooden platter on the hearth, the first such food that the men had eaten since leaving the Naskapi village at dawn three days hence. Finally sated, the two finished with several dippers of water and got to their feet.

During the short time while the messengers ate, conversation between the council members and tribal emissaries gradually died out. A tense expectancy hung in the smoky air around the council fire.

Days later, as Nesatin mulled over the final decision that he had pushed through the council, getting the unanimous vote that he wanted from the outset, a slight feeling of disquiet continued to mold his thoughts.

Chieftains of all the bands would make the final decision for their band based on the reports given by their emissaries that attended the council. Their agreement with the decision of the council was regarded as a formality, but necessary nonetheless. A decision for all-out war against the pale-skins would involve all the bands of Anishinabeg north of Kitchi-Gami. His mind sorted through the points he had made to obtain the required unanimous council decision for war. He felt a sense of accomplishment that he got the necessary vote the first time around. All the men had finally agreed that the settlement of the pale-skins must be destroyed; for fear that other foreign invaders would eventually follow. Once agreement was reached for war, he had pushed for an attack during the Time of Falling Leaves, rather than attack during the Time of Green Grass, when the enemy would likely expect an attack. As time wore on without an attack, they would grow complacent, making them more vulnerable. He had pointed out that a delay until the Time of Falling Leaves would ensure that any survivors of the all-out destruction of their settlement would go into the Time of Whiteness without the food they had stored; they would not survive. He was proud of his strategy, but still…

He came to realize that the talisman worn by the pale-skin chieftain was at the core of his disquiet. The tale the messengers related to him, and the council, told of a man called Nipishish, a pale-skin captive whose association with the Naskapi was making him the talk of Nitassinan. Over time this man became one with the Naskapi. It was revealed that the Talisman of Life was given to this man's chieftain, in recognition of an affair of honor, from a war chief called Chisasi, of Antanak's band. Although Sachem had nothing to do with the gift, he later approved of Chisasi's action.

Nesatin knew that Sachem's acceptance of the gift of the talisman made it no less important than if Sachem himself had given it to the pale-skinned chieftain. He preferred that his people not go to war against their Naskapi kinsmen, but if Sachem upheld the sanctity of the Talisman of Life, and he would, then all-out war was inevitable. He exhaled in exasperation, as he paced back and forth in his wigwam.

His wife and other family members occasionally glanced up from their work as their chieftain paced. None spoke or caused any distraction, knowing what he was about. Word had flown from wigwam to wigwam as people talked of the decision for war.

All but the youngest among them knew what would happen once it started - how their daily lives would change. Fear would initially spread through the women of the band, then stoic acceptance at the inevitability of their men's penchant to play the game of war each season. The call to battle always began with the tribe's best warriors, selected from among their husbands and sons. As the ranks thinned in a long war, as this one would surely be, the warriors became younger and younger. The women of the tribe knew these things from a lifetime of listening to the war talk. But, this time the scope was without precedent, for this time the drums called all the Anishinabeg to prepare for war.

When it finally ended, as it must, many men would be missing from the lodges of all the bands of the people.

❧

HALFDANSFJORD

For the first time, Chisasi brought the chieftain of his band, Antanak to the settlement of the Norsemen. They appeared toward day's end at the edge of the snow covered barley field, a long line of men on snowshoes trudging toward the north gate of the settlement.

Antanak was somewhat taken aback by the village of his new friends. The scale and strangeness of the dwellings and the multitude of strangers with strange habits overwhelmed him for a time, but like his war chief, Chisasi, the welcome provided by the Norse ensured that he did not feel unwelcome for long.

The Naskapi crowded through the north gate and spread out in the commons as was their custom, greeting friends, and mingling with the populace.

When Chisasi walked through the gate with Antanak at his side, he greeted those he knew with a smile and the salutation of his people, but his eyes darted around the crowd looking for one man. He finally saw Halfdan, and the man that he knew would be at his side, the man he had heard was here, the one he had come to see. Kejo was also with Halfdan, but Chisasi's focus was on the man at his side.

Chisasi smiled at Antanak, gesturing with his chin across the commons. "Come, there is Halfdan and Kejo. I want you to meet one of the other men that are with him." The two men wound their way through the crowd, greeting familiar people, moving toward Halfdan and those with him.

"I see Kejo and the Haudeno, Deskaheh, with Halfdan, but who is the other man, the big one dressed as one of the people," asked Antanak?

"He is Halfdan's war chief. His people know him as Gudbj. Our people know him as Nipishish. He is why I wanted us to come here at this time."

"I have heard this name. Do you know him well," asked Antanak?

"No, I only saw him once before he left here on the expedition that led to his capture by Glooscap and his men. The first time I came here to this place, Halfdan killed one of his own men after they violated our two young women. He gave the other man to us, for our justice. Nipishish was a part of that. As you know, he has fought for our people. Sachem's band and many of the forest bands of our people talk of his exploits."

Halfdan and those with him paused when they caught sight of Chisasi and Antanak coming toward them.

Halfdan greeted the two men with the traditional Naskapi greeting, one of the few phrases that he felt comfortable with. The other men added their own greetings; Gudbj, Deskaheh, and Kejo also replied with traditional Naskapi greetings.

Chisasi and Antanak answered in kind, acknowledging Gudbj, Deskaheh, and Kejo apart from the other men.

"Your Naskapi improves, Halfdan," observed Antanak. "Soon we will be able sit and talk together without the help of another."

Halfdan laughed. "I hope so, but that is one of only a few phrases that I know." He gestured toward Kejo. "He has taught me many words. Pishekat, a maiden living here with us, has also been teaching me about your people."

Chisasi and Gudbj repeatedly made eye contact during the course of the general conversation. This did not escape notice.

Gudbj broke the spell. Acknowledging Antanak with a smile and nod, he spoke directly to Chisasi. "I have wondered about you. It has been many moons since we saw one another. We have much to talk about." His copious hand signs included his friend Kejo, who stood next to him. "Kejo and I bring greetings from Sachem and Glooscap."

While Gudbj spoke, Chisasi could not help but notice Antanak's facial expression. To say Antanak was surprised at the facility with which Nipishish spoke Naskapi would be an understatement.

"You speak the language of the people well, Nipishish," Antanak said. "We look forward to hearing the message from Sachem and Glooscap."

"Aye, I am one with the people now. Your concerns are my concerns. Kejo and I have many things to tell everyone."

Speaking directly to Chisasi he continued. "I am glad you and Antanak are here, Chisasi. We did not have time to become acquainted before I left with my men to explore Nitassinan. Much has happened across this homeland since I was last here. The drums of war have been heard in the south. The Anishinabeg become restless. We must talk of these things."

"I, too, am glad we are here, Nipishish. To find you here is a good thing. We have heard your name. We will want to hear your stories," Chisasi said. His respect for the man was apparent. He and Nipishish, both tall men, were equal in that regard, and they had a history, albeit brief, but sufficient for each to respect the other.

Nipishish laughed. "I do not know about the stories, but we have much to talk about."

"There will be time for stories," said Chisasi, "There is always time for that."

"Good, so be it then."

Deskaheh leaned close to Halfdan during this exchange, translating for him. Halfdan half listened, his mind occupied with watching his friend speak to the Naskapi. *He truly is one with them. I see now that his value to me and to our people in this land is incalculable. He knew this long before I did. That is what he meant when he told me that he had changed. Thank the gods he has changed.*

Halfdan held up a hand, to stop the conversation. "Gudbj, tell them I want all of us to meet in the council chambers, you, all of the Naskapi, and our council. Everybody has a stake in this and I want all of them to hear what is said." At a questioning look from Tostig, he added, "I will not call another Thing; gossip alone will get the word out to the people about what we say."

Tostig nodded his understanding.

Gudbj told the Naskapi what Halfdan had said.

"Tostig, you and Deskaheh contact the council members. Tell them to meet in the council chambers after the evening meal. Gudbj, you, Chisasi, and Kejo gather all the Naskapi. I want every man there. This is too important for anyone to hear second hand."

"The forest Naskapi men, too," asked Gudbj?

Halfdan's curt nod and the hard set of his jaw bespoke the deep concern that he felt over the course of events that he could not control.

———❧———

Frida had taken control of the effort to feed the forest Naskapi women and children, and make them feel welcome. It was a daunting task. Thora and Ingerd were right with her in her efforts, but the problem was that the Naskapi women came from a small extended family group that spent every waking moment of every day either looking for food or repairing their meager clothing and possessions. By comparison, Norse society was rich beyond their comprehension.

Although communication was not really an obstacle, it took consider-able time for the small group to even appear to relax. Even then, the din and gaiety of the Norse women and female children confused and intimidated the Naskapi, especially the boy.

He stayed by himself for the most part, refusing to join. His eyes darted around the interior of the longhouse, not unlike a wild animal in unfamiliar surroundings. His demeanor fairly screamed of an inner turmoil.

Frida was troubled that she could not seem to reach the Naskapi women, or the children for that matter. The Norse girls had done their best to make the Naskapi girls welcome, but it is difficult for children to maintain an inter-est when the object of that interest does not respond.

Frida watched Ingerd trying to deal with them. Ingerd had made every effort to engage the two women in conversation. Although her facility with the language was limited, she could communicate. They were at least some-what accustomed to her, while she herself, and the other women, were alien to everything in their experience.

Ingerd chanced to make eye contact with Frida, and she walked over.

"I know, Frida, it is frustrating. We have done our best. They have been fed, and our people have done everything possible to welcome them. Gudbj explained them to me. These forest Naskapi live in small bands, like this one. Usually they are an extended family. They roam the forests and lakes, trapping, hunting, and fishing. Seldom do they see anybody at all, even their own people. Occasionally they travel to a Naskapi village to trade their pelts for something they need. Other than those infrequent visits they see nobody. He told me they are like wild animals around strangers; they have no social skills of any kind. Do not feel badly that we cannot engage with them. What we have here with them at this moment is all there will ever be."

Frida nodded her understanding. "At least we got them warm and comfortable, and their bellies are full."

Kejo entered the longhouse at that moment, instantly becoming the focus. The Naskapi clustered around him. He talked to them for a time; they seemed to relax. He singled out the boy, beckoning him forward. "You will come with me."

The boy said nothing, but some of the wildness slipped from his face.

Kejo approached Frida and Ingerd, the boy in tow. "The boy comes with me to the council, Ingerd."

"That is good, Kejo, he is not happy here with us." She placed a consoling hand on the boy's shoulder.

The boy did not shrink away from her touch; the dark eyes held hers in unblinking regard.

Kejo looked at the boy. "He will be alright. His band is not accustomed to strangers."

After Kejo and the boy left the longhouse, the woman and girls went back to their normal work. The Naskapi women sat with them while the Norse women and girls spun fibers of wool into skeins of thread that others among them wove into cloth on the looms. These processes were unknown to the Naskapi women, but when some of the Norse women began plying their steel awls and needles to fashion leather clothing, finally a connection occurred.

As time passed into the early evening hours, both groups had settled down once common ground was identified. The buzz of conversation, laughter, and good-natured banter common to any such gathering filled the air. Certainly there were communication problems, but it did not seem to dampen what appeared to be a normal gathering of gossiping women, doing what they did every day.

The long shadows of early evening held sway when men began to gather in the council house. As usual, the interior was somewhat smoky from the hearth and the many whale and seal oil lamps that furnished illumination to the environs while adding to the haze hanging near the ceiling. The golden glow of the many flickering yellow flames reflected from the haze overhead, shimmering and pulsating as they bathed the room and its occupants in an ethereal, almost spectral luminance.

The long trestle table where most gatherings of the council occurred would not accommodate all the participants because of the presence of so many Naskapi men. A loose quadrangle had been formed of four tables beside the long hearth, to take advantage of the warmth and light, creating enough seating for every man. The tables were not joined together. Enough space had purposely been left to accommodate the free passage of individuals back and forth as needs dictated.

Halfdan had been pacing back and forth in the center of the quadrangle, gathering his thoughts while he watched the men arrive and take a seat. His lieutenant, Tostig stood off to the side nearby, positioned to do Halfdan's bidding when necessary.

Many of the Naskapi warriors that came with Antanak, Chisasi, and Kejo had never seen the gyrfalcon, or a dog as large as Fang. Both animals were in the quadrangle, the bird on his perch, the dog close by Halfdan, watching the arrival of the men with the detached, yet alert interest common to their kind.

Over time the gyrfalcon had become accustomed to the activity in the council chambers, where he lived. This level of activity was not normal, so his actions – rapid head movements, side-to-side shifting on his perch – indicated a certain degree of agitation at the moment.

Fang, of course, went wherever Halfdan went. The only way Halfdan could go anywhere without the big dog, was to tether him.

Halfdan became aware that the Naskapi were fascinated by his animals. Gudbj, who had not seen the gyrfalcon until his recent return, was obviously talking to the Naskapi about that very subject, so Halfdan beckoned them over for a closer look.

"They have never seen a bird that big before. Neither have I." The question in Gudbj's voice was obvious.

'Tell them it is a gyrfalcon. It came from the same place that Fang came from. Essipit of the Thalmiut sent it to me," Halfdan said.

Gudbj translated for the Naskapi. Those so inclined spent a few moments examining the tethered bird, their animated gestures and conversation bringing a smile to many of those watching, including Halfdan. But, none got close to Fang. The baleful yellow eyes watching their every move ensured he was not approached too closely.

Their close look at Halfdan's animals completed, the Naskapi rejoined their compatriots along the outside of two of the trestle tables. The Norse men were similarly positioned along the outside of the other two tables. No attempt had been made to seat the two groups in this way, it just naturally happened. In numbers, they were almost on par, with the Norse men numbering a few more.

As the men took seats, Halfdan realized they had segregated themselves. Whether intentional or not, he realized he did not want them to be apart. Unity was the whole idea here. He glanced at Gudbj, who sat between Kejo and Chisasi among the Naskapi. The two men made eye contact.

Gudbj stood and joined Halfdan. Even after their forced separation the two men still had an innate ability to communicate without words. Gudbj nodded slightly in greeting to Tostig, and grinned at his chieftain.

Speaking directly to the Naskapi, Gudbj held up his arms for attention. "Hear me my brothers. You and these men are my people." He gestured toward the Norsemen. "We have come together to talk of many important things. We cannot be separated on these things. Instead of setting apart, let us all mingle, so we look like the group we must be. You know these men; they are not strangers to most of you. Our destiny is together. The gods have willed it be so." The Naskapi stirred somewhat, but nobody moved.

He turned toward the Norsemen, who did not know what was said. "I told them we should mix together. We are not two groups anymore. Some of you already have friends among these men. Sit with them. Our destiny in this land is with them. We must act like we are one with them."

He again made eye contact with Halfdan. A slight change of the man's expression gave him to know that he was on the right track.

Repeating himself in both languages, he walked back and forth in the table's center. "Come, everybody up." He motioned repeatedly for everybody to stand and mix. "Move around and find a new place to sit, among your other friends."

Surprisingly, considering the considerable difference in the two cultures, the mixing happened with good natured grumbling from both contingents, telling both Halfdan and Gudbj that the men agreed with them.

It did not take long before all the men were seated once again. Gudbj and Halfdan watched the process with a certain amount of amusement, for when the shuffling was finished, the two men looked at one another when both realized that little mixing had occurred, although all the men had changed seats.

Halfdan just shook his head at Gudbj's shrug – things were as they were. Only the passage of time would make a change.

"Alright, you tell all of us what you have come for. Handle it however you want,' Halfdan said. "Tostig and I will help if need be."

Gudbj nodded in agreement as Halfdan made for his high seat. Before Tostig followed, he made eye contact with Gudbj, a man he deeply respected.

"I am glad he picked you to replace me, Tostig."

Tostig started to disagree; he did not want anybody to think that he was replacing a man such as Gudbj.

Gudbj smiled, clapping a hand on Tostig's shoulder. "It is alright. My capture finished my time here. I hope what I am doing now will provide our people with the permanent home that they deserve."

Tostig did not trust himself to speak, so he just nodded.

"Watch my friend and our chieftain, Tostig. Guard his back, as I did. He needs you now."

"I will do that to my dying breath, Gudbj. It is my honor."

"Good; I knew that." Giving Tostig's shoulder a final squeeze, he looked around the room, his eyes settled on Kejo. He moved toward the man, speaking over his shoulder to Tostig. "Kejo and I will speak now."

Tostig watched him a moment, then turned to join Halfdan. He made eye contact with his chieftain.

Halfdan's eyes held Tostig's attention as he walked toward his accustomed seat next to his chieftain. Halfdan bobbed his chin slightly. Tostig felt a thrill of satisfaction as he realized the sword had been officially passed by Halfdan from Gudbj to him. As he took his seat, he knew that a change in hierarchy had just occurred between the three men involved. He, Tostig, was now Halfdan's lieutenant, his war chief, and a man to be reckoned with. It was altogether satisfying to know that both the men he held in the highest regard wished it so.

The council went far into the night. Halfdan expected it would take quite some time to get it all out, and then reach consensus, but not all night.

Amazingly, few adults in the other four longhouses were asleep; instead they lounged or sat around talking, too keyed up to relax.

When Frida realized the estimate to complete council business that Halfdan had given her had passed without any word from any of the men involved, she rounded up food and the women to cook and carry it into the council chamber. Shortly after she broached her request, she and a procession of women laden with kettles of chowder and stew, trenchers of meat and fish, and the utensils to eat with, entered the council chamber. Without a word, the women arranged all of it along the hearth and left the way they came. Frida made eye contact with Halfdan as she sat her kettle down. The appreciation on his face needed no words. She grinned at him and followed the others out.

While most of the men gathered around the hearth to eat, Halfdan reflected on what had been accomplished, and what had not. His stomach felt sour, his throat burned, probably from stress, he thought. Food did not sound good at all.

His mind returned to the business at hand. He thought it unusual for such a large group of men to spend so long in discussion about a common problem without any dissent. The aim of every man in attendance, for the first time ever, was to find a solution, not to squabble and disagree on what course of action needed to be taken.

Actually, he told himself, to call it a common problem was not correct either. The Anishinabeg were a problem for his people, not the Naskapi, yet they had made it their problem out of a common bond of trust and friendship that he had no real part in. Once again, he silently thanked the gods for Gudbj, the man who made all this possible. He felt no jealousy of any kind toward his friend for what he alone had accomplished, only relief and gratitude.

He glanced at Gudbj, standing beside the hearth talking to Kejo and Chisasi. The man gnawed at a joint of meat, tearing at it with his teeth, while talking between mouths full. More than a little of the contents of his mouth sprayed out while he talked, a situation not lost on his companions. He emphasized his points with stabs at the air with the meat joint. Whatever the topic of discussion, it was not something of a serious nature, because all three men suddenly erupted in laughter. Kejo punched Gudbj or Nipishish as they called him, in the shoulder, bringing on more laughter.

Several of the Norsemen sitting nearby, either grinned, or laughed with them, although they did not understand what was said, the laughter was contagious.

Realizing they were laughing without understanding, Nipishish switched to Norse, repeating the story of Ingerd and the mice, that occurred while they waited out the storm in their snow shelter, complete with copious gestures of emphasis with the meat joint.

Before he finished the second telling, laughter had seized all within earshot.

Halfdan heard the story, too. Although he did not react with the same exuberance as the others, he did laugh because it was funny, especially the way Gudbj told it. He glanced toward the doorway, as if expecting Ingerd to suddenly appear. *She might not think it funny to be the brunt of all this male humor at her expense,* he thought.

⊷⊶

At that moment, in another longhouse amongst a large group of her friends and acquaintances, including the forest Naskapi women, and Pishekat who had been acting as their interpreter, Ingerd felt no humor. One of her friends asked her about Ivar. She knew that somebody would broach the subject. When it finally happened she found the topic still pulled at the open wound in her heart and mind. She knew it always would. Before replying to the direct question, her eyes travelled over the group of women, briefly pausing on Rannveig, who had asked the question, before moving on. All were friends and close associates, some more one than the other. Did she like them all? No, she did not. She had been with most of them since Iceland and Greenland. Like any similar group there were points of stress, or disagreement between individuals, that always served to hold them slightly apart, neither ready to let their guard down, to go back to the way things had been between them. Such was the case with Rannveig.

The two women had the unintentional ability to grate on one another's nerves. Ingerd felt no animosity toward the woman at all. She had asked a reasonable question. Ingerd just preferred not to talk about it.

"I do not want to talk about that."

Rannveig made no reply.

The others returned Ingerd's stare as her eyes swept the room. She noticed most had assumed expectant postures. Their facial expressions were altogether open and friendly, some more than others. Varying degrees of sadness tempered many of their expectant expressions. They all knew that she had lost her son, but they did not know the details. Secretly, each wanted to know the details, all of them.

She had thought Thora or Frida would ask her. When neither did, she took that to mean they preferred to leave the deeply personal issue to her; if she wanted them to know she would tell them.

That was not the case, though. Frida suddenly jumped into the silent void with both feet, broaching the thorny question of Ivar as only she could do.

"Ingerd tell us the whole story. We all want to know. Telling us might make you feel better. All we know is that the Haudeno captured Ivar," Frida said, looking around at the other ladies, "What happened after he was captured is the question we have."

Ingerd looked at her friend a moment without answering. Her hesitation bespoke the mental struggle that threatened to tear her soul from her body.

Frida got up from her seat by the hearth. She wrapped her arms around her friend, hugging the other woman fiercely to her breast. Drawing back slightly, she studied Ingerd's face at arm's length.

Thora joined the two, enfolding both with her arms, saying nothing. Her touch was enough.

"Tell the story, Ingerd. Thora and I will be with you," Frida said, her voice husky with emotion.

Ingerd exhaled loudly. "I will try."

Beginning slowly, her voice flat, seemingly drained of emotion, Ingerd began her story at the point where she and the others arrived at the village of the Haudenosaunee. She told them that Glooscap, the Naskapi war chief of Sachem's band, had told her that the expedition was a war party; a dangerous mission, and that the outcome all depended on the Haudenosaunee reaction to the intrusion.

Her audience was raptly attentive. None had ever before heard such a tale. Those sitting at the back crowded forward so as not to miss any of the unfolding tale.

Telling them that, although Sachem had dispatched Glooscap and a large Naskapi war party to find out what happened to Ivar, she tried to convey the notion to her audience that their intent was for a peaceful parley, providing the Haudenosaunee wanted to talk to them.

The women were being given a glimpse into two alien cultures. With the possible exception of Thora, because of her association with Deskaheh, all this was new to the spellbound assembly of women and girls.

Ingerd realized that she had captured their entire attention. As her tale unfolded, she warmed to the telling, describing the scene in front of the village in minute detail, as only a woman could. Intuitively knowing what her audience wanted from her, she described that part of the village she could see, the clothing of the people, the sounds, smells, everything that she recalled from the parley. Her voice remained flat, still without emotion. She felt none in the telling. Her tears had long since dried up.

As best she could recall, she related the conversation between the principles in the parley beginning with the roll of the captive Haudenosaunee maiden. She told of Glooscap's instructions to the young woman in full view of the armed Haudenosaunee warriors pouring from the village gate. He told her that the fate of many people hung in the balance if she could not convince Deganawida of their peaceful intentions. Glooscap then released her to her people.

The mental pictures that her tale painted of the Haudeno chief Deganawida, his war chief Sakohkea, and Glooscap, war chief of the Naskapi made her audience feel as though they had been there, had seen these things with their own eyes. The tableau created by her words gave her listeners the ability to see what she had seen, a rare gift among storytellers, and one that Ingerd did not know she possessed until now. Truth be told she had never before addressed such a large group.

The tension, sadness, or anger, her words instilled in her listeners ebbed and flowed like a living thing, if one was to believe the play of emotions across every face. She knew that she had her audience's attention, but she remained unaware of the effect her words were having. Her eyes remained downcast. Her words continued in the same monotone, almost without inflection, as she moved back and forth before them.

Her struggle to understand the strange languages at the parley became her listeners struggle as she told them of Sachem's calumet pipe of peace, what it looked like, and what it meant to all there. Without the calumet that Lothar presented to Deganawida from Sachem, she told her listeners, she doubted the parley would have occurred, or that they would have been allowed to go in peace when it concluded.

The mental pictures that came to the minds of her audience as she continued her tale, of the fire the Haudeno had kindled for the parley, the grim faces of the participants gathered in a loose circle around the fire for warmth, the open hostility of the large group of Haudeno warriors nearby, the stoicism of the women and children gathered between the warriors and the village entrance, had her audience leaning forward in expectation as they became enthralled by the story.

Ingerd happened to look up from her pacing directly into the face of a beautiful young woman that she had not noticed before. She took a breath in her monologue, pausing for a heartbeat, when the two made eye contact. Although it had been sometime since she had last seen her, she knew this young woman to be Vigdis. At one time she and Ivar seemed destined for one another.

She has matured so much I hardly recognize her, Ingerd thought pensively. Knowing the last few thoughts she had to share with her audience would deal a crushing blow to Vigdis, she pressed on, telling them of Ivar's part in the brief parley, and how his decision had dealt her a blow from which she might never fully recover.

Describing Ivar's adopted parents was especially difficult. In spite of her animosity toward them, for no other reason except that her son had chosen them over her, she described the couple as she saw them, thereby conveying a vision of two capable and caring people. Not exactly how she wanted to convey them to her friends, but she spoke the truth and that is how the couple emerged from the truth.

Her story drew to a conclusion. She told her listeners that with the passage of time, she realized that Ivar had not really had a choice. If he had chosen to leave with his natural parents, there most certainly would have been a conflict in which many people would have died. Everything was in place for such a conflict. During the parley, open hostility hung in the air; a simple misstep would start a battle that nobody present could stop.

Her final few words were especially poignant. She told them how she had paused at the brow of the knoll to look back, for a final sight of her son. There was none, he was gone, forever.

Her eyes travelled over the face of every person in her audience. There were few dry eyes. "That is all I have to say about this. Do not ever ask me again what happened that day. It is finished." She gave the cutting sign that always ended a conversation among the native peoples. It seemed natural to end it that way.

Chancing to look at Vigdis once more, Ingerd would always remember the look of devastation and anguish on the face of the beautiful young woman.

Twin rivulets of tears coursed down her cheeks as the full import of Ingerd's story took hold. She twisted her smock in anguish. Ivar would never come back; she would never see him again.

Things were not much better with the men attending the council. A great deal of emotion, running the gambit from denial to anger and outright rage swept through the men at Gudbj's final assessment of their situation. He confirmed the suspicion most had that the Anishinabeg would attack them, and continue to attack them until all resistance ended. All the men would be dead. The women and children that survived the onslaught would be taken away to a life of slavery.

The Naskapi drew back from participation as the meeting convulsed with the inflamed emotion running rampant through the Norse contingent. As it now stood, nothing could be accomplished in the din. Men came to their feet, shouting to be heard.

Gudbj stopped his pacing in the center of the quadrangle. His glance took in the scene of bedlam. He made eye contact with Halfdan, shaking his head once at the volatility of these men.

Halfdan inclined his head at his friend, a slight smile on his face. He took no part in what passed for a council among his men. Content to let them rant, he poured himself another cup of broth. Nothing would be accomplished by his intervention at this point.

Giving up for the moment, Gudbj selected another joint of meat from the diminished pile on one of the trenchers and returned to his seat with the Naskapi, tearing at it while he watched.

Kejo and Chisasi stole occasional glances at him without verbalizing their thoughts, a good policy in the circumstance since they would have had to out shout the others to be heard.

Halfdan drank the remainder of the broth, slowly and deliberately placed the empty cup on the table, and got to his feet. It was time to stop this before a fight, or worse, developed; emotion alone had taken control. His eyes traveled quickly over his men. The din began to quiet as individuals realized that their chieftain was on his feet.

Thorgill had his back to the tables and did not see Halfdan standing in the quadrangle. His famous temper had gotten the better of him in a disagreement with Hrafen, kinsman to Thorgeirr that had nothing to do with what the others had been vehemently discussing. Accustomed to getting his way in any confrontation, Thorgill had met his match in Hrafen. The man did not know how to back up, or give way. Of all things, given the gravity of the question before the council, the disagreement was about a woman. Not a specific woman, rather what each thought would be the ideal woman.

The raised voices of the two became the only two raised voices in the room as the other men gradually quieted when individuals realized that Halfdan wanted their attention. Suddenly aware they were alone in discussion, their arguments cut off in mid-sentence when the raised voice of their chieftain abruptly ended their discourse, but not before most of the other men knew the topic.

"We will all want to know what you two think about women after we decide the future of our people. Until that decision is made, try to focus on the subject at hand."

Both men held their positions for a heartbeat while they looked at Halfdan and their comrades, many of whom were grinning.

"Our chieftain has called, Thorgill." Hrafen put a hand on his friend's shoulder, the ghost of a smile around his mouth and eyes. "I think he wants us to sit down and listen."

"Aye, I think he does," Thorgill agreed, nodding sheepishly to Halfdan as he followed Hrafen back to the bench.

The room erupted in good-natured chiding and laughter at the men's expense.

The Naskapi smiled at the humor, although only those around Nipishish actually knew what had been said.

A silence descended, like a dark impenetrable covering over the men while they waited for Halfdan to speak his mind. All eyes were on their chieftain.

"Most of us have taken the words of Nipishish to heart, judging by your reactions. That is good." Purposely using his friend's Naskapi name for the benefit of the Naskapi men, and to indicate his own approval for the name by using it in his conversation, Halfdan turned to Nipishish and those around him.

"We have heard your opinions on what the Anishinabeg will do to us. Now, what must we do to prevent that from happening?" His eyes went from Kejo, to Chisasi, and to Antanak while Nipishish translated.

Without preamble the answer came from Antanak. "You must abandon this settlement before they attack you."

When his words were translated a stunned silence descended over the Norsemen like a pall. Then they all started talking at once.

Halfdan raised his arms above his head to quiet them. His eyes did not leave the face of Antanak while he waited for order to return.

"Why do you say we must abandon this place without a fight?"

"You cannot win the fight, you cannot. You are too few. If the Anishinabeg find your settlement abandoned they will burn it to the ground. That will be the end of it."

Halfdan stood rigidly silent, unable to accept what he had been told. "Do the rest of you agree with Antanak, that we should abandon Halfdansfjord?" His glance moved from Kejo, Chisasi, and of course Nipishish. All three nodded without comment.

Still rooted in place Halfdan directed his attention to the rest of the men seated around the tables. Normally they sat in all possible attitudes from boredom to excitement. But now, he noticed that they all seemed more attentive, even though a language barrier existed among them, the gravity of the topic had their undivided attention. As he made eye contact with the other Naskapi, all nodded or voiced their assent.

He began to pace back and forth in the quadrangle. A tense silence endured for a time. As he paced he continued his examination of the individuals of the assembly without really seeing them while his mind grappled with this new twist. The others honored his silence. None of them seemed to know what to say in the circumstance.

Halfdan stopped in front of Gudbj. "Tell me what you think of this Gudbj. You have lived among the Naskapi since last summer. You know things that I do not know. Surely there is some solution short of abandoning everything we have accomplished in this land, to go somewhere new, where we will have to begin all over?"

Nipishish stood and translated Halfdan's words for the Naskapi in a loud voice before answering his chieftain. He looked around the table until his eyes fell on Deskaheh.

"Deskaheh, come and help these men understand what I will tell my people," said Nipishish, gesturing to the table where he had been sitting.

He made eye contact with Kejo. "Help him, Kejo."

Kejo nodded and passed the word around the tables to his men to know what to expect when their former enemy did the bidding of Nipishish.

Beginning slowly and using the copious hand signs to which he had grown accustomed, he laid out the situation as he saw it, as Glooscap, Kejo, and Sachem had told him it would be.

"It is known that the Anishinabeg will never allow us to live here, unless we defeat them in battle. The Naskapi have always lived in Nitassinan, but the Anishinabeg only tolerate them so long as they stay out of their hunting and fishing grounds. Starvation sits on the shoulders of all the people in this land every winter. These needs dictate their policy toward others in their land. There is only so much to share. They will not share with strangers in their land."

He paused a moment. "There is just one small chance that we can stay as we are."

Utter silence greeted his words. He paced a moment, head down, letting the tension build and ensuring he had every word of his short announcement at the ready.

"Before we left to come here, Sachem told Kejo and me that the fate of all here at Halfdansfjord rests with the Anishinabeg chief, Nesatin. He is the leader of the Kitchi sipi people, the same warriors that attacked you here last summer. Nesatin is the principle chief of all the bands of Big River People north of Kitchi Gami. If he listens to us there will be peace."

Chapter 10

STIRRINGS ACROSS THE LAND

Early in the morning, two days after the council meeting ended, Kejo, Nipishish, and the other Naskapi men of the expedition began the return journey to their village. Travel conditions had changed little during their time at Halfdansfjord, but the men knew that if they did not begin the return journey soon, while the ice and snow was solid enough to hold their weight, that the chance of worsening weather conditions and rotting ice would necessitate their lingering until after the spring thaw.

In similar fashion to the trek northward to Halfdansfjord, the return began with the promise of a beautiful day. Would the clear, cold conditions persist through the new moon, or would a storm catch them as it had before? Only the gods knew these things.

Ingerd and Nipishish parted with neither feeling remorseful pangs. Ingerd had grown accustomed to the frequent partings with her man. Besides, she had her friends all around her, supporting her. That is why she came home, to be with these women that she loved. Only other women understood the depth of sorrow that continued to tear at her over the loss of her only natural child. She knew her man had a mission to perform for all of them, and she felt a deep pride for what he was doing. Nothing short of death would stop him from achieving the goals that he felt were the will of the gods. She made no attempt to dissuade him. She could not dwell on the inevitable loneliness that separation occasioned; later perhaps, but not now. He told her that he would return in the spring or early summer. For the present, that was good enough.

The forest Naskapi went on the return journey, wanting to spend the remainder of the winter with their kinsmen, to trade and visit. Although the inhabitants of Halfdansfjord certainly made them feel welcome, the small bands of people that made up these forest Naskapi were a different breed. They did not normally seek the companionship of other members of their own tribe, much less an entirely alien people such as the Norse.

Although their existence in winter was literally hand-to-mouth, they knew no other way but the reliance on the cunning and skill of each member of their small extended family groups. Their snares and deadfalls provided the bulk of the meat that sustained them. There was no need to share this occasional bounty with a village or even another forest band. Their nomadic, frugal existence furnished what little they required. The fur pelts and meat of the animals they caught were theirs alone. It was their choice to be nomads. It was their way; they liked moving about over the vast landscape.

As time passed, deep snow accumulated over the countryside. Most of it blew with the wind until it piled up against an obstacle. Thick ice built up over the lakes and watercourses, covered over with deep snow drifts from the winds of the frequent storms.

Halfdan sat alone in his high seat near the long hearth of the council chamber. Thralls kept the fire burning, not that he was aware of their comings and goings, but he would have noticed the creeping cold without the warmth of the hearth. In truth, his mind was far away, and not in the present. He always went over the happenings of the day, intent on each event, trying to make certain that nothing important had been missed, by him, or any of the other leaders. He recalled a discussion from an earlier meeting, when it was suggested that they go after the next Anishinabeg scouting. The subject never came up during this latest council, so he let it drop. Given that they now knew what their fate at the hands of the Anishinabeg would be, attacking a small scouting party might make the participants feel better, but it would accomplish little else for his people. The fate of Halfdansfjord depended on Gudbj and Kejo. His friend had told them that only a thin chance existed that their lives would remain as they were now, that they could remain at Halfdansfjord. It all depended on the Anishinabeg chieftain, Nesatin. He alone would make the decision for peace or war.

His thoughts shifted to his friend Gudbj. The debt they all owed him and Kejo for a chance to plead their case with Nesatin, was incalculable. He shook his head, smiling at the thoughts that tumbled into his conscious mind. He felt in his heart that Gudbj and his companions had completed their ten day journey before another storm caught them in the open. Winter travel over any long distance became a foolhardy venture as the winter wore on. The violence of the winter storms and the intense cold of this winter was a topic of conversation among all the people as they remained confined in the warmth and security of their lodges and longhouses.

Even outdoor activity at Halfdansfjord had ground to a halt for the most part. The two ships under construction would not be ready when the ice went out, as Halfdan had hoped. The men worked between the storms whenever conditions allowed, but finally everything in the shipyard became locked in ice and crusted snow, forcing even the hardiest to give up until spring.

—— ∞ ——

With the passage of several moons, the days began to lengthen, heralding a change of season. Prevailing winds began the seasonal shift from north to south, bringing a gradual thaw to the frozen northland. Every cloudy day brought wet snow well into the beginning of the Time of Green Grass, adding little to the winter's accumulation but markedly increasing the misery of every living thing as the temperatures warmed and the thaw began in earnest.

Break-up on the rivers came first as the ice pushed up pressure ridges and then broke into huge slabs, creating ice dams that caused flooding over all the lowlands. A crescendo of groaning and cracking sounds made by the shifting ice were heard day and night as the ice began its journey down to the bay of Halfdansfjord where it piled up against the solid expanse of pancake ice already there.

The surface of the ice covering the lakes began to rot in the heat during the day. Refreezing at night, its surface became rough and opaque. Groaning sounds could be heard, a sure sign that the solid pack was beginning to shift as its anchor to the shoreline melted away. Within days, most of the shoreline was ice-free, leads of open water yawned open across each lake. In another moon most of the ice would be gone; greenery would be seen peeking from the bared earth, as the warmth of the Time of Green Grass awakened the land.

———∞∞∞———

Slightly farther south, the warming trend affected the village of Sachem sooner than the environs of Halfdansfjord. Impatiently waiting for early spring conditions to allow for travel by canoe, Nipishish and Kejo busied themselves readying equipment, including the canoe they had selected for their journey to meet with the Big River Anishinabeg. They watched the river daily, waiting for the floating ice to melt as it flowed north in its journey to the bay. The river would be clear well before all the ice melted on the lakes. This entire hazard to travel by birch bark canoe had to be gone before they could leave.

As before, the men and older boys congregated most days in the council house to visit while performing winter tasks. Equipment and weapons were repaired or produced during these impromptu, but important social interactions. The men taught the boys many of the skills needed to make war, trap, fish, and hunt.

While replacing a cracked thwart in the canoe he and Kejo were working on, Nipishish stole an occasional glance at his son Lothar. A small group of boys, one of them Lothar, were busily engaged in the fine art of flint knapping. Nipishish made eye contact with Kejo, pointing with his chin toward the group seated in a semi-circle before their teacher. The two men watched the unfolding drama while they worked on their canoe.

Many men possessed a certain facility with flint knapping; enough to sharpen or reshape broken arrowheads, spearheads, or tool points, but today the boys were under the tutelage of Kakatshu, the tribe's master projectile point and tool knapper. He had just finished breaking long, leaf-like spalls from a lump of dark, rose tinted chert with a hammer stone. Handing one to each boy, he showed them how to hold the spall in a piece of leather to protect their hands from the sharp pieces that would result from knapping the projectile points they were learning to make, while he explained how to shape a spall into the point each was particularly suited for. Short spall flakes became all manner of arrow points while longer flakes were more suited for spear points, knife blades, or scrapers.

For their part, the boys watched Kakatshu intently while he demonstrated the use of a deer antler tine to snap a tiny flake from the underside of the spall he held firmly in the leather pad in his left hand.

Kakatshu, a short, dark, thin-faced, wizened man of indeterminate age, frequently looked up at his pupils as he worked, watching the boys closely as they tried to replicate his deftness with the antler tine. He found humor in much of life; his facial expression wore that look much of the time, even when concentration on a particular task momentarily furrowed his brow, as it had now. The look of concentration dissolved as his face split into the creases and clefts of mirth at the sound of a loud snap. It was a sound that he always expected at such times.

He chuckled aloud. Lothar had broken the spall he was working on into two pieces.

Lothar made eye contact with Kakatshu, his consternation plain to see, especially given that his companions also laughed at his expense.

"It is alright Lothar that is how we learn." His dark eyes swept over the other boys, causing them to swallow the laughter rising in their throats.

"We will always break some of the spalls, no matter how careful we are. Remember what I said about them.' His eyes swept his rapt audience. "You must hold the spalls along the entire length, tightly between your fingers and the heel of your hand, while protecting your hand and fingers with the leather pad. When you apply downward pressure against the edge you are working on, the spall will snap in to if you do not have a tight hold."

He reached out and took the two broken pieces from Lothar. Turning them in his wrinkled hands, he examined them a moment before handing them back to the boy. "What can you make with these two pieces of flint?"

The boy shrugged, examining each shard with a critical eye. "I will make arrowheads of them."

"Good, that is what I would do." He waved a hand for his pupils to continue their work. While they worked, he selected a long piece of chert, and in a short time turned it into a spear point.

He glanced toward the men, many of whom had witnessed the exchange. Catching Nipishish's eye he held up the spear point. "For you, Nipishish."

The beautifully wrought spear point spun through the air between the two men. Nipishish deftly caught it. Turning it over in his hand he examined the workmanship. Testing the sharp edge with his thumb, he grunted in satisfaction, nodding his thanks to Kakatshu.

Observing the schooling of the boys, Nipishish was struck by the rapidity with which Lothar had assimilated into the Naskapi culture. His son was like he himself, he was one with the Naskapi. *His facility with the spoken language is every bit as good as mine, maybe better. Like me he has crossed a line, he is Naskapi.*

Nipishish found this new awareness of his son somewhat unsettling, because he himself was responsible for Lothar's being here. To look at him now, comfortable in his surroundings, dressed as everyone else, giving as good as he took from the other boys, it seemed hard to imagine he had ever been Norse. Except for his long blonde hair and blue eyes, he no longer was.

Lothar seemed taller to him, and he had filled out. The gangly boy was becoming a man. He had come into his own since Ivar's capture by the Haudenosaunee. Much of the transformation, the transition to what he was now, had been forced by events that transpired since then. *He seems to have taken to it like a duck to water. He has become his own young man. Our shared destiny has made him better than he was. He has grown up right in front of me, and I hardly noticed,* thought Nipishish. The two made eye contact across the room.

Lothar got to his feet, stretched, and walked over to his father. From his facial expression he obviously had something to say.

Nipishish and Kejo watched him, waiting...

Speaking in Naskapi, Lothar got right to the point. "I want to go with you." He glanced at each man as he spoke.

The question surprised Nipishish. He glanced quickly at Kejo, the ghost of a smile forming on his face. "You want to go with us? This is not a hunting trip."

"It is a mission of peace. You go as representatives of Sachem. Having your young son with you will be a good thing. The Anishinabeg will know you are serious."

Nipishish chuckled at the temerity of the boy. "I am proud that you came up with this on your own." He glanced at his friend. The look on Kejo's face also conveyed a feeling of pride in the boy.

"He is right. There is little danger; our mission would be good training for him. Nesatin and his council might regard Lothar's presence as a good sign," said Kejo.

Taking but a moment to reach the obvious conclusion in the circumstance, Nipishish clapped Lothar on the shoulder hard enough that he staggered back a step. "Alright, you can go with us."

———

The journey consumed the better part of two uneventful days by canoe. It could have been done in a single long day, providing a departure at first light, but the men did not want to arrive in the evening, feeling the full light of day their best bet for success.

Sachem had told them what he expected from the overture of peace that they were to convey on his behalf, presenting Nesatin with a calumet and the wampum belt. This wampum was a special sort, consisting of strings of dark shell beads with a purple tint. Being rare, the dark shell beads were more valuable than the more common beads made of white shells.

As before, Lothar was entrusted with the buckskin case containing the calumet and wampum. He took this trust seriously for one so young, knowing the importance of this meeting to both the Norse and Naskapi people.

Dawn of the second day of travel saw the camp coming to life under lowering, gray skies sagging almost to treetop level. A steady, windborne, cold drizzle had begun during the night. The trio crawled from their brush shelter, rolled up their sleeping robes, and prepared to launch their canoe for the final paddle to the Anishinabeg village. Everything was damp or sopping wet, including their buckskins, which would become sodden and shapeless if the drizzle continued. The good thing about buckskins was that they kept you reasonably warm, even when wet and they dried out to form a good fit to the frame of the wearer, for the most part.

After relieving themselves, cakes of pemmican were quickly consumed, followed by a piece of jerky to satisfy man's need to chew on something to assuage hunger pangs, the canoe was launched, and they set out.

They had on all the clothing they had with them, including pullover parkas, mittens, and fur hats. Kejo occupied the stern steering position, Lothar sat hunched in the middle, and Nipishish knelt in the bow, providing the timing for the paddle stroke. The other two matched his efforts closely, with Kejo providing the course corrections.

"You look cold, Lothar, the paddling will warm you up pretty soon," Kejo observed, chuckling.

"I am not any colder than you," the boy shot back, sitting up a little straighter.

Kejo smiled at the pluck of the boy. *If he is as cold as I am, he is cold indeed.*

"We will be there before midday," said Kejo, the only one who had ever been to the village. "The village is on the west bank of this river, where it flows from a connected system of long, narrow lakes. They will see us long before we land on the beach in front of the village."

"Good, that will be better than paddling in and surprising them," said Nipishish over his shoulder.

"We have not talked about our roles in this parley with Nesatin. The first Anishinabeg to see us will only know we are strangers. They will recognize us as Naskapi, even you two until they get closer, but none of that will matter. Lothar, when they are close enough to see us plainly, I want you to stand slowly and hold up the wampum so they cannot fail to see it. You can sit back down when they have seen it, but hold it in plain view all the way in to their village. This is important; otherwise we will never reach the village without trouble with them. They will respect the wampum. After we get there, and you have identified Nesatin, watch me for a nod, then hand him the wampum."

"I understand, Kejo," said Lothar, turning his eyes on the man.

Kejo nodded. "Nipishish, when we arrive at their village one of the men in the people crowding around us on the beach will be Nesatin. You will not know which one he is, for his appearance will be like all the others around him. Follow my lead; I will not acknowledge him until he speaks. He will see immediately that you and Lothar are not Naskapi. If he speaks to you directly, answer him directly. A great deal hangs on his first impression of you. It is possible that he will have heard tales of your fighting skill. If so, that will be valuable. He is a man similar to Sachem, he does not waste words. Answer him the same way you would Sachem, because his words are strong and he cannot be deceived. He alone will decide about you and your people. He will be curious that Lothar is with us. That he is your son will carry much weight with him and his people."

"I will do the best I can to convince Nesatin that we wish to live in this land in peace with the Anishinabeg." Nipishish held his paddle stroke a moment. Placing the paddle athwart the canoe, he turned toward Kejo. "I imagine he and his council have already made their decision to drive us out of this land."

It was more of a question than a statement. "They will have decided on war, I am certain of it. Nesatin can change that course if he wishes. That is why we are here, to convince them that Sachem would view that decision unfavorably. Your task will be, if you get a chance, to show Nesatin that your being here will not have an impact on his people. You will not deplete the animals they hunt for food. That will be a big question for him."

Conversation died of its own accord as attention was directed back to the task before them. The river was in full flood, so the normal slow current that meandered north through the many lakes before emptying into the bay of Halfdansfjord, did so with considerably more force, requiring constant diligence and effort on the part of the trio, to both make headway and avoid outcroppings of rocks and snags. While negotiating a particularly treacherous area of outcroppings of every sort, another canoe came into view as it rounded a bend in the river well ahead.

A loud whoop from the strange canoe left no doubt they had been seen and identified as strangers. The four men stopped paddling, allowing the current to carry them downstream to meet the strange canoe in their river.

"Anishinabeg," hissed Kejo unnecessarily, given they could not be another so near their village. "When we get closer, Lothar, stand up and hold the wampum aloft. Nipishish, just paddle enough to hold position and to keep the bow pointed up stream. They know we are not their enemies."

No weapons were in view among the four men, all watched the occupants of the other canoe intently as the intervening distance closed. One of the Shinabeg suddenly raised a hand, shouting the traditional greeting.

Kejo and Nipishish replied in kind.

The two canoes were within about three canoe lengths now, close enough for easy communication. Kejo and Nipishish stopped paddling. The canoes slowly drifted downstream on the current, in close proximity, their occupants silently taking the measure of one another.

Lothar stirred in preparation to stand as he had been instructed. The Shinabeg fastened their attention on him. His light skin tone and the lanky blonde hair sticking out from the fringe of his hat were hard for them to miss. They also studied Nipishish for the same reasons, knowing that neither of them were Naskapi, although they dressed like Naskapi, and they were in the company of a Naskapi.

Lothar stood carefully, mindful not to upset the unstable canoe while extending the wampum over his head. "Ho, we bring greetings from Sachem."

Hearing the boy speak in good Naskapi surprised the four men. His mention of Sachem and sight of the wampum sobered them. Watching the boy continually try to catch his balance got a laugh from one of the Shinabeg, as the bobbling motion of the other canoe defied the boy's efforts to hold it steady. Lothar did his best to balance the unstable platform, but equilibrium was precarious at best and worsening.

Abruptly the boy sat back down, knowing that if he did not all of them would wind up in the river.

The brief period of levity ended with a direct question from one of the Shinabeg. "Why do you come to our land?"

"Sachem sends us to talk to Nesatin. We bring the wampum of our people, and the calumet of peace to present to him and the Kitchi sipi Anishinabeg." Kejo did not elaborate further, nor did he need to.

The man who had asked the question said nothing further, studying each of the strangers while he decided what to do with them. He knew that the two companions of the hard looking Naskapi were the pale skins of the village on the bay's north shore. He had been among the warriors that attacked that same village late last summer. But, he also knew that the decision of what to do with was not his to make. Nesatin would want to see them for himself. Making up his mind, he glanced at Kejo. "Come, we will take you to Nesatin."

Their arrival at the village had not gone exactly as Kejo had thought it would. The Anishinabeg gathered on the beach as expected, but Nesatin never identified himself. After the large crowd had milled about until every individual got a close look at the pale skins, the trio from Sachem was finally taken inside the village where more people came forward to look them over.

As expected when in close proximity to people they thought of as their enemies because of the fighting last summer, and the casualties suffered at the hands of the pale skins, the Anishinabeg were hostile toward Nipishish and Lothar. There were no overt incidents of their hostility, but the threat hung in the air like smoke.

Later, they were taken into a large circular wigwam were they were forced to wait for some time. Impatience at this treatment began to affect them, especially Lothar, who passed the time by pacing.

Nipishish and Kejo had both taken a seat when they got tired of standing, or walking around examining the wall hangings. At the moment, both men lounged comfortably against a couple of the many backrests scattered about the large room.

"They hate us," observed Lothar, his agitation at the protracted waiting plain to see.

"Aye, they do hate us," said Nipishish. "Be patient, Lothar. Perhaps this parley with Nesatin will change that."

As if on cue, his words were hardly out before a group of men filed into the council house. They stepped onto a slightly raised, pelt covered dais against the circular inner wall, and took a seat in a loose semi-circle.

The two men and the boy froze in place, conversation died in their throats when the five Shinabeg council members filed in. The only light in the gloom of the large room came from the flickering flames of the fire in the long central hearth. Deep shadows lent a surreal quality to the faces of the two groups as each examined the other, making it difficult to assess facial expressions and body language. The silence built tension.

In appearance, the men were all similar insofar as dress. Dark brown skin tones predominated. To a man, their faces were long and angular. Deep creases through cheeks and foreheads, with crowsfeet deeply etched around their eyes, bespoke of a lifetime spent out of doors in all conditions. Taken together, these characteristics imparted to each dominate facial feature an indication of inner strength. The men looked like what they were, leaders of their tribe. Some wore their hair in two braids, one, the oldest among them, had long straight, black hair streaked with gray.

Another man, the most striking and intense of the group, sported a high scalp lock, woven with porcupine quills and hair, bits of leather, and stiffened with grease to hold it upright. Unlike most of the others, his face and bared upper arms were tattooed. Nipishish recognized in the man's fluid movements, and the way he handled the unfamiliar weapon that he was a seasoned warrior.

Nipishish and Kejo made eye contact when the man got to his feet and walked into the flickering light near the hearth to examine the axe. Nipishish had a questioning look on his face.

Kejo leaned close. 'He is called Shingoos, Nesatin's war chief." Both men then got to their feet. Lothar joined them from the other side of the room.

"Sachem sends his greetings, Nesatin," said Kejo, identifying the chieftain for his companions. "I bring you the wampum and the calumet." He glanced at Lothar, giving him a slight nod. "Lothar, son of Nipishish, received them from the hand of Sachem. He presents these gifts to you and your council."

Lothar stooped over to retrieve the medicine bundle from the floor. He paused, waiting a sign from Nesatin to approach. The young man felt a chill course through his body as his eyes travelled from man to man, briefly pausing at each. The hard, brown faces conveyed no sign of friendliness or feeling. His eyes stopped on Nesatin. Giving the man his full attention, he waited for a sign or word as to what he should do next. The black eyes of the Anishinabeg chieftain looked him over from head to foot. He returned the steady gaze of Nesatin without flinching, although he felt unease for the first time. He approached the dais at a hand sign from the chieftain.

Nesatin held out a hand for the bundle. The black eyes never left the face of the young man.

Lothar stepped forward and passed the bundle to him.

The chieftain set it aside without looking at it, his eyes still on the young man. "You have no fear of me, of us?" He waved a hand at the council.

"Aye, I do have fear, Nesatin, but I am not afraid."

Some of the council laughed aloud at the pluck of the young man. Nesatin's facial expression did not change. "That is good. If you live, you will be a warrior one day, like your father." He waved a hand of dismissal at Lothar, as he made eye contact with Nipishish. The two men sat in silent regard for a moment.

Nesatin's eyes shifted to Kejo. "Why do you bring these pale skins among the Anishinabeg?"

Before his friend could answer the direct question, Nipishish took a step forward to answer for himself. "We have come here in peace, Nesatin. I stand before you so that I may know what is in your heart. I want you to know what is in my heart, in the hearts of my people. These things I have come to tell you and your council."

Nesatin said nothing for a moment. If he was surprised at Nipishish's fluency with the language of the people he gave no sign. He glanced at the members of his council. None made eye contact with him, their attention on Nipishish, indicating to him that they agreed to a man that he was to speak for all.

"We do not want you or your people in our land. The council of the bands has voted for war. The vote was unanimous, there will be war." He paused, watching Nipishish narrowly, gauging the man's reaction to the finality of his statement.

"You reached your decision before I had a chance to plead our case with you. I stand here before you and the council to do that, if you will permit it. You, Nesatin, are the chieftain of all the Kitchi sipi bands of the Anishinabeg people. Your word carries a heavy weight with your people. I ask you, man to man, to let me speak of matters that concern all of us in this land." The forceful personality, heartfelt words, and bravery of Nipishish impressed the council.

"Why should I listen to your words? We are many, you are few. What you think matters not to us." A rumble of assent rose from the council.

Nipishish sighed inwardly, nodding his understanding. He paused a moment, trying to order the chaos of his thoughts. His eyes sought Kejo. He gleaned nothing from the stony face. He then realized that the outcome was strictly up to him, nobody else could help him convince these men not to war against his people. He had always known that it would be this way. Kejo had been but the instrument to convey him to this place of destiny. The gods had picked him for this effort. Except for the peaceful intent conveyed by the wampum and the calumet he felt he would never get out of here alive. He made eye contact with Lothar. The boy watched him closely, a look of trusting acceptance on his face. He turned back to the council.

"My friend, Kejo, brought me and my son to your village. I allowed my son to come here with us, to show you that our heart is open, that our intent in this land is to live among the Anishinabeg and Naskapi in peace. Like you men," he waved a hand to include the council, "I have known much fighting, much war. We are warriors; it is our duty to fight our enemies. I am not your enemy. My son is not your enemy. My people are not your enemy."

He paced back and forth, his habit when talking like this. Coming to a halt after a few moments, he faced the council once again, making eye contact with each man before continuing. "We are few in number, but our people will not give up without fighting for their new home, to the death if that is the will of the gods. We want to share the bounty of this land with your people, as we do with our friends the Naskapi. Our big canoes bring trade goods from afar that our people would want to trade with your people as we do the Naskapi." He paused, waiting for a response. When it came, the question threw him off his present tack, because it was not directed to him.

Nesatin looked past the standing Nipishish to Kejo, who had remained seated while Nipishish made his plea.

"Tell us why the Naskapi have befriended these pale skins, Kejo."

Kejo got to his feet. He made eye contact with Nipishish as he stepped forward, approaching the council.

As Kejo began to speak, Nipishish took a seat next to his son. A single shake of his head to Lothar conveyed his opinion of their chances of swaying the council's decision. He listened to Kejo begin his tale. Knowing it would be all about him, he did not wish to feel like an idiot, so he sat down rather than stand with his friend while he told the whole story of his time among the Naskapi.

"It is a long story, Nesatin. Where do you want me to begin?"

"At the beginning."

Kejo sighed in resignation, but after a time he warmed to the telling. It did take a long time to tell, for it was a good tale. With his embellishments, he felt that he was telling a great tale, from which a legend had been born among his people. The fire burned to embers twice, requiring women to haul in armloads of wood to keep it going. He told them everything he had witnessed and everything he had heard about his friend Nipishish, and his people the Norse. The council was visibly impressed that a prisoner had fought against a common enemy while held captive. A rumble of understanding swept through the council when he told them how Nipishish was his hated enemy in the beginning, for killing his friend Pantoo, and how he had come by the name Nipishish after the fight with the Haudeno war party. He brought his tale to a conclusion by telling the council that Sachem had decreed that Nipishish would learn the language of the people and some of the people, including himself, were to learn the Norse language at the same time. Nipishish would learn these things by living in the longhouse of Glooscap for a moon, and then in the lodge of Kejo for a moon. He gave the cutting sign and returned to his seat with the other two.

The formality of the question and answer period was over. The council conversed in subdued tones for a time. When finished, Nesatin signed for Nipishish to approach.

A man that sat next to Nesatin said, "Show us the axe."

Nipishish smiled to himself as he slipped the sling for the axe from his shoulder. He had known that somebody would ask to see his axe. Removing the doubled loops of the sling from the axe he passed it haft first to Nesatin.

The chieftain, surprised at the weight of the weapon, balanced it in his hands, while examining it closely. As men are wont to do when presented with an edged weapon, he tested the edge with his thumb. A surprised grunt managed to escape despite his normal reserve. He examined his thumb for damage. Rubbing the dark metal of the bearded blade, he sniffed at it, then licked a finger and rubbed spit on the blade, bringing forth its luster. He looked up at Nipishish.

"What is this axe head made of?"

"We call it iron. The axe head is forged in a hot fire and pounded into shape while it is hot."

With a grunt of apparent appreciation Nesatin handed the axe to the man next to him, the one that had requested to see the weapon.

The man stood and walked over to the hearth. Bending down to take full advantage of the flickering light of the flames, he closely examined the blade and handle.

He swung the axe through the air testing its weight and balance. An exclamation escaped his lips in spite of his aloof bearing. Nesatin watched from the dais, apparently unmoved. The other three council members joined the man at the hearth, each in turn examining the battle axe.

Nipishish turned to Kejo, a question in his eyes.

Kejo spoke from his seat on the floor, his voice lowered for privacy. "Shingoos is the war chief of Nesatin. I do not know for certain, but he probably led the attack on Halfdansfjord."

Nipishish nodded. He had known that the man was no ordinary warrior when he first saw him. He watched Shingoos narrowly, as a predator watches its prey, taking the measure of the man.

As if sensing that he was watched, Shingoos turned his head away from his companions, making eye contact with Nipishish. The eye contact was brief; almost a searing caress, but it forged the two men as implacable adversaries.

Kejo had watched the byplay with amusement. "He will make a dangerous enemy."

"If he makes that choice, it will be the will of the gods. I came in peace." He looked at his friend, and his son who had joined them. A broad grin split his face asunder. "I make a better friend than an enemy."

Kejo and Lothar laughed dutifully, but Kejo quickly became introspective.

"Whether they fight or not has already been decided. Nesatin can change certain aspects of the decision if he wishes, but the outcome will stand. Shingoos had his say long before we came here. So did the other council members. There are many men that played a part in the decision that are not here for this parley, they are members of other bands of the Kitchi sipi Anishinabeg. Nesatin alone speaks for all his people. He will tell you his terms. You must hope that he decides to let you live here in peace, or he gives you an opportunity to leave Halfdansfjord in safety. It will be one or the other. Your people cannot defy them, they are too many."

"I guess we are about to find out." He gestured with his chin as the men at the hearth began to return to the dais. Shingoos walked over to Nipishish, and handed him the axe. Neither man spoke. Shingoos turned away and returned to his seat.

Silence hung over the assembly like a pall. The council lounged against backrests, studying the trio across the room. Nesatin bent forward from his backrest, crossed his legs, and rested his extended arms on the knees. His eyes travelled from Nipishish to Kejo, both of whom watched him intently.

This silent treatment is intended to make us uncomfortable; it is working, thought Nipishish. In spite of Kejo's little speech of a moment ago, the delaying tactics of the council were obviously a ploy that was wearing thin with him. He was visibly agitated.

Nesatin noticed the subtle change in Nipishish. He smiled inwardly, knowing that he had made them nervous.

He ignored Nipishish, focusing on Kejo instead. "Sachem has befriended the pale skins, he may regret that. The Anishinabeg will not befriend them. The pale skins must leave this land, or they will all die. Tell Sachem that I will keep his gifts, but we will not smoke the calumet with you."

"I will tell Sachem these things. He will not be happy that you refused his offer of peace." Kejo got to his feet as he spoke.

Nipishish and Lothar followed suit. "How long do we have to make our decision?" Nipishish asked.

"My scouts will keep me informed of your actions. Sometime between this Time of Green Grass and the Time of Falling Leaves, Shingoos will come at you, if you have not abandoned your village. These are my words. Now, go in peace." Nesatin gave the cutting sign, the parley was finished.

Far to the south, warmer days had already fully awakened the land of the Haudenosaunee from its winter slumber. After the drabness of winter, the many new shades of green were pleasing to the eye as grasses and broad leaved plants began to cloak the land.

A kind of frenzy gripped all living creatures, the air filled with buzzing insects and chattering birds. Bear sows had birthed their naked and helpless cubs in the den. Over time, the tiny creatures had grown into little furred bundles of energy. Hungry and wasted after her long winter's nap, the sow dug through the snow still covering the den's entrance into the open air and began to forage. She ranged far and wide, cubs in tow, eating anything and everything in her need to replenish the body fat that had sustained her over the long winter, slowly building back her strength in the process.

Moose, deer, and forest caribou roamed about, voraciously feeding on the new growth springing from mother earth, newborn charges underfoot. Animals of every species and size sought their kind. The northland was in the throes of another mating season.

For the people, fresh meat and fish filled the cook pots, and sizzled over the cook fires in every longhouse. The reawakening of the land brought a new sense of being, a new sense of hope to every person.

Runners began to reconnect the far-flung tribes and bands of the Haudenosaunee, to see how the people had fared over the long winter. Councils were called to plan the annual trading expeditions.

In similar fashion, the war chiefs of every tribal unit called councils to plan the punitive raids against the tribe's many enemies, as the constant need for slaves and booty of all kinds was an integral part of every summer's activities. Each tribe raided independently for the most part, unless the need arose to band together so as to field a large combined force of warriors. In that event, a war chief was chosen to represent all the tribes, to coordinate their combined efforts. In years past, Sakohkea had been the unanimous choice of the five tribes of the Haudenosaunee. He was easily the most feared and most ruthless of all the war chiefs. Men wanted to follow such a man into the heat of battle.

—∞—

As the sun plunged into a bank of dark clouds to the west, dusk came to the village of Deganawida. A southerly breeze off the water brought a damp chill to the air. The village was a beehive of spring activity.

Fur robes and bedding festooned sections of the palisade wall and horizontal poles erected between uprights throughout the village, blowing in the breeze to air them out. It gave the woman and girls of the tribe a rare opportunity to wield clubs with gusto to beat the dirt and vermin accumulated over the winter from their bedding and robes. It was a satisfying opportunity to be outside for a change, and visit with neighbors that had spent the winter cooped up.

The women had talked about the dark clouds in the western sky as the sun set. While they worked someone invariably mentioned the weather, passing a comment that the signs were favorable for rain or wet snow later. Weather was always unsettled in early spring, and often a favored topic of conversation. Sometimes Orenda was slow deciding which it was to be, winter or summer.

Insulated from the chatter of the women and girls, an event of a more serious nature was taking place in the council house. Flames leaped from the long hearth, pushing back the natural gloom of the windowless room. The heavy warmth of the fire, accentuated the smell rising from the packed humanity. Firelight reflected from the surface of water buckets scattered about, and from the bangled raiment of the men and older boys that sat in various attitudes of attentive silence in the circular wigwam.

One man was speaking to the assembly, and he had their undivided attention. Near the back of the room, standing on one of the platforms attached to the inner wall, a group of young men listened intently to the speaker, Sakohkea, as he told his warriors what to expect over the summer insofar as war parties were concerned. It was the same every summer, but there were always new details to work out, and that was what he was doing.

Raids against Naskapi and Anishinabeg bands occurred throughout the summer, as needs dictated, or in retaliation. This summer, scouting parties would again watch the pale skins at their village. Deganawida wanted to know what they were doing, and where they were doing it.

The rapt young men were the same five that were attacked by the wolf pack while trapping during the winter, Okwáho – the former Ivar, his constant companion, Otetiani, Ganeodiyo, Igoo, and Gyantwaka. They had become fast friends through shared experiences, especially Okwáho and Otetiani, because they were the oldest of the boys and young men of the Cokanuk band of the Haudenosaunee people. The arduous daily training to become warriors over the winter further bonded them. They made the rituals and drills that taught them the art of the warrior into contests. The dominate pair in most contests of strength and martial arts were Okwáho and Otetiani. They were the ones to beat, and the other three young men did their best, but their two friends were fierce competitors.

Okwáho had matured considerably over the winter. In the process his manner and even his appearance underwent a transformation. Except for his slowly darkening blonde hair -- now worn in a bear grease stiffened roach, like his friends -- and blue eyes, nothing remained of the Norse boy that had been captured. He looked, acted, and was exactly like his four friends. The young man was Haudenosaunee in mind and heart. Right now, Ingerd, his own mother would not have known him. As time went on he would strive ever harder to be more of a Haudenosaunee than any of them.

His outgoing personality, intelligence, and physical toughness made him popular among the people. Young females of the band vied for his attention, but thus far he had expressed no interest. His daily focus, his dream, was to become a famous warrior, like his father Odatshedeh, and his idol, Sakohkea.

During the hectic days of summer, when everything done by the people away from the home village would be accomplished, his journey on that long path would begin with expeditions to trade with the Anishinabeg. Sakohkea split the band's young men between the six groups of warriors that would soon take the field; purposely separating any groups of close friends. His thinking on this was well known. In a life or death situation he wanted his warrior's reactions to be all about what was best for the group, and not about feelings of friendship between individuals. It was the only way to survive in their hostile world.

Each year, the trading season began in much the same way. Groups of warriors, with their young charges in tow, launched canoes along the rivers and across the lakes in all directions from the village, to trade with the villages sited along the shorelines all across the land. In similar fashion, other groups from other bands of Haudenosaunee and other tribes set out from their villages to do the same thing.

By tacit agreement the beginning of this period of trading was a time of peace, even between traditional enemies like the Haudenosaunee, Naskapi, and Anishinabeg. A sense of animosity existed at each trading site, but the participants usually conducted the bickering and impassioned banter associated with bartering for goods to a good natured level. Without this mindset, such an annual undertaking would be impossible.

The trade goods carried by each group of the Cokanuk band of Haudenosaunee, as well as most of the other groups scattering out from their villages, were many and varied. Among them choice pelts from the winter's trapping, surplus winter robes, baskets and bark boxes, pottery, surplus dried herbs gathered by the women and girls last summer, and an assortment of wooden and bone or antler utensils and tools, as well as specialty items peculiar to a particular tribe, were the usual fare. Later, when garden produce surplus to the needs of the band was harvested, it, too, was traded. Pregnant bitches and recently weaned whelps became sought after trade goods. Two pregnant bitches, two young males, and small cage of whelps was a part of the cargo. A lively trade in pack dogs was usually a part of any gathering, both ensuring new bloodlines and promoting desired characteristics in these valuable pack animals and food sources during lean times. Packs of trade goods and the dogs were evenly distributed between each canoe.

—— ❊ ——

Throughout the time of daylight the four loaded canoes had been paddled northwest, upstream against the lazy current of the river, through connecting lakes, toward their destination, an Anishinabeg village. The thought occurred to him that the trip home would be much easier downstream.

Mosquitos hung over the water and the grass along the riverbanks and lake shores in dark clouds, pestering the canoe's occupants each time they paddled through one. The bear grease and ground cedar berry mixture used to repel the pests worked well, and each canoe carried some.

There were ten of them all told, four warriors, one for each canoe, and six young men. Seawi was the leader. One of the young men was Okwáho; he was two summers older than the other three.

Over a winter of trapping together, the taciturn Seawi had grown to like the brash youngster that the tribe had adopted. He had selected him as one of the two young men to help paddle his overloaded canoe, the expedition's largest.

Okwáho's shoulders ached from the strain of paddling, but he never missed a stroke in his dogged determination to overcome any hardship, any obstacle. Seawi had told him and Danegea, the other young man, at dawn when they set out, that their destination would be reached today well before darkness. Except for their companions in the other three canoes, they had not seen any people since leaving their village the day before.

"Smoke! I see smoke over the tree tops!" yelled Okwáho, pointing with his paddle. Their canoe happened to be in the lead when they paddled around a bend in the river, the forested riverbanks opened into a broad savannah along both banks. Columns of smoke rose into the still air from a large, palisaded village sited on a knoll overlooking the savannah and the river beyond.

As they drew closer, a number of barking dogs ran from the open village gate, fanning out across the savannah and along the riverbank. So far, no people came from the village proper.

The four canoes grounded on the beach. "Hang onto our dogs, or we will not be able to trade them," called Seawi to his companions. "Keep those others away!"

A few well aimed kicks kept the village dogs at bay.

"Here they come," observed Danegea, bobbing his chin toward the village gate. Six men walked rapidly across the savannah toward the four canoes. They were armed.

"Unload our goods," directed Seawi, walking away to meet the Shinabeg men.

This being the first trading stop, the other three men directed their charges in how to spread the robes atop the grass to display their wares to best advantage. By the time Seawi returned with the Shinabeg men, the packs had been unloaded and the goods were being spread out on each robe for display.

No greetings were passed back and forth. The Shinabeg gave each of the Haudeno men the once over, but hardly gave the young men with them a second glance, except for Okwáho. He received their attention.

One of the Shinabeg turned to Seawi, a question in his eyes.

Seawi gestured toward his charge. "Tell him who you are, Okwáho."

The young man got to his feet from the pack he was pulling trade goods from and walked closer to the group of Shinabeg with Seawi.

"I am called Okwáho." The boy spoke simply and directly to the man he assumed to be the spokesman for his companions. He stood an arm's length in front of the Shinabe, making direct eye contact with the man, his height placing him almost at eye level.

The man looked him up and down. "Okwáho." The name rolled easily off his tongue. "How do you come to be here, with these Haudeno? You are a pale skin from the village to the north." He gestured in the general direction of the distant Halfdansfjord.

A slight smile transfigured the face of Okwáho. "Aye, I came from Halfdansfjord. It was long ago to me. I am no longer of that place. I am Haudenosaunee. These are my people now. I am one with them."

The Shinabe digested this revelation in silence. His companions said nothing. He grunted noncommittally, gesturing to one of his companions, and bobbing his chin toward their village.

This man turned toward the village and raising a war whistle to his lips, gave a long shrill signal. The parley was over; people began pouring from the gate, to spread out over the savannah as they made their way toward the group on the riverbank.

Okwáho and the other young men watched the colorful tableau of the crowd of people moving toward them excitedly, commenting back and forth, for they had never before seen the like.

⸺⸜⸝⸻

The traders retraced their route toward home from the village of the Anishinabeg, leaving at midday of the second day. As usual, every piece of their trade goods had been replaced by one or more items gotten through spirited barter with the people of the Shinabeg village.

The novelty of trading with an enemy people had quickly worn off for the young men, replaced by the knowledge that their next meeting would not be as amicable.

For the occupants of the four canoes, the journey downstream on the indolent current required little effort beyond the occasional flick of the paddle for all except the man in the stern, who still must steer.

"I am happy to be away from there," said Okwáho from his position in the canoe's bow. "They did not like us being there."

"I did not like being there either. We are their enemies," said Danegea.

"It would not have taken much for a fight to break out. We would have had no chance with our weapons in the canoes."

Seawi snorted from the stern. "It would not have mattered if we had weapons in hand, there are always too many of them."

Okwáho turned to look at him. "How do we fight them?"

"We never engage them in pitched battles. Our raiding parties strike when least expected, hitting fast and then running away. It is the only way for us."

Silence prevailed for a time while the two young men digested what Seawi had told them. The shadows lengthened as the sun sank in the western sky. The air grew colder along the river in the shadows of the dense forest that lined the riverbanks.

"Watch for game, fresh meat will be good in camp tonight," ordered Seawi.

Their canoe was well in the lead of the other three, gliding soundlessly on the current, when they rounded a sharp bend in the river.

Being in the bow, Okwáho saw the cow moose and two young calves before his companions, as they foraged on water lilies along the riverbank. All three had their heads underwater. His bow was already in hand, an arrow on the string, ready for an opportunity to present itself. Without pause, he drew to the arrow's head, and shot in one fluid motion.

The arrow struck his target, one of the milk fattened calves, in the paunch, angling forward into the vitals, the killing shot taught to him by his father on his first big game hunt. The animal bolted, jerking its head from the water at the sudden pain, before running a few steps, to collapse dead at the water's edge. The cow and her surviving offspring, frightened at the commotion, ran from the water in a flurry of spray, disappearing into the forest gloom so quickly that nobody else had time for a shot.

"Good shot," exclaimed Danegea! "You had already shot before I saw them." The trio beached their canoe next to the carcass of the moose calf and leaped out onto the shoreline.

Okwáho grinned at his companions. "Look how fat he is!" He touched the carcass with the tip of his bow in tribute to the spirit that had dwelt within. Although young, the animal already was taller and heavier than a mature adult of any other deer species.

Seawi made eye contact with Okwáho. A slight smile transformed the face of the man. He nodded in appreciation. "Good, now you two get him butchered. We will camp here tonight. I will kindle a cooking fire to roast our meat." He turned around at a hail from the river, raising his hand in greeting. The other canoes headed inshore to the landing spot, the fading light just sufficient to make their contact.

Sometime later, the satiated group of traders lolled around the dying fire in their sleeping robes, their distended bellies a testament to the prodigious quantities of half-raw meat they had consumed. All that remained of the moose calf was a small pile of boned meat lying on the animal's hide.

Conversation ebbed and flowed for a time, until sleep claimed them.

HALFDANSFJORD

The spring thaw brought a flurry of activity to the settlement. On one fine, sunny morning, Halfdan called everyone not engaged in something vital to congregate on the landing beach around the two ship frames to dig them out.

The framework had lain indistinguishable as the skeleton of ships, buried under many feet of deep snow for much of the winter.

The crowd pitched in with enthusiasm, happy to be outside in the open air and sunshine after the long winter. Concerted effort over the course of an entire day left the ships and the shipyard exposed to the sun's feeble spring heat. Rather than just throw snow back away from the two frameworks, a line of people formed to convey baskets and buckets of snow down to the water's edge, getting it out of the shipyard proper. In this way, the earth's surface would dry out quickly, cutting down or eliminating the period during the thaw when the exposed earth became a sea of deep mud. What little snow and ice remained on the frameworks and in the shipyard proper quickly melted while timbers, planks, and other frame members thawed as well.

Over the course of the next few days, planks sprung out of position by the crushing weight of the snow were forced back in their place where possible, or replaced. All things considered, no extensive damage to either ship framework was sustained.

Halfdan had been in the midst of the snow removal, the effort was that important to him. He had worked side by side with Hallsteinn, the most knowledgeable of the shipwrights. With the snow removal behind them and work on the ships was more ongoing, he asked the question that had nagged at them both.

"When will they be finished?"

Hallsteinn sighed and looked at his chieftain, both hands on his hips. "I knew you would ask that. Truthfully, I do not know. It depends on many things, as you know. All the materials are here, so work will go along as fast as it can. If the weather holds, I think we will have them in the water by the new moon. On the other hand if a bad spring storm comes, maybe not." His expansive shrug spoke volumes left unsaid.

Halfdan nodded, crossed his arms, and looked out over the bay. He knew what they would see out there one day this summer. He did not want to think about the loss of these precious ships.

He locked eyes with Hallsteinn. "You are in a race against time, Hallsteinn. The terrible winter has taken its toll on our plans." He raised his chin toward the bay. "Anishinabeg canoes will cover that water again. I do not want those ships sitting here unfinished when that happens. I am depending on you and your men to see that there are not."

"We will do our best, Halfdan." His eyes fastened on the grim visage of his chieftain.

"I know you will. Keep me informed." Without waiting for an answer, Halfdan turned and walked back toward the gate.

Hallsteinn watched him go, somewhat humbled by the task at hand and the trust placed on him by his chieftain. His eyes travelled over the men working in the shipyard. As he returned to his work, he clenched his jaw as a determined feeling came over him. *With these fine men, a lot of luck, and the help of the gods we might be finished by the new moon.*

Chapter 11

HARD CHOICES

Nipishish, Kejo, and Lothar returned to their village as quickly as possible after the parley with Nesatin. Word spread faster than normal through Nitassinan that the Anishinabeg had rejected Sachem's peace offer regarding the people of Halfdansfjord.

The people soon knew that a dark mood had seized their head chieftain at the bad tidings. None could recall such a thing ever before occurring. Sachem was known throughout the land, by friend and foe alike, for his wisdom and even temper. This business with his kinsmen, the Anishinabeg, was a different situation. He came to regard the slight by Nesatin as a personal insult. He held his own council for the first two moons of early spring, finally ending his period of reticence by sending emissaries to all the principle settlements of his people. The Naskapi people across the length and breadth of their homeland knew something important was brewing when the chiefs and war chiefs of every Naskapi band were summoned to Sachem's village for the biggest powwow in living memory.

Activity in Halfdansfjord slowed slightly when the two new ships were launched. Thorgill and Hrafen picked their six man crews from the many volunteers and set out from the settlement's landing beach on a shakedown cruise that was expected to last into the new moon. As always, a sailing brought out the entire population to see the ships put to sea.

Halfdan stood at the forefront of the crowd watching the sailing with a critical eye when two hunters came to report to him. Unable to hear them in the din, he motioned the men off to the side.

"Something has the Naskapi all stirred up, Halfdan," said the hunter Grimr. He motioned toward his constant companion on the hunt. "Thorkell and I met up with two different canoes of Naskapi men on their way to summon the chiefs of all the bands to the village of Sachem for a big powwow."

Halfdan glanced from man to man.

Thorkell held his tongue, as usual preferring that Grimr do the talking.

"Did you talk to them?" asked Halfdan of Grimr.

"Not the first canoe, they just waved to us. The second canoe stopped briefly to talk. They told us that they were on their way to the village of Antanak and that the call has gone out to all the Naskapi. It is the Anishinabeg, they are preparing for war."

Halfdan's jaw clenched as his mind grappled with this new information. "How long ago did this happen?"

"Two days ago since we talked to them. We headed right back with the meat we had."

Halfdan just nodded. He stood watching the two ships as they came about, set a course to the west to weather the headland, and soon disappeared from view.

"There is something else, Halfdan." Thorkell entered the conversation. "The men told us that three smoky fires will be set on every high hill whenever the wind is calm. The three columns of smoke will tell every man that sees them of the powwow." He stopped watching his chieftain narrowly.

"The guards reported columns of smoke to the southeast just after dawn," acknowledged Halfdan.

Grimr took up the thread for his friend. "The men were anxious to continue their journey, so we parted company. As they paddled away they had one more surprise for us. Antanak and Chisasi will stop by here on their way to the powwow."

Halfdan facial expression conveyed a question; he impatiently bobbed his chin at Grimr.

"Sachem has called for you to come to the powwow. Antanak and Chisasi are coming here to take you with them."

Halfdan's expressive face momentarily registered surprise before he recovered his composure. "Chisasi will have at least two canoes full of warriors, so they will make a fast journey here. If they leave the Loon Lake village as soon as they receive the summons they could be here as early as nightfall, or perhaps sometime tomorrow morning."

"I doubt they will stop overnight, Halfdan. The summons is urgent; the men told us it had never before occurred. That is why we hurried back here."

Halfdan's eyes appraised the two men. "You have done well. Now, go find Helge. Tell him I want the council members in the council chambers right away." Without a backward glance he strode off purposely for his longhouse. The council chambers and his quarters occupied the same building.

The men of the council had listened intently as Halfdan told them what he knew. They all sat around the same long trestle table that had witnessed many such meetings, in the same smoky room, against the backdrop of the hearth fire that warmed their backsides. Most wore glum expressions for they felt they knew what was coming.

"We have discussed this issue at length, except for what I am going to tell you now." He paused a moment, his eyes travelled over these men he knew so well. "If the Anishinabeg attack before I return, I want everybody to board the ships and leave our settlement. While I am gone I want to know that my people are safe. We can build another settlement somewhere, we cannot replace those we lose fighting a hopeless battle. We know how they will come at us. This time their numbers will be overwhelming. You must put out groups of scouts to warn of their approach from the south. You all know what to do; I will leave you to make your own decisions based on the reality of your situation."

"Who accompanies you, Halfdan," asked Brodir?

"I will take Frida, Fang, and Ingerd if she wants to come. That is enough."

The men were not surprised at his choices. If they had reservations they were not voiced. Several humorous comments about the dog came from around the table.

Halfdan grinned at them. "Fang would not let me leave without him."

Suddenly serious again, he continued. "Encamp on that island just off-shore of the river that flows by Chisasi's village. It is far enough away from here that the Anishinabeg may not look any further north if this settlement is abandoned when they get here. You might be able to see the smoke when they set fire to our home."

A growl swept through the council. The indignity of running away, and having their home burned to the ground by an enemy that they were not going to fight was hard to endure.

Halfdan resumed pacing back and forth in front of the table, letting them vent for a time.

"I will look for you there when we return. If I do not find you there, we will stay with the Naskapi and go to Antanak's village until somebody comes for us. If they have not attacked by the time I return we may consider return-ing here. It all depends on what we find out at the powwow."

Before anything further could be said, the blast of a guard's horn warned that something might be amiss. The council chamber quickly emptied as the men ran from the building and turned toward the north gate, where the warning came from.

The guard's extended arm pointed in the direction of the river that would bring the Naskapi to Halfdansfjord. "Naskapi come," shouted the guard!

The feeble light of a single torch illuminated the way for a file of men car-rying three canoes across the barley field toward the gate.

Halfdan waited at the gate for their arrival. Most of the council met the column of warriors about midway in the field, many of them helping carry the canoes into the settlement.

Frida walked up to Halfdan and laid her hand on his arm, a serious expression on her face. "Ingerd will not be going with us. She left at dawn yesterday with two guards and a group of women and older children to gather eggs from the seabird nesting grounds." She absently pointed in the general direction of the bay to the east, invisible in the darkness of night.

Halfdan nodded. "She probably would not want to go anyway. She has not been back from there very long."

"She is still withdrawn over the loss of Ivar, so it is difficult to say what she would have done." She paused in thought a moment as they watched the approach of the Naskapi. "I am ready whenever you decide to go. We each have a pack. All you will need are your weapons. I have mine."

He smiled at her in appreciation. "We will know soon.' He nodded in the direction of the bobbing torch. "I imagine they will stay the night and leave with first light."

That was not to be. The Naskapi ate and rested for a time in the warmth of the council chamber. Chisasi and Antanak told Halfdan and the council that this summons of all the Naskapi leaders was unprecedented in their experience. Something very important was afoot. The men were in a hurry to be on their way, so shortly afterwards, with some still chewing the last of their late meal, and with Halfdan, Frida, and the dog in company, they paddled their canoes rapidly away to the southeast. The darkness quickly swallowed them from the view of the people seeing them off. Later the sliver of a new moon would light their way.

The watchers on shore stood a moment staring into the darkness before turning to the yawning gate of Halfdansfjord. Most sought their sleeping robes, while others congregated in the council chambers to talk over the momentous events that were transforming their lives.

VILLAGE OF SACHEM

Two days hence, after a single overnight camp, during late midday of a clear windy day, the three canoes beached in front of Sachem's village, amid more canoes than anybody had ever before seen in one place.

A large crowd of village residents and visitors from other bands milled about between the landing beach and the village gate. Word passed quickly that Antanak and Chisasi had arrived.

Greetings were exchanged with the new arrivals. Halfdan and Frida created quite a stir initially, with people juggling for a closer look. The fact that they came with Antanak and Chisasi obviously carried considerable weight, because no trouble arose from the fact that they were strangers.

Fang became an object of admiration by many of those that came for a closer look at Halfdan and Frida, with her flaming red hair on full display. All kept a respectful distance from the big, unfriendly looking dog. Halfdan occasionally dropped a reassuring hand to the big head in the face of all this unaccustomed activity. The village dogs that happened by did not bother with the common nose touching greeting, no doubt sensing the big dog sitting beside the strange man was not interested in friendship.

The novelty of the pale skinned strangers soon wore off after everyone had had their look, and people went about their business. It was apparent with the mix of men and women that gathered in their own small groups with friends and acquaintances they had not seen for some time, that most, if not all, of the visiting warriors had brought a few women with them. The women could be seen in animated conversation scattered throughout the milling crowd.

Judging from the wares that began appearing on robes around the edge of the main crowd, many people, visitors and residents alike, came to the pow-wow to trade. With this new activity, the focus of the crowd slowly changed from visiting to trading, the two being mutually compatible.

Halfdan and Frida continued to nod and smile, but their faces began to show the strain of smiling all the time. Both saw and greeted the warriors that Kejo had brought to Halfdansfjord during the preceding summer, but beyond those brief glimpses of a familiar face, neither recognized a single person beyond those they came with. Any discomfort they felt at being strangers among all these people changed quickly when Frida spied a familiar grinning man working his way through the crowd.

"It is Gudbj," she said, with a lift of her chin.

"I see him." Halfdan and Frida walked to meet their friend.

Although the two men had not been apart for long this time, they clasped one another's forearms in an iron grip, their obvious joy at the reunion plain to see.

Frida looked from one to the other happily. She smiled broadly at the man who accompanied Gudbj.

The man's hard face softened somewhat, but he said nothing.

The moment passed, and the two friends broke the bonding contact.

Gudbj gestured to the man that accompanied him. "Halfdan, this is Glooscap, the war chief of Sachem."

The two men greeted one another with a nod, their mutual respect and regard for one another obvious.

"I have heard much about you, Glooscap." He gestured to Frida. "This is my mate, Frida."

Glooscap appraised both, especially Halfdan. "Nipishish has spoken of both of you many times. You are welcome in this place. Sachem requests that you come to the council now." His eyes swept the crowd, until he found the tall figure of Chisasi. He glanced at Nipishish.

"I will get them." Nipishish wound his way through the crowd toward Chisasi and Antanak. He could be seen talking to them for a moment, and then the three of them came back toward Glooscap and Halfdan.

"Frida, you will have to stay here with the others," said Nipishish. "I am to interpret for Halfdan otherwise I could not be at this council. It is for the chiefs of the nation only. I do not know how long this will take."

She looked at the men; a slight smile curved her mouth. "I knew that when I came. Do not be concerned." She glanced out over the crowd. "I saw Kejo a moment ago; talking to the women we came with. I will go talk to him. And, I will be making new friends." With a toss of her red hair, she strode away, hips swinging, because she knew all of them were watching.

Halfdan shook his head and grinned at the others. Nipishish appreciated what had occurred, but the Naskapi remained stoic. They obviously did not understand what had just occurred nor did they know what to make of such a woman.

All of this byplay had taken but a few moments, but Glooscap demonstrated his growing impatience with a single word of command as he turned away, heading toward the village gate. "Come!"

As Halfdan followed the others into the village, he examined the sights and sounds curiously. Similar in many ways to the Loon Lake village of Antanak, the only comparison in his experience, he observed that this village was considerably larger. The people they passed on the way toward the largest building within the encircling palisade, the round council house, examined him closely, but in an open, not unfriendly manner.

The crowd around the council house entrance shuffled aside as they approached, and Glooscap entered without pause. The gloom of interior was illuminated by a smoke hole at the top of the domed roof and light streaming through the single entry.

Glooscap took a seat with the other members of Sachem's council. The large assembly was silent while the new arrivals found places.

Halfdan followed his companions as they took seats among the large group of men that shuffled around making room on the hides that covered most of the floor. Perfunctory greetings were exchanged during this process, giving him time to examine his surroundings. He felt that every man was watching his every move. He crossed his legs comfortably at the ankles and his eyes travelled around the room. Gradually he became accustomed to the weak illumination, and details swam into sharper relief.

A small circular fire pit, with a bed of coals from which a few tongues of flame licked at the air and tendrils of smoke rising toward the smoke hole overhead, separated the council from those assembled before them. Halfdan realized that he sat among all the leaders of the many bands of the Naskapi people scattered throughout Nitassinan. He felt they all knew who he was, and why he was here. It sobered him that he was here at the invitation of Sachem himself. The thought sent a chill through his body. He examined the council closely; now that he could see them plainly, as he tried to determine which of them might be Sachem. His attention focused on an old man, his straight black hair streaked with grey, whose eyes fairly bored into him. He knew immediately that this was Sachem, the man he had heard so much about, and the man to whom he and his people owed their very existence in this land.

"Nipishish, tell Halfdan that I am glad he came to this place." When Sachem spoke all sound ceased among those assembled.

Nipishish turned to Halfdan to translate.

Halfdan stopped him with a raised hand. "I understood." Switching to the language of the people, he answered as best he could.

"Thank you for inviting me."

A sound of surprise and approval swelled through the men at Halfdan's ability to understand and give voice to a few words of their language.

Sachem smiled slightly, inclining his head in assent.

Nipishish slapped his friend on the knee. "Good, you have made an impression on them. Sachem is pleased."

"I hope so. Our fate is in his hands."

The low buzz of conversation and the normal sounds made by men shifting position occasionally trailed off when Glooscap got to his feet.

"Many of you have come far. Every band of our people is represented, except those that live far across the great salt bay to the west. Eventually they, too, will hear of this powwow. Sachem has called all of you here to seek your wisdom on the actions being undertaken by our kinsmen, the Kitchi sipi Anishinabeg." He gave the cutting sign and sat back down.

From his place among the council, seated with his legs crossed, back resting comfortably against a backrest, Sachem's eyes travelled over the expectant faces of the chiefs of his people. Being old, as such things are reckoned, one might think it would be hard to hear him from a seated position, but that would not be the case at all. He always spoke in a strong, modulated voice, not especially loud, but the timber of his voice carried his words to all his listeners without fail.

As the assembly became aware that their chief's eyes travelled over the faces of all the men arrayed before him, muted conversation died away, to be replaced by an absolute silence that fell like a curtain over the council house. Sachem began to speak.

"For two moons I have searched for the wisdom to make the right decision. To take action or not to take action in the matter of the Anishinabeg rejecting our offer of peace that was presented to Nesatin by Kejo and Nipishish. This offer was made so that Halfdan and his people can continue to live among us in peace, as he wishes, and as I wish. Many of his people already live among us. You all know this. We cannot continue to do this peacefully without the agreement of the Anishinabeg. Nesatin has already given his ultimatum – he will allow Halfdan and his people to abandon their village and leave Nitassinan. If they do not, he will send his warriors to kill all of them and burn their village. You have been summoned here to personally give this council your answers to the two questions that I have struggled with. Do you consider that Nesatin has insulted us as a people? Is it to be peace or war because of this? I have made my decision, now I want to hear your opinions before I say what we will do as a people."

Halfdan sympathized with Sachem, for he had faced this dilemma many times. A good leader must always consider what he says and does in the name of those he leads, so as to be certain that his actions are not in his behalf alone. Sometimes that balance was hard to achieve. He watched the byplay between the council and the assembly with special interest, and listened carefully as Nipishish furnished a running translation of what was being said. As time passed he came to realize that the majority of these men, the principle chiefs and war chiefs of most of the Naskapi bands, spoke with passionate conviction. They had formed an opinion beforehand.

As full darkness enveloped the land, tapers of pitch pine in bark containers of sand were brought in to illuminate the council house. The dancing tongues of flame reflected from the domed interior, imparting a surreal quality to the grim faces of the men who listened intently to the progression of their peers as each had his say.

Outside, few people slept. They had congregated around the council house, waiting for word, wrapped in their sleeping robes. A fire winked here and there, but most sat stoically, hunkered down in the warmth of the heavy robes, content with the expectation that the decision of their supreme leader would be forthcoming.

For Frida, the whole affair had been enjoyable, even considering the gravity of what was taking place among all the tribal leaders. Kejo had not stayed among the women long. Like most men, he soon tired of their chatter, and went away to seek others of his kind. Frida began the long wait in the company of the women she had come with. They joined other women in one of longhouses and were made welcome. As time passed, she had a bowl of stew with her friends while she made new friends from the women that came and went from the longhouse. She dozed on a pile of warm robes for a short time after conversation lagged.

Back in the council house, the powwow went on long into the time of darkness. By the time all present had their say, the sky had begun to lighten in the east.

A unanimous consensus had been reached. They, too, considered the action taken by Nesatin to be a personal insult to Sachem, and to the Naskapi nation.

Sachem received their decision without visible emotion. A short time later, he got to his feet. The room became quiet. His orders came quickly. They were short and to the point, for he had thought of little else for some time. He directed his chieftains that lived closest to the Kitchi sipi Anishinabeg villages to set lookouts to watch their movements. When it was known that they were preparing to venture forth to make war, signals of smoke, drums, and the word carried by runners would spread the alarm over Nitassinan. When this alarm came, every band of Naskapi were to dispatch canoes filled with all the warriors they could muster to converge on Halfdansfjord, where the challenge would be met. No questions followed. Sachem's explicit orders broached no further discussion.

The chieftains began to file by to pay tribute to Sachem. Some had not seen or talked to him for many seasons.

As men began moving toward the entry door, Glooscap announced that food had been cooked for all of them. It was on the hearths in one of the longhouses. People would show them the way, so they could eat before beginning their journey home.

Halfdan and Nipishish stood by and watched the line of men pay their respects to Sachem. Halfdan thought it strangely moving that so many powerful leaders of the many bands of the Naskapi Nation paid such tribute to this man that they obviously held in high regard as their supreme leader. He studied Sachem's every movement as he talked with the leaders of his far-flung nation. The respect and affection shown to his chieftains by Sachem, and they to him, told Halfdan much about the character of the man.

Nipishish continued his briefing. "He will want to talk to us, Halfdan, so be patient until the others have left. Glooscap will stay with him. The rest of the council may also want to talk to you. What they are doing is unprecedented for them. It was a big decision to stand up to their kinsmen, because they far outnumber the Naskapi."

"I know what it took to defy the Anishinabeg chieftain. I think this is more about what they regard as an insult to their Sachem, rather than a desire to stand with us against them. We Norse are just being swept along with them." He paused when he saw the look on his friend's face.

"Do not misunderstand me, Gudbj. I am thankful to have them as our friends. Without them and your relationship with them, we would have been killed or run out of this land, long ago."

Somewhat mollified, Gudbj, was about to answer, when he saw the last of the chieftains leave his audience with Sachem. "He will call us over now, I think."

Glooscap leaned forward to whisper to his chieftain. Sachem's eyes sought Halfdan and Nipishish; a wave of his hand beckoned them forward.

"I am not sure I know what to say to him, Gudbj."

"You will know, Halfdan. You are here by his invitation. That is an honor accorded to few men. Speak from your heart. Answer his direct questions truthfully. He will know if you do not. You will be surprised at what he knows. He will test you with what he knows about you and our people."

The two men got to their feet and walked toward the supreme chieftain of the Naskapi Nation.

Antanak and Chisasi had not left with the others. They held back, wanting to be with Halfdan and Nipishish to offer their personal support, to stand before the supreme council with them.

Nipishish and Halfdan nodded a greeting to the men, their facial expressions conveying their thanks.

"I will translate for you as you need me to," said Nipishish softly.

Halfdan made no comment. Like Gudbjartur before him, he did not derive comfort from the fact that he towered over the short, slight chieftain. On the contrary, the man possessed an understated presence, an aura that overwhelmed the conscience of those he came close to. His attire was simple and common, without adornment of any kind. This accentuated rather than detracted from the power of his persona. Halfdan was impressed before a word was spoken, and that was not easy to do for he had always felt in complete command of any situation. It occurred to him that that was why leaders were chosen by their followers, they stood out, stood above the fray. That this simple man was a leader to be reckoned with was immediately apparent by his bearing and the intelligence and intensity of the black eyes deeply recessed in the lined face.

As they stopped before Sachem, Nipishish greeted him with the traditional Naskapi greeting. Sachem returned the greeting, smiling broadly at Nipishish, as one would a close friend. He greeted Antanak and Chisasi in like manner. With convention satisfied all around, he then directed his attention to Halfdan. The smile dropped away somewhat, but the wizened face remained open and friendly.

Halfdan repeated the traditional greeting. His attempt seemed to please Sachem and the council. Every man openly glanced with approval at the Talisman of Life hanging from Halfdan's neck.

The council members returned the greeting, smiling in welcome before Sachem spoke.

"I am happy to have you here among us, Halfdan. Nipishish has told me many tales of you, that you are a great chieftain of your people."

"I am honored to be here with you, Sachem. My people have many friends among your people. I am thankful for the opportunity to live in peace among the Naskapi people, to prosper together in this beautiful land."

Sachem's eyes shifted to Chisasi. He beckoned with a bob of his chin. "Chisasi told me a tale about you one time when he came to see me. About you and our Axeman, Nipishish, and the justice you both meted out to your own men over two of our young maidens. Nipishish has told me his side of this, now I want to hear it from you."

"Aye, it happened. They were punished." Halfdan minimized the incident purposely, not wishing to elaborate on something that happened so long ago.

"Why did you kill your own men, Halfdan?"

Halfdan's face contorted with the memory, the force of his will and the anger engendered by the memory came to the fore. He spoke vehemently. "They violated my orders and raped those maidens. In doing so, they endangered the safety and existence of my people in this land. I killed one of them myself. The other I gave to Chisasi for his justice. I did this because I wanted to be friends with him and his people. Those men deserved to die for the safety of my people."

Sachem watched the struggle on Halfdan's face as he fought to regain his composure as Nipishish translated.

Sachem nodded in understanding, his eyes never leaving Halfdan's, but he said not a word about the incident. He took Halfdan by the arm. "Come, we will sit and smoke the calumet and talk of things."

Halfdan realized that the first question had been a test, as Nipishish had told him. Over what seemed like a protracted period of time, he was asked many more questions as Sachem used the answers to take his measure as a man, and the leader of his people. Halfdan increasingly realized, as he sat and smoked with these men, that Sachem carefully assessed every word that was spoken by any of them. When he spoke, his depth of understanding of any topic under discussion amazed him.

Out of the blue he asked Halfdan why he had built two more ships and what they would be used for. Sachem smiled slightly at the look of surprise on Halfdan's face at the question, but he seemed satisfied at the answer.

There were a few comments or questions by other council members, but most of the questions came from Sachem. As the session with the supreme chieftain continued, Halfdan came to realize the special place his friend had with these Naskapis, especially men like Glooscap. Halfdan knew the whole story of the two men, but watching them together made him aware of the trust and high regard that each had for the other. It made him a little jealous; he himself had lost the best friend he had ever had when Gudbj was captured. But that he was on a mission ordained by the gods was evident. Without the special relationship his old friend had with these people, he and his people would likely be dead. As his eyes travelled around the faces of the men he sat with, he knew for a certainty that that single event made all of this possible.

HALFDANSFJORD

Halfdan and Frida returned from the powwow to the worst possible news. When asked how things were, Tostig had to answer his chieftain directly.

"The egg gathering party that set out by boat to the seabird hatchery in the east bay just before you left with Antanak and Chisasi for the village of Sachem, has met with disaster."

Instantly, a look of fury suffused Halfdan's face. Frida placed a hand on his forearm, her way to calm him. It usually worked, but this time it did not.

Halfdan inhaled sharply, trying to control himself. He spoke through gritted teeth.

"Tell me, man!"

Tostig swallowed, his anguish plain to see.

"It was supposed to be a two day affair. When they did not return as planned I sent Helge with a large group of armed men in one of the new ships in search of them. They did not know exactly where to look, but they sailed along the north shoreline of this bay until they got to those high cliffs where seabirds roost. There they found the party's two burned out ships' boats on a beach near to where they had camped the night before. This was right where the cliffs begin where the birds roost. Back in the forest, they found where the group had camped for the night, and the butchered bodies of the two guards, three of the older women, and one boy, who had obviously fought beside the men. As for Ingerd, and the other two women and four children, three girls and one boy, there was no sign. A war party had carried them off." Tostig paused to give Halfdan a chance to speak.

The entire council and several people had quietly gathered as Tostig made his report. Halfdan's eyes travelled over his people as Tostig spoke.

Tostig's poignant pause was brief; Halfdan gestured impatiently for him to continue.

Helge walked up at that moment. Tostig glanced at him, a look of relief on his face at the interruption. "Tell Halfdan what you found after the bodies were found."

"We gathered the bodies and loaded them on the ship. They had been butchered, the worst any of us had seen. Skeggi the Tracker pieced together what had happened while the bodies were loaded. There were four canoes of warriors, he thought about ten men. Our men killed two of them, Skeggi found their graves in the forest. There were at least two of them wounded judging by the blood trails between the campsite and the beach where they pulled the canoes up out of the water. One of my men found an arrow that the war party had not picked up. Deskaheh said the war party was Haudeno. From the markings on the arrow shaft he said they were warriors of the Ganadoga band. We have not seen them before. He said they live far away from here."

"Did you go after them?"

"No, I decided not to pursue them, Halfdan. Too much time had gone by since the raid occurred. Skeggi figured they hit our party in the morning of the day before we found them. They were long gone with their captives."

Halfdan nodded, at a loss for words. He looked out over the crowd that continued to swell, the waters of the bay, and the nearby countryside while he ordered his thoughts. Frida had not left his side. They made eye contact. He knew that she had been crushed by the loss of her best friend, but being a strong woman, nothing could be gleaned from her facial expression. She squeezed his arm and turned away without a word, walking toward the gate. He knew she went to seek Thora and her other female friends. A deep sadness gripped him. For the first time he realized that Chisasi, Antanak, and the other Naskapi men and women that he and Frida had accompanied stood by quietly while he sorted out the troubles of his people. He made eye contact with Chisasi.

The man's face did not change, but a slight shake of his head conveyed his feelings to his friend.

Halfdan's eyes travelled over the crowd standing silently by. He found Deskaheh standing near the council members and beckoned him forward.

"Deskaheh, tell Chisasi and Antanak I want them to attend a meeting late this afternoon. I want to be certain they understand what has happened and what I want from them. Arrange for food and lodging for all of them for the night. We must talk about this that concerns all of us together."

The man wordlessly acknowledged and turned away and made his way through the throng to do Halfdan's bidding

He spoke to Tostig. "No more expeditions for any reason without a large enough armed force to protect them."

He looked at the other council members. "Meet in the council chambers at day's end. Invite the people. We must do something different. At this point I am unsure what is needed, but I want to hear your ideas."

<hr />

VILLAGE OF THE GANADOGA HAUDENOSAUNEE

Ingerd had been clubbed senseless during the dawn raid that ended with the capture or death of everyone in her party. The war party that captured her had not escaped unscathed. She did not know how many there had been originally, but she later recalled that one of the two wounded died the second day of travel. From the looks of the other one at the time, she knew he would not recover from his wounds. They hid one canoe in the forest during the first day, because there were not enough people to paddle it. That left five able bodied warriors in three canoes with two other women and four children besides her. She and the four children wound up in the same canoe with two warriors. They had forced her to sit in the middle and paddle. One of the young girls kept sniveling and crying in spite of warnings from one of the warriors. Without warning he hit her over the head with his paddle. She did not lose consciousness, but the blow gave her something to cry about. As she started to cry again, rubbing the top of her head, the man killed her in a fit of rage. He hacked the small body repeatedly with a tomahawk, splattering her blood over the other occupants of the canoe. Ingerd recalled her horror at the senseless killing of an innocent child and the sight of the man tipping her lifeless body out of the canoe. Without a word he picked up his paddle and continued as though nothing had happened. The other warrior said not a word about the incident. She had never seen such cruel, savage men. She had known they were Haudenosaunee. To think that her son Ivar had become one with them crushed her heart.

She had sustained a head wound behind the left ear in the attack that led to her capture. The wound went untreated. Her captors never allowed her enough water to wash the wound herself. The dried blood finally dropped away and the deep cut healed on its own, leaving a prominent ridge of scar tissue. Her hair fell out around the scar and she realized that she was deaf in that ear.

She did not understand why her captors hated her so; she had done nothing to them. The only thought that was paramount each day was to survive somehow. As a slave, her life since arrival at the village had become a blur of abject misery. She was forced to work in all weather, both inside and outside. When her day ended, she received her single meal of the day, and then she was securely tied to a support post at the entrance of one of the longhouses. This position left her exposed to the elements. In spite of the extreme discomfort of being tied hand and foot, and being chilled to the bone, each night she rolled up in the filthy, vermin infested robe they gave her, as best she could, and fell into an exhausted sleep.

In the beginning thoughts of Gudbj and their life together occupied her thoughts as her mind gradually retreated from reality. She would smile at the recollections, thankful to the gods for her time with this exceptional man. A feeling of pride at the sons they had raised swelled her heart. When she thought of Ivar and Lothar they were little boys, not the young men that they had become. Mercifully, thoughts of Ivar as a member of the same tribe that held her captive no longer intruded in her mind.

Visions of the egg hunting party of her friends and their children who were captured or killed flitted through the fog of her consciousness from time-to-time. She had no idea what had happened to them. She imagined that the two women who survived were also being worked to death. The children that survived would be adopted into the tribe she supposed, that is what had happened to her son Ivar. As time passed, she thought of them less and less, and finally not at all.

The women that controlled her every movement were merciless. They worked her from dawn to dark every day, with little food and no rest between chores. Somewhere in the recesses of her mind she knew that one day she would be killed for breaking some unknown rule, or because they had tired of her. They obviously intended to work her to death. She lost track of the passage of time.

Orders from her captors came in the form of screams, kicks, and blows. She could not understand their language and few of their signs. No attempt was made to teach her a single word of the language. Her mind slowly numbed to her surroundings. The treatment she received as a slave she could not comprehend. The thought processes of her once active mind became snippets of her past life as sanity slowly slipped away.

Near the end of a day, during the Time of Falling Leaves, a wretched crone slowly scraped fat globules and bits of dried flesh from a green hide pegged to the ground. Filthy, vermin infested hair once the color of corn silk hung in tangles from her head. The exposed skin of her face, hands, and bare feet were dirty, greasy, and scabbed with insect bites from inattention. What fingernails remained were cracked and broken to the quick. Her hands slowly pulled the bone scraper across the hide, the movements lethargic, unconscious. Her mind no longer functioned, she felt nothing. They had broken her in mind and body. Nobody that had known her would have recognized what remained of a once beautiful, vibrant, and happy woman.

She did not resist or react in any way when two warriors took her arms and drug her away to one of several upright posts near the village center. They trussed her securely upright, wrapping the leather rope around her entire body, atop a large pile of wood that encircled the post.

That which had been Ingerd stared with vacant eyes at the boisterous crowd that gathered, uncomprehending. Burning torches kindled the wood she stood upon. Her bloodshot eyes stared out over the crowd, her face twisted in confusion, until the flames begin to lick at her body like the heads of dancing serpents. Then the otherworldly screams began. Too quickly for the crowd of laughing people, the leather ropes burned through, and the twitching body slid into the flames.

Much later, after the fire burned to a deep bed of hot coals, nothing remained of the woman, or the post that had secured her; all were gone, consumed.

Many seasons came and went before a lone man finally discovered what had happened to her. His search became a legend.

HALFDANSFJORD

Almost as an afterthought at the end of the council meeting, Halfdan made a surprise request.

"Some of our people will stay with the Naskapi, but there are too many for all to stay. Over time perhaps more can join other native groups. There is no point in building another settlement on the mainland, where eventual attack is a certainty. If we are forced to leave here I am thinking about one of the big islands we passed on the way down here. One of them would be safer than this place on the mainland." He paused, looking at his captains.

"Athils and Sweyn are the most familiar with the inland sea. I want you men to explore the biggest islands for a place that has what we need to build another settlement if we are forced from here. You know what we need, so find an island that meets our needs. You decide how to accomplish your task. If you make contact with Thorgill and Hrafen in their new ships, put them to work on this, you will finish faster. Return here as quickly as possible."

He paced for a time, his men watched him silently. They had talked about all of it. The final decisions were for Halfdan alone to make.

"The Anishinabeg could come at us any day. I want the three remaining ships to take turns patrolling to the east and offshore along the eastern shoreline to the south, to provide a warning. You men figure out how to cover the routes the Anishinabeg will take here, and set your schedule to patrol. One ship must be out there day and night, unless there is a storm, in which case the Anishinabeg will not attempt to cross the bay in their canoes." His mind quickly went over everything he had requested of his captains. He hoped he had not forgotten anything. A few more details came to mind.

"The Naskapi will also provide a warning system, so watch for their signal smoke."

"When the ship captain on patrol sees them, he can return here much faster than the Anishinabeg can get here by canoe. Our tower guards will sound the alarm that the ship is returning. When that happens I want every woman with small children ready to board the ships and be taken to safety at Antanak's Loon Lake village. They are expecting them. There will be no exceptions." He reacted to the facial expressions of some of the men.

"We have discussed this endlessly. Our mothers and their children must be safe; we cannot fight effectively against such odds if we are worried about them. Any woman without small children can stay and fight if they wish; I leave that up to them."

Frida came to mind. *I would not want to be the man that tried to make her leave.* He smiled to himself at the thought.

The council broke up then. They had their orders. The waiting began in earnest.

At dawn the next morning, the two ships assigned to explore the habitable islands of the inland sea set sail under clear skies and a freshening wind from the southwest. Few watched the sailing; they were too busy with the tasks at hand.

People were well aware that the order to move, if and when it came, would come quickly. Every mother of small children kept personal possessions for themselves and their children ready to carry aboard the ships.

The manufacture of extra weapons then became the priority. Herjolf the Bowyer and his mates worked as quickly as possible turning every bow stave into a finished bow, to replace bows damaged and broken in combat. Others twisted new bow strings from sinew. A large group of men and women straightened and fletched arrow shafts, fitting each with one of the new broad head points arriving daily from the smithies. Another group of craftsmen worked with Jorundr the Carver hafting new battle axes, hand axes, and spears as quickly as the heads became available from the smithies.

Helge had other work parties outside the palisade walls renewing or repairing the sharpened obstacle barriers around all four sides of the walls that had been so effective in the last attack of the Anishinabeg. Many of the attackers pushed from behind by the mass of their fellows, fell into the ditches just before the barriers, to become impaled on the long, sharpened points of the saplings secured to the barrier's framework.

The workers also dug new, or renewed old concealed pit traps with the sharpened stakes that had crippled and killed many of the attackers. When finished, each pit trap was concealed by a few fresh pine boughs with a little dirt scattered about.

All the citizens of Halfdansfjord knew not to walk near the outside of the palisade walls, for all had heard the screams of the enemy warriors impaled on the maze of booby traps lying in wait for the unwary.

Smoke belched from the smithy daily as the four smiths and their helpers turned out projectile points of all kinds. Iron bar stock, used to fabricate everything from swords to arrowheads, was quickly exhausted. Bog iron was brought in daily by the bucket full. The smithy's helpers smelted these bog iron nodules of their impurities by packing them atop a deep bed of charcoal in the clay furnace, weighting the clay lid down with a big flat rock. The charcoal was then set alight from the bottom and the big, double bellows soon had smoke pouring from the top of the furnace as the charcoal column within ignited. The raw bog iron nodules became white hot in the process, combining with the burning carbon of the charcoal; they melted into a mass of fairly pure carbon steel and slag that trickled down through the red coals of the burning charcoal. The men working the clay smelter knew not what happened inside the furnace to cause this miracle; they just knew how to do the work. When the miracle occurred, a rivulet of white hot molten steel flowed from a clay spout at the bottom of the furnace and into the stone forms waiting to receive it. From these bars of steel the smithies fashioned all manner of tools, utensils, and weapons.

———

Toward days end, Brodir lounged with Thorgeirr and Bjorn on a long bench against the outer wall of the council house. The bench was shaded from the hot afternoon sun, and afforded a good view of the commons area. The bench had become a favored spot for settlement leaders to lounge toward day's end while quaffing a mug or horn of mead. The three men were so engaged as they watched the activities around the commons.

"Tostig is to be relieved tomorrow during slack tide. It is up to us who relieves him," said Thorgeirr to his companions.

"Aye, it is up to us. I have been here longer, you go," answered Brodir.

"Nay, I propose a contest. The loser goes."

"I agree," said Bjorn. "A contest is the best way to decide."

Brodir took a long pull on a drinking horn of mead, eyeing his two companions over the lip of the horn.

"What manner of contest?"

"Knives thrown to the mark. Give me your axe." He held out his hand.

Brodir chuckled, handing Thorgeirr his hand axe.

Without another word, Thorgeirr got to feet and walked the short distance to the commons largest tree, an ash. He bent down slightly and hacked a blaze in the tree's bark. The distance to the tree was five or six paces; a pretty good distance to throw a knife accurately. The ash tree had many old blaze marks hacked in its bark from contests of yore.

Thorgeirr walked back and sat down on the bench. His eyes went from Brodir to Bjorn. A smirk twisted his bearded face.

"Each of us gets one throw with his knife. The man closest to center mark gets to call the shot to relieve Tostig tomorrow at slack tide."

Brodir snorted and got to his feet, pulling his knife from its scabbard.

"Nay, from a sitting position, anybody can do it standing up," said Thorgeirr, the smirk still in place on his face.

Brodir took his seat, feeling another good draft of mead was called for.

Bjorn had already emptied his mead cup.

"I am ready to throw," he said, jerking his knife from the scabbard and throwing in one fluid motion.

The knife thudded into the tree trunk on the right edge of the blaze mark's center.

"Good throw, Bjorn!" Brodir's big right hand crashed into his friend's back.

Without hesitation Thorgeirr's knife sped to the mark, sticking in the tree just above dead center of the mark.

Brodir and Bjorn both looked at him, and then at each other. Words were unnecessary. Thorgeirr's throw was the one to beat.

Brodir took another pull on his mead. His powerful right arm swept up, and recoiled down. The knife blade flashed in the air as it sped to the tree, turning over once, to stick quivering in the mark.

Nobody said a word as they got to their feet. As they walked to the target tree trunk it was plain to see that the three knife blades had stuck into the mark within a hand's breadth of one another. Nobody spoke as they bent down to examine the three knives.

"Well, I do not know who won, but I do know that I do not want either of you throwing a knife at me," said Brodir, throwing his hairy arms around the shoulders of his companions.

"Nor I," said Bjorn. He used his finger to measure the difference between the three knives. He looked at Thorgeirr. "I think you won."

Brodir looked from Bjorn to Thorgeirr. "I agree, he won, but not by much."

The men pulled their blades from the tree, which took some doing given their penetration through the bark and into the hard outer wood layer of the ash tree.

As they walked back to the bench, Bjorn mentioned the reason they had the contest in the first place.

"All right, Thorgeirr, you won. Tell us who is to relieve Tostig tomorrow at slack tide."

"Brodir relieves Tostig, and you relieve Brodir."

"Fair enough," the two men answered. Conversation lagged for a time as the men retreated into their own thoughts. Thorgeirr left first. Bjorn followed shortly thereafter, telling Brodir he was going to find Ingunn, as if Brodir did not know that.

Brodir chuckled at Bjorn's retreating back. *That woman runs his life. He did not used to be like that. Women, who needs them?* In spite of his own admonition, he began to watch his thrall Genevra come and go as she and other thralls prepared the evening communal meal. Normally he did not care about women. They seldom intruded on what he considered the important details of a man's life. He was a man's man; his life revolved around his associations and interactions with other men that he liked and respected. When he wanted a woman, he took one from among the thralls.

He had never coupled with Genevra. In the past she had not appealed to him. Lately, he realized his attitude toward her had changed. He was actually watching for her rather than just watching her.

It all began after she lost her baby last winter. Why she lost it did not concern him; whelps were a woman thing to him, he had no interest in children at all. Still, her whelp would have meant another thrall for him, not that he needed any more, just another mouth to feed.

Thoughts of losing the services of another thrall began to make him angry again. That and the fact that Sigmund and Genevra had actually hoped he would free her so the whelp would be a freeman. By the gods, what insanity that was; to free a slave, never this side of the Underworld. He felt a sense of satisfaction that the romance between the two began to come apart after she got fat with child. The thought that Sigmund finally broke it off mollified him somewhat.

Some time ago, he did not know exactly when, he began to notice that bearing a child had changed Genevra's looks for the better in his opinion. Her face was beautiful, but the body needed improvement to attract his attention. Her breasts were much larger and her hips had filled out and widened. These attributes were to his liking. He wanted to rut with a rounded, well-endowed women when the spirit moved him.

Genevra walked out of one of the longhouses carrying two kettles suspended from a yoke across her shoulders. She turned toward the council chamber, almost directly toward Brodir.

She feared the volatile man, although he had never mistreated her beyond yelling for her to bring one thing or another. Aware that he had been watching her, she averted her eyes as she passed him and entered the council house with her burden of stew. She heaved a sigh of relief to be out of his sight. Her relief was short-lived, when she saw him walk through the door and head in her direction.

"Put those kettles on the hearth," Brodir ordered.

She did as she was told. Laying her yoke on a nearby bench, she turned to face him. Coldness gripped her heart, she knew what was coming.

He gestured toward the platforms that lined all four walls. People often sat or napped on them, so all were covered with various fur robes, some even sported privacy curtains.

She selected one of those, removed her smock and undergarments, climbed on the platform and lay down. She was not surprised that she felt no revulsion. Truth be told, she always enjoyed sex. Multiple partners were a part of her life, and she determined long ago to make the best of it. Brodir was just another man, in a long line of them since Sigmund stopped paying attention to her. He was not bad looking; it was just that he was a big, brusque, hairy man that she would not have chosen had she ever been given a choice. No resistance could be offered, nor would resistance even occur to her. She was a thrall, his property; he could do whatever he wished to her.

He came to stand at the edge of the platform. With a slight smile on his face, he quickly undressed and joined her.

"Are you surprised that I have decided to lie with you?"

"Nay, not really. I knew someday you would claim what is yours by right."

"Aye, and this is the day."

Later, she recalled her surprise that he did not just crawl on her and make quick work of it, like most men did. Brodir actually fondled her, caressed her, and showered her with kisses, before consummating his mission. The whole process was without conversation, which was fine with her. She knew his ardor would require frequent dampening, now that they had coupled. She decided the experience was not that bad, especially if it kept her on his good side.

All four ships had come together in the inland sea, heaved to within hailing distance of each other, and Athils had just finished briefing Hrafen and Thorgill on Halfdan's request.

"There are many islands out here, but I think we may have already found two that we could live on. One is about 5-leagues off the east shore, not far from Halfdansfjord, and the other is a big island about the same distance from the west shoreline," shouted Thorgill through cupped hands. "We found them yesterday."

"We are closest to the one on the west side of this inland sea if you want to go explore it. It took two days to sail around it, because we had to shelter overnight from a windstorm. There are landing beaches on the west shore and the southeast shore," added Hrafen. "There are also three small islands between the island and the mainland."

"All right. Hrafen, show me this island of yours. We will land, spend the night, and do a little exploring," said Athils, always the spokesman for his taciturn friend, Sweyn.

"Sweyn, you and Thorgill do the same to the island he found. We can meet back at Halfdansfjord tomorrow. Halfdan is anxious to get the word on these islands."

A wave of assent was all Sweyn could manage. He gestured at Thorgill to take the lead.

Thorgill's crew sheeted home the sail, and the ship heeled to the press of the wind as the helmsman brought her around on an easterly course.

Sweyn and his crew did the same. Following in the wake of Thorgill's ship, they headed toward the island Thorgill had found off the eastern shoreline from their settlement at Halfdansfjord.

Chapter 12

EVACUATION

Halfdan found that he spent a part of each day trying to allay the concerns of his people. In doing so he naturally helped them with their daily tasks while they talked. He wanted to put their minds at ease, but this became more difficult with the passage of each day. It was the waiting. The attack all knew was coming drove the conversations. They wanted an answer to the same nagging question: 'Will we have to leave Halfdansfjord?' For the first time as their chieftain he had found he did not have a ready answer.

Frida had always been his sanctuary, his confidant, but even she had not been able to help him with this. She tried to offer suggestions, but only half-heartedly, knowing that only he could make the final decision. Besides she had her own demons to confront. Both she and Thora had become introspective over the loss of Ingerd, especially since nobody really knew what happened to her. It dominated their conversations. All the women that had performed their daily tasks together were affected in much the same way; Ingerd had been liked by all of them. Thoughts of Ingerd continually inserted themselves into their daily tasks making it difficult to focus. The entire affair left Frida with an uncharacteristic hesitation, an inability to make plans or decisions. She apologized to Halfdan, but he waved it off as an unnecessary aside to what they as a people had to confront. At the time it angered her that he felt that way about the loss of her best friend, but later she chided herself for being so shallow in the face of the monumental task that lie ahead for her husband as the chieftain of their people. They continued to talk every night in bed, about the day's problems, and what loomed ahead. It seemed their uncertain future had all but replaced the happy life they had previously taken for granted. The small, normal things, the enjoyment of everyday life seemed to be gone now.

For Halfdan, after all the talking with his people, and all the council meetings, no ready solution presented itself. Defying the Anishinabeg was tantamount to suicide, he knew that. Because of that fact and to protect his people his dominate thought remained to load up everybody on the eight ships they now had and leave this place. If they did that he would have his men burn their settlement to the ground. It gave him a certain perverse pleasure – leave nothing but ashes for the Anishinabeg. He also knew that they would not care that he had destroyed everything. That is what they wanted after all; nothing left of the Northmen in their land.

The answers he sought to the problems they faced as a people were figuratively crushing him. He was aware that his burden had played havoc with the relationship that he and Frida enjoyed. Everyone tried to avoid bothering him if possible. He knew that all were feeling that he seemed about ready to explode. He mentally waved all their concerns away, knowing he could do nothing at the moment. Oh, people spoke when spoken to, but he was fully aware of their furtive looks. He could not salve their anxieties, nor they his. He hoped the passage of time might set things to rights; only the gods knew.

The thought of abandoning the settlement that was the first real home many of them had ever known plagued him. But, at the same time he knew there was no real choice. He liked to think he would not order the abandonment of Halfdansfjord until forced to; however, to delay might seal the fate of his people. He felt like he carried the weight of his world on his shoulders. Only solitude and time away from the decisions he must face each day could soothe his raging emotions.

One morning, in the first few days of the quarter moon, in a bid to get away from the constant demands of leadership, he and Fang went for a walk. Dense fog had rolled in off the bay during the night, obscuring the settlement's landing beach where they walked. His hair and beard streamed with water from the cloak of the Fog Giant. He angled down toward the sound of the bay's surf lapping ashore. The short wavelets made a hollow, gurgling sound as they came ashore in the stillness of the fog.

His mind was a jumble of thoughts. Knowing his people were more than capable, especially when confronted by lifestyle changes such as faced by all of them now, he nonetheless was ill at ease. Virtually the same questions had been repeated by everyone that he had talked to, and the implications haunted him. His dog sensed this as he walked behind his master. Halfdan stopped suddenly. He turned around to speak to the dog.

"You know that something is wrong with me. I wish you could help me decide what to do about all of this."

Fang sat down on his haunches when the man turned to him. His tail scribed a short arc on the pebbles of the beach.

Halfdan rubbed the great, wet head with affection. "Ah, you do not know either. Come on, let us walk to the top of the cliff."

He reversed his direction and headed west. He could not see the dog in the murk, but he knew that he followed close behind. Straining to see his way in the fog, he walked slowly, placing each foot carefully lest he lose his balance. As he recalled from infrequent walks in this direction, the pebble beach would end at the trail to the cliff's top.

When he finally found the narrow trail to the top of the cliff, he nearly tripped over it, as the relatively smooth beach suddenly ended; giving way to the almost vertical rock face of the cliff that overlooked the bay. The rock slab surface of the treacherous trail was slippery with dew. He placed each foot carefully, one before the other on the slippery rock, as he progressed uphill, occasionally bending forward at the waist to place his hands ahead on the steep trail to ensure he kept his balance. *Perhaps this is not such a good idea,* he thought.

"Watch your step, Dog." He grinned to himself at the thought of the four legged animal losing his footing.

Fang followed along behind, his wet nose twitched, testing the damp air. The smell of the sea, with a hint of the cloying stench of something dead came to him on the heavy air.

Halfdan thought he must be getting close to the end of the cliff trail. Seldom had he taken the time to hike to the top, especially on a foggy day, so he was unsure. He realized the fog was thinning as he climbed, near objects had lost their fuzziness as the opaqueness dissipated. Tatters of the damp blanket that had held his senses in check gradually fell away. The air between the fog top and the bottom of the leaden clouds sagged with moisture. Haze imparted a fuzzy texture between the layers, but the air was clear enough to see a goodly distance in spite of this impediment. He turned in a half circle, surveying the area to the south and southeast, looking for columns of smoke rising through the still air of the fog layer, the Naskapi signal of danger. None were to be seen to the limit of his vision. Here and there a hilltop poked through the top of the fog layer. To the west, out over the coast of the inland sea, the fog layer had become patchy as the morning breezes freshened under the influence of the sun's warmth. He saw open water here and there. Thoughts of the men on the four ships he had sent out there came to mind. He knew there would be no problems with the new ships on their shakedown cruise. Thorgill and Hrafen might have a few issues with crew coordination as they broke in their new crews, but the ships had been built by experts, and they would perform as they should.

Thoughts of the missions of Athils and Sweyn came to the fore. They could return as early as tomorrow, with information on habitable islands they had found. In thinking about these two men and their ships, he came to make a decision that he had avoided. If they found an island suitable for settlement, he would evacuate the women with small children before the Anishinabeg made their move, rather than wait for a warning that the attack was imminent. With the evacuation accomplished, everybody that remained at Halfdansfjord would not have to worry about the mothers' safety.

He felt more at ease now that he had grappled with one of his major decisions. Not feeling the need to return to the settlement just yet, he took a seat on a damp ledge, and leaned back against a handy flat rock. Fang jumped up beside him, and he pulled the dog's front quarters onto his lap.

The two sat that way, looking out over the panorama before them. The man slowly relaxed. His mind gradually cleared until he began to doze in the warmth of the morning sunshine. The dog glanced occasionally at the man as his eyes moved here and there, examining the countryside as far as he could see. Finding nothing requiring his attention, he looked at the man once more. A feeling of lassitude and contentment came over the normally watchful animal. He sighed, licked his chops, and lowered his head onto his forelegs that crossed the man's lap. He blinked a couple times, closed his eyes, and dozed.

The next midday Sweyn and Thorgill arrived back at Halfdansfjord. By the time Athils and Hrafen came in later, the shadows had lengthened, and the council had gathered around the chamber's trestle table for the evening meal.

With their two ships secured on the landing beach, the last two captains to arrive and their crews headed for the council chambers, where they knew other members of the council and most of the population would be gathered as they got something to eat, and talked about their day with friends and kinsmen.

Like any day in their free and open society, people gathered almost daily in the big council chamber at day's end. Kettles of stew or chowder warming on the hearth, trenchers of meat joints, and baskets of bread beckoned. Most of those gathered visited in subdued tones, or sat watching what others were doing.

Children of all ages were a part of the mix. Like the adults, all were engaged in some activity, only with them it revolved around some mischief, playing games, eating, talking with their friends, chasing their friends, a dog or cat that happened by, or some such. Adults seldom admonished the children, although anybody could do so, they just seemed to run amuck without supervision, especially during any gathering. Amazingly they stayed away from the trestle table where the leaders habitually sat; apparently knowing intuitively that to cause a commotion there might not be in their best interests.

The only difference in this gathering and any other was that almost everybody in the village was there, or at least among those that came and went. Halfdan had noticed that the chamber was literally bulging at its seams with his people. He looked up from a bowl of chowder occasionally as he watched the goings on. He was looking up when his last two captains and their men entered the chamber. He waved Thorgill and Hrafen over.

"Get something to eat, and then we will talk."

Athils and Sweyn were sitting together as they normally did. As they ate a bowl of chowder, they had their heads together talking about the islands they had found and explored. Athils glanced at Halfdan, who had finished eating and sat with his legs crossed over a corner of the table, picking his teeth with the point of broken skewer.

Halfdan got to his feet and refilled his cup with the thick broth of the chowder. Drinking it down, he tossed the empty cup in a basket of other dirty food containers.

On the way back to his high seat, he spoke directly to Athils. "All right, let us hear about these islands you found."

The room gradually quieted as people focused on the table of their leaders.

"Sweyn and I came across Thorgill and Hrafen after we had been out there for three days. As you know there are many islands in the inland sea, but there are only two that we landed on and explored that have everything we would need to build another settlement. Hrafen and I landed on a big island that he found a couple days before. We spent the night ashore, but we had to keep two big fires going so the white bears did not eat us."

The men at the table all laughed at what they considered a joke.

"No, he is serious," added Hrafen. "We have never seen so many bears in one place. Game animals of all kinds are in abundance, including every kind of seal I have ever seen. That is why there are so many bears."

"How big is this island," asked Halfdan?

Athils beckoned Hrafen with a lift of his chin. "Tell him what you found, Hrafen."

"I thought the island was part of the west coast of the inland sea when I first got sight of it. It took two days to sail around it. The strait between the island and the mainland is narrow, because I suspect much of it is shoals of mud from several big rivers that flow into the sea there. I do not know how many. I did not explore that, only the island. There are three small islands in the strait also." He paused, his eyes on Athils.

"There are beaches along the south shore, that is where we landed," said Athils. "We pitched our tents, made camp, and then split into two parties and did a little exploring. There are many lakes, all the timber we would ever need, game animals in profusion, including the bears we mentioned, moose, caribou, and deer. The south side where we landed has several valleys close to the landing beach that would provide shelter from the wind. Hrafen and I think this island is big enough that we would not be able to hunt it out, and it is far enough away from the Anishinabeg that they probably would not bother us. We found signs of other natives, but we think they are Naskapi who hunt on the island." He looked at Hrafen, who nodded in agreement.

"Sweyn, what did you find," said Halfdan.

"We explored an island that is just a few leagues from here. Thorgill will tell you about it," said Sweyn expansively, for him. He waved a hand to Thorgill.

The other men laughed dutifully at Sweyn's reluctance to talk, or be the center of attention.

A smiling Thorgill got to his feet. "I have not seen the other island that you just heard about. It sounds ideal. The island that Sweyn and I explored is unique, I think, because of the natural fjord on the south side that gives complete protection to any ship there, and protects a perfect site to build another settlement. It is not a big island, and it is not visible from the mainland. We sailed around it in half a day. There are many small fjords and safe harbors all the way around the island. The island seems to have everything we use, timber, lakes, streams, and clouds of ducks and geese, but we saw no large animals beyond a beach full of seals. It is close to the mainland here, but the open water of the inland sea is often rough through there. I do not think the Anishinabeg would try to invade us there because of the open water. It would be dangerous by canoe, I think." He left it at that, his eyes on Halfdan, waiting for him to speak.

Halfdan nodded his thanks for the reports. Getting to his feet, he began to pace around the long table where his men were seated.

"It sounds like either of these islands would be good for us. For now, I would prefer that we try to stay closer to this shoreline, because of our many Naskapi friends. If we have to evacuate our settlement later, the big island* to the west may be the best place for us. We will have time to thoroughly explore before making up our minds. Tomorrow morning I want the mothers with children evacuated to the smaller island** that Sweyn and Thorgill explored, rather than wait until we know the Anishinabeg are coming." He paused, looking around the room.

"It appears most of you mothers are here, that is good. Now you know what we are going to do. You will be told when to be ready to board the ships."

He expected some discussion from his captains. There was none. His men had expected him to tell them what he wanted. To a man they knew the struggle their chieftain had gone through with this business that faced their people.

Halfdan smiled at them. Every man made eye contact with him. "So be it then. In the morning, load up everything they will need to camp on the closest island for a while. I want all eight ships to transport them and their goods. Tostig, you are in charge of the ships. Put Helge in charge of putting the encampment to rights. Make fast work of this. I do not know how much time we have left. I will stay here with a small force until such time as the work on the island is finished, then I want you all to come back here with four ships, leaving four ships safely beached in this fjord you found. Leave only enough men with the women and children to protect them from any problems that might arise. All the rest of you, every available man, come back here. We will use the four ships full of armed men against them. It worked well the last time they attacked us."

*Present day -- * Akimiski Island, ** Charlton Island -- James Bay, Canada*

He paused a moment. "Who is out on picket?"

"Thorgeirr, I was to relieve him in the morning," said Tostig.

"Send somebody to recall him. We will not have picket ships out anymore. I want a man atop the cliff during daylight hours. It is easier and more effective than manning a ship. The guard can see over the bay for many leagues, and sound a horn to warn us immediately that he sees something."

Halfdan looked at his men. "Have we forgotten anything?"

"What about our livestock," asked Tostig? "We cannot leave them here if there is to be a siege, they would only be in our way."

"You are right. Move all the small livestock to the island. Leave the horses; they can fend for themselves until we round them up after this fight is over." He asked a direct question. "Do we still have sufficient dried food left over from last summer to sustain us during a long siege?"

Tostig's answer included another issue that nobody had mentioned.

"Aye, we are sending dried fish and meat to the island. We will have more than enough remaining for a siege. There is also this year's barley crop. The grain will be dry enough to harvest soon, and the crop is so heavy we will have more grain than we have ever had at any one time. We can harvest it while waiting for the Anishinabeg. They will set it afire if we do not harvest it. The stand is so dense and heavy that it could set fire to the west and north palisade walls. The shocks can be piled in one of the ships for transport to the island."

Halfdan nodded appreciatively. "You are right, Tostig, make it so when the time comes."

"I will, Halfdan." He looked around the table until his eyes fell on Helge. "You had best build a granary, too, Helge."

"Aye, I will." He grinned at the table at large. "I knew you would find more to do. I think we will need to make beer out of some of that extra grain."

The others laughed, knowing that Helge always got the work done without complaint, and he made good beer.

Their people had always made beer from excess barley not securely stored in varmint proof granaries. Beer, a food source from time immemorial, had long been a favored way to save the barley berries from the legions of such pests. The swollen barley berries left from the beer making process was then fed to the livestock. The pigs especially seemed to relish the yeasty taste of the spent grain.

Halfdan smiled to himself as he watched his men in their good-natured chiding of one another over who made the best beer. Others of a more serious bent talked over what he had decreed for all of them. He felt great pride. *Anything can be accomplished with such men at my side.*

The meeting broke up soon after, the men joining the crowd of onlookers. Tostig sent Hrafen to recall Thorgeirr's ship, so he could come in before full darkness. Other men were dispatched to each of the longhouses, to make certain that all the mothers knew where and when to assemble with their goods and children the next morning. There were no surprises, the people expected the evacuation, just not this soon, but all saw the wisdom of an early departure.

They had a plan, one that might work with a little help from the gods.

The island was beautiful to behold, and seemed to have an abundance of small animals. Clouds of ducks and geese filled the air as they came and went from the lakes and sloughs nearby. Not a single large land animal, beyond seals, had been seen. No white bears had been seen either, allowing the livestock tenders to heave a collective sigh of relief.

Although not as protected as Halfdansfjord from the incessant north wind and frequent rain squalls off the vast reaches of the inland sea, the island's dense spruce forest to the north filtered the worst of the onslaught. The south facing beach overlooked a narrow fjord. This fjord was oriented in such a way that the stunted timber clustered thickly around its three sides afforded some protection from the elements except an easterly wind. The fjord inlet, the only access point to the protected fjord, opened to the east and could not be seen from the waters of the inland sea until a looker was close inshore.

All eight ships had been utilized to transport the 85-women and their children, as well as the large group of men to build the encampment, to the island. With Sweyn and Thorgill in the lead, each vessel dropped their sail and entered the fjord cautiously, powered by sweeps alone. In line astern, each ship had a man in the bow plying a plummet to determine depth of water under the keel in the unfamiliar anchorage. In short order all eight ships had beached on the north shore of the fjord and their crews secured them.

Tostig dispatched armed men in three directions to secure the landing site and explore inland for possible threats. Within the hour they returned and reported to Tostig and the other captains.

Helge's group came in first. His report put the leaders at ease.

"We found no sign of anybody else here. There are lots of small wildlife of all kinds, but we saw no large animal sign or bear sign." Helge pointed off in the direction he came from. "There is a big peat bog over there, where peat can be cut and dried for fuel."

"Good, get some men out there with slanes to start cutting and drying a fuel supply."

The rest of the people disembarked and scattered out to explore the beach area and the nearby forest verge.

Each ship carried some of the livestock they had brought off the mainland with them. The younger animals had never been aboard ship and their panicked bleating and bawling frayed many tempers of the participants trying to get them on and off the ships expeditiously. By dint of shouted oaths, the application of a rope end when needed, and more than a little pushing and shoving, the task was accomplished.

The livestock were released from their confinement during the short voyage and roamed at will on the island, while under the watchful eye of some of the older children, who kept them from straying too far. Fodder of many varieties was abundant. If the need arose in the future, there were plenty of materials close at hand to build livestock shelters and pens. It all depended on the length of their stay. For the time being, the animals presented no problems, they never strayed far. Each night they sought their accustomed security, to bed down in close proximity to the people that protected them.

Lemmings in unusual numbers were among the small animals of the island. Always a favored food animal, they soon became a part of the daily fare.

The succulent rodents were fat, easy to harvest, and their meat provided a seemingly endless supply for the stew pots.

The encampment's children became the hunters of this multitude. In the beginning, no expertise was required to hunt animals that had never before been hunted by man. Throwing sticks, clubs, and bows and arrows all worked equally well. Stomping even worked in the packed masses. Stealth was unnecessary with the little critters. The cacophony of shrieking pursuers, the favored method of the hunt, actually helped in the harvest. After the rodents became wary of the shrieking methods employed, some of the men showed the children how to set up catch nets between stakes driven into the ground. This method worked much better than those previously employed on the scurrying rodents.

Hunting always involves butchering, and most of the children got quite adept at removing the hide and entrails to make them ready for the stew pot. This odious task was certainly not as much fun as the chase, but necessary nonetheless.

The animals were so easy to catch that the frequency of the hunt as well as the numbers of the hunters had to be modified, taking into account the current need for more meat for the larder. Like everything else with children, the novelty eventually wore off. Many of the girls and smaller boys went on to other pursuits, leaving only a few of the older boys with the sense of duty to continue.

Tostig and Helge shared responsibility for the building efforts. Except for the 50-man security force with Halfdan, virtually every other available person was present on the island. Everyone got into the spirit of the effort and suggestions came from all quarters as the construction efforts progressed.

The perfect weather had allowed the large contingent of men and women workers to erect the necessary windbreaks for the tents. Selected spruce was felled, cut to length for posts, and set into the ground one axe handle apart. The long limbs that were cut off the tree trunks before the posts were measured and cut were stripped of their small branches. These supple, stripped limbs, laced horizontally between the upright spruce posts, became the wattle walls. The tops of the windbreaks thus created were taller than a man.

The quadrangle of tents was protected from the wind behind the four wattle windbreaks. These were purposely not joined at the corners, but overlapped so the people could walk in or out at each corner. The wattle was not daubed, the normal circumstance with such structures, because of the temporary nature of the encampment. The wattle windbreaks not only diffused the wind, they created a sense of openness for the occupants, and their overlapped corners eliminated the need for gates.

It was decided during the construction of the encampment that a wattle, three-sided, roofed shed would be needed for the communal hearth. Although the camp was temporary, nobody knew how long it would be needed, so everything had been done with a certain degree of permanency for the comfort and security of the residents.

The concerted effort by many people had quickly produced a comfortable and secure bivouac on the north shore of the fjord, with the desired southerly exposure to take advantage of the sun's warmth. The natural stands of black spruce and the wattle windbreaks protected the residents of the encampment from the constant aggravation of the wind and frequent rain squalls. Enough of a breeze remained after filtering through the trees and the windbreaks to afford some protection in the encampment from the clouds of insect pests that hovered over the water of the inland sloughs and lakes. Smudge fires and clothing that covered everything but faces and hands also helped in this effort.

Two days after arrival, and after a day of hard labor, the end of the hectic building period on the island was declared to be finished. All the major building projects were completed; all that remained were incidentals. They had done it in just two complete days, and Tostig and the people were very pleased with the outcome.

The tired people had gathered around the peat fire in the communal hearth for their evening meal. Braziers and oil lamps lit the interior of the shed, reflecting off the inside of the sod roof, the yellowish light illuminated the faces of all present. People milled about, getting something to eat, and then leaving to let another do the same. The hearth shed was not big enough to accommodate everyone at once, but then, it was not intended to.

A waxing three quarter moon rose in the east to shine over the island. People coming and going around the hearth shed commented that the moon seemed especially bright for its phase, almost as if it were a harbinger of the god's pleasure. With their lives in a state of flux, a feeling that the gods approved of their actions was certainly welcome.

First light the next morning brought into view gray, lowering skies with a threat of more rain. Tostig and several other men were shaking off the chill of morning around the communal hearth, drinking cups of hot broth left over from the night before. They had been talking about the eight ships of the flotilla drawn up beam-to on the broad pebbled beach of the island's fjord. Neither the ships within the fjord, nor any of the tents and shelters inside the wattle windbreaks could be seen except from the inlet entrance to the narrow fjord. It was thought to be an ideal place of concealment.

Some supplies had remained securely stowed aboard while the encampment was built. Now that storage and dwelling structures were built, it was time to empty the holds of the ships.

"As soon as everybody is awake and had something to warm their bellies, get gangplanks rigged from the ships' sides to the beach, so we can get the rest of our cargoes unloaded." Tostig said, speaking to the group at large.

Shortly thereafter people began pitching in to unload the remainder of the dried food, and both hard and soft goods. With more arriving every moment after they bolted down a cup of hot chowder, the job was finished quickly.

Tostig and the other captains had let others do the unloading while they talked over plans for the day.

"I am anxious to get back to Halfdansfjord. As soon as the men are assembled, we will set sail. I have thought over how many men to leave here. All the women and many of the older children are adept in the usage of some form of weapon, so I have decided to leave only 12-men. These men, with some of the women to help, can crew the four ships remaining in the fjord if necessary. The ships are their lifeline, should the Anishinabeg find this place."

His decision had come without hesitation or discussion. This was the first the other men had heard of his decision. A doubt over the correct actions to take insofar as the island's security detail had pulled at the edges of his conscious mind. He kept it tucked away, but it was always there, and he felt its lurking presence. Initially he did not know that the ships' captains agreed with his assessment, for he had not asked them. Tostig had been chosen by Halfdan as his lieutenant. To a man, that was good enough for his fellow captains.

Imbued with a forthright nature, his leadership qualities had matured to the point that even the bluster of Thorgill, Hrafen, and Brodir could not sway his opinion once made. He was no Gudbjartur, but he was a good, strong man, secure in his own skin. Affirmation of his decisions came from an unexpected source.

"Halfdan left the size of the security force for the protection of the women and children that are to remain on this island up to you, Tostig. To me, that means you speak for Halfdan." Brodir pulled at the matted curls of his beard.

"I appreciate that, Brodir. Although I harbored some doubt, now that I made my decision I will stand by it. As for the disposition of the ships, I have decided to leave the four largest vessels here. We will all return to Halfdansfjord in the four smaller ships. All four are less than half the length of Halfdan's Steed of the Sea, and Thorgeirr's big ship, and will be quicker to maneuver in a fight."

"I think we all agree with your decision," said Bjorn. "It takes fewer rowers to propel them, leaving more men to fight."

The others agreed. Without further discussion the men scattered to the four ships, where everybody not remaining on the island had begun boarding.

As always for a sailing, those left behind straggled down to the shoreline. One of them was Thora and her young son. She had harbored a feeling of disquiet that only worsened as time went by. She had vehemently resisted Halfdan's decree that all the mothers and their young children were to be evacuated to a place of safety until this business with the Anishinabeg came to an end. It was the possible end that bothered her, but she begrudgingly gave in to her chieftain. Deskaheh had been paramount on her mind while she worked with the others on the island encampment. She wanted to be with him and the rest of her people, not stuck on an island away from everything that mattered to her for only the gods knew how long. She missed Frida, and her heart still ached over Ingerd. The continuing hostility of some of the native tribes had made life increasingly hard to fathom, not to mention the danger posed for all of them. Life could have been so wonderful in this land if everybody just got along, but she knew that would never happen, ever.

All of this was going through Thora's mind as she moved along the beach with the others, following the ships as the men aboard pushed out from the shoreline. She was not alone, all the women harbored similar thoughts.

The long sweeps rattled through the sweep holes in the ships' sides, and the crews began the rhythmic rowing that propelled the four ships toward the fjord entrance. Shouted farewells went back and forth with more than the usual emotion, as those ashore expressed their heartfelt appreciation for all the hard work that had been done in their behalf. First one ship and then another raised its sails to the masthead as they cleared the fjord entrance, heeled to the press of the wind, and sped away east toward Halfdansfjord.

The men were going to do battle with an implacable enemy, and nobody knew what the outcome would be. All felt in their hearts that many faces would disappear from among their people. That was a certainty. This might even be the beginning of the end for the Norse people in Vinland. Only the gods knew.

⁂

Thora watched the ships out of sight, sighed resignedly and returned to where she had left her son. She had kept a watchful eye on him as she moved along with the crowd on the beach, so she knew he was still playing in the patch of sandy dirt beside the moose hide she had spread for them to sit on. He was as she had left him, completely absorbed in the tableau of strategically placed pebbles, little pieces of driftwood, and rocks in the make-believe world he had created for himself.

Busy with his diorama, the boy did not look up when Thora stepped onto the hide and took her seat. She reclined against the Thalmiut backrest that she never took for granted. Since Halfdan and Frida brought them back... *How long ago was that; last summer, the summer before?* She could not recall exactly.

The simple, rawhide bound, wooden frames were replicated by Norse wood-workers, becoming a feature of every longhouse. Collapsible and handy to recline against, the backrest eased a tired back. She had always been thankful for the comfort they provided.

Gathering her sewing onto her lap she watched her son for a time, marveling that he was so absorbed in the world he had created. He sat with both his fat little legs thrust out front. In the v-shaped area created between his legs, to the limit of his reach, he had placed the pieces of his world, interconnected by trails traced in the sand by his fingertips.

Her mind wandered as she began her work again. Thoughts of Ingerd and Frida came to mind, as they always did at such times. Thinking of Ingerd always brought tears to her eyes. She swiped ineffectually at the mist that blurred her vision. She missed Ingerd horribly. Deep in her heart, the feeling of dread that always rose up choked her. Shaking the feeling away, she concentrated on Frida. They had spent tearful times together, both trying unsuccessfully to quell the anguish that thoughts of their dear friend inevitably brought to the fore. Frida was a strong woman, but even she could not stop the flow of tears. She missed Frida; missed talking to her, missed just seeing her each day. Not knowing what had happened to their friend was the worst of it. They knew in their hearts that Ingerd was lost forever to them, but their struggle continued nonetheless. The passage of a lot more time would be required before the dull ache left their hearts and minds, if ever.

Thora's focus changed when she saw Rannveig and Gudrun approaching. She quickly got control of her raging emotions before greeting them. She welcomed the company, glad to push her previous thoughts into the background. Soon she found herself engaged in animated conversation with both of them, as though they had been there with her all along.

Both women were carrying their babies in the same kind of cradleboards used by the Naskapi. Over time, all the Norse women had adopted the cradleboards for their babies; they just made sense, leaving the mother's hands free to do her work.

Both women also carried their sewing bags over their shoulders, in addition to their cradleboards. After propping the cradleboards up against a large boulder protruding from the ground next to Thora's moose hide rug, they sat down. Pulling their sewing out, they both began to work without conscious thought. Conversation flowed unabated for a time on the good and bad aspects of their lives on the island. They all agreed that the island was beautiful, and now that a slack period had presented itself after their encampment was completed, they further agreed that exploratory walks in the near future to see the sights were in order. They did not like living in tents again, as they had before Halfdansfjord. They decided that they missed the comfort and warmth of the longhouses -- tents were so drafty. But, at the same time they all agreed with the decision to get them moved to a safer place. After talking about everything that had happened recently the conversation finally settled on the one topic nobody wanted to address.

"I am afraid for our men," said Rannveig. "There are so few of them. How can they fight all the Anishinabeg warriors that will attack our settlement?"

Gudrun quickly agreed. Both women looked to Thora for an answer.

Thora did not respond immediately. Looking back and forth from the women to her work, she seemed to be considering her answer. During this silent period, she used a length of twisted wool yarn, in which she had tied knots corresponding to the length of her son's arms and legs, to cut out the front and back pieces of a pair of loose-legged trousers with her scissors. Finishing one piece, she looked up at the two women.

"We all have thought of little else. Truthfully, I do not know the answer. I am glad that I do not have to make the decision."

"Last summer our men fought them to a standstill," offered Gudrun hopefully. "Maybe they can do it again."

"Frida told me that the Anishinabeg war chief called the retreat when he saw Halfdan's Talisman of Life, given to him by Chisasi. That is why they left. I do not think that will happen next time."

"I had not heard that before," said Gudrun. "What does Deskaheh say about the Anishinabeg, Thora?"

Thora's eyes went back and forth as she looked at each woman in turn. "He said they will keep attacking us, until all the men and most of the women are dead. They will take the survivors away for slaves."

"By the gods! What of the children?"

"He said most would be adopted into the tribe."

"Now I am wondering why we did not just move away and find another place to live," said Rannveig.

"It is too late now. Deskaheh told me that Halfdan and the council decided that would not work either. Any new place would probably have similar problems," said Thora.

Her statement effectively ended further speculation. Their silence spoke to their feelings of helplessness and isolation from events on the mainland.

Unknown to anybody on the island, events in and around Halfdansfjord were taking a turn. Whether that turn would be good or bad for the survival of the Greenlanders in Nitassinan remained to be seen.

⸺◦◦◦⸺

HALFDANSFJORD, FIVE DAYS LATER

The moon's brilliant crescent would grow steadily smaller and dimmer until about sixteen days had passed, and then the night sky and the land below, would be as dark as it gets for two full nights before a sliver of the new moon would reappear. Traditionally, it was a period when bad things happened.

Chisasi and a large group of warriors had arrived at Halfdansfjord the evening before for that very reason, the coming darkness. The long column came from the riverbank to the northwest, as usual, and the tall form of Chisasi led them as they wound their way through the stubble of the recently harvested barley field toward the north gate.

The tower guard sounded no alarm horn. He recognized Chisasi at the head of the column of armed men as their Naskapi friends from the Loon Lake village of Antanak.

Beyond a cursory nod to the tower guard's greeting as he walked through the north gate Chisasi offered no verbal response other than a single word, "Halfdan?"

The guard pointed toward the council chambers and Chisasi headed that way.

Most of his warriors dropped out of the column as they passed through the edge of the commons, where much of the settlement's daily activities took place. Greetings were exchanged as the men mingled with those engaged in various activities around the many sheds and tables.

As he walked to the council chambers, Chisasi thought it unusual that there were so few women about. Intense activity at the smithy was evidenced by black smoke billowing from the roof's smoke hole. The men and a few women scattered out over the commons worked on weapons in various stages of completion. Through the open south gate, he also saw that there were only four ships visible on the landing beach, where there should be eight ships. He knew then that the warning he carried would not be a surprise to Halfdan.

Chisasi and six of his men entered the open double doors of the big long-house to find Halfdan in conversation with a group of his men. He recognized them as the leaders of their people. *We have arrived in time for a council with them,* he thought. *That is good.*

A look of pleasure crossed Halfdan's face when he saw Chisasi. He got to his feet to greet the man with whom he had developed a friendship. Those with him mingled easily with their visitors, making the Naskapi men feel welcome around the table.

Chisasi noted that Deskaheh had been seated near Halfdan. He voiced the traditional greeting of his people to him, which Deskaheh returned.

After pleasantries were dispensed with, and with Deskaheh's help, Halfdan got right to it.

"What brings you here, Chisasi," asked Halfdan?

"Antanak sends his greetings to you."

Halfdan responded in kind.

Chisasi pointed to two of the men with him, neither of whom Halfdan knew. "These men are two of many that Sachem has sent to call our tribe to war. All the bands will send men here to your settlement as a result of the summons from Sachem, to meet the Anishinabeg. My men and I will wait here until the others come. We will face the Anishinabeg together, with all of you." He swept his arm to include all of Halfdansfjord.

Halfdan understood some of it without translation. His face registered surprise as Deskaheh translated and he understood the full import of Chisasi's words.

"Why would you do that? The Anishinabeg are your kinsmen."

"Nesatin insulted Sachem when he rejected his overture of peace. Sachem does not think the Anishinabeg will want to fight if we all join with you and your people. We will give them this choice." Chisasi smiled. "Besides, we often have disagreements and we fight once in a while; it clears the air and fosters respect."

Halfdan considered this momentous twist in the fate of his people as Deskaheh finished his translation. He did not feel like returning Chisasi's smile, not yet. What he felt was humility, a feeling he was not accustomed to. The Naskapi were risking everything to side with his people.

Halfdan slowly shook his head in wonder. His eyes travelled over all those watching him and Chisasi, finally settling on the war chief.

The hard man who had become his friend watched him closely, his face once again showing no emotion. He waited while Halfdan, obviously struggling to understand what his announcement meant to the Norse, regained control of his churning thoughts.

"I am humbled by this, Chisasi. That your people would do this for us..." His voice trailed off. "You risk everything to give us hope, Chisasi."

"Battles between all of us in this land happen almost every summer. It has always been so. We have fought the Anishinabeg before. We will fight them again. The battles end when honor is satisfied. Warriors return to their villages, most living to fight another day."

Halfdan digested this revelation in silence, still moved by what he considered a supreme sacrifice from the Naskapi Nation. If it came to a fight, many would die in spite of what Chisasi said. He knew it and so did Chisasi.

"When do you think they will attack?"

"They will come during the dark of the moon."

"I would do that too," said Halfdan, nodding with approval. "We have a few days, then, from the dark of the old moon until the sliver of the new moon appears in the night sky."

Chisasi inclined his head in agreement.

"So be it then." He waved Chisasi and his men to seats at the long trestle table. The first of many meetings on strategy began.

Over the next three days there would be many more such gatherings of leaders as canoes filled with warriors poured into Halfdansfjord.

※

South of Halfdansfjord, all along the main watercourse leading to the bay where the settlement was located, canoes filled with Naskapi warriors rode on the slow moving current toward the rendezvous ordered by Sachem, the supreme leader of all of them.

Greetings were exchanged with new arrivals, but the general air was subdued as most men held council with their own thoughts. The warriors were mentally prepared for war. Whether that happened remained to be seen, but the reality of the situation dampened all but the occasional attempt at levity.

All-out war with a numerically superior foe was a sobering thought. Many battles had been fought over the years with the Anishinabeg, with the reasons for conflict running the full gambit from minor disagreements to the attempted purloining of hunting or fishing rights. A few skirmishes normally solved the issues so that the aggrieved tribe or band felt vindicated and everybody could go home satisfied with the outcome. This time the grievance was too serious to solve with a few gestures and feints. An affair of honor was involved.

On this final day of the journey that had been long for many of them, the rigors of daily travel showed on the drawn faces of many of the paddlers. Their numbers kept swelling as other canoes full of men joined the flotilla from tributaries along the way as they all progressed down the river toward the bay. The numbers were unprecedented. With bands of Naskapi scattered all over the vast homeland of Nitassinan, never before had there been so many of them in one place.

A large group of canoes clustered in mid-river, floating on the slow current like a raft of dry leaves. Except for an occasional flick of a paddle to alter course or position, the men rested on their paddles as the current bore them downstream.

Many of the canoes in this particular group came from the village of Sachem. Their numbers fluctuated as new arrivals came and went. The focus of attention was the canoe that held Glooscap, Nipishish, Kejo, and Atkaa. New arrivals wanted the latest gossip, but they also wanted to see the famous pale skin.

Nipishish smiled and nodded at the new arrivals, all strangers to him. The men regarded him with open curiosity as everyone rested on paddles held athwart their canoes and visited with friends and acquaintances not often seen. Introductions, cursory at best, were shouted throughout the scattered canoes as they drifted downstream. Nipishish's eventual acceptance by the men of the other bands resulted from his camaraderie with everyone else as well as his friendly overtures toward them. Conversation and reverie gradually subsided, giving way to the drudgery of paddling.

Most of the strangers to him had only heard tales of his exploits that were fast becoming the stuff of legend among the people. The man was held in high regard by the Naskapi, most of them anyway. A few of the new arrivals were more reserved than the men that saw him daily. Jealousy is a natural human condition, and it manifested itself in this gathering.

Nipishish took the overall attention in stride, as he did most things in life. He encountered jealousy occasionally, even among those he lived with. He recognized that he was an outsider, no matter what had transpired since his capture and subsequent bonding with the band of Glooscap. He was still not Naskapi, although he felt like he was. Being an interloper among them would always set him apart. Any indication of jealousy or anger toward him never failed to awaken a feeling of unease. He was finely attuned to any sense of impending danger. His open, enthusiastic nature could change instantly to something else entirely. In his world that is how one stayed alive. His close friends, Glooscap and Kejo, were acutely aware of his volatile nature. They knew that this trait was the reason he had been Halfdan's war chief, his second in command.

Canoes continued to come and go, promoting an often boisterous air as the milling flotilla floated down the river. A shout from a canoe near the outer edge of the main cluster, changed all that.

"Gudbj, Gudbj!" The shout rose above the hubbub of many voices.

Surprised, Nipishish turned toward the sound of his name, seeing a paddle waving above the press. At a distance, he did not recognize the man at first, nor was the voice familiar. Although he was attired like all of them, he sported a short beard, a dead giveaway -- he was obviously a Norseman.

The canoe that the man rode in jostled its way forward toward Nipishish. As it drew closer, the man shouted joyfully once again.

"Gudbj, it is me, Snorri!" The words were in the Norse language.

It took Nipishish a moment to switch his thoughts from the sound of the Naskapi language he had grown accustomed to, and back into the Norse of the past.

"Snorri?" His face reflected the surprise and confusion he felt over an encounter he had not expected. "It has been a long time. I have not seen you since we were captured."

"Aye it has."

The two canoes were side by side now; the occupants gripped the gunwales of each to keep them together.

"Where is Gaut?" Nipishish asked. Recalling that the last time he saw Snorri, Gaut the Hunter had been with him as a captive.

Snorri looked around at the milling canoes. "He is here."

"I heard that only two men of my expedition were still alive. Until I saw you I did not know which two."

Snorri nodded, his face wore a pained expression as he blurted out some of his story. "We thought we were going to be killed in the beginning. They kept us separated, so I did not even know that anybody else was alive. Then word came from Sachem and everything changed. We became one with the people and most of them gradually accepted us. Both of us have mates and my woman just had a little boy." He grinned.

Other men of the group had been conferring with friends and kinsmen from canoe to canoe, but their conversations trailed off as the strange sound of the Norse language had its effect on everybody within earshot. The guttural language began to agitate some of them.

Noticing this, Kejo spoke for the first time. "Speak in the tongue of the people, Nipishish, so that others may understand."

Nipishish turned to look at his friend. He nodded when he caught the chin bob, suddenly aware that the friendly atmosphere among the occupants of the nearby canoes had undergone a subtle change, and not for the best.

Snorri, always one who did not require constant direction to get the drift of any situation, switched to Naskapi. "I have heard this name, Nipishish, and I have heard the tale of how you got that name. Axeman, it suits you, Gudbj." He bobbed his chin in a gesture to the axe, slung over his erstwhile commander's shoulder. "I see you still have the axe."

"Aye, I do. It is an old friend."

The general mood among the men that had stopped talking when the sound of the Norse language intruded gradually changed. The buzz of many conversations gradually picked up as though nothing had happened.

The gaggle of canoes continued their drift downstream, the milling continued as men came and went. Nipishish's conversation with Snorri ran its course and the two canoes drifted away from one another.

After a time, Nipishish turned and winked at Kejo. Both men knew and understood what had been averted by the change of spoken language.

Kejo smiled at his friend. "You are one of us now, Nipishish. You do not look like we do, but we can overlook that."

Glooscap and Atkaa, the other occupants of the canoe, both laughed aloud.

"No he does not look like us," said Glooscap, normally a man not given to public displays of humor or affection. "He is beginning to think like us, though."

The others grunted without comment. By unspoken agreement, first one and then another began to paddle and the canoe moved away from the others.

Nipishish watched the countryside ahead unfold as they picked up speed. For a time they were almost alone on their stretch of river. He noted that the shadows had begun to lengthen as midday gave way to late afternoon. He recognized the mouth of the stream where he and Halfdan had taken his sons and their friend Yola on their first big game hunt. Memories of the hunt flooded his mind. It all seemed so long ago. *Little Yola,* he thought. *What a waste of a young boy's life.* He had not thought of the hunt or the loss of Yola for some time. So much had happened since then; it was hard to focus on the past, or the future for that matter, with so much happening in the here and now.

His introspection brought forth fleeting thoughts of his sons. Ivar was gone for good. That he knew for certain. The thought that he might fight his own son one day sobered him. Stranger things had happened in this life. Lothar, on the other hand, had enthusiastically embraced the Naskapi culture, as had he.

Random thoughts came and went as the riverbanks sped by. He started slightly as a raft of ducks burst into the air from the still water formed by a back eddy, surprised as they dabbled in the shallows for food on the bottom. Their quacks of alarm had others of their kind taking flight further downstream ahead of the swishing sound made by the passage of the canoe.

His thoughts returned to what Glooscap had said earlier. *I have begun to think like them. Their people seem more like my people now, than my own people.* A kaleidoscope of individual Naskapi faces appeared as his brain processed this revelation. He heard their voices, saw their smiles, their frowns, and heard their shouts. He smiled at the sound of their laughter as memories flooded through his conscious thoughts.

Since he and Ingerd had been apart for so long, even his thoughts and cravings for her had lessened with the passage of his time among the Naskapi people. When they were together, it was a happy time for both of them. He still loved her as much as he always had, or at least he liked to think so. There were no other women in his life, but he still had cravings. There was no reason for Ingerd to be away from him. It had been her choice. She had missed her good friends, Frida and Thora. She wanted to be with them rather than with him after the loss of Ivar. He understood that, her desire to be comforted by other women, but it was not good for their continued relationship, of that he was certain. He knew that she would always mourn the loss of Ivar. His thoughts of their son were more pragmatic. Ivar was a young man, he had made his choice, and that was the end of it as far as he was concerned. At the first opportunity after he arrived at Halfdansfjord, he must have a talk with Ingerd. It was time to determine if they intended to pick up their lives together and continue forward or continue to lead separate lives. He wanted an answer.

The forces that had governed life in this land had forged his heart and soul into another entity, another man. He realized that he had come to a fork in the trail of life. He would never again be Gudbjartur Einarsson, for he had chosen the other fork. He was Nipishish, the Axeman, Naskapi warrior.

His thoughts were jarred back to the present, when a hail from the canoe ahead of them announced that they had entered the bay and Halfdansfjord was visible on the far shoreline. He saw the columns of smoke rising into the still, humid air from the early evening cook fires. *It will be good to see everyone again. Hot food will be good for all of us.*

Chapter 13

DAYS OF RECKONING

At a hail from the south tower guard, Halfdan climbed the ladder to the tower. In answer to the question on Halfdan's face, the guard pointed along the shoreline to the east.

Light from the setting sun could be seen flashing off the paddles of many canoes as they streamed into the bay from the wide mouth of the distant river. Still too far away for details to be seen, the two men watched them closely.

The guard, Einar, normally Sweyn's helmsman when their ship was at sea, glanced at his silent chieftain. Unable to contain himself, he asked the question that had occurred to him when he first sighted the flashes of sunlight off the wet paddles, before he actually saw the canoes.

"How do we know they are Naskapi, Halfdan?"

Halfdan looked at the man. "We do not know, Einar."

Einar looked back at the mass of canoes, now scattered across a large area of the bay, obviously heading straight for the settlement. "I cannot tell who they are until they are almost here. I felt like I should sound the alarm. It looks like there are about 100-canoes. That could be 400 to 500 warriors." His voice rose in pitch as he finished making his point.

"When to give the alarm is your decision. I will never fault a guard that gives a false alarm, as you know. With the warriors that are already here, we have them outnumbered." He clapped Einar on the back. "There are two reasons I am not concerned, besides having them outnumbered. You alerted me to what you thought was a threat. That is good." He pointed to the southwest. "The enemy will come from that direction, around the south point at the mouth of the bay. You were at sea when they attacked last time, so you could not know the direction they came from." He started down the ladder. "The Naskapi pickets will send up smoke signals by day and signal fires by night when the Anishinabeg come. Then you will need to blow your horn, Einar."

Now that he understood a few things about what to expect, Einar felt better about his unfamiliar duties. He had been briefed on his duties, but not to the extent that Halfdan had just briefed him. His eyes swept the horizon in a half circle. The mass of canoes drawing closer with each stroke of their paddles held his attention for a moment before he looked back to the west at the sun's golden orb, its intense light defused by the heavy humid air. As the sun began to sink below the horizon, he looked back at the canoes. *They made it in time for hot food,* he thought, sniffing the air as the smell of roasting meat came to him from the fire pit.

NIPISHISH AND THE NASKAPI WAR PARTY

The flotilla continued to swell until there were now more than 100 canoes carrying between 500 and 600 warriors. More would join them during the third and last day of travel, making for a combined force of 650 to 750 men, a truly awesome host.

As the group of canoes around his own continued to paddle toward the distant settlement, Nipishish's mind replayed the chain of events that brought all of them here.

The council of all the tribal bands decision came after two days of heated debate that ended in deadlock. Sachem, as only he could do, gave a long eloquent speech giving consideration to the arguments of both sides. He then made the only decision possible given the circumstances. If the insult was allowed to pass without response, he reasoned with those present that much worse would occur next time. Mutual respect between possible adversaries had always been the only way open to peaceful coexistence. He further convinced the council that compromise eventually fostered disdain that ultimately led to more conflict. He wanted a strong response to this insult to the Naskapi people.

A large force would be gathered from the bands and dispatched to the town of the Greenlanders. Sachem's decision to confront the Anishinabeg in concert with the people of Halfdansfjord directly left little chance for compromise. Every Naskapi band was represented in this effort; there would be no turning back now.

It was generally felt that the Anishinabeg, under the war chief Shingoos, might decide after seeing the combined forces arrayed against them to hold a powwow rather than attack out of hand. If they decided to talk first, many lives could be spared. Only an apology to Sachem personally would be acceptable. Nobody really thought that would happen.

The problem between disparate peoples had always been one of mistrust and the inability to communicate well. It had always been so between the Naskapi and the Anishinabeg, although they were kinsmen. With the perceived insult by Nesatin's rejection of the Naskapi overture of peace, the kettle had boiled over.

At the conclusion of the final council before the call to war went out to all the Naskapi bands, Sachem chose Nipishish to be his personal emissary, because he understood the customs and language of both peoples.

Nipishish was humbled by the trust and responsibility this placed on him. This was not to say that he was in charge, he was not. His duty to Sachem involved ensuring the relationship between the Norse under the command of Halfdan, and the Naskapi did not present problems due to misunderstandings. The command of the Naskapi host fell to Glooscap, Chisasi, and the other war chiefs of each band. He thought this a cumbersome command structure – too many leaders – but felt a consensus would be reached making either Glooscap or Chisasi, both held in high regard by all the bands, would emerge in command of the Naskapi contingent.

Reflecting on the council meeting, Nipishish had to chuckle at Sachem's ability to manipulate all of them. The old man listened to every argument, and always managed to make a decision based on common sense that only a fool would disagree with. By choosing Nipishish as his emissary he placed responsibility on the one person among them with the most to lose, and the most to gain, thereby behooving him to make the best effort possible for all concerned. *A wily old fox*, thought Nipishish, laughing aloud.

"What is so funny?" Kejo said, interrupting his rhythmic cadence of paddling.

"I was just thinking how Sachem made me his emissary. He is a wise old man," Nipishish said, shaking his head in wonder. "Out of concern for you and to help you get over the loss of your friend when I was captured, he made you responsible for teaching me the ways of the People, the man who hated me the most. This was a wise thing to do."

"Yes, my friend. That is why he is the Sachem, he protects us from ourselves," Kejo said, smiling at Nipishish.

Conversation was interrupted as more canoes joined the flotilla from the last river that flowed into the bay prior to their arrival at Halfdansfjord. After greetings were exchanged, the combined canoes continued toward the settlement of Halfdansfjord, intent on finishing their long journey before darkness ended another day.

※

With the palisades of Halfdansfjord beginning to come in sight to the distant west, Nipishish found that he had conflicting emotions about this mission, about being here at all. Many moons had come and gone since his visit last winter, when they had brought Ingerd back. He knew there would have been many changes at Halfdansfjord: people died, babies were born, kinships forged, others dissolved for whatever reason; life had gone on and he had not been part of it.

"You must be glad to see your village again," observed Kejo, from just behind him."

Nipishish stopped paddling and turned to Kejo while considering how he felt. "I will be glad to see most of them, and that they have survived. On the other hand I am apprehensive about their continued survival, and about our survival." He gestured out over the large flotilla. "We have come to make war against a stronger enemy. Many of these men will die." He resumed paddling while he sorted the jumble of thoughts his own answer to Kejo's question had engendered. Given the grim resolve of the large group of warriors he accompanied from the Naskapi town of Sachem, he felt that this war would cause the women to wail throughout Nitassinan at their losses.

He estimated there were at least 150 men in the 35 canoes that set out from the beach at first light. Since that day, many more had joined them along the way. He had lost track, but in an earlier conversation with Kejo they had come to the conclusion that there had to be at least 400-500 warriors now, not counting those that had arrived in the recent past. They missed the final count by a considerable margin.

That his companions shared his thoughts was evidenced by a statement from Glooscap from the rearmost position in the canoe.

"These fights with the Anishinabeg happen from time to time. We have never had an all-out war with them before, just a few battles until everyone is satisfied and goes back home. This time they have lost respect for us. We have come to teach them to respect us once again."

"Aye, I have heard these things, but this time you have also come to defend the right of we Norse to live here in peace. I am afraid that fact alone will make this war different than the battles of the past."

"He is right, Glooscap," Kejo said. "It will be different because all of us will be fighting from behind the palisades of Halfdansfjord. That is not the way we normally fight with them."

The men lapsed into silence, the only sound the rhythmic splash and gurgle of the paddles propelling the canoe through the water.

The final night of the quarter moon shone weakly over the northland. The sliver often likened to a finger nail moon would shine for this last night before the full darkness of the moon blackened the night sky.

Over the past two days, the final contingents of Sachem's warriors had arrived. There could still be stragglers, but the war chiefs agreed that most had arrived. Naskapi warriors quickly integrated with the permanent residents of Halfdansfjord into what was hoped would be a cohesive fighting force. The process had been interesting. Nipishish worked tirelessly with all concerned, making certain the disparate groups of men -- many Naskapi warriors had never even seen a Norseman before -- accepted one another. That this transformation happened at all spoke well of the warrior's adherence to the wishes of Sachem and the efforts of his emissary, Nipishish.

Initially, each new group joined others in camps already set up on the grass flats adjacent to and on three sides of the settlement palisade, as well as the stubble of the harvested barley field. Other camps were scattered along the wide expanse of gravel beach in both directions from the south settlement gate. Soon after arrival, the men carried their canoes into the woods to the north of the barley stubble, and concealed them.

The hectic activity within and around the settlements palisades was quite a spectacle and one that occupied a portion of every conversation. Never in living memory had anybody ever before seen so many men gathered in one place at any other time.

Food for the multitude was a concern from the outset. The Naskapi expected to subsist entirely on water and the jerky and pemmican each carried. These trail rations, took care of much of the immediate needs while all manner of fresh meat augmented the diet. As time wore on however, a transition from the food stores remaining in the settlement's larder from winter occurred, so as to preserve the dried rations for later use during the coming battle when fresh meat was unobtainable.

From the beginning of the influx of men, all four ships were engaged in hunting whales. The sheer mass of edible meat and fat from a single carcass made even the smallest whale a valued asset. That the hunter's efforts were successful was evidenced by the dismembered carcasses of whales of all sizes scattered along the beach, and the cries of wheeling seabirds overhead.

Many of the Naskapi had never seen a whale, much less eaten the slightly fishy meat. It did not take them long under the prodding of their leaders and Nipishish before the daily beach scene involved a mix of everyone available butchering the bounty. A portion of the meat was consumed, but most ended up on drying racks over smoky fires to feed the multitude during the expected siege.

Winking lights from the many cook fires each evening gave some indication of the numbers of warriors encamped around the settlement. The fires also conveyed to the prying eyes of Shinabeg scouts that a large number of Naskapi had joined with the Norse.

Halfdan and the other leaders had decided during their endless conferences that every single man, except for those aboard the four ships and the widely scattered pickets, would spend this final night inside the settlement. Attack was expected sometime tomorrow.

Because the Naskapi had joined with the Norse in defense of the settlement, the alliance leaders felt that there would be a powwow with Shingoos and his leaders before the actual attack. If attack could not be averted by powwow, it was expected that the Shinabeg host would continue to assault the settlement day and night until it was overrun, or the war ended, one way or the other.

On this final night before the attack, the palisades surrounding Halfdansfjord fairly bulged with the mass of men inside. The gates were closed and barred. Several sentries were posted in both towers and at each corner of the palisade. Not a canoe remained of the 150 or so that had been scattered about on the beach. All were concealed from sight, scattered out in the forest to the north.

The four ships had left the beach under sweeps until clear of the land after midnight on this last night of the fingernail moon. Crammed with a mix of Norse and Naskapi fighting men, it was hoped the ships would provide a formidable edge for the defense of Halfdansfjord. After rounding the southwest point of the inland sea they scattered out close inshore to watch and listen for the approach of the enemy that would be coming along the shoreline from the south. This picket line of ships were to shadow the Anishinabeg when they were sighted, conveying the alarm to the settlement via signal horns.

To a casual observer the silhouette of each ship had undergone sinister looking alterations to enhance its ability to cause severe damage to the expected masses of canoes and their occupants. A splayed cluster of heavy, sharpened poles were affixed on either side of the bow of each ship, the sharpened end about a foot above the water's surface, to act as a battering ram as the ships sailed back and forth through the canoes. Tanned hides would be rigged on tightly braced rope lines along each side of the ship. During attack these hides would hang loosely along the ship's gunwales at chest height to provide some protection from incoming missiles.

Halfdan had made it clear that the ships were their last option for escape. If the settlement were lost and had to be abandoned, each of the four ship captains had a rendezvous point along the northern coast where they would expect to pick up the survivors for transport to the island where the women and children awaited developments. The Naskapi crewmen could remain with them or return to their own villages.

With the ships and canoes away, no outward sign remained of the numbers of fighting men within the palisade walls of the settlement.

The rumble of male conversation in two languages filled the chamber, as they talked over the day's events, and the state of readiness that they all hoped was in place. Every available seat and bench was filled, with the overflow standing in small groups about the big room. Women were also scattered about, some talking together while others had joined one group of men or another, listening for the most part, as strategies and concerns were bandied about. Occasionally, the sound of laughter rose above the conversation.

Halfdan smiled at the laughter that seemed to emanate from one particular group that included his mate, Frida, and some of her female companions. Something humorous had all of them laughing. He was glad they could find something funny to laugh about. He could not recall when he had last laughed. He glanced at Nipishish, who sat directly across the table. They made eye contact, but neither spoke.

The men with them around the long table consisted of Naskapi war chiefs, the four Norse ship captains, Brodir, Bjorn, Sweyn, and Thorgeirr, whose ships had been left safely on the island with the women and children, and other individuals of both groups that had just claimed a place to rest their tired feet.

Halfdan again glanced at his friend, who was in conversation with Deskaheh. In spite of the trouble descending on all of them, he had worried since he revealed to Gudbj that Ingerd had been captured by a Haudeno war party. His friend's stoic acceptance when he heard of her capture surprised him at the time. It had not affected the important work that Gudbj did as Sachem's emissary, but he knew the knowledge ate at the man, it had to. He had been aware that the two men had spent whatever free moments opened for them with their heads together while Gudbj picked Deskaheh's brain. He well remembered the day that Deskaheh came to him after he had examined the place where the battle and abductions occurred. He had held up an arrow that he had retrieved from the scene, telling his chieftain that the Haudeno war party that captured Ingerd were men of the Ganadoga clan, of the Haudenosaunee people. Now he was telling Gudbj.

Halfdan would later recall that his friend had begun to withdraw within himself after he had been told all that Deskaheh had to tell him. He never shirked his duties to all of them, but the happy man that had been Gudbjartur Einarsson – Nipishish to his Naskapi brothers – changed that day. What his friend did with the information Deskaheh gave him that day would not be known for many seasons.

Although the Anishinabeg certainly knew of the presence of the Naskapi, the expected powwow did not occur. The assault did not occur when Halfdan and the Naskapi leaders expected, nor did the attackers all come from the same direction as they had the previous summer. The attackers also did not wait for the dark of the moon as expected; they came in the early morning darkness of the finger nail moon. They had learned a valuable lesson the previous summer. This time, without warning the assault began.

The principle war chief, Shingoos headed an enormous force comprised of warriors from all the scattered bands of Kitchi sipi Anishinabeg. Because of this, it was prudent for him to split his forces. When the word went out to begin the long journey, the fact that his warriors came from so many scattered bands ensured that he had a continual stream of reinforcements entering the assault.

Later the Naskapi allies of the Northmen would find out from their own villages that the Anishinabeg host had streamed by practically every village without incident, as they utilized the waters of the navigable creek and river courses leading to the bay of Halfdansfjord.

Out on the inland sea, the four picket ships did not slow down the invasion as intended, nor did they provide an early warning to the settlement. Many canoes slipped by the ships without being seen in the darkness against the land. At the same time the creaking of the sweeps, and the gurgles and splashes of the ships' bows cutting through the water, made the ships' presence known to those stealing by close inshore.

The defenders of Halfdansfjord awakened on the first morning to an attack under the cover of darkness that nearly overwhelmed them by its surprise and the sheer force of the numbers involved. They came from three sides simultaneously, in waves preceded by clouds of arrows. The pits and barricades claimed many attackers' lives in the darkness, but quickly lost their effectiveness as subsequent waves simply went around them. The initial attack's purpose, other than to create mayhem, was to cloak the activities of the large groups of men whose mission was to set fire to the settlement's log palisade. That they were successful became apparent as fire caught hold on all four sides of the palisade. Horns and war whistles sounded withdrawal, and the Anishinabeg pulled back out of the light cast by the flames gradually catching hold in the upright logs. The first assault ended as suddenly as it had begun.

The palisades were set alight before the defenders awakened fully to mount a defense, although the parapets along three sides had been filled with sleeping men. When the alarm came, it was already too late. The upright palisade logs, dry with the passage of time, readily ignited in the intense heat of the fiercely burning pitch that the attackers smeared between the logs before setting them alight. As the leaping flames diminished in the choking clouds of smoke, smoldering coals within and between the logs continued to eat away at the fabric of each log. The men that did the deed melted away into the darkness.

Sporadic feints by the Anishinabeg came with the dawn, just often enough to keep those trapped within the settlement from relaxing. The fires licking at the palisade diminished in volume, becoming smoking coals for the most part; but, in spite of efforts to put them out, several sites scattered along each palisade wall burned into the interior of individual logs to slowly eat them away.

The clustered canoes of the recent Anishinabeg arrivals fell prey to the four ships for a time as they sailed back and forth, crushing the fragile craft under their spiked bows. The ships were only effective while the canoes were still in deep water. Close inshore with insufficient water depth and room to maneuver, the ships were forced to stand away and try to disrupt those still streaming toward the landing beach.

While joined in close combat during this period. Thorgill's ship caught fire from fire arrows and horns of live coals thrown aboard, nobody would ever know for certain which. Fire in a wooden ship quickly becomes uncontrollable, and so it happened here. The mixed company of Naskapi and Norse abandoned ship. None reached shore, either drowning or speared like fish in a barrel by their Anishinabeg foes. The burned out hulk of the new ship drifted ashore later, a constant reminder of defeat.

The other three vessels quickly disengaged, sailing away to the west. Out of the fight, they deployed to the bays and inlets as Halfdan ordered previously, to await the final outcome and to be available to convey the defenders of Halfdansfjord to the island with the others.

⸎

Beginning during the night after the first full day of the assault, the leaden skies began to release a light drizzle. Those within the palisade walls felt that the gods had intervened in their behalf for the drizzle soaking the countryside was the only thing keeping the palisades and buildings of Halfdansfjord from burning to the ground.

The attacks continued intermittently, almost halfheartedly. No attempt was made to carry the settlement and end it. Shingoos and his men taunted the defenders. Not unlike a coyote playing with a mouse. Eventually tiring of the game, the coyote would flip his prey into the air, eating the squirming little body in one gulp. Insults were hurled back and forth by attackers and defenders alike, each trying to outdo the other with their bravado. The Anishinabeg were playing a waiting game, waiting for the fire do its work on the palisade. Then the attacks would end it all.

During the early daylight hours of the first all-out assault, and always preceded by a cloud of arrows shot from the parapets, the south gate would fly open and about 100-fighting men attacked straight at the nearest body of Anishinabeg. This method of battle had proven effective during the attack of the preceding summer. Not so much this time; the Anishinabeg were expecting it, the element of surprise was missing. One such group had almost been annihilated before the signal horns sounded recall. Such an attack was not attempted again.

Losses on both sides mounted steadily, with most of the casualties being from arrow or spear wounds. Close combat after the last attempt by the mixed group of Naskapi and Norsemen was abandoned as too costly. No attempt was made by the Anishinabeg to push any perceived advantage to actually scale the palisade. Each attack involved three of the four palisade walls simultaneously, the one facing the fen being too boggy for an effective attack. Each time it was the same; the attackers closed within arrow range and a missile exchange ensued. The plunging flight of the arrows from both sides came into the settlement proper, and down on the attackers with about equal results. The strategy of the Anishinabeg war chiefs was obviously one of attrition. They had the defenders outnumbered by at least 5 to 1. They could afford to wait for the casualties among the defenders to reach an unsustainable level, or the smoldering fires eating away at the upright logs to bring down a palisade wall. Either way their final victory was inevitable.

⸺ ⚬⚭⚬ ⸺

Three days later, the drizzle had ended. Another gray dawn revealed a countryside and settlement ravaged by the siege. Tendrils and columns of smoke rose into the heavy, still early morning air. The smell of scorched and burning wood filled the air. An accompanying heavy odor of pine pitch told the defenders pitch pine wood and faggots had kindled the fires that still might cook them alive.

Bucket brigades struggled to deal with the fires that the drizzle had not extinguished. Most of the water they poured over the vertical palisade from the top fell to the ground below without quenching the coals that had eaten into the wood.

Men crowded the parapets, passing sloshing water buckets to those at the forward edge. By the time these buckets made it from the well up through the lines of men passing them forward to each wall, only about half the water remained. The well was now the only source of water within what remained of the palisade as the small rill that had previously run through the settlement had stopped flowing, either dammed or diverted by the Anishinabeg.

Halfdan had been inwardly fuming at the ineffectiveness of the bucket brigade. There simply were not enough buckets available to make it effective. Men had told him that areas of the palisade walls were growing hot to the touch. He realized that nothing could be done to quench the smoldering fires that stubbornly resisted every effort. He ruefully contemplated the lowering skies. *Great Thor, open the sky and bring a deluge.* Shouts from the west palisade drew his attention. He left the commons to make his way toward the shouting that had increased to a din of angry voices.

As he topped the parapet ladder, he saw what had made his men so angry.

"Our horses wandered out of the forest to see what was going on. They are cooking and eating them, Halfdan!" Falki said angrily, pointing an accusing finger toward the cook fires to the west of the palisade. "They have hunted down and killed every one, including the new colts."

The Naskapi warriors among them knew of the value they placed on the horses, but their understanding of the brief conversation was limited at best. However, the anger on the faces of the Norsemen they understood without translation.

Halfdan looked on in silence as he studied the scene just beyond arrow range. The carcasses of their horse herd, most already dismembered and apportioned among their brethren, were plain to see scattered around the evening cook fires of the Anishinabeg. The only outward sign that he was every bit as upset as those around him was the clenching and unclenching of his jaws. He looked at those grouped near him, watching for his reaction. His eyes settled on Falki.

"What do you want to do about this, Falki?"

The measured tone of his chieftain's voice gave Falki pause. He correctly sensed there was more to the question than any of them could address dispassionately.

"I want to attack them right now for killing all our horses." He looked out at the virtually unbroken wall of enemy warriors milling about. Shaking his head in both understanding and disgust at what he perceived of the situation, he locked eyes with Halfdan.

"You would tell me that we can do nothing. There are too many of them. The enemy has us trapped in here. If we leave the security of this settlement to attack them, every man would be lost. It would not be worth it for the horses, for they are already dead."

The hard eyes of Halfdan held Falki's attention. He said nothing for a moment in answer to Falki's assessment. His eyes travelled over the swelling group of angry men, settling on Falki. "You are right. We can do nothing without losing more men needlessly." He stepped to the ladder and climbed down from the parapet without another word.

The men watched him go, and then turned their attention to Falki, who shrugged. "Like he just said, we can do nothing. Our dead horses are not worth getting killed over."

—⟶∞⟵—

Tostig saw the look of rage on the face of his chieftain as Halfdan walked quickly toward the council chambers. He knew that something was about to happen that would affect them all.

Halfdan turned toward his lieutenant. The two came together near the empty animal pens.

"Gather as many leaders as you can find quickly." In answer to the look on Tostig's face, he added, "We must abandon the settlement tonight, before one of the palisades burns to the ground and they get inside." He bobbed his chin. "Go!"

As such things happen, word passed quickly through the defenders. The time had come. Nobody disagreed, their situation was hopeless.

THE ISLAND

The plight of Halfdansfjord and an unknown number of the people fighting to defend it became apparent to those on the island as the attack entered what would become its final day. Thoughts of their friends and kinsmen fighting for their survival occupied their minds every waking moment. The finality of it all was plain to see in the distance. Smoke by day and the dull glow of flames reflecting from the smoke by night. People talked of little else.

"They cannot go on. I do not see how they have lasted this long." Thora spoke from the edge of the growing group of people that had gravitated to the point of the island closest to the mainland.

As the day wore on, people naturally began to gather here, women with their children and babes in cradleboards. The few men on the island followed as they finished their work or brought it with them. The last man to arrive, Helge, stopped beside Thora just as she finished her observation. She glanced at him, a question in her eyes.

As their leader here, he felt that he should say something, but he did not have an answer for her. He shrugged, shielding his eyes from the glare of the bright sunlight off the water as he studied the distant smear of smoke on the horizon.

"I agree with what you said, Thora, it will end soon. There is nothing we can do except wait for somebody to come and tell us what happened. Halfdan sent us here so the woman and children would be safe." He bobbed his chin toward the mainland. "Whatever has happened at Halfdansfjord will bring an end to it soon. It is the will of the gods."

Other conversations trailed off as Helge began to speak to Thora. The crowd pulled in closer to hear.

Helge's eyes travelled over the others. He was acutely aware that they all were watching him closely. He sighed in resignation; uncomfortable to be seen as one that might have answers when he knew in his heart that he did not have the answers they sought. No one did.

"Between dark tonight and dawn tomorrow I want a guard posted here on this point to warn us if the enemy comes. I do not think they will come here, it is only a precaution. They do not know we are here, I hope, so that is in our favor. Until we hear from our people about the outcome of the battle do not kindle wood cook fires. Use the peat for your fires, it has almost no smoke." He shook his head, and scuffed at the ground with his foot. "I do not know what to tell you, except that all we can do is wait. Tomorrow we may hear from someone about what has happened."

The people knew he was right. Everybody felt his frustration in varying degrees. It was the not knowing that nagged at them. They began to straggle back to the encampment, the men at least looking forward to the final meal of the day.

Sometime well after darkness had enveloped the island, the second lone guard to assume the post, with nothing to occupy his mind during the wee hours of the night, watched the unworldly shimmer of the flames as they played along the cloud bottoms in the direction of Halfdansfjord, thinking that they had grown brighter.

The overcast had rolled in before sundown. He sniffed the air; the slight westerly breeze bore the smell of rain somewhere to the west of the island.

I hope it does not put out my fire, he thought, as he spread his hands over the small brazier that held a handful of glowing charcoal. Rubbing his warmed hands together he enjoyed the chill that coursed through his body from that small comfort. He smiled at a sudden thought, and dropped in another piece of his dwindling charcoal supply. *The next guard will need to bring his own charcoal.*

ESCAPE FROM HALFDANSFJORD

About three hours of darkness remained of this, the final night of the attack. Reconnaissance patrols had earlier returned the word that the fen to the north was unguarded by the Anishinabeg.

A silent double cordon of grim-faced men faced the west palisade wall. Halfdan, Chisasi, and Glooscap stood at their center, ready to repel the final attack should the palisade collapse. The logs of the west palisade showed the glow of coals scattered throughout. In many places the coals had eaten clear through, leaving small gaps. Those facing the palisade hoped it would stand upright just a little longer.

Behind this cordon, Nipishish and Arni the Hunter hurried an unbroken line of men, and the few women and older children remaining in the settlement, out the north walk-through gate that opened into the fen. With the last of them out the gate, a low whistle from Glooscap alerted the cordon of men, and they, too, began to file through the gate.

Once clear of the settlement the single file continued without pause through the bog toward the stygian gloom of the nearby forest. Behind them the men that were the last to leave the settlement, formed a rear guard for the others.

Once the escapees were in the forest, the canoes that had been hidden previously were recovered and transported to the nearby river. The escape plan entailed a contingent including Halfdan and Frida that would go overland to the west from the river to rendezvous with the three ships for transport to the island. Most of the escapees were bound up the river for the village of

Antanak, including a majority of the former residents of Halfdansfjord that preferred living with the Naskapi rather than starting life all over on an island.

———

Halfdan, Frida, and the others with them paused atop a promontory ridge that offered an unobstructed view of their erstwhile settlement. The fire had spread since they escaped. Some of the longhouses were aflame; soon all would be gone, just a heap of glowing embers all that remained of their home in this land. Nobody said anything for a time; the scene they witnessed below sobered them all.

Thoughts of the dead left behind occupied Halfdan's mind as the flames danced in his eyes. Tostig had fallen from an arrow through his eye, just a short time before the escape commenced. The man had been like a rock to him, he would be missed.

There were so many dead, both Northmen and Naskapi that they had to utilize one of the longhouses for storage until such time that the bodies could be tended to according to custom. But, the gods had intervened, as they so often did. All would be consumed in the fire that was destroying Halfdansfjord. The Valkyries had claimed the dead as their spirits ascended in the fires that consumed them, both his men and the women who fought beside them to the end. He also knew that the Valkyries would bear the Naskapi dead to Valhalla, as warriors fallen in battle that fought beside their Viking brethren. These warriors would roam the netherworld together until Ragnarok ended the world forever. This he fervently believed, as did all the survivors of this great war with the Anishinabeg host.

He looked away from the fire as Frida took his hand in hers.

"Come Halfdan, we must go before they come after us."

He shook his head. "They will not come after us, Frida. I heard the wail of the war whistles as I walked out the gate. Shingoos knew that we were leaving, I feel certain. He let us go. It is over."

———

In the half light of early dawn a bedraggled group of dirty, weary people, smelling of smoke, walked from the forest verge and onto the pebbled beach of a small cove a little north of due west from the ashes of Halfdansfjord. As the crow flies, the distance was barely 3-leagues, but they were not crows and it had been a hard slog in the darkness of the dense, brush-filled woodlands that they had traversed to get to this place.

At the far end of the cove a ship swung at anchor, her bow facing the incoming surge of the flood tide. The crew aboard her had been waiting two days here, one of the three predetermined rendezvous points to pick up survivors from the battle that raged to the east. Each night they saw the flickering glow in the night sky from the slow destruction of their home. All the ship's crew could do was wait for it to end, as it surely must. The eyes of the lookouts, at least, frequently swept the shoreline around the cove hoping to be the first to catch sight of their people.

The wail of a horn told Halfdan they had been seen from the ship. He responded with a wave.

The signal caused a flurry of activity aboard the ship. The lookout called forward, "One of them is Halfdan!"

"I see him," answered the captain, Hrafen.

Moments later, the crew had the anchor in and the tide and a pair of sweeps brought the ship into the beach.

For Hrafen and his crew, watching the soot covered and disheveled people walk along the sloping beach toward them, before wading into the shallows to come aboard told them all they needed to know about what had happened at Halfdansfjord. First one and then another sat down in the clear frigid water to wash off the dirt and accumulated grim of their ordeal, without regard for what the water might do to the weapons all of them carried.

The willing but grim-faced crew offered a hand up over the side as the people began to come aboard.

"Where are the others?" Hrafen faced Halfdan squarely after giving him a hand aboard, his expression clearly showing the depth of his feeling at seeing his chieftain in this state.

Halfdan did not answer right away, instead wrapping Frida in a dry robe that Hrafen handed to him. The others that had come with him took shelter from the wind, most sitting down with their backs against the hull.

"There are not many others," said Halfdan. "More than half our people have been killed in the fighting. I split those left into three groups and some of them headed for their respective ships. We will meet those who elected to go to the island later today, the others..." His voice trailed off.

Hrafen watched Halfdan, waiting for him to continue. He did not.

"Many people went with the Naskapi," said Frida, taking up the story for Halfdan. "We think more people went with them than are going to the island. Some went with Chisasi, and some with Glooscap. Others went with the other bands. We do not know how many, or who they are."

Hrafen and his crew had listened with rapt attention to Halfdan and Frida. Now that the dispersal of their fellows was known, the crew naturally sought out friends and acquaintances to hear their stories.

"What about Thorgeirr," asked Hrafen? He dreaded not knowing what had become of his former captain and kinsman.

"I do not know," said Halfdan.

A voice from the stern provided the answer. "He is in Valhalla. He fell in the last assault."

Numbness came to Hrafen. He clutched the rail as he stared out over the cove. Thoughts of his friend cascaded through his mind for a time. Gathering himself with an effort of will he turned back to Halfdan, who sat with his back to the hull, an arm around Frida.

"We sail on the slack tide. The flood slows, so it will be soon."

His chieftain answered with a desultory gesture of his hand.

HALFDANSFJORD

With the dawn, the Anishinabeg assault that followed the collapse of the western palisade wall in a shower of sparks met no resistance, the defenders were gone. The war chief, Shingoos was at the forefront of the attack. He and his warriors knew that the defense by the pale skins and their Naskapi allies would crumple when the fire finally destroyed the palisade, allowing them inside the settlement for the first time.

A body of warriors immediately went in pursuit of the pale skins until the shrill wailing of the war whistles recalled them. None questioned the decision of their war chief to let them go. Wherever they escaped to, they were gone from here, and that had been the reason for this war.

Shingoos walked through the abandoned settlement, looking with interest at the dwellings, sheds, and pens that had survived the fire arrows of his warriors. What he saw was a complete settlement that had survived the siege virtually intact, but without the hated pale skins that had lived here.

Everything of value that could be transported by canoe was systematically looted from the five longhouses and attached storage sheds. Most of it would prove to be too heavy for the long pull to the home river system. It took the personal intervention of Shingoos to prevent men from trying to take the heavy iron kettles they found on every hearth. The initial greed of the looters soon gave way to orders from their leaders to take only the dried meat and fish; leave the rest.

In an orgy of destruction common to war, everything that could be destroyed was destroyed. Superstition alone prevented the victors from desecrating the Norse and Naskapi dead that had been either left where they fell, or arranged by the defenders as the battle wore on in an unbroken line along the bottom of the four palisade walls. All the weapons were taken, but the bodies were left to be consumed in the fires to come.

When the vast flotilla of canoes paddled from the landing beach at Halfdansfjord, every combustible part of the once vibrant settlement was in flames. Visible for many leagues in all directions, smoke and flames rose from the site for days.

⸺⧤⸺

Much time had passed since the darkness of the moon began the ordeal at Halfdansfjord. Except for frequent rain showers or squalls accompanied by everything from light breezes to a full blown gale, the gods provided what one would expect on a small island near the southern extremity of a vast inland sea. A full moon shone over the island and its people once again, ensuring that none would soon forget the events that had changed their lives following the last full moon. For now, it appeared that they were safe from further attack.

The waters teemed with fish, seals, and whales. Meat in the form of deer, small game, and waterfowl of all kinds were abundant on the land itself.

All three ships had come into the cove on the south side of the island with those that had survived the war with the Anishinabeg and wished to begin life anew with their own people rather than with the Naskapi. Without exception they were shocked by what had been lost in people and culture. All told there were only 150 some odd of them, including the men women and children that were already there when the ships came in bearing the survivors. Many familiar faces were missing and their beloved settlement was burned to the ground, gone forever. As stories were told and personal observations came to light it became known who had joined with the Naskapi, and who had made the final journey to the afterlife. Even at that, the whereabouts of many of the people would remain an unknown.

A majority of the women remained hopeful that they would someday know the answers to the questions each had. For some, the eternal optimists among them, their hopes even extended to a resolution that included a happy reunion with their friends. The men harbored no such thoughts. Pragmatic by nature they knew in their hearts that their friends and kinsmen were just gone. It did not matter whether they were dead, or swallowed up by this immense land, they were gone.

As their chieftain, Halfdan knew that the way of life they had always enjoyed as a people had been essentially destroyed by the Anishinabeg. Nothing would ever again be as it had been before. Because of the ongoing threat of a similar disaster, he knew that building another settlement was not the answer either. This summer, next summer, or one that followed, the Anishinabeg, or some other hostile native people would find them, no matter where they were in this land.

Their only option for survival was to join with the natives of this land. He knew in his heart that the alien culture of the Norse would never survive the ravages of time standing alone as they had in Halfdansfjord. His people were not ready for that reality, yet, but in time they would all see the obvious.

One cool morning some days later, after he judged that sufficient time had elapsed for his people to mentally deal with the trauma that still could destroy them, Halfdan called them all together. Knowing that he must allay the rampant gossip and give his people a new direction, he hoped his ideas would give them a sense that there was still a chance to live in this land that they had all grown to love.

In any such council, the leaders sat together before the assembly in a show of solidarity. Before the battle there had been eight ship captains and Halfdan. Now, two captains remained, Bjorn and Hrafen. The others were in Valhalla.

Halfdan let them all have a say, it was the only way for them to accept his decisions without rancor in this instance. During most of the daylight hours on that particular day, and in spite of often heated conversation ruling the gathering, three options emerged for all of them. He conferred with his captains for a time. Then he used the options the people had chosen to tell them what he thought was best for them.

"Alright, you have all told us what you think, and we have considered your choices. Our numbers are almost equally divided between the three choices you have made. That will make it easier, I think. We have lost many good men and women. Six of those men were our ship captains. We lost one ship, leaving us seven ships and three captains, including me. I will keep Steed of the Sea, Bjorn will take command of Thorgeirr's ship, and Hrafen will take command of Athils ship. The other four smaller ships need new captains. Bjorn and Hrafen will train men that want to assume command of one of them. Many of our men have the experience at sea to command a ship, but I leave it up to them to decide." He glanced pointedly at Helge and Hallsteinn the Shipbuilder. "Those that wish to return to Greenland may do so after Bjorn and Hrafen get new captains trained. You can go with them when they go to Greenland to replace the supplies we have lost." He stood from the log where he had been seated with Hrafen and Bjorn, and paced slowly back and forth. "The group that wants to settle farther away from the land of the Anishinabeg on the big island to the west can take two of the remaining ships with their captains that want to settle there also."

"What will you do, Halfdan?" Helge asked the simple question that was on the mind of everyone.

"I was chosen to lead you. I will do that until you decide that you want another chieftain." He caught Frida's direct gaze on him. He smiled slightly at her. "Frida and I have talked of these things, as you might expect. We will stay on this island. We have many friends among the Naskapi. By being close to the mainland, we can keep those friendships alive. With all of you who decide to stay here with us working together we will turn the encampment that you have made into our new home. I would wish that all of you wanted to stay here, but I understand what drives you and I will not stand in your way."

For the time being, they were all together. The intense desire for change and the natural passion that drove many of them would dim with the passage of time. The heated arguments that had formulated their decisions would become less important, especially when they all realized that their best option was one that kept them together until they assimilated with the native peoples. Doing so was the only lasting option for the Norse people, and most would realize that on their own.

After the council Halfdan spent his time in relative seclusion, his mind sorting through the events of the recent past. It was easy to do; everybody was still busy with the myriad tasks that resulted from making the encampment into a permanent settlement. Thoughts of Gudbj again came to the fore. He recalled seeing Gudbj helping get everyone away safely when they evacuated Halfdansfjord, but the man had not been seen since. Deskaheh had also disappeared about the same time, so he thought the two had left together. Gudbj had become more and more circumspect during the final days of the siege, and Halfdan felt that the two men had hatched some plan that included finding what had happened to Ingerd. Halfdan queried Thora about plans that Deskaheh might have shared with her, but she knew nothing. In fact she had not known that her mate had disappeared until the three ships arrived with all the survivors. She was not concerned. Halfdan knew of Deskaheh's unannounced comings and goings. The man would return whenever he and Gudbj finished their mission.

Work began the following morning to replace the tents with permanent dwellings for those that wished to remain. The wattle and daub windbreaks protecting the tents from the incessant wind and rain showers were readily adapted to become the outer walls of two longhouses connected to a fully enclosed byre between them to house the livestock. A single, sod-covered roof overlaid the long structure. People could tend the livestock during bad weather and walk back and forth between the dwellings as necessary, without having to venture outside. As time passed, the settlement would come to resemble a miniature Halfdansfjord, but without the palisade walls.

Helge and Hallsteinn the Shipbuilder took command of the two ships that were to remain for the use of the island's residents. Their prime function would be fishing and whaling. Steed of the Sea would be used exclusively for trade with the Naskapi and Thalmiut and transport to and from the mainland.

The new captains for the two remaining ships were quickly deemed competent and they in turn soon had trained their crews. Small supplies of hides, dried meat, smoked fish, and other various and sundry essentials were accumulated sufficient for a start on the big island.

One morning on an outgoing tide, and just before the next full moon the expedition to the big island to the west set sail. None of those left behind, nor any of those that sailed knew how the whole affair would turn out, but it was their choice to go and nothing was done to dissuade any of them from their chosen course.

⌘

NIPISHISH AND DESKAHEH

Many moons came and went since the fall of Halfdansfjord. During the hurried evacuation of the settlement in the darkness prior to first light, groups of survivors hurriedly made for one of the ships waiting at the three rendezvous points to transport them to safety.

Two of their number melted into the forest. Nobody saw them go, nor were they missed until the ships arrived at the island.

Since that time Nipishish and Deskaheh had steadily paddled the canoe stolen from the Anishinabeg toward their destination, the village of the Ganadoga Haudenosaunee. Initially, travel had been by day, over waterways and lakes familiar to Deskaheh but increasingly new to Nipishish. They were now deep in the country of the Haudenosaunee. They had thus far avoided detection, but both knew that could change at any moment. As they drew nearer their destination all travel was shifted to the cloaking darkness of the night. They could ill afford detection by any Ganadoga warrior now that they were coming into that clan's home territory.

Each morning before first light, they sought the dense foliage of an island or the forest verge, hiding themselves and the canoe securely while they slept. No fire was ever kindled and the men subsisted on the pemmican and dried meat or fish trail rations common to all travelers.

Something had awakened both of them from a sound sleep just before the cloaking darkness enveloped the land. Neither man knew what it was but they separated to examine the lake island where they had spent the time of daylight.

Nipishish had found nothing amiss. He waited for Deskaheh's return near where they had slept. The slight snap of a twig and the swishing sound made by foliage with the passage of a body, alerted him to the man's approach.

Deskaheh shook his head at Nipishish's questioning glance.

"I saw nothing out of the ordinary. I think a moose cow and calf made the sounds that woke us up. I killed the calf and pulled the carcass into the forest. After we butcher it out, I will take the meat to trade."

Later, after returning to camp with the boned carcass of the calf rolled in its hide, the men huddled together, talking in low tones. While they talked they consumed the still warm liver and the chewy heart of the calf. Both belched contentedly when finished. To say the bloody fare was delicious missed the mark by a goodly amount. It was the first fresh meat they had eaten since before the Anishinabeg attack and siege of Halfdansfjord.

Both men knew the time had come to separate, as they had planned. Deskaheh would go on alone to the village of the Ganadoga clan, a distance of about half a day's travel. Only he could successfully get the information that they sought. Although he was originally from another clan, he was Haudeno. Over the course of this canoe journey he had gradually transformed his appearance, from a resident of Halfdansfjord to what he had been. In this way he would not attract unwanted attention from anyone in any of the villages of his people.

Nipishish would remain securely hidden on the island until Deskaheh returned from his reconnaissance. Knowing his wait might be the better part of two days, he appropriated a succulent chunk of fresh meat to augment his pemmican and the few pieces of dried meat that remained of his rations. The bloody liver had quickly relegated his dried rations to a less than satisfactory status. Even raw, he preferred the fresh meat.

Both men looked similar in appearance, clad as they were in buckskin clothing, their bodies lean and hardened by travail. But, Nipishish was taller, sported a short beard, was more heavily muscled than the average native male, and his skin, even that burned dark by exposure to the sun, was several shades lighter than his companion's skin. He could never pass for a Haudeno warrior, while Deskaheh could, even though he had been away for a long time. Deskaheh's hair had grown out over time, as he assumed the various aspects of the Norse culture, but during the planning stages for this journey he had shorn it away, leaving the telltale scalp lock.

Nipishish was amazed at how the scalp lock changed his friend's appearance. The leggings, vest, and other accoutrements that Deskaheh wore would be enough like that worn by the Ganadoga that the man would attract little to no attention when he appeared among them.

For all intents and purposes, Deskaheh had transformed himself back into the Haudeno warrior he had been when Gudbj captured him so long ago. He examined his friend closely in appreciation.

"You look ready, Deskaheh. Shaving your head has completed the transformation. They will not be suspicious. I doubt they will give you a second look."

Deskaheh grunted in acknowledgement. "Aye, I am ready. I will take the moose calf to them, to trade for pemmican and dried meat for our return journey. Trading will give me a good reason to be among them."

"When will you go?"

"We are less than half a day's journey from the Ganadoga village. I want to arrive around midday, as people normally do who have come to trade.

"How will you explain the Anishinabeg canoe?"

Although Haudeno and Shinabeg canoes were similar, Deskaheh's use of the canoe from another tribe could pose questions.

"I have thought about that. I will tell them it drifted up on the landing beach of my village and it was better than the canoe I had been using."

Nipishish chuckled appreciatively. "That is not too far from the truth, we did find it on a beach. Of course we found it in the middle of the night, and I doubt the Shinabe owner would have given it to us."

Deskaheh snorted, and grinned foolishly in the darkness. "I am happy you agree with my tale. And, so will the Ganadoga. It will satisfy their curiosity about me, if they have any."

Nipishish felt that he was growing lazy. He had sharpened his axe and knife several times, whittled toothpicks, wooden figures, and a new spoon for his belt pouch. On the second or third day, he had forgotten which, he fashioned a good looking fish spear that he used to spear a fat pike cruising for prey in the shallow waters of the shoreline of his island. Now he was out of ideas.

He had to be careful moving around the island by day. If he was not sleeping his time was spent concealed in an area of heavy brush, whittling or fashioning one of his creations. He was stiff from sitting, or lying supine, or with his back against a handy tree trunk. It would feel good to stand erect for a change, to walk erect, rather than stooped, something he was loath to do in the circumstance.

After the two days that he expected the return of Deskaheh became three, then four, his mind conjured up myriad problems that his friend may have encountered in the village. He decided to wait one more day before taking matters into his own hands. He would swim to shore and go overland to the village to look for Deskaheh. The thought of swimming to shore from his island engendered a feeling akin to fright in him. He swam well enough to stay on the surface for a short distance, but he flailed the water enough to cause a commotion that might be seen or heard, and he doubted he could stay on top long enough to reach the shore. The only way he could ensure success would be to use a piece of driftwood to help him stay afloat. His mind was processing these thoughts when he was snapped back to the present by a scraping sound from the shoreline; the sound of a canoe being pulled through the brush. It came from that end of the island where Deskaheh had launched their canoe four days hence.

Just in case it was somebody from whom he wanted to remain concealed, Nipishish moved through the dense undergrowth carefully, gently pushing limbs and branches aside, consciously placing each foot, as he made his way toward the source of the sounds he had heard.

A low chuckle came from his forefront.

"I hear you, Nipishish. You cannot sneak up on a Haudeno warrior."

Nipishish stood erect and grinned at Deskaheh. "If it had not been you, I would have been ready." As he examined the man's appearance, taking note of the heavy pack he held in his hand, he raised the head of his axe far enough to bring it into view.

Deskaheh shook his head appreciatively.

"What have you found out," asked Nipishish without preamble.

Dreading the question, Deskaheh had steeled himself for this encounter with his friend. In spite of having thought his response to the inevitable query through thoroughly, he found he could not deal with his answer at the moment. Shaking his head, the pain plain to see on his normally inscrutable face, he pushed past Nipishish and wound his way through the brush to the spot in the island's center where they had camped.

Nipishish watched the man until he disappeared in the dense undergrowth. A chill coursed through his body. A sense of foreboding, of doom, seized his psyche. He shook himself and followed after his friend.

Unbeknownst to either man they shared a similar pain and because of that shared pain, neither wanted to talk about Ingerd, not right now.

Nipishish found Deskaheh kneeling on the ground in the clearing kindling a fire with a tiny bow and drill he carried in his belt pouch.

"What are you doing? Somebody will see the smoke."

"It does not matter; they know I am camping here for the night."

"How do they know that?"

Deskaheh looked up from his efforts at the tiny fire he had coaxed into being. "I told them that I camped here before coming to their village." He gestured to the pack he had brought from the village. "I have a young goose in the pack. We need a fire to cook it."

The details of his friend's absence momentarily forgotten, Nipishish joined Deskaheh on the ground.

"A goose!" He exclaimed, dumping the contents of the pack on the ground. He picked the goose up by its neck. Turning it back and forth, he examined it closely, while squeezing its fat breast.

"It is a good fat one you have brought. It has been a long time since we had a fat goose." Without further ado he ripped the feathers from the bird's body, leaving the plump carcass dressed in its layer of down, which he dropped into the pile of feathers as he stood up and headed off for the shoreline.

"I will find some watercress and plantains to stuff the body cavity," he called over his shoulder. "You can find some of those little onions to go with them."

Deskaheh watched him walk away, relieved that the goose had momentarily defused the tenseness he felt in the circumstance, and diverted his friend's attention onto another subject. *I will have to tell him eventually. But, if it pleases the great spirit, Orenda, it will not be right now,* he thought. He got to his feet and stepped into the brush to begin his search for the elusive wild onion.

Later on, the shadows had lengthened as the day progressed to its natural conclusion. A promise of drizzle during the night, or at least by tomorrow sometime, was contemplated by the two men as they lounged by their almost smokeless fire.

They had hauled a few rocks from the shoreline to build an impromptu ring around the goose that rested at the edge of the fire pit, in a bed of coals. Earlier, in preparation for cooking their meat, Nipishish had completely encased the carcass in a layer of mud, to hold in the steam generated in the cooking process, and to keep the meat from burning before it was cooked through. Judging from the smell wafting from the cracks in the fire-hardened casing, the goose was about cooked.

Nipishish rubbed his hands together and grinned at his companion.

"What do you think? Is it cooked?"

With a twinkle in his eyes, Deskaheh replied in the affirmative. "It smells done to me."

Nipishish picked up the two short lengths of tree limb he had cut earlier, and passing the other ends to Deskaheh, the two men faced each other over the fire pit, clamped the limbs around the ball of baked mud containing their goose, and gingerly lifted it from the coals of the fire pit to the ground. Steam rose into the air from a large crack atop the ball of baked mud. A distinct odor of baked goose rose to their nostrils.

The men dropped to their knees and began breaking the baked mud away from the goose. As they did so, the layer of down that had encased the carcass of the goose after the feathers were plucked, came away from the meat with a slight ripping sound, leaving the body of the bird completely cleaned of down and pin feathers.

Sometime later, a loud belch rose from the inert form of Deskaheh as he lay stretched out in the grass of their small clearing. Nipishish was in similar condition. Of the goose, nothing remained but a pile of bones. The two men had eaten every shred of the tender, succulent meat, including the neck, heart, gizzard, and liver that Nipishish had stuffed into the body cavity with the plantains, water cress, and onions. They had even eaten the juice soaked greens.

"I know how hungry I was for meat, but I think that was the best meat I have ever eaten." A loud, rumbling belch escaped his open mouth. Both men laughed.

Deskaheh agreed with his friend's assessment of their meal. "I traded my last two pieces of moose calf for that goose, yesterday, before I started back here. A young woman had it. She did not want to part with it, but I finally talked her into a trade after I showed her how good the two back straps looked."

The statement transformed Nipishish. Perhaps it was the mention of the woman that had bartered the goose. He was silent a moment as his eyes bored into Deskaheh, who felt the intensity before looking up.

Deskaheh made eye contact. "Aye, I found out what happened to Ingerd. It is bad, Nipishish. She was there in that village. She is dead."

Nipishish said nothing. His eyes and face had hardened to a stone mask. They alone bade Deskaheh to continue.

"You know that she would be worked until she could no longer work. She was a slave, nothing more. When she could no longer work they killed her."

Still Nipishish did not speak. A crushing sorrow filled his breast, coursed through his body, like that brought on by a chill wind. He had known it would be like this, that she would not be rescued. Too much time had passed. He had felt that she no longer lived, felt it to the depth of his soul. Had they been able to get here sooner, there may have been a chance.

The two men made eye contact. Nipishish bobbed his chin, a question in the fierce eyes.

Deskaheh dropped his gaze, shaking his head, unwilling to look into his friends eyes, or answer his question.

"How did she die?"

Deskaheh again looked full into those baleful eyes, a look he had not seen in them for a long time.

"She died at the stake, in their fire. You know this is how they kill prisoners."

Nipishish gave no sign he had heard. He sat still a moment longer, got to his feet, and began gathering his meager possessions, stuffing them in one of the travel packs they both carried.

"Come, Deskaheh, we go now. I do not want to be in this place anymore."

In a matter of moments they were gone from the island, headed north into the gathering darkness that follows the setting sun. A pattern of ripples caught the fading light as they opened out from the bow of the canoe as it knifed through the calm waters of the lake. A loon cried in the distance. The splash of some animal along the shoreline or a fish falling on its prey seemingly went unnoticed by the men as they bent to their task.

Not a word passed between them as they went along their way. Both men processed their feelings in silence.

They rested from their travels at the village of Glooscap for several days. Nipishish remained at the village, Deskaheh continued his journey.

The people were happy to have Nipishish return to them, but all quickly noted that he was not the same man that had left with the warriors for the fight with the Anishinabeg. He did not share Ingerd's fate with anyone, although both Glooscap and Kejo asked him. As time went by he withdrew more and more. Finally, one morning before dawn he was gone. It would be a long time before anyone saw him again, or he had a meaningful conversation with anyone.

DESKAHEH RETURNS

Many days later, an exhausted Deskaheh pulled his battered canoe from the sound. Thora saw him before he saw her, and ran shrieking down the beach toward him. The two came together about halfway. His transformation into a Haudenosaunee warrior for the mission that he and Gudbjartur had undertaken took many of them by surprise, but Thora did not seem to notice. After all, she has seen him that way before. It was the inner man that she loved. His appearance had nothing to do with that love. Surrounded by the people, they made their way to their new home.

After a short rest and some much-needed food, and with Thora and their child at his side, he spent that day and half the night telling his tale to everybody on the island that had gathered in one of the longhouses. The people hung on every word. More than a few tears were shed by the people over Ingerd's fate. All knew in their hearts that she was dead, but hearing the details almost overpowered her many close friends, especially Thora.

Deskaheh spent considerable time alone with Halfdan and Frida relating the more personal aspects of his tale.

Halfdan later told Frida, that he doubted he would ever see Gudbj again. As it happened, he was right.

———⊛———

Chapter 14

DEMON

Nipishish watched the village from a knoll that gave him height above the river valley floor and a panoramic view of people coming and going through the gates. Close enough to study his enemy, yet far enough from the activity to avoid accidental detection.

He had chosen the knoll for the dense brush that covered its slopes, and the single spruce tree that grew out of the dense brush at the top. He carefully examined the entire knoll for human sign, found nothing, and satisfied himself that few, if any, people ever climbed through the dense brush to the top. That was good.

He determined that the tree was where he would conceal himself. Climbing high enough up into the tree to get an unobstructed view of the settlement, he began building his lair of spruce boughs. Woven across several main branches about halfway up the tree, on the back side from the village, and against the trunk, the platform of boughs gave him a place to stretch out while he was watching, as well a secure place to sleep. When finished, he climbed down the tree and carefully checked from all angles. He could not see his lair from anywhere on the ground, and he knew where it was. Satisfied that he would be undetectable from ground level or from anywhere around the tree, he climbed to the platform of boughs and settled in to wait.

He would spend a day and night concealed in this particular lair, watching, before selecting his target.

After the sun set on the first day, he rose from the bed of spruce boughs where he had lain concealed, stretched, and relieved himself against the tree trunk, spreading his scat over the nearby branches as necessary. He never noticed the smell, nor would anyone else that happened to pass under the tree, for it was not an uncommon odor in the forest. He thought his scat smelled similar enough to that of a bear that it would not arouse the suspicion of anyone passing close by.

His weapons consisted of a short, powerful bow, quiver of arrows, belt knife, and the ever-present axe. His personal needs were simple; a piece of dried meat or fish, or the still warm hearts of his victims washed down with water from his water skin. Beyond that he needed nothing. Unconscious of and unaffected by the passage of time, he had become a base animal, no longer bothered by the normal thoughts of man, but supremely aware of every sound and smell in his proximity. He had gradually become feral, a dangerous predator, his whole being focused on watching and waiting. That is what he did, day after day, watch his enemy, and then he picked his target and the time to strike.

The village, a typical palisaded enclosure of 20 to 30 longhouses was the principle village of the Ganadoga Haudenosaunee. He estimated that there were about 200-300 people in the village.

He chose his prey carefully from those that journeyed out from the village. His focus was war parties, but he also chose hunters, fishermen, anybody that left the safety of the village, man or woman. He studied his enemies carefully before he chose a target. The dark of a moonless night was his preference, because it instilled terror in his prey, but daylight was more normal because that is when the people of the village were afield. His intent was to exact revenge against the people of this particular band, to kill as many of them as possible, all of them if possible, before they finally got him. He was under no illusions about that. What he was doing required great skill and lots of luck. His enemies were superb fighting men. They would all hunt him relentlessly. He relished that aspect of what he was doing. The challenge of continually avoiding them on their own ground appealed to his sense of adventure. But, one day his luck would run out and he would be seen out in the open, or his current lair would be found. Then he would fight his final battle against them.

Three winters had passed since this vendetta began. During the height of the cold winter, conditions sometimes forced him out of the forest and into one of the Naskapi villages. Those that knew him well thought his fixation on that which had changed him would eventually be satisfied, and he would rejoin the people. That had not happened. If anything he had become more withdrawn, more introspective, and more dangerous to his enemies.

He turned up in a Naskapi village from time to time, where he had many friends, but for the most part he remained cloistered from others. His friends were concerned about him, because his transformation had been so severe from that which he had been, in another place, at another time, that he no longer resembled that man. His comings and goings were frightening to most people; he appeared and later disappeared, without offering an explanation and usually without a sound. The village guards never saw him until he was standing before them, so adept had he become at the stealth that kept him alive in the environment in which he lived. Not even the dogs barked, rather they slunk away, frightened at the smell and sight of the apparition that suddenly materialized in their space.

He was more animal than man, a dangerous predator of other men; scruffy, dirty, completely focused on his mission. What he was doing possessed him; it had become his reason to exist. He no longer had any human feelings. Mercy for others was not a part of what he had become. Such things had been ripped away by a personal loss that he could not accept. He existed to kill.

Even to a close friend, the change in the man was so profound that he would have been unrecognizable at first glance. His eyes were empty of feeling; his face devoid of expression. The stained buckskin clothing he wore blended naturally with the deep forest, the place where he lurked. The stains and splotches on his buckskins broke up any discernible human shape when he concealed himself. His hair and beard had grown long and unkempt. If it got in his way he wacked off the bottom some, twisted it a couple of times, and tied it in a knot. A nondescript fur hat effectively broke up any symmetry with the shape of his head that a watcher might detect. Lying prone in heavy brush, the hunter would have been virtually invisible.

Before beginning his final approach to his victims, the final stalk, he tied a thick rawhide bearskin pad, hair side down, to the bottom of each foot, much as one would don snowshoes. They served to distribute his weight over a much larger area than his moccasin clad foot. The thick bear fur distorted the shape of his foot, leaving almost no discernible imprint beyond a slight scuff on bare ground, and little to no sign at all in the groundcover of the forest. The pads ensured that anybody that found his spore would not think that a man made the sign. He wanted it to be as if he had never been there.

Many of the natives of this heavily forested land had an ancient legend about a man-like demon they called Death Wind. It was said the wind moaned through the forest like a demented spirit when he was on the hunt. This man was the manifestation of that demon, that spirit of the forest, and the men and women that became his prey were terrified that the legend had returned, to prey on them.

He had originally gotten the idea from conversations with his friend Deskaheh. The man had told him much about his people, the Haudenosaunee. Nipishish had been interested in learning about them, and Deskaheh provided answers to all the pointed questions that he asked.

Over time the kernel of an idea formed in the mind of Nipishish while he listened to the tales spun by his friend, especially those tales of the legend of Death Wind, the spirit of the deep forest. At some point during these sessions, without conscious thought, Nipishish began to actually become in his own mind the contemporary manifestation of this demon of the forest.

Death Wind had always been the people's way of explaining the loss of entire war parties, of individuals, of small parties of women and children foraging in the forest. It was known that children were never harmed by the demon. They wandered back to the village, speechless with terror, having never seen the demon that massacred the adults that they had accompanied.

A war party would immediately take to the forest to run the demon to ground, but beyond a scuff mark or two at the scene, a broken twig, or bent over blades of grass, no complete tracks were ever found, nor had anyone ever seen the demon. The victims were always found, though, sitting upright back to back, or propped against a tree trunk, hearts ripped from their chests, and their empty eye sockets staring into eternity. The missing hearts were never found. The putrid smell of the demon lingered over the scene of the carnage. Had the war party known that the demon always ate the hearts with considerable relish, terror would have seized the bravest among them.

VILLAGE OF DEGANAWIDA

"The demon that walks like a man has killed many of our people. This is the second summer that he has preyed on us. We know he watches everything we do. The women are afraid to venture from the village. The only way they will go into the forest to forage is with a strong guard. Even then they get little work done because they are afraid." The emissary from the Ganadoga clan of the Haudenosaunee Nation spoke to the council of Deganawida with passion.

He continued. "Right now there are five men afield to try something new. They volunteered to try to lure him into a trap. We have never tried to lure him into a trap. He put us on the defensive from the beginning. If he does not fall into this trap, we…" His voice trailed off.

"Why do you not send all your warriors into the forest to hunt him down and kill him," said Sakohkea, from his place in the council seated at the center of the packed council house?

"We tried that, it did not work. He is not a man, Sakohkea, he is a demon. Warriors have taken the field many times to run him to ground. They never see him. He does not leave many tracks, nor any sign for them to follow."

Sakohkea snorted in derision. "No man can move without leaving some sign."

The emissary spoke through gritted teeth, struggling to maintain his temper in the face of Sakohkea's disbelief.

"He can do this thing. He is not a man. We think he is Death Wind, come to kill all of us."

An audible intake of breath swept the assembled warriors. An unnamed demon was one thing, but the legendary Death Wind was quite another.

In the ensuing silence, one of the assembled warriors, a distinctive young man with his dark blonde scalp lock festooned with the two eagle feathers of one that had distinguished himself as a warrior, voiced what the silent throng was thinking.

"How do you know the demon is Death Wind?"

The emissary turned toward the speaker. He nodded his recognition of the young man that was fast becoming a famous warrior among the people.

"I myself have heard Death Wind's moan in the forest before he strikes, Okwáho. The demon can only be Death Wind that takes the eyes and hearts of his victims."

Murmurs of superstitious dread swept through the assembly in the council house. Okwáho looked at his companion. An unspoken message passed between the close friends. The two young men watched the council closely, gaging the reaction of their leaders.

Beyond Sakohkea making eye contact with each of them, there was little reaction from the council of elders.

"I think my father now believes that the demon is Death Wind," said Otetiani, leaning toward Okwáho to make himself heard above the rising conversation.

"What do you think?"

Otetiani's black eyes fastened on Okwáho. His friend's intense, pale blue eyes always served to unnerve him somewhat.

"You and I are not true believers of all these mythical creatures that appear to the people from time-to-time. I dismissed this man's tale as just more myth, but when he told us that the victims had their eyes and hearts taken, I began to think that this might be more than just a myth."

"I agree. When the others settle down, I want to ask more questions about what they have found after Death Wind strikes."

Otetiani grunted his assent. "That is good; you ask better questions than I do."

The two grinned at each other, and turned their attention back to the council where one of the elders signed for quiet.

Deganawida leaned toward Sakohkea and spoke briefly. Sakohkea got to his feet, his eyes travelled the length and breadth of the assembly. Voices died away.

"Are there other questions before the council decides what is to be done?"

Okwáho had been waiting for just such an opportunity. He stood, so as to be heard and recognized.

A slight smile curved the corners of the war chief's mouth, softening the cruel visage. He had expected further questions from Okwáho. He inclined his head expectantly.

Addressing the emissary directly, Okwáho spoke loudly enough for all to hear.

"Tell us about one of the scenes of carnage, Juraken, so that we might know in our minds what to expect in the hunt for this demon." He took his seat again; content to let his question foster other questions. If something was missed he would ask other questions until they had the complete tale. He was known and appreciated for this ability to draw others out.

Juraken nodded his understanding to Okwáho, pausing for a moment while he gathered his thoughts. He had always been impressed by this pale skin son of Odatshedeh. The young man was a pale skin, but nobody would ever say that to him, for his heart was pure Haudenosaunee. It was said that this young man would one day be a leader among the people, for he was held in high regard for one so young. He looked around the room at the others and then began his tale. He looked directly at Okwáho for a time, and then his eyes wandered over the council and the crowd of men as he related his tale, emphasizing salient points with copious hand signs

"Since the beginning of this full moon there have been two attacks. The first one came on the first of two days that a group foraged for berries and mushrooms. The demon came in the night while they slept. There were six warriors to guard the five women and a young girl, so we know that somebody stood guard while the others slept."

"How do you know this," said a man in the back of the room.

"The demon spared the young girl. He has never hurt children. We do not know why."

The man paused a moment before continuing. His face twisted in anguish as he struggled to maintain his composure.

"At dawn, the young girl, my daughter, awakened to find every person in the camp dead. One of the dead was her mother, my mate." Juraken lost his struggle then, his composure slipped away, burst asunder like bubble on the water. The room grew silent, while he struggled to regain himself. After a moment he continued the gruesome tale.

"My daughter returned to our village right away, she could not remain in the camp for fear of Death Wind. She heard his voice moan through the forest."

Murmurs of incredulity and unease swept the assembly.

When they quieted, Juraken continued. "I know it is hard to believe in these things. It is hard for me to believe what my ears have heard and my eyes have seen. But, I have heard the voice of Death Wind; he lurks in the forest. There is nothing I have ever heard before that is like the sound he makes. It starts as a stirring through the forest, the leaves of birch trees flutter as if a breeze is blowing, but there is none. That fluttering is followed by a kind of keening sound that grows in volume until the tree tops begin to sway as from a strong wind. It is then that you hear the moan of Death Wind in the distance. It is an unworldly sound."

More than one man in the assembly felt a chill course through his body, for not every man is imbued with the same degree of courage, especially concerning the spirit world of legend. These men could face any enemy they could see in battle with bravery, but the unknown tended to terrify them. To face this manifestation of evil that had always been known as Death Wind among the people caused the bravest among them to quail to a certain degree.

"After my daughter returned alone to the village to tell us what had happened, a large party of men followed her back to the camp. Everyone had been butchered, their blood was everywhere. The demon poked out their eyes, and cut their hearts out. All the bodies had been arranged in a circle with their backs inward. Death Wind used a forked stick to hold up their heads, so that the first thing you noticed was their empty eye sockets staring into eternity."

Juraken hung his head a moment while he struggled with his raging emotions. He looked up, and his eyes swept the attentive assembly.

"One man's head was missing. His head had been cut from his neck with a single stroke of something big and sharp. The demon has never taken a head before. Like the missing hearts we did not find it at the scene of the carnage. Death Wind returned the head to the village during the following night. It was found sitting atop one of the prisoner poles in front of the council house. It was a sign from the spirits to strike fear into our people. Now we are all afraid. That is why I have been sent here to ask you, Deganawida, for your help."

The assembly went crazy for a moment at the thought that Death Wind had overcome the security posed by the palisade surrounding the village as well as eluding the two guards.

A hand sign from Deganawida restored quiet after the uproar ran its course.

"How did he get by your guards?" asked Odatshedeh from his place with the council.

"I do not know, but neither of them saw or heard a thing out of the ordinary. It was a dark night; the crescent moon had already set when he came during the time before first light. The wind was blowing. That made it hard for the guards to hear an intruder, if Death Wind ever makes a noise that can be heard. They both said they heard a couple of dogs growling, but when they stopped growling the guards thought no more of it. With the dawn, both dogs were found cut in half at the shoulders. We have no weapon that could cut a dog in half with a single stroke. The dogs would have died instantly, without a sound. I was sent here to tell you about what has been happening to us. We cannot fight the demon alone, not when he can come and go in the village as he wishes."

"Did you find the demon's tracks," asked Okwáho. "He must have left his sign in the dirt of the village."

"Death Wind has never left what you could call a track. No sign of his trail in the forest has ever been found. Dead bodies are all he leaves for us to find."

———

Midday of the second day that he watched the village, Nipishish selected his prey. Five warriors walked from the village gate and into the forest. They intended to fish judging from the net one carried over his shoulders and the long fishing spears that each carried. They were not in a hurry, so he thought they might not have far to go, especially given that half the time of daylight had gone. He lost sight of them after they entered the forest. He had noted that people coming and going from the village generally used one of three well defined trails when moving through the area where he lay concealed. One of those trails followed a draw that ended on the banks of a small lake behind his position to the north. He shifted position so he could see a small section of the draw in the hopes he would be able to see which trail they had taken. After a time, his vigilance was rewarded when first one, and then the other four warriors wound single file on the hoped for trail in the direction of the lake. After that he lost sight of them.

He went back to watching the village. Activity in and around the village lessened as the day wore on. If the five warriors did not return before dark, he would go after them along their back trail.

His mind wandered and became blank as he lay prone on the bed of boughs, the warmth of the afternoon air lulled him and his eyelids became heavy. During his slumber he remained unconsciously aware of the normal sounds of the forest: the snapping of insects, the cries of the birds, the strident barking of a village dog that suddenly became yelps of pain, and the smell of the spruce needles under him. Finally lulled to sleep by his benign surroundings, he remained so until awakened suddenly with a start.

Slowly opening his eyes, he remained frozen in position, aware that something untoward had awakened him. Nothing out of the ordinary could be seen in or around the village. Smoke came from the wigwam smoke holes as the village women stoked the cook fires to warm the final meal of the day. The smoke rose into the still air of the surface to drift away to the south and disperse into the forest.

Smoke! That is what woke me up. I smell smoke, he thought. He turned his head slowly, examining the countryside in proximal relation to his position. As he shifted slowly a slight smear of smoke could be seen in the direction of the lake to his north. Sucking his teeth, his attention fastened on the almost invisible thread of grey rising into the still air and dispersing in his direction.

He glanced to the west. Although he could not see it, he knew that the orb of the sun would be sinking from view, bringing his friend the darkness to the land. *They have built a fire. Perhaps they intend to camp for the night.* His mouth widened slightly in what might have passed as a smile. The eyes did not change, remaining lifeless. *Building a fire could get them killed.*

Sometime later, he crept down from the tree. Standing immobile against the dark tree trunk for a time, he listened to the sounds of the night, sniffed the air, and watched for telltale movement around his position. Beyond the lingering faint smell of wood smoke there was nothing untoward that he detected. He bent down and tied the fur pads in place on his feet. Straightening up, he again stood immobile for quite some time listening to the night sounds. Satisfied, he crept down off the knoll through the underbrush and into the cloaking darkness of the deep forest.

Moving from tree to tree, he crept inexorably in the direction of the lake, his course dictated by the continual smell of smoke in his sensitive nose. All senses continually on full alert, he paused often and listened carefully for sounds alien to the forest before creeping forward to another tree to begin the whole process anew.

During one such period of rigid attention, the noise of an animal eating the ferns growing in profusion underfoot came to his ears. He was so close he heard the rumblings from the animal's stomach yet, being downwind, his presence had not been detected. Unless he made a noise that the animal heard, he would not be detected. Thus far he still had not seen the animal in the natural gloom of the forest. Knowing it was a big moose, probably a lone bull; he remained frozen in position, waiting for the animal to make a move so he could follow up with his own move. Being this close he could only move in concert with the animal to avoid detection.

This game with the moose continued for some time. With the moose foraging in the general direction of the lake where the five warriors were encamped, he thought it prudent to just follow along.

As he moved slowly along, more or less together with the moose, a plan began to form in his mind. The smell of smoke went from an occasional whiff to a heavier smell of smoke as they drew near the Haudeno camp. Nipishish marveled that the moose did not balk from the smoke as the acrid smell increased, but he continued his unconcerned grazing, moving slowly toward the lake.

The slight flicker of light from a fire up ahead reflected off the bottoms of leaves and pine needles. Knowing they were very close now, he put his plan into action by leaping from concealment directly at the bull moose that loomed head. The animal's head was down for another mouth full when he slapped him across the butt with his bow.

The animal, finally aware that something had materialized in his space, jumped sideways in fright and ran directly away from that which had frightened him.

Close behind, ran Nipishish, using all the cover available, he stole within a matter of feet from the campfire of Haudeno warriors before going to ground. He watched with what amusement he was capable of as the moose charged through the Haudeno camp, scattering men and embers from the fire before disappearing into the forest beyond.

The surprised Haudeno warriors shouted and gestured at the trotting moose as it disappeared in the darkness. What was a fairly normal event for them did not put them on alert or raise their suspicions. Gradually they returned to their former conversation and interrupted meal. None had an inkling that certain death watched them from the darkness.

Nipishish watched all this unfold from his prone position in the heavy brush. His unkempt appearance, bearded face, and nondescript outline blended perfectly into the landscape.

The men began to roll up in their sleeping robes, leaving one of their number to stand the first watch. The guard made a circle around the campsite, selecting a spot at the edge of the forest to begin his watch.

Nipishish settled in to wait for sleep to claim the men that encircled the tiny fire pit. He knew the guard was there, but could not make out his outline in the dark backdrop of the forest. One of the other men grunted something unintelligible, got up from his robe, and walked into the brush directly toward Nipishish to take a wet.

He stopped an axe handle from where Nipishish lay concealed, pulled his manhood from beneath his buckskin pullover, and began to piss in the brush.

Nipishish coiled to spring at him, but quickly realized that the man was likely blinded by the last flickering flames of the fire. He slowly relaxed.

Although the man's eyes travelled over the darkness before him, he did not see the prostrate form at his feet. He continued his stream for the longest time, finally waving his member back and forth, and slinging piss out over the brush at his feet.

Nipishish closed his eyes to receive a brief stream of piss full in the face. As suddenly as it began, the stream stopped and the Haudeno returned to his robes without a word to the guard lying in concealment.

With piss running down his face, Nipishish did not move a muscle. By the time the men around the fire were fast asleep, the piss had dried in place, and a ghostlike apparition began to slither forward toward the guard's position. Utterly soundless his approach remained undetected. He finally reached a point where he saw the man seated facing the camp with his back against a tree trunk. Altering his course somewhat, he moved toward a point behind the tree that the guard leaned against.

It took tremendous strength and endurance to sneak up on a man that waited in readiness to protect his fellows. Nipishish barely touched the ground as he crept forward, his knees and elbows often the only points of contact. Feeling the ground in front for obstacles, he carefully moved sticks and brush aside as he inched forward. Focused intently on his prey, he closed the distance inexorably, making no more noise through the brush than a snake stalking its prey.

The Haudeno sentry lounged comfortably against the bole of the tree, his sleeping robe covered his shoulders against the night's chill. He had been fighting off a spell of drowsiness, so he got to his feet and shook himself. Taking a couple of hops in place and shrugging his shoulders seemed to help. He returned to his robe and leaned back against the tree. Suddenly his head was wretched violently to the side by a powerful hand over his mouth and nose. He struggled mightily, unable to make a sound; his last conscious thought was a searing pain across his neck as the knife blade nearly decapitated him, killing him instantly.

The warrior's killer slowly relaxed his vicelike grip on the man's head, and lowered the still form to the side. Without pause he slithered forward, killing the other four warriors in the same silent manner, without a sound being made by any of his victims. His work done, Nipishish crept into the brush to conceal himself to wait the coming dawn when he would complete his work.

Just after first light, five gore covered bodies sat in a tight circle facing outward with legs extended. Their heads were propped upright on a sharpened forked stick that had been shoved down into their chests at the juncture of neck and collar bone. To ensure the bodies remained in their posed position, Nipishish tied them together at the elbows with their own pullovers.

Earlier in the ritual, the eyes had been levered from the skull of each dead man with a knife. Then the chest was sundered between the ribs on the left side with an axe blow. Separating the ribs far enough for his hand to gain entry into the chest cavity, he reached in, grasped the heart, and ripped it from the body.

He rolled the five hearts up in a leftover pullover and placed the packet in his pack for later. The hearts tasted better cooked, if he had the time and could kindle a fire, but he would eat them regardless. He thought they tasted like pork, one of his favorite meats from another time. Taking a moment to survey his work, he nodded in satisfaction, and melted into the woods.

Had the dead Haudeno warriors been able to hear, an unworldly sound muted by distance would have come to them, a keening wail that seemed to come from everywhere and nowhere all at once. At the peak of the terrifying wail, the tree tops trembled as though a slight breeze had come, but the five bodies that bore witness felt none.

It took several days for the war parties to find the missing men. The five men went missing the day they were expected to return to their village and runners were dispatched to the other nearby Haudeno villages.

Deganawida had decided to respond to the Ganadoga Clan's plea for help, and it was a war party from his village that found the missing men.

Circling vultures led them to the spot.

A party of six young warriors spread out in a line within hail of one another, moved rapidly through the forest. The sky opened up over a fen, and without the cloaking cover of the forest canopy, the man on that end of the line, Otetiani, saw the circling buzzards as he stepped into the fen.

His shouts drew the others in.

"Buzzards are onto something dead," he pointed into the northern sky as his friend Igoo joined him in the fen.

The other warriors joined them.

All were close friends and had spent their boyhoods together, except for one of them. He had joined them four seasons ago as the adopted son of Odatshedeh. Much had happened in the land of the Haudenosaunee since that day. After humble beginnings among the people, that young man, Okwáho, had blossomed into what he had been born to be, a leader of men. He had not been appointed the leader of this party by the war chief of the Cokanuk Band of the Haudenosaunee people, but that is what invariably happened when the party consisted of young men. The others deferred to him and the war chief, Sakohkea, knew that when he sent them on their mission.

"I do not have good feelings about those vultures, Okwáho," said Otetiani.

The tall young man fastened his piercing blue eyes on his closest friend. He grinned at him.

"Nor do I. Let us go see what they have found."

The war party waded through the fen and fanned out in to the forest as before, heading in the general direction of the circling vultures.

They were the first search party to arrive, quickly followed by several others. The scene that greeted them reduced even the hardest warrior to silence. Most stood in a kind of shocked hush at the enormity of the rage that had been visited on these dead men. Some could not look at what remained of the five men that many of them had known. Men from the Ganadoga clan were especially affected, for they had known these men all their lives.

Although the six young men sent out by Sakohkea were certainly not the principles in this gathering of warriors, their leader had never been one to keep silent before his betters. He had nodded a greeting to the war chief of the Ganadoga warriors, the largest group present, and stood by respectively while the others handled the disaster in their own way. Still not knowing of the specifics of the plan that had gotten these five men butchered, his curiosity finally got the better of him.

He got Otetiani's attention with a bob of his head toward the war chief. The two men approached those grouped with the Ganadoga war chief. They stopped in front of him and listened to the subdued conversation while waiting to be noticed.

Okwáho would never know that these same Ganadoga men had directly contributed to the death of his natural mother, Ingerd, three seasons before, nor did he know that she was even dead. Those things had happened in another time and place, when he was someone else entirely. To look at him now, it would never occur to the casual observer that this stalwart Haudenosaunee warrior was also, Ivar the Northman. He seldom thought of his former life. The most formative portion of his life had been spent as the son of Odatshedeh. He was one of the people, a Haudeno warrior to his core.

The subject of conversation among the men grouped around the war chief shifted, and his gaze came to rest on Okwáho. The war chief, Ongwata, nodded a greeting to the young man.

"I am troubled by what I have seen here, as we all are. How did this happen, Ongwata? Juraken told us of a plan that brought these men here. What was that plan?"

"It was not really a plan, Okwáho; it was more of an idea. These men volunteered to try to lure the demon into a trap. I do not know what their plan was." He gestured vaguely toward the bodies. "Whatever they decided to do, it did not work. We all need to take to the field, all this summer, to confront this demon. We must stay in large groups for safety. Even at that I do not know how to fight this demon that none has ever even seen."

Looking skeptical, Okwáho stated what was obvious to his way of thinking. "The demon killed five seasoned warriors that had taken the field to trap him. If he can do that, he can kill any of us, at any time that he chooses."

Ongwata's eyes narrowed somewhat as the young man spoke. He had heard all about him from Sakohkea, who held him in high regard. He glanced from Okwáho to Otetiani.

"What do you think we should do about this demon?"

"I do not know what to do about him," said Otetiani. "We have never seen him. Nobody is alive that has seen him. I agree with Okwáho, and so do the others in our party, the demon will take us when he wants to."

Every man present, regardless of clan, had gathered around the war chief of the Ganadoga clan to hear what was being discussed. Few had anything to add to what had already been said. During a pause in the dialogue, a voice came from the back of the crowd.

"Nobody calls this demon what it is. It is Death Wind! I heard him a few nights ago just before dawn."

He suddenly became the focus of attention as the group parted, leaving him at its center facing Ongwata. Many of those present drew away from the man, not wishing to be near anybody that made mention of the horror known as Death Wind. Most men thought that to deny the spirit's existence would somehow protect them and their families. That had not worked well for any of the victims of Death Wind's recent depredations.

The speaker gestured at others standing with him. "We all heard the moaning wail. I have never before heard such a sound in the forest."

"How far away was this sound from you," asked Ongwata?

"I do not know, it seemed close at hand. Others that heard its wail said that it seemed close at hand to them too."

"Yes," said another. "I was in the forest at the other end of the village from, Deshay." He indicated the first speaker. "The wail sounded very close by me. I ran back toward the village with several other people."

Nobody laughed at this admission of fear. Just talking about things that most preferred not to talk about had many of the men glancing over their shoulders, their unease apparent.

Okwáho felt a chill course through his body at all this talk of demons and spirits. Like all primitive peoples that lived close to nature, the fear of the unseen, the unknown, the unclean, rode on their shoulders wherever they went, especially in the half light of the dense forest which was their home. It was easy for a man to conjure up things that might lurk in the gloom. The fact that these same thoughts now manifested into a tangible demon, one that had long ago reached the status of legend, was horrifying to contemplate.

On the other side of the clearing from where the Haudeno men grouped in conversation, and within earshot, leaning against the bole of large ash tree that stood in heavy shadow, the object of their concern listened closely to the conversation.

He had chosen his cover carefully. Brush and saplings obscured the bole of the tree he leaned against, leaving a small, unobstructed view of the proceedings that he watched. The heavy shadow of the deep forest did the rest. He knew that if one of them looked directly at his position that he would not be seen, his concealment was so complete.

It pleased him to be this close to his enemies without their knowing he was there. He could hear every word spoken. He knew that most of them would feel as though they were being watched as their conversation moved toward the discussion of the spirits they feared above all things. That was natural for a hunter, a warrior to have senses tuned to that level of perception. They all knew that he, Death Wind, was out there, somewhere, waiting. He used that fear, fed it with the bodies of the slain, and nurtured it with his savage treatment of his victims.

Even the voice of the demon was his invention. In the early days of his wanderings, thoughts of Ingerd and the manner of her death was still fresh in his mind. The first time he killed, the sound had sprung from his mouth unbidden from the pure joy he experienced as he savaged the remains of his victims. It seemed so natural to him that he just continued without conscious thought, knowing that the sound would serve to further terrify his enemies.

While listening to the subdued conversation of the warriors he had heard one voice in the throng that seemed familiar, that stirred a remembrance in him. He began to watch that young man closely, trying to place the voice. It had been many seasons since he last saw his son. As he watched and listened he began to realize that the young man with the two eagle feathers was Ivar. He also knew that he was his enemy. That fact evoked no feeling or emotion in him. He would kill him as he would any other enemy, without thought or feeling.

He listened to the conversation about Death Wind run its course. The tall young man with the two eagle feathers had occupied a prominent place in the conversation. He watched him closely. He knew that he would see him again as the hunt went on, season after season.

He watched the men begin to stack dry wood against and atop the circle of dead he had prepared for the living. They kindled a small fire off the side of the pyre and men carried bundles of burning grass to set the pile of wood alight in several places. Soon, flames engulfed the entire pyre and greasy black smoke rose into the air as the body fat flowed from the corpses, ignited, and helped to consume them.

While he watched all of this from his place of concealment, he saw the tall young man turn and look directly at him, or at least it seemed that he did so, although he could not possibly see him. The moment passed quickly, but he knew that his presence had left an imprint on the soul of the young Haudeno warrior that he would never forget. *He felt that something was watching him. That is good. Such a thing might keep him alive for a time.*

With that, he gave the throng around the pyre one last look, his eyes dead, his mind vacant of any feeling, moved slowly around the bole of the ash tree, and melted into the forest like a puff of smoke.

—❧—

"What is it, what is the matter?" asked Otetiani. He had noticed his friend studying the forest verge close at hand.

Okwáho shook himself, as from a chill.

"I do not know. I thought somebody was watching me."

Otetiani looked in the indicated direction. "I do not see anything." He snorted. "We all feel strange. It is this talk of spirits. It is nothing."

"Oh, it was something all right. I know when I am being watched. Get the others, let us go look around that big ash tree." He gestured toward the towering tree.

Their curiosity peaked, their senses on full alert; the six young men fanned out and examined the area around the ash tree. Okwáho gave the base of the ash tree his full attention. A thick carpet of leaves covered the area, the detritus of many seasons, and he could glean nothing unusual from his preliminary examination. A nagging doubt pushed him on. Dropping to hands and knees he crawled slowly around the bole of the tree. Suddenly he stopped.

"Come here. Easy, do not step near the trunk. Get down on your hands and knees," he ordered his companions. He pointed to an area in the leaves against the trunk. "Tell me what you see there."

All six of them, their heads close to ground level, looked intently at the area indicated.

"I see a slight depression in the leaves. That is all I see," said Gyantwaka, pushing up on his haunches.

"Exactly," said Okwáho. "That is what I see, too. How about the rest of you?"

"I do not know, maybe," offered Ganeodiyo.

"The leaves are not broken. It is just a depression. It means nothing to me," said Otetiani. "Why, what do you think it is?"

"I think something was standing here a moment ago," said Okwáho, getting to his feet.

"What?" asked Igoo, his eyes wide as he got to his feet, looking around and into the dark forest.

The others quickly got to their feet and assumed a stance of readiness, although none knew why they reacted in that way.

"I do not know what stood here, but something mashed that carpet of leaves down." Okwáho leaned over to examine a mark in the bark of the tree. The light was bad, making it difficult to see exactly what had drawn his attention.

"Look at this." He pointed at the slight mark. "Something sharp made that mark in the bark."

Otetiani voiced his opinion with a loud snort.

"I think your imagination is running wild. I agree that the mark was made from something sharp, but what was it? A dry branch could have broken off higher up the tree from a gust of wind and made that mark." He tossed his hand in a gesture of dismissal. "Here comes Ongwata. You will have to explain all this to him now."

"No, say nothing. I have to think more about these things," said Okwáho, as he turned to meet the war chief before he got to the tree.

"What is it? Have you found something over there?" The war chief's eyes bored into his.

"No, not really. I thought I found something, but the others weren't sure about it. It is nothing, Ongwata."

Shortly thereafter, each war party headed off toward their particular village. All had agreed that they would continue the sweeps over their territories in the hopes that they could keep the countryside so stirred up that the demon would move on to other easier prey. During all the conversation it did not occur to anyone to ask why all the victims had been from one band alone. This question would later come up at a council, but no reasonable answer would ever be found.

The smoke of the pyre still rose into the air to disperse through the treetops in the slight breeze that blew off the lake, when the last of the men disappeared into the forest.

The tall young man stopped and looked back at the base of the ash tree, indistinct in the gloom of the forest. He felt another chill course through his body. He knew for a certainty that he had been right, something had stood there. But, he would never know how close he had been to what had been there. The mark in the bark of the tree had been made from the edge of a very sharp axe, as the entity he knew as the demon had leaned back against that very tree trunk while he watched the warriors gathered at the scene of his slaughter.

Like many things in the life of solitary stealth that he led, the lair he had found and lived in for the past three seasons of his unrelenting war of vengeance had been found by accident. He had found the cave while desperately looking for a place to hide from the men that had very nearly gotten him one day. They had been so close he had clearly heard their shouts. The snapping of branches and splashes in the water of the river that he clearly heard to his rear told him his flight from them was about to end badly if he did not find concealment. He had waded down the river in the hopes of avoiding them, but they stayed right on him, knowing he had not left the water. Coming to a steep defile that eons of river water had worn through the solid rock of the canyon, he had quickly examined both sheer walls of the defile for handholds, so he could climb from the water undetected. His wet moccasins left no discernible imprint on the almost sheer wall of the defile. Always damp from spray as the river water plunged through on its journey downstream, the defile seemed to beckon to him. Carefully he began to climb upward on the uphill side.

Quickly he climbed as high as he could get before his Haudeno pursuers hove into view below. In his frenzy to escape he found a small evergreen, grasses, and scrub, tenaciously clinging to a narrow ledge. The ledge offered enough concealment for him to slither in behind the tree and scrub just as his pursuers burst into the beginning of the defile below. He burrowed into the thin layer of dirt and lichen at the base of his cover careful to avoid loosening any material to fall below and reveal his location.

The men shouted back and forth over the roar of the cascading water, a note of frustration in their voices.

Nipishish was so close he heard every word, in spite of the sound of rushing water.

Their minute examination of the area yielded them nothing, so they soon continued downstream.

He knew they would be back. In a short span of time they would know that they had passed him and would return to try to cut his trail, to find where they had lost his spoor. That was how the deadly game was played between the pursuers and their prey. He did the same.

Using the small evergreen to shield his face and the outline of his head, he carefully looked over the edge of the narrow bench he lay on and surveyed the river basin to the limit of his vision. Nothing was to be seen, but he knew they would not give up that easily. If he had made a move away from his concealment, he knew that he would be seen. One of their favored tricks was for one man to linger behind in concealment, to watch the area where they had lost the trail. Should their prey become impatient and move away from a place of concealment, and into the open, they would come whooping in triumph after him.

No, he had known they would do this. He was stuck like a moth in a spider web. He would have to wait right here on the ledge all night if need be, not daring to move, not daring to attempt to continue his dangerous climb in the dark. Perhaps sometime after first light returned tomorrow, he could make good his escape.

The Haudeno warriors had come back before darkness cloaked the land, but they did not find him. Now, around mid-morning of the following day, long after he had seen the last of them, he unfolded from his narrow sanctuary and stood erect. His legs and back muscles twitched and crawled as the blood coursed back through parts that had been asleep most of the previous night. He stood unmoving while feeling returned to his cramped muscles.

He stood absolutely immobile on the ledge for a very long time, partially concealed by the small evergreen tree. Sectioning off the semi-circular panorama to his fore, he minutely examined each slice of the countryside for anything that did not belong where he saw it. His body pressed back and molded into the cliff face at his back. It is doubtful he would have been seen by anyone even though he stood erect. Attired in nondescript leather clothing, hair and beard gone long and scraggly, and with his head topped off with a fur hat that distorted its outline, he blended perfectly with the multi-colored granite of the cliff that he stood against.

Finally satisfied that his enemies were gone, he carefully turned around on the ledge and examined the cliff still above where he stood. A crack the width of his fist seemed to run all the way to the cliff's top. Reaching above his head, he jammed his fist in the crack, tested his purchase on the rock to either side, and pulled himself up the length of his arm until his feet found toeholds on the cliff face. He repeated this process, hand over hand, gradually working his way up until another small ledge presented itself. The crack he had been using continued on through this narrow ledge and upwards. He had not noticed the ledge from below, and he had been looking for anything that would give him an advantage in his climb. Off to the side, level with the ledge, a v-shaped hole appeared in view as his eyes came level with the ledge. It was not very wide, but curiosity got the better of his normal caution, and he went hand over hand along the ledge until even with the hole in the cliff face. He saw immediately that it was a cave, the extent of which was not immediately apparent. The highest point of the v-shaped opening extended just half its length up the cliff face from the ledge, the reason it had not been visible from below, while the other half extended below the inside edge of the ledge that he gripped in both hands.

Pulling himself up as far as possible, he braced his feet against the sheer cliff face, and grabbing the sides of the opening in first one hand and then the other, he swung himself up onto the ledge on his right side with his face directly in front of the cave opening.

He reached into the opening as far as he could. As he conducted this arm's length survey he quickly realized that the cave was much larger than the bottleneck entrance indicated. By turning sideways he was able to wriggle inside far enough to sit up. Dark as the bottom of a well inside he could not see the full extent of his discovery, but he was satisfied nonetheless. He smiled to himself, a rare thing these days. *This could be a good place to hide*, he thought.

With the cursory examination of his new discovery finished, he climbed back out to the ledge and carefully unfolded himself from where he had lain, winding up with his back to the cliff face. The ledge he stood on was not as wide as his feet were long, as evidenced by the fact that his toes hung out over the edge. He looked both ways along the ledge, seeing that it narrowed down and finally ended just beyond the cave entrance in one direction, while the other direction seemed to continue out of view, indicating continuity. He moved slowly in that direction, arms out from his sides for balance, hands feeling carefully for purchase on the cliff wall. Coming to the point where the ledge had disappeared from view, he peered around the corner and saw the ledge come out on an expanse of bedrock. For the first time in a long time, he felt excitement as he realized what this cave and its dangerous access could mean to his security. *Even if they find where I am hiding, they can only come at me one at a time. Eventually I would kill all of them,* he grunted thoughtfully.

Later that same day he went back to have a good look at the cave with a pine faggot and dried grass to make a torch. He discovered that the cave was exactly what he needed to survive alone.

The narrow entrance widened into a single room high enough for him to stand erect, and wide enough to move about or lie down. Besides the security it offered, he found a water drip that with minimal excavation would provide him all the fresh water he needed.

Animals had used the cave over the years, but not recently. He found no evidence of bears being among the past residents in the scat scattered over the sloped floor. Being trapped in a small cave with a bear determined to hibernate for the winter was not appealing to him. *My own stench should keep animals from ever using this cave again. Nothing will ever want to be around me again,* he thought ruefully.

He noticed a draft in the cave the first time he had inspected it with the torch. The considerable smoke from the torch was being sucked out through the back of the roof, and out a hole he could see daylight through. *That is how the small animals have been getting in here,* he thought. They did not seem to use the narrow ledge, and now he knew why.

It took careful sleuthing to find the hole from the outside that animals used to come and go, but find it he did. The cool air flowing from the hole, he now thought of it as a chimney, confirmed his discovery. To exclude animals from the cave he arranged a nondescript pile of rocks that looked perfectly natural over the top of the chimney that closed it off as an entrance for strays, yet still promoted the circulation he desired through the cave itself.

He thought the cave to be a perfect combination of protection from the elements and security from those that hunted him. He found he could even kindle a small fire because of the draft without worrying that he might choke to death in accumulated smoke and fumes. The sticks and limbs of an abandoned packrat nest in one corner provided fuel for many such fires.

He ranged far and wide over the countryside, but whenever his wanderings brought him back he began to spend more and more time in the cave. It offered the only security he had ever found since he began his odyssey of the hunt. He felt relaxed and secure while there, something that had eluded him over all this time.

The fat of the animals he killed was used as fuel for an oil lamp he had made from a geode found in a creek bottom. With the wick he had braided out of dry grass floating in a puddle of melted fat, the small flame illuminated and warmed the cave, providing enough heat in the process to partially cook the meat or fish he ate each day.

The cave allowed him to gradually accumulate a few meager possessions. Grass and leaves packed into a dry, natural depression on the cave floor, covered by a moose hide, provided a comfortable bed. A backrest filched from a berry gathering group of Haudeno women and set up atop his extra skins provided a good comfortable place to contemplate his next move, or work on his many projects. Birch withes suitable for arrows lay flat on the rock floor. He collected the best he found during his wanderings, and bundled them with split spruce root as a binding to keep them straight while the wood cured and dried. Bow staves split from the outer living layers of the elm tree, just under the bark and including a good wedge of heartwood cured at the same time. He had broken the tip off his bow jumping down from a tree awhile back. His repair had produced a shorter, more powerful bow, but he did not like the balance – arrows had a tendency to overshoot the target. When the elm staves were cured out he intended to select the best of them for a new bow. The new bow had to be short, because he carried it and his arrows in a bow case off a shoulder and down across his back.

Crudely tanned leather for moccasins and clothing accumulated. He planned to make a full set of new, less odiferous clothing over the next winter, while he holed up like a bear during the worst of it.

During periods when he stopped looking for his prey – something that he felt increased their terror of Death Wind – the cave offered enough security that he could relax while warriors hunted him far and wide over the land. He felt they would never find his hiding place. With enough meat and fish air dried in the cave, his needs were such that he could linger for long periods without having to assume the risk of foraging expeditions outside.

The wolf sat on its haunches watching the man kneeling at the lakeshore, seemingly unperturbed by his proximity to a mortal enemy.

Earlier, the man had tensed, his hand stealing to the haft of the axe on the ground at his side when he detected the movement of the wolf. He watched the animal glide soundlessly as smoke through the forest verge.

The animal came to a stop as he walked into the open, standing still for a time at the tree line as he studied the man. Apparently satisfied he then angled toward where the man knelt on the lakeshore gutting the large pike that his fish weir had snared. He sat back on his haunches like a dog, watching every movement of the man. The great head moved slightly as the sensitive nose tested the air.

Noting that the big male wolf was in prime condition, Nipishish also noted that his muzzle was grizzled, almost white. Dried blood stained the grey and black fur on his near flank. A split nose and split ear crusted with more dried blood, and minus its tip spoke of a recent battle. He *lost the fight to hold onto his pack to a younger more dominate male. It happens to all of us, old fellow,* he thought, lips compressed in a grim line. He threw the wolf the guts and head of the pike, then rocked back comfortably to see what he did with the offering.

The animal distained to look at the fish offal; his unblinking eyes remained on the man. That he did not feel threatened was obvious by his being a matter of feet away, that he remained sitting, and that he did not even look at or shy away from the offal as it skidded to a stop near his feet.

Nipishish did not utter a sound. The wolf and he communicated in silence, their actions did the talking.

He went back to butchering his pike, occasionally stealing a glance at the wolf. His knife split the long body of the pike to the tail. Then, ripping the backbone and most of the rib bones from the twin slabs, he slung them over a shoulder and turned his regard back to the wolf.

The animal sat as before, at the forest verge, closer than he had ever been to a live man. Although he appeared relaxed and unconcerned he was in fact tensed for flight, ready to melt into the darkness of the forest if necessary. His tongue lolled from his mouth, saliva dripped from the tip as he mouth breathed to cool his body in the damp heat of the day.

Finished with the fish and tiring of the game he played with the wolf, Nipishish rose to his feet. Without a backward glance he walked quickly into the safety of the cloaking forest. Being in the open anywhere, especially along a river or the shoreline of a lake made him feel vulnerable. He did not like the feeling.

As he moved deeper into the forest he caught the faint sound of bones being crushed as the wolf ate the fish head. He stopped a moment, cocking his head to catch the sounds. *I would have wagered that he would eat the head first. When he is done with the head he will eat the guts, too.*

He shook his head at the idea of a wolf and a man being neutral toward one another. Such things did not happen. *I have seen the last of him. He will sleep off his full belly and go find another pack of his people.* He was wrong about that.

— ∞ —

The wolf quickly consumed the pike head and guts, and licked the gore from his chops and forepaws. His eyes had never left the spot in the wall of trees where the man had disappeared. Getting to his feet he stood there a moment, his eyes examined the area, coming back to the spot where the man disappeared, as if he expected him to appear once again. He made a circle of the area along the lakeshore where he and the man had first come into contact, his sensitive nose gathered in the strong odor of the man, and his brain categorized the spoor. Not unlike a dog circling to find the best possible spot to lie down, the wolf followed his tail in a circle, stopping with his nose pointed in the direction the man had gone.

Some primal instinct took precedence then and he followed after the man. The gods had decided that day that they would need each other.

— ∞ —

Shortly after leaving the wolf, the man climbed a tall ash tree and reclined comfortably athwart a deep fork of the main branches. From this vantage point he surveyed the countryside, listened to the heartbeat of his world, the arboreal forest, and tested its warm breath with flared nostrils. He projected his whole being into the dense forest ahead; his senses were bared to its stimuli. Senses tuned to the slightest deviation from the norm, he missed nothing.

He took one of several available avenues to his lair, always heading in its general direction, while at the same time making certain that his destination would not be apparent to those that might cut his back trail. He was under no illusions about the skill of the men that hunted him each and every day. One single mistake on his part and they would have him.

He hated them for what they had done to Ingerd, and to him, but at the same time he could almost forgive them, for they knew not any other course; they killed all their enemies at the stake, purifying their bodies in the flames. It was their way. He could tender them a grudging respect for being the brave men that they were, warriors of their people, but he would kill all that he could for as long as he lived. He had sworn an oath to his gods, Odin, Thor, Frey, Freya – all of them – and he knew they waited and watched him every day. They knew, and he knew, that one day his time would be finished. He would fight the good fight, to the last, and the Valkyries would come for him. He embraced these things. His closely held beliefs were his true self, what made him a man, which made him what he was. To the core of his being he was a Viking of old, true to his beliefs and the gods that dictated them. He was also a warrior of the people, and duty bound to them as well. His bond with them would not stay his course. He had chosen the remainder of his life. He embraced his fate.

His back trail held no threat on this day, for only the wolf followed him. He did not know this, nor would he have been able to elude the animal had he known that he was being followed.

He always gained access to the cave via the only route open to him – the narrow ledge. Earlier in his residence in the cave, he had thought about digging the chimney out enough to gain access that way. But, after living there for a time he came to the conclusion that there were too many big rocks in the way, and if he made a hole big enough to accommodate his body, a bear could get into the cave as well. The only reason no bear had ever used the cave was that the only way in for a large animal to gain access was the narrow ledge, and a bear could never negotiate the ledge entrance without falling to its death onto the rocks below.

Unbeknownst to the man, the wolf saw him settle into concealment in the brush atop the cliff that contained his cave, to watch his back trail for intruders before descending to the ledge and the cave entrance. The animal lay unmoving in the scrub watching the man.

Shortly thereafter, his patience was rewarded when the man got to his feet and crept off the hilltop where he had lain concealed.

The wolf lost sight of the man, but his sensitive nose never lost the trail of his quarry. As he stalked ahead following the scent of the man he came to the cave's chimney atop the hill. Issuing from the pile of rocks at the chimney's top, he caught the strong, familiar scent of the man, and heard him moving about in the cave below.

And, so an association grew between man and wolf. No effort to bring it about was made by either of them, it just happened with the passage of time. Both were lobos, solitary hunters. Whenever the man left the cave, the wolf followed after him. They gradually began to roam the forest together, the man and the big male wolf, both outcasts of their kind.

The man threw the wolf his extra human hearts and generally shared his food with him. But, still, he had never uttered a word to the animal. Occasionally the wolf foraged the nearby forest. Oftentimes after these forays, the man found some remnant of the kill at the cave's entrance, the wolf's way of sharing his kills with the man.

Although the wolf had never entered the cave with the man in attendance, he was always close by. As their association matured, one day the wolf did enter the cave. From that day on he came and went as the spirit moved him. He and the man trusted one another, their spirits joined, they had become one.

As the unworldly butchery continued over the land of the Ganadoga Clan of the Haudenosaunee, people reported hearing the chilling howl of a wolf accompany the keening of Death Wind through the forest after each incident. The most dubious mind could no longer ignore the horrifying implications. Spirits walked the land together.

EPILOGUE

HALFDAN AND HIS PEOPLE

Seasons came and went over the northland. The survivors of Halfdansfjord and certain of the natives of Vinland continued their friendly association. Lonely Norsemen joined with willing native women. The new couples divided their time between the Norse people and the various clan villages of the women's people.

The three largest ships were used for trade. Bjorn and Hrafen undertook the long distance trade with the Tornit and Greenland, while Halfdan, Frida, and the old crew of Steed of the Sea continued the previously developed trade with the villages that could be reached from the inland sea. The villages of Essipit's Thalmiut and several scattered bands of Naskapi, including the band of Chisasi, were regularly contacted in this way.

Helge and Hallsteinn with the two smaller ships established a lively trade with all the same villages in the bounty of the inland sea. They spent every summer at sea, fishing, sealing and whaling, covering both the east and west coasts of the inland sea in the process. For the first time in living memory all these native peoples had a dependable source of food with enough surpluses for winter storage.

With the passage of time the general Norse population lost a man here and there as individuals decided to leave the sea and join permanently the tribe or band of their choice.

Halfdan had foretold that this would happen. He both encouraged and approved of this assimilation process, knowing full well that it was the only way for his people to survive in this savage land.

A few men even joined with the Thalmiut of Essipit and the Tornit people of Inuktuk in the far north. Dropped off by one of the trading ships on route to Greenland, they were seen occasionally by other trading ship crews, but because of the vast distances they eventually just disappeared with the nomadic people they had joined.

Life assumed a settled routine as time passed. Relations with the scattered bands of Naskapi had always been good, and that continued. The Norse and Naskapi remained firm allies that depended on one another to confront any issue or threat together, as a single people, whether it be food supplies or common enemies.

Babies were born, people died, skirmishes and wars with the Haudenosaunee and some bands of the Anishinabeg continued each summer. It had been so as far back as anyone could remember.

THE ISLAND

The travail suffered by the survivor's in their flight to the nearer of the two inland sea islands had faded from active memory and conversation. They put the loss of everything they held dear behind them, and forged a new life from the ashes of the old. It was their way; it was what made them conquerors wherever they chose to go. The survivors of Halfdansfjord were happy with their choice of a new place to rebuild their lives. Their island*, while small by comparison to some of the others in the inland sea, furnished the 70-some odd people that remained there with everything they needed for happiness, security, and sustenance.

It was a mixed bunch; assimilation was welcomed and encouraged by the leaders, but given the circumstances it would have occurred naturally without their input. Most of the men had found mates; for all knew that it was the only way for their people to survive. Without children any developing culture would wither and disappear eventually.

Halfdan still led them, but summer trading called him away frequently, to sail the sea he loved in his beloved ship. These voyages transformed the man, bringing a sense of inner peace that had been absent for a long while. Frida always went with him, welcoming the relief the voyages brought to both of them. Halfdan's responsibilities had forged him into the man he was, but the respite provided by putting the problems of command aside for a time remade the man's psyche.

One fine day between these trading voyages, after many moons without any word from the other group of settlers, Halfdan became concerned about them. Their original intent had been to settle on the big island** on the west side of the inland sea. With no word about their wellbeing or anything concerned with them he could not answer questions that were coming from his own people with increasing regularity.

So, with Hrafen being available while waiting for a cargo load for his next trading voyage to Greenland, Halfdan dispatched him and his crew to investigate.

*Present day — *Charleton Island, **Akimiski Island, James Bay, Canada*

HRAFEN SAILS WEST

The ship was gone for more than two moons. Part of that time was spent aground between the big island and the mainland, waiting for the right combination of wind and tide to refloat the ship. This happened twice between the island and the mainland where the shallow strait became a mud flat at low tide. Because of that hazard, Hrafen abandoned the area in favor of sailing all the way around the island to check both approaches to the large river estuary that became the focus of their search. During those many days of searching the only sign found of the two ships and 50 - some odd people that had sailed in them was the wreckage of a ship's boat in the rocks at the head of a small cove on the northwest side.

The expedition had not occupied the big island for some reason. Their intent had been a landing in the bay on the southern shore, but that had not happened because Hrafen and his men could find no sign that they had been there.

Two of Hrafen's crewmen were Naskapi men that would act as interpreters should contact be made with the bands that occupied the area along the major river estuaries on the southwest coast of the inland sea.

During their second ship grounding several canoes loaded with Naskapi warriors came to see who they were.

Had it not been for the presence of the two Naskapi men as members of the ships' company, this encounter had the potential to turn out differently.

As it was, some of the new arrivals were the kin of Hrafen's crewmen. The encounter became like a large family gathering as food and current events were shared. As a result the whereabouts of their lost colonists was discovered.

Several days later, after Hrafen's ship floated up out of the mud flats, he and his crew set sail and laid a course for the south, where the Naskapi visitors had told them their friends would be found. Their friends had chosen the south shore of another even larger river* and estuary than the one west of the big island on which to settle.

The local Naskapi had welcomed the new settlers, trade relations had been developed, and two turf-walled longhouses had been completed.

Both ships were drawn up on the beach when Hrafen's ship sailed into the estuary. What he and his crew saw as they beached their own ship was a typical Norse village whose inhabitants had already begun their assimilation process with the local Naskapi bands. People of both cultures crowded the landing beach to welcome the new arrivals.

Several days later, thoroughly rested and rejuvenated, Hrafen and his crew rowed from the estuary and set sail on an easterly course, to report back to Halfdan.

Present day — Albany River — southwest James Bay, Canada

PEOPLE OF NITASSINAN

Nipishish no longer put in his infrequent appearances at the village of Sachem. Kejo or Glooscap, his closest friends, had not seen him for many seasons. Both understood what drove him. They always thought that some-day he would return, but he never did. Most of his old friends knew in their hearts that his mind was gone, that his war with the Haudeno had taken his soul.

For a time, people of the small roving bands reported seeing him occasionally. His wild appearance, the smell of carrion that announced his presence and the wolf that travelled with him scared them more each time. He stayed with them a day or two and then he and the wolf simply disappeared, as they had come, without a word or sign, creating no more disturbance than a slight breeze, and leaving nothing to mark their passage. People did not know why he came; he brought nothing, took nothing, and said nothing. Some thought he came because of his kinship with them. Others were not so certain. His presence among them began to scare every band that he visited into silence, for fear of what he had become, for fear of what they knew he could do to his enemies.

Although he was never a threat to any Naskapi, they all came to know that he was the spirit of the forest that people talked about, the demon that the Haudeno people called Death Wind. No longer was he Nipishish, their friend and a man they had admired.

Eventually, enough of the story became known about why he had become Death Wind. Its telling became a favored topic during the telling of tall tales by many of the Naskapi bands. Embellishment of the actual facts of the matter added to the intrigue created, making the legend of Death Wind as real to the Naskapi as it was to the Haudenosaunee.

Finally, the object of the legend that possessed the people of the land came among them no more. He and the wolf were gone. He would be seen just one more time, and then not by a member of the Naskapi Nation.

During one summer skirmish the redoubtable Glooscap died leading a war party against the Haudenosaunee of Sakohkea. His loss affected the people for longer than anyone could have foretold. Sachem, old and toothless now, but still revered as the principal chieftain of the far flung Naskapi Nation, was especially affected by the loss of Glooscap, his war chief in many engagements with the enemies of their tribe. Sachem withdrew inside himself, spending most of his time reclined against a backrest in the council house, alone with his thoughts. None of the people bothered him in his reverie. One day, without input from the council of elders, he came to a decision, calling for Kejo to attend him.

As those that gossip will, the names of various warriors had been bandied about. People had anticipated that Kejo would be among those summoned to stand for war chief of the people. It came as a surprise, even to those professing to have all the answers, that Kejo was the only man summoned by Sachem. This fact indicated to the gossiping network that was active through the tribe that Sachem had already made his decision, the summons was a formality. Somewhat later, with tension among the people increasing dramatically as the closed session with Sachem wore on, a rather subdued Kejo walked from the council house. Nobody would ever know what had been said at his meeting with Sachem. Kejo even looked different to those that had waited impatiently for him to appear, so that all of them would finally know. The weight of his new responsibilities and the mantle of war chief had literally transformed him in the eyes of the bystanders. Assuming the place of Glooscap, a legend among the people, would not be an easy task, and all knew that. Sachem had left him in no doubt of the difficulty that he faced. Many prominent warriors felt that they would be chosen. When all were passed over, it left some feeling slighted – not a desirable circumstance with a warrior. It would be Kejo's task to prove his worth to these men, to reinforce their value to him and to the nation. This he must do to some degree with all his warriors. In verification of the continued wisdom of Sachem, Kejo did just that, becoming a resourceful, reasoned, and fearless leader like his friend, Glooscap. Men would follow him anywhere, not because he demanded it, but because he led them. Kejo was the tip of the spear, the man responsible for the security of a nation.

HAUDENOSAUNEE - PEOPLE OF THE LONGHOUSE

The hunt for the demon continued throughout the land of the Ganadoga Clan. Every Haudeno warrior from every clan of the Haudenosaunee Nation had tried to run him to ground as the seasons passed. He struck at will, both inside villages and throughout the vast forest land. The darkness of the night became a time of fear for all the people throughout the deep forest that was their homeland. Nobody had ever actually seen him; a shadow perhaps, or the feeling of a presence nearby was as close as he let them come. Some thought they had been close to catching him, but he always managed to simply disappear. He seemed to leave no spoor. Wolf tracks were occasionally seen, but even they were lost in the detritus of the forest floor, making the task of tracking either of them virtually impossible.

In the past, victims of the demon had been members of the Ganadoga Clan. That changed one winter when a group of trappers from the Cokanuk Band were butchered singly while working their trap lines. Unlike all the other attacks, the six men that trapped together were not mutilated. This was the first time that the demon did not take their hearts, the first time he did not put out their eyes. All six men had fought the demon to the death, each dying from a single killing stroke that cut through their bodies. The demon left them where they fell, and he and the wolf melted into the forest.

The warriors that later found the missing men along the trap line, saw that the demon had struck during a snow storm. Had they been close by, the cloaking snow would have eliminated all sign. As it was, had they not known the lay of the trap line, they might not have ever found the bodies of the missing trappers.

After this incident, the councils of the Cokanuk and Ganadoga Clans arrived at the same opinion, but separately and without the other clan's participation.

Okwáho made a statement in the council that he attended in the village of Deganawida that started the warriors to thinking about why the demon had previously only attacked the people of the Ganadoga Clan.

"Death Wind has always taken the eyes and hearts of his victims. This time he did not. He allowed the victims to fight for their lives."

Sakohkea challenged him with the obvious question. "Why do you think he treated our men differently?"

"I do not know. He may be sending us a message, sending the Ganadoga a message, too."

"What message?" Odatshedeh interrupted the rising voices.

Okwáho considered a moment, his eyes on his father. "Death Wind does not regard our clan like he does the Ganadoga. They have done something to kindle the hatred he has for them."

"I heard that the Ganadoga burned pale skin slaves in their fires several seasons ago. Perhaps that is why Death Wind preys on only them; he was a pale skin before he became the demon."

Okwáho could not identify the speaker in the pandemonium that erupted with his statement. Every man in the council house tried to offer an opinion.

Sakohkea quickly restored order. Knowing the statement had come from Seawi, he beckoned him forward so that all could hear his words. "Tell us what you know about this."

Seawi came before the council. He spoke loudly enough that the assembled warriors also heard his tale. "Women and a few children of the pale skin tribe were captured in a raid. The women became the slaves of the Ganadoga, and they were eventually worked to death or worked until they could work no longer, just as we do with our slaves. Some children were adopted into the band, the others were killed. All the women died except one. She became crazy and would not work; the Ganadoga burned her at the stake." He gave the cutting sign, ending his tale.

Okwáho gave no sign that the tale in any way connected to him. He had no way of knowing that the slave woman of Seawi's tale had anything to do with his natural mother, Ingerd, nor would he ever know.

"I agree with Seawi," said Otetiani, looking at his friend for confirmation of that statement, as he so often did.

A slight inclination of Okwáho's head and the ghost of a smile around the blue eyes let him know that he agreed, too.

Deganawida cleared his throat, a sure sign that he was about to enter the conversation. Silence quickly came over the assembly.

"There may be a connection between the demon and the pale skin prisoners of the Ganadoga people. If there is a connection, then the demon is a pale skin. The Naskapi will know of this. Question any Naskapi prisoners before they are killed. If this Death Wind is a pale skin, he is a dangerous enemy of our tribe." He paused, getting to his feet, so that all could see him plainly and hear his final words. "I cannot believe that any pale skin can outwit the warriors of our people. Every other raid against our enemies will stop until this demon is run to ground." He pointed to Sakohkea. "Tomorrow, you take our men into the field and meet with Ongwata and the warriors of his Ganadoga Clan. Combine forces and find this spirit, this demon, and rid our forests of him forever." The cutting sign told the assembly that their chief had spoken.

The council house rocked to its foundation by the roar of approval from the warriors of the Cokanuk Band of the Haudenosaunee Nation.

———

The massed hunt of the combined forces of the Cokanuk and Ganadoga clans swept the countryside for Death Wind. While they hunted the demon through the vastness of the surrounding forest, the demon struck their villages, for the first time targeting the village of Deganawida.

He did not harm any of the women or old ones that were asleep when his attack began. Deganawida himself, as well as the members of his council of elders, slept blissfully through most of it. Neither sentry survived his visit. In the hours just before dawn, each man died from a single massive stroke of the demon's weapon that decapitated each of them.

After the demon dispatched the sentries, the village dogs set up a frightful din, waking all the village people. Shortly thereafter every loose dog inside the village palisade walls was either dead or dying, literally torn to pieces.

Deganawida and all the able bodied elders of the village armed themselves and stormed from their wigwams at the racket set up by the dogs, but found nothing in the village save carnage at every hand.

In the ensuing silence after the attack on the village dogs, the keening cry of Death Wind and the mournful howl of a wolf reverberated through the nearby forest and off the palisade. People would later state that the keening and howling seemed to come from everywhere at once.

With the exception of Deganawida and the elders, not another person ventured from the longhouses that morning until the sun shone full on the village, pushing back the shadows from where the demon might lie concealed. Only then did the frightened villagers slowly creep from the security of their longhouses. They were greeted by a scene of carnage the likes of which they had never before seen. The body parts of many of their dogs were scattered about like leaves before an autumn wind. The carcasses had all been sundered by the demon and his wolf companion.

The next night he attacked a secluded Ganadoga village that had thus far escaped his rampages. This time he slaughtered people and left the dogs untouched. Only the children awakened from their night's sleep in one wigwam. All the adults were dead; throats cut, eyes cut out, and hearts ripped from their chests. The heads of the four sentries had been thrown to the village dogs. Death Wind and his wolf dined on the hearts of the slain in the village council house, while the village slept on. In defiance of those adults and children that he spared he kindled a cook fire in the communal hearth to sear the hearts of his enemies. His audacity defied comprehension. It challenged the manhood, the warrior ethos of the men that hunted him.

He and the wolf retired into the forest after that last attack, well before dawn, to hide and await the return of the men of the clan.

As it happened, instead of hiding in the forest he should have gone back to his lair under cover of darkness.

Word quickly spread through the warriors of both clans still on the hunt for Death Wind, that the demon had struck both villages while they were afield hunting him. What he did and did not do to those in the villages both enraged and perplexed the men. Why he savagely butchered the one and largely spared the other was something they did not understand. As it happened, it was something they would never understand.

As their time on the hunt occupied most of one summer, allowing little to no time for normal activities, warriors of both clans grew increasing angry and jumpy. The demon was never seen by any of them. Men had seen the wolf in the distance from time to time, ghosting through the trees to quickly disappear from view. The demon left few tracks and never enough spoor to establish his escape route. It was frustrating, to say the least. Many arrows were wasted shooting at shadows and perceived movement in the darkest recesses of the forest. One such incident did connect, but the shooter never actually saw, or heard his arrow strike.

During early evening on the same day of his last attack, just before the sun dipped below the treetops and the last of the usable light faded in the forest, Death Wind showed himself for the first time.

Sakohkea had a large contingent of warriors of the Cokanuk Clan pushing downhill through the dense copse of a small canyon. Among them were Okwáho and the circle of young men that he was often seen with. The men had kept one another in sight as they progressed forward, but the daylight was fading rapidly. It was doubtful they would finish pushing down the canyon before darkness came in earnest.

Okwáho bent over to pass under a fallen tree in his path. When he straightened up he came face-to-face with the demon. He started in surprise, knowing the demon had revealed himself for some reason known only to him.

Neither spoke. Each examined the other in silence for a heartbeat. No hint of recognition came from either.

The man stood a matter of feet in front of Okwáho, looking him over from head to foot.

The young man felt no fear at this encounter; on the contrary he perceived no threat from the man before him as he had no weapon in hand. Although Okwáho had bow in hand, with an arrow nocked on the string, he did not raise the weapon. The seasons of hatred he felt while hunting this man, for that is what he was, a man, rather than the demon of myth, fell away as he confronted him. He saw that the man had been wounded; fresh blood darkened the front of his buckskins, he could hear his labored breathing. The stub of an arrow shaft protruded from the right side of his chest. Fresh blood stained his lips, and blood dribbled from one corner of his mouth.

The arrow has pierced his lung, thought Okwáho. A slight rustling in the leaves of the forest floor drew his attention. It was then that he saw the wolf watching him narrowly from the side. *He is a big one,* he thought.

Without having uttered a word, the man turned and began to walk into the shadows.

It was then that Okwáho saw the axe hanging from a strap across the man's back. Like a lightning bolt, the man's identity came to him.

"Father?" Okwáho spoke the word in a language no longer familiar, while his mind grappled with what he knew to be true about the man before him.

The man stopped and turned back to him.

They looked at each other for a moment in time, neither able to speak. The man turned away without a word or sign of recognition, disappearing into the gloom of the forest.

Two men burst on the scene, apparent distant witnesses to what had just occurred. Both looked at Okwáho in confusion.

"Why did you not kill him?" One asked angrily. "He is the demon, Death Wind."

Okwáho just shook his head, in seeming denial.

"I will go after him," said the man, moving in the direction of where he had seen the demon disappear into the forest.

"No!" Okwáho hollered firmly. "You will let him go."

"Why should I, who will stop me?"

"I will stop you." Okwáho faced the other man defiantly; his body stance, half drawn arrow, and commanding tone left no doubt of his resolve.

"The demon is our enemy, we can finally kill him. What is the matter with you? Why did you not kill him when he was standing right in front of you?"

"He is my father!" Okwáho ground out the words through gritted teeth, barely in control of his emotions.

The arrival of Sakohkea and Odatshedeh partially defused the unfolding drama, as those present acquiesced to the war chief.

Both men had heard Okwáho's words. At a sign from Sakohkea, Odatshedeh raised the war whistle to his lips and recalled the other men. The others arrived quickly, forming a group with their war chief, Okwáho, and Odatshedeh at its center. Tension was palpable.

Sakohkea reached out and gripped Okwáho's upper arm, a move unusual for him. "What is it; what has happened here?"

Okwáho looked full in the face of his war chief, glanced at Odatshedeh, and then dropped his eyes, the mental anguish obvious in his facial expression. Regaining his composure with an effort, he answered Sakohkea, a man not known for his patience.

"Death Wind is a man. He has taken an arrow in the chest; he is dying. I did not recognize him until he turned away and I saw his battle axe. There is no doubt in my mind that he was my father, Gudbjartur Einarsson, Nipishish the Axeman, as the Naskapi call him."

Sakohkea and Odatshedeh were rendered momentarily speechless. Both men had seen Okwáho's natural father and mother before, at a parley when they had accompanied Glooscap and a large party to try to recover their son from captivity in the village of Deganawida. The possibilities at what motivated the man Nipishish to become the Death Wind of legend raced through the minds of both men. The two men made eye contact. Each realized at the same time why these years of slaughter and butchery for the Ganadoga Clan had come about at the hands of what everyone supposed was a demon. One of the pale skin women captives that the Ganadoga burned at the stake had to be the natural mother of Okwáho, the mate of Nipishish.

Okwáho had watched his war chief and his adopted father closely while each processed what he had just told them. In the telling, he realized the full import himself, and things began to fall into place for him. A great sadness came over him. Largely forgotten memories came to the fore. He struggled to put them aside as Sakohkea spoke to him.

"Nipishish was driven mad by the loss of his mate. I understand what has caused all of this death for our people. For that this man must die. Do you understand, Okwáho?"

In full outward control now, the stoic acceptance of fate that he had learned from these people cloaking the feelings he held inside, the young man inclined his head in assent. His heart hammered against his rib cage, his chest felt hot on the inside from the depth of his feeling, but he clenched his jaws and the fiery blue eyes he turned on the men around him conveyed the depth of his intense emotion. He drew to the side of his companions, still holding the bow at the ready he looked from man to man. His eyes came to rest on Sakohkea, for it was he that would make the decision whether to go after the man, or let him go.

"I told you, he is dying. You can order us to go after him, and we will, but he will not be found. It is almost dark. In all this time we have never found him. He let me see him, because he knows who I am and that he is dying. He has been close to me before, I felt him, but I did not see him until he wanted me to see him." He half drew his arrow. "I will die doing it, but I will kill the first man to go after him. Let him go, he is beaten."

Sakohkea watched his protégé approvingly. *He defies me in front of my warriors. I know of no other man that would do that.* His eyes shifted to Odatshedeh, who had watched the unfolding drama somewhat closer than most of the others.

"This son of yours is a fighter," he said, in a voice tinged with a hint of admiration. The cruel face and hard eyes conveyed no acceptance of the defiance, however.

Odatshedeh shook his head once in acknowledgement, knowing better than to voice an opinion when one had not been requested.

The others were silent as the war chief's glance took them all in. Most averted their eyes, not willing to attract his personal attention.

Okwáho felt like he was about to die. He accepted his fate for defiance, whatever it happened to be. He knew his life hung in the balance. His war chief could kill him where he stood and not a single man would intervene, including his adopted father, Odatshedeh. This he knew.

Suddenly, Sakohkea stepped inside of an arm's length from the young man, his face so close that Okwáho felt the hot breath of death dry the moisture from his eyes. He did not blink or draw back, but stood his ground before the threat of Sakohkea's presence.

Sakohkea grabbed each of the young man's upper arms in a vice-like grip, his face still close.

Okwáho held his ground.

"No man alive has ever defied my will. You are alive because I choose to keep you alive. Do not make a habit of defying me, Okwáho, you will not survive the next time you do so." He released his grip and turned away. As he stepped by Odatshedeh, he winked at his friend.

Odatshedeh was too surprised to show any reaction to the unexpected gesture from his thoroughly unpredictable war chief.

"Come, it is time to end this," Sakohkea said over his shoulder as he headed toward their distant village.

His men looked at each other without comment, and one by one they followed after him. The last to leave were Okwáho and Odatshedeh.

Neither spoke for a moment. Okwáho's attention was directed momentarily into the gloom of the forest, where he had seen the man disappear. He made eye contact with Odatshedeh.

"You have brought much pride to our wigwam, Okwáho. Nahcomis loves you like our lost son, and so do I."

Okwáho looked at his adopted father. No words came to him. He, too, felt a love, a kinship with this fine man. But his heart was torn asunder by what had just occurred. It would take the passage of time to assuage his raging emotions. Shaking his head once he averted his eyes from those of his adopted father and turned away to follow after the others.

Odatshedeh watched him go. A sigh came from deep within. He cast his eyes down to the path he must follow, and moved off behind his son. As Sakohkea had said, it was over.

END OF THE LEGEND

Close by, a man leaned against the bole of a big spruce, concealed in the deep shadow of the evening forest. No attempt had been made to escape. Had his enemies pursued him, they would have found him. That the young man let him go and guarded his escape meant nothing to him. He had witnessed the entire drama unfold with his son and the men with him. He felt nothing about what he had witnessed. His mind no longer harbored any such personal thoughts. His breathing was labored. Frequent coughing brought bright blood into his mouth that dripped off his lips and filtered down through his beard. He knew he was finished.

Summoning the last of his considerable reserves, he moved off in the direction of his lair, the wolf close behind. The long journey had ended; the legend of Death Wind, the spirit of the forest was finished, as all things must end. He had exacted his revenge; he and the wolf had fought their fight.

Only the gods know why the wolf disappeared with the man, or what the end for both of them was. Nobody ever saw either of them alive again.

EONS PASS

Time passed for the people as it always had. As the seasons became memories for the living, the accomplishments of those that lived before receded and disappeared from the memory of man.

ASSIMILATION

The ashes of Halfdansfjord blew away on the wind and were ground down to eventual nothing under each winter's onslaught. Trees and brush grew up over the site until its former existence was hidden by the mists of time.

The cliff wall containing the cave entrance, the former lair of Nipishish the Axeman, eroded away slowly over the centuries. The access ledge to the cave entrance was ground away by the ice of many winters, rendering the cave itself inaccessible. Finally, the entire cliff face and hillside above cracked off from an accumulation of ice one winter, and fell into the river defile below, damming and rerouting the stream. The only evidence that a cave had ever existed there was a small partially rock-filled hole in the vertical cliff face. Rodents and other small vermin continued to come and go into the cave through the chimney from the hilltop, until it too was blocked by the demise of the cliff face below, thereby eliminating all external influences over the cave environs or its contents.

The proud ships of the Norse settlers disappeared from the inland sea and the Greenland Sea as the men that crewed them grew old and died. The ships themselves rotted and fell apart from disuse and neglect, ground to bits by the ice of winter and mixing with other detritus along the former landing beaches or on the bottom of the sea.

The Norse people assimilated with the pre-historical natives – Naskapi, Haudenosaunee, Thalmiut, Tornit, and yes, even a few with the Anishinabeg.

Those Norse people that originally settled along the banks of the present day Albany River, western James Bay, Ontario Province, Canada, fleeing the beginnings of many centuries of severe winter weather eventually found themselves permanently assimilated with the ancestors of the Mandan and Arikara Indians of the upper Missouri River Basin in what is now North Dakota.

The genetic makeup of the Norse people that assimilated with the pre-historical natives of North America, diluted by more than 1000-years, or 50-generations of human time, survives in some form, but the physical characteristics that set them apart from others of that time has disappeared forever from the modern ancestors of the peoples with whom they joined so long ago.

A climate event lasting about 500-years, from approximately 1200-1700AD, known as the Maunder Minimum, or Little Ice Age, held much the northern hemisphere and much of North America in a savage winter grip that led to the displacement migration of many pre-historical peoples to areas of more benevolent weather farther south from the Canada they had always called home. Among them were the Norse descendants along the Albany River, to the Upper Missouri. There may have been other small Norse groups that joined with other native peoples in what is now the United States to survive; we may never know the full extent of their assimilation. Based on the Athapascan Linguistic -- origin southwestern Canada -- grouping of their languages alone, it is known that the pre-historical ancestors of the Apache and Navajo Indians migrated to the American Great Plains and eventually to the American southwest, where they still reside today. There may be many other displacements of entire pre-historical Indian cultures during the Little Ice Age that we will never know about.

Perhaps, someday an archaeologist on the eternal hunt for answers to the enigma surrounding the Norse settlers of Greenland will happen on something that will tell us what happened to them. Where did they go? Right now, only the gods know the answer to that one for certain.

PRESENT DAY

Jim Raven thanked God that he had made it back to the Haudenosaunee Reserve in Ontario, Canada before his grandfather passed away. Now two weeks after the funeral that had seen the fine old man laid to rest, he still found himself thinking of little else. Pangs of remorse still assailed him in waves for not spending more time with the man that he had venerated since childhood. Stories of the ancient ancestors were haunting examples of his grandfather's gift for storytelling. Now, all the untold tales of his people would forever go untold, for he was the storyteller of his band and nobody else had the gift, or the interest, it seemed.

ASSIMILATION

Born James Raven Wing in upstate New York of a white mother and Iroquois father, Jim felt the stigma of being a half breed through all of his formative years. Some of his friends thought it was pretty neat for him to be half Indian, but they weren't half Indian, so it was easy for them to say that to him. He knew what he was and the hurt of rejection because of it plagued him until he finally put it aside, forever. Or, so he thought.

Jim vowed that he would one day play down his ancestry, never admitting to anyone that he was of mixed blood. He did a good job of it, too. Dropping the Wing from his name, becoming just Jim Raven, helped somewhat. Only a couple guys that knew him through college and graduate school ever guessed. As for the others, if they did guess, they never said anything.

His black hair and dark, often brooding eyes, bespoke of a heritage other than purely white, but his relationships with co-workers and friends were never defined by ethnicity. As time passed it became fashionable among the uninformed to be able to claim Indian ancestry. Even then he did not. At one half Iroquois, his name was carried on the tribal rolls, a happenstance that concerned him not at all. Beyond an abiding affection for his paternal grandfather that he took for granted he had no interest in that part of his heritage.

Jim's father had been a proud Canadian high steel worker all of his working life. A member of the Mohawk First Nation tribe, with many others of his ilk, he remained fearless while erecting the high steel skeletons of buildings in New York, Toronto and Montreal, until he plunged to his death, like so many before him.

His father's death crushed Jim's spirit, but his pragmatic mother insisted that the large insurance payout as a result would allow her son to pursue whatever higher education degrees that he desired.

He chose geology, a discipline in keeping with his love of rock climbing. He ultimately gained a master's degree in geology and had his choice of employers as a result. Although his chosen field was an abiding interest for him – he loved the work – two unrelated passions developed out of his geology fieldwork, rock climbing and fishing.

Without the encumbrance of a female in his life, every day off saw him engaged in one or both of these pursuits.

After his grandfather's funeral he took the opportunity to backpack into an area not far from the Iroquois Reserve in Canada where his grandfather had lived that also just happened to be on his way home, more or less, to northern New York. The hike lasted the last week of his vacation and covered a portion of a particularly beautiful area of southern Quebec, situated along a small stream drainage north of Trois-Riveres and the St. Lawrence River.

The stream's origin was the wilds of western Quebec, which suited his purposes given his propensity for solitude. Many of the fish species available locally abounded in the stream. His particular favorites being crappie and bluegill, those were his focus, but anything that went for his flies suited him just fine. He kept what he could eat and returned the others to the stream for the next lucky fisherman.

His perusal of a topographical map of the watershed had revealed the possibility of the unsullied areas free from towns and other hikers that he preferred. For that reason he chose this particular stream, or that's what he thought at the time.

Being able to drive to within a reasonable distance from his desired destination, given his time constraints, was important for his schedule – a week would pass quickly – so it must be four days in and three days out, at the outside.

He did not realize until later that he seemed to be drawn, or led, to this particular area of the watershed. The topo map showed a deep defile that the stream had cut over the centuries and he zeroed in on that, knowing from the map gradients that a good climbing cliff might be found there.

Without really realizing that he hurried toward the cliffs that he hoped were there, he reached the defile at dark the second day, having gotten a late start on the first day while he drove to his jumping off spot for the hike inland.

The cool, damp dawn that revealed the sheer cliff on the uphill side of the defile filled him with joy. His geologist's brain analyzed the fact that a part of the uphill cliff face had collapsed into what must have been a deep streambed defile at one time, creating a small lake, and rerouting the stream itself. At the time, he did this unconsciously.

As he waited for the full light of the day to reveal the details he needed to begin his climb up the cliff face, he assembled his fly rod and tried his luck in the small lake at the cliff's base. As often happens in such pristine conditions he quickly caught all the brook trout he could manage for breakfast.

Later on, he viewed the cliff face from every angle he could to determine his best avenue of ascent. He quickly determined that his pitons would be useless, because except for a vertical crack that was too wide to use them, the cliff face was almost smooth. *This is going to be a tough one,* he thought ruefully.

The wide crack began about 10' above the talus from the collapsed cliff face, continued to the top, and as far as he could tell from the ground, it was the only path of ascent available to him. Shouldering a coil of nylon rope, a few pitons just in case, and his other climbing accoutrements, he made his way to the base of the 200' escarpment.

Sometime later, he lay on his back at the top of the cliff catching his breath. *The crack in the cliff face was tailor made for climbing. I am not sure I could have made the climb without it.* His gloved fist wedged nicely in the crack, and had allowed a relatively simple hand-over-hand ascent. His mind sorted through the details of the climb as he lay resting.

Levering himself up onto his elbows he surveyed his immediate surroundings, his field of view restricted by the dense forest. Standing up, he carefully walked to the cliff's edge and gazed at the stream below. For the first time, he noticed a jumble of rocks and gravel filling what could be the entrance of a cave, well to the side of his path of ascent up the cliff face. He determined to investigate that as he repelled down.

Finding a good crack to hammer a piton, above what he thought might be a cave entrance, wasn't difficult. Feeding his rope through the piton's eye, he arranged the ends along both sides of a tree in line with his intended route down, and dropped the remaining rope coil off the cliff. In the unlikely event the piton gave way the tree would snag the loop in his rope. *Can't be too careful climbing by myself,* he mused.

With the belay loop in the rope gripped in his right hand, he stepped off the cliff to repel down to the jumble of rocks he wanted to investigate.

Positioning himself securely at the bottom edge of the jumble of rocks, he saw that he had been correct, it was a cave entrance filled with rocks and gravel. Throwing a few rocks over his shoulder he quickly saw that he could push them inside the cave easier. In a few minutes he had worried out a hole big enough to allow his body ingress. His flashlight revealed that he had found a fairly roomy cave. With a combination of rope and brute strength, he finally wiggled his torso completely inside. Securing the lifeline under a handy rock, he crawled in far enough to sit upright.

As the beam of his flashlight played over the interior of the cave, it came to rest on a pile of bones against the far wall. A chill coursed through his body when he realized it was the skeleton of a man. A few feet away were the bones of what looked like a big dog. He was so overcome by his discovery that he froze, his mind emptied of thought, and he just sat there.

The archaeologist's facial expression registered disbelief as he sorted through the photos that Jim Raven had presented to him. Jim reached over and arranged them sequentially atop the table both men were bent over.

"This is the order in which they were taken," said Jim. "I tried to take pictures from every possible angle, so we could better determine what it is we are looking at."

"Phenomenal! I have never seen anything like this in Canada." The archaeologist's excitement at Jim's discovery was palpable. "Much of the earth is too acidic; there is too much moisture to preserve anything like this. These bones look to be ancient."

Jim laughed at his friend's enthusiasm. "They are ancient. Nothing has ever disturbed them. Animals have hardly gnawed the bones. I found a few with the ends chewed off, but most of the bones are in good condition for their obvious age.

Dr. Andrew Norin, originally from the small Minnesota town of Hovland, was a college and graduate school chum of Jim's. The man was almost beside himself as he studied the photos arranged on the table in detail with a large, illuminated magnifying glass.

"What kind of camera did you shoot these photos with?"

"My phone, it's all I had. As I said, I tried to get shots from all angles."

"You did a great job. When we go to study this site, we will of course, get grid photos so we know exactly where all of this is resting."

Jim glanced at the man, offering no comment to his assertion.

Andrew continued with his running commentary. "It looks like this man was lying on a sort of pallet when he died." He looked closer among the bones of the ribcage. "What is this down among the ribcage bones?"

"It is an axe, a battle axe, I think. Most of the handle is still attached. I believe he was holding the axe when he died." He proffered an envelope. "Here, I saved these photos for last."

The close-up photos showed the battle axe and a knife, both made of ferrous metal judging from the rust, displayed away from the skeleton, with one of Jim's pitons for scale. Andrew held each photo individually under the magnifier, saying nothing until he had examined each. When finished, he made eye contact with Jim.

"You found these in a cave in Quebec, Canada?"

Jim nodded. "Tell me what you think they are."

"They are Norse, Viking weapons, both of them. This discovery defies logic, and flies in the face of conventional wisdom."

"You are certain, Andrew?"

"Yes, I will stake my reputation on it. Nothing like this has ever been discovered in North America."

"Wait, what about the weapons discovered near Beardmore, Ontario, just east of Lake Nipigon? I read that many people thought they were Norse weapons."

"They are authentic Norse artifacts - a sword, axe head, and some kind of iron bar - that you can see today in the Royal Ontario Museum. The argument about them is that scientists felt they had been planted."

"Well, the battle axe and knife in these photos were not planted, because I just found them last week in southwestern Quebec. Both belonged to the man that died with them on his person."

"Jim, I cannot tell you how important this discovery is to Canadian ar-chaeology, to the entire world's archaeology. Why didn't you bring some of this back with you, so it can be examined?"

Without answering directly, Jim held out another large envelope. "I brought these for you to test. DNA testing should tell you all you need to know."

The envelope contents were three sealed plastic bags containing two each hu-man front teeth, two each canine front teeth, and one short piece of shaped wood.

⁂

One month later, the DNA results were in. Andrew called Jim to his office; he wanted to personally deliver the momentous test results.

Andrew handed Jim the sealed report.

"That is your copy. The man was pure Norse. He was about 45-years old at the time of death, which occurred between 980AD and 1050AD. That is as close as they can come. The canine teeth are from canis lupus, a male gray wolf that was past his prime. The piece of wood, that you told me was part of the axe handle, is chokecherry. It was cut around the year 1012AD in the James Bay area of Canada. Dendrochronology is currently a little more ac-curate than DNA insofar as the dating and origin of wood are concerned."

Jim just nodded slightly, a far off look in his eyes.

Unable to contain himself any longer, Andrew got right to it. "Jim, your discovery is huge. We must go to the site and make a proper examination for the sake of science."

Coming back to the present with an obvious effort, Jim said, "I will never take anyone there. I did not bring anything but the teeth and a piece of wood away from that place, and I never will."

"Why, for God's sake? Your discovery belongs to science, to mankind."

"Bullshit! It belongs to none of us. It belongs to him alone, him and his wolf. The cave had been sealed from the inside. That is why they lasted until I found them. His spirit led me there. He sealed them in before he died, so that I would find them. When I left the cave, I resealed it as I found it. I will never go back there."

Incredulous that his friend thought this way in the face of such a discovery, Andrew paced the room, marshalling his raging thoughts. He stopped suddenly, facing his friend.

"What do you mean you were led there? Is this some of your Indian bullshit?"

"Call it what you will, I was led there. It was my destiny to find the place where he died."

Andrew snorted in disgust. "How can you say that? You cannot believe such drivel."

"Listen to me, carefully. I will say this only once. If you interrupt what I am about to tell you, I will walk out of here and you will not see me again."

Andrew watched him narrowly.

"You are one of the few that know I am half Iroquois, Mohawk to be exact. I have always played down my heritage, my ancestors, and their beliefs. After this recent event happened to me, I feel my association with them to the core of my being. I cannot explain it to you, I don't even understand it myself, but it is real. My grandfather died recently, as you know. He was the storyteller of his Mohawk tribe. I now realize that it is my Mohawk tribe, too. One of the many legends that he passed down to me that was passed to him through generations of storytellers of the people was one about a spirit of the forest that they called Death Wind. This man that I found is Death Wind."

"You cannot seriously believe that, Jim," said Andrew passionately. "You are an intelligent man, how can you accept the validity of an ancient legend, much less actually believe it?"

Jim made to leave at the interruption.

Andrew threw his arms up in supplication. "Wait, please wait. I was not interrupting you. I am just overwhelmed." He waved his hands in the air. "Please, continue, I apologize."

Mollified somewhat, Jim continued. "Like you, like all white people, the white part of me dismissed the stories of my grandfather as poppycock. Oh, I enjoyed hearing them, because they were interesting stories to hear. He obviously believed fervently in the stories that he related all of his adult life. I now believe them, too. When I entered that cave and saw what was in there, my mind retreated to some other place. I have no memory of the rest of that day. The reason I am so certain about his identity, is because I was with the spirit of this long-dead man and with the gods of his past for a brief time in that cave. The connection is so vivid that I think it is possible that I am related to him in some way, that we have a kinship that crosses time."

Andrew sat wordless for a time, occasionally glancing at his friend, trying to assimilate the impossible.

"Have you ever had your DNA tested? That would tell you if your hypothesis is possible."

"Yes, I have, and yes, I have the Y-chromosome, Norse haplo-group marker R1A1."

"Could that have come from your mother?"

"No, it had to come from a male. My father carried that marker. So, you see Andrew, at some point in the distant past, a male relative of mine was at least part Norse. My grandfather also related a legend about a pale-skin warrior that became a famous war chief of my people. Perhaps he passed this marker to me."

"This is truly incredible, Jim. I can see that you believe every detail of this legend, but it is so far-fetched that I am having difficulty accepting it without further examination of the remains, if then."

"That will never happen, Andrew, believe what I say to you. That man is my ancestor and I will never reveal his final resting place to anyone." The intensity of his feeling was obvious, broaching no further discussion on the subject.

Andrew said not a word; the very idea posed by Jim had stolen his thought processes.

"While you are pondering all of this, I have one more part of the legend of Death Wind for you. For me it was the clincher." He grinned slightly at his friend, pausing for effect.

"Death Wind always ran the forest in the company of a gray wolf."

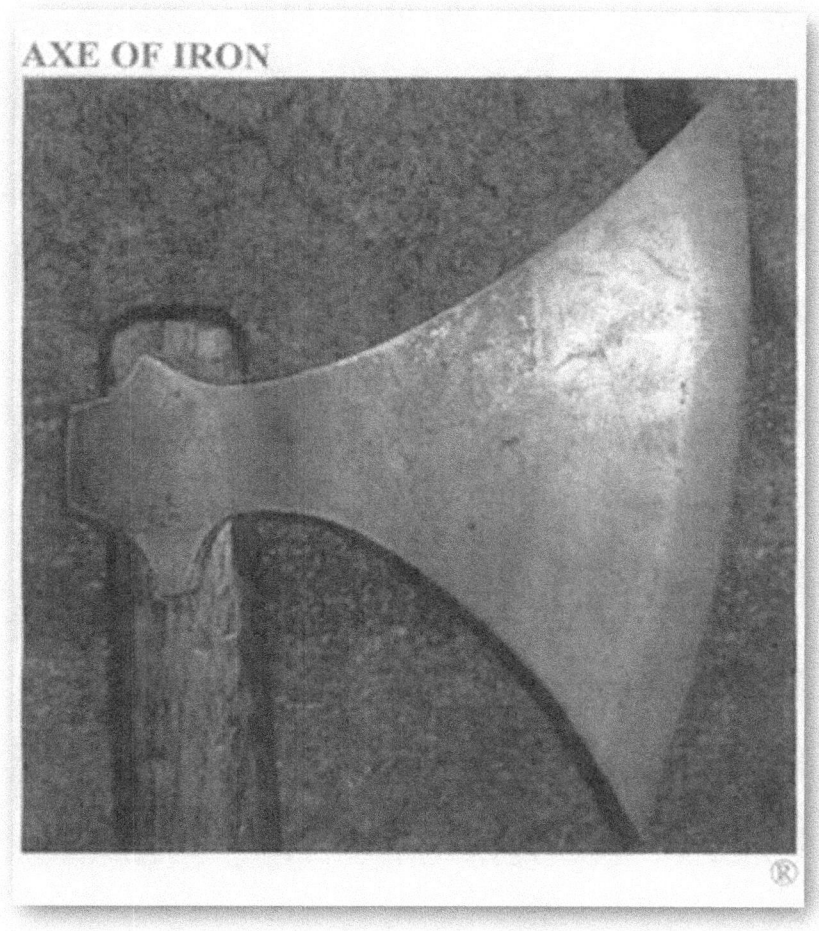

AXE OF IRON

AUTHOR'S POSTSCRIPT

NOTE ABOUT THE INDIAN LEGEND OF DEATH WIND

My idea for the Haudenosaunee legend of Death Wind came from the life and times of Lewis Wetzel, a real man of the colonies that lived in the 18th century. His adult life became a vendetta against the local Indians of the wild frontier of what are now northern West Virginia and the Ohio Valley.

Little substantive information exists about him, except that he killed Indians. That fact fit right into my needs for this novel.

The paucity of information about Wetzel gave me all the leeway required to assign the protagonist of my Axe of Iron series, Gudbjartur Einarsson, the mantle of this legendary Indian killer from the early days of the American colonies.

For those readers interested in such things, I offer the following reference.

LEWIS WETZEL

"Lewis Wetzel was a well-known and controversial frontiersman who lived in the Ohio Country in the years of the American Revolution and the early nation.

Wetzel is believed to have been born in 1763 although sources of information about his early and later life do not always agree. His family moved to the Ohio River Valley in the area that is now part of the northern panhandle portion of West Virginia in 1770. At least one member of his family was killed by American Indians. Wetzel and his brother were captured by American Indians in 1777 but managed to escape to Fort Henry (now Wheeling, West Virginia).

Lewis Wetzel became notorious for his violence against American Indian peoples in the Ohio Country. His actions compounded the already high tensions between the region's American Indians and the white settlers who continued to pour into the Ohio Country -- which was supposed to be reserved as American Indian territory. Wetzel did not care for military discipline and often acted as a lone assailant.

Having mastered the technique of reloading a single shot flintlock rifle on a dead run, Wetzel was feared as a man whose weapon never seemed to be empty. Some American Indian peoples in the region came to call him "Deathwind".

Accused by General Josiah Harmar of the murder of several peaceful American Indian groups in 1788, Wetzel was held in Marietta but escaped before trial. It is not known with any certainty how Wetzel spent his last years. He is believed to have died in Mississippi at the home of a relative in 1808.

Wetzel County, West Virginia is named for Lewis Wetzel."

From Ohio History Central: http://www.ohiohistorycentral.org/w/Lewis_Wetzel

ARCHAEOLOGIST, DR. ANDREW NORIN

Although fictitious, I felt comfortable using the name Andrew Norin because he was my maternal great, great grandfather from Hudiksvall, Sweden, who took ship to America in the 1870's. All of which is meaningless to anyone but me.

GLOSSARY

NORSE TERMS

Aesir – the principle gods of Teutonic mythology, Odin, Thor, Tyr, Balder, Forseti, Heimdall, etc.

Brattahlid – the farmstead of Eirik the Red near the inland end of Eiriksfjord, Greenland.

Einvigi - duel to the death. Challenger chooses the weapons. Usually swords and shields but can also be knives. Usually fought on hides staked to the ground, with both men clenching a length of leather strap in their teeth.

Eiriksfjord – site chosen by Eirik the Red, in 986, for the first of the two known medieval Norse settlements on Greenland's southwest coast.

Freemen - largest social order among the Norse. Men capable of owning land. Women could be free but could not vote or own land.

Frey – god of fertility, crops, peace, and prosperity.

Freya - goddess of love. Sister of Frey.

Frost Giants - populated Niflheim, a world of cold, frost, mist, and ice.

Furdustrandir - wonder Beach or Marvel Strand. Thought to be the forty-mile stretch of white sandy beach located south of Cape Porcupine, Labrador, Canada.

Gotar - people of Gotland. One of the two main Germanic tribes, the other being the Svear, which became modern Sweden.

Hel - goddess of death and the ruler of the realm of the dead. Daughter of Loki, who rules the abode of the dead. Hel lives among the roots of the world-tree, Yggdrasil, and has the appearance of a rotting corpse.

Helluland - flat stone land, Baffin Island, Canada.

Leifsbudir - Leif's Booths or Leif's Camp. Found in 1962 on the north-eastern tip of Newfoundland, Canada, by Helge and Anne-Stine Ingstad, of Norway. Carbon dated artifacts from the site indicate an approximate date of AD 1000. It remains the only substantiated Norse settlement site ever discovered in North America.

Loki - god of discord and mischief. At Ragnarok, the twilight of the gods, he will lead forth the hosts of Hel.

Lysufjord — the second of the two known Norse settlements on Greenland was located on the southwest coast about 400-miles north of Eiriksfjord.

Markland - woodland, Labrador, Canada.

Mead — a fermented, alcoholic combination of honey and water favored by many Germanic tribes.

Niflheim — a cold land in the north; the abode of fog, frost, and ice. One of the nine worlds of Norse mythology.

Njord - god of winds, navigation, and the sea. Father of Frey and Freya.

Nordsettir - northern hunting grounds of Greenland. The region along the northwest coast as far as 80° north latitude in waters free of pack ice during the Medieval Warm Period.

Odin - god of war, wisdom, and poetry. The Valkyries attend him in the Hall of Slain Warriors - Valhalla.

Otherworld - world after death.

Ragnarok - twilight of the gods. The final battle between the gods and their enemies that leads to the destruction of mankind.

Skyr, Skyrr - mildly fermented drink made from the curds of soured milk. A high protein, nutritious drink favored by Norse people.

Steerboard - large oar secured on the right aft side of the ship; a combination rudder and keel. Possibly the origin of the term starboard, or right side of a boat or ship.

Svealand - land of the Svear, one of the Germanic tribes that became modern day Sweden, the other main tribe being the Gotar.

Sweep - large, long oar, used to propel a ship in calm wind or close quarters. Usually plied from a standing position, the long sweeps were thrust out through holes spaced equidistant along a plank below the ship's rail.

Thing - the *h* is silent, thus literally *Ting*. An annual assembly that served as the governing body of Norse society, at which any Freemen could bring their concerns before the chieftain, or lawspeaker, for the rule of law. Although women could be heard at a *Thing*, they had no vote.

Thingvellir - literally "Parliament Plains" - the site of the Norse Althing general assembly on Iceland.

Thor - god of the sky and thunder. Thor may have been the favorite of all Norse gods. His hammer was a much-favored amulet worn by both men and women. As in any Germanic combination of *th*, the *h* is silent, thus literally *Tor*.

Thrall - slave or chattel of a chief or freeman. Not a Norse word, therefore the *h* is pronounced.

Trencher - a wooden serving platter of various sizes to fit the task at hand, usually with carrying handles at either end.

Underworld - realm below the surface of the earth in which the spirits of the dead reside.

Valhalla - Odin's Hall of the Slain in the Underworld where the Valkyries take the heroes killed in battle.

Valkyries - handmaidens of Odin, who select the heroes from the field of battle and transport them to Valhalla.

Vinland - an area somewhere in southeastern Canada or the northeastern U.S. Disagreement and conjecture surrounds both the meaning of the name and the location of the place.

Wadmal - tightly woven wool cloth used for clothing; also panels sewn together to make sails and tents. Virtually waterproof due to the tightness of the weave.

Yggdrasil - horse of Yggr, that is, Odin. A giant ash tree, the world-tree of Norse mythology. Odin impaled himself on a spear and hung from the world-tree for nine days to discover the secret of the runes. Believed to be supported by three main roots: one each in Asgard, the realm of the gods, Niflheim, the realm of the dead, and Jotenheim, the realm of giants in the earth. An eternal tree will survive Ragnarok.

Sources:

Webster's New International Dictionary, (G & C Merriman Co. Springfield, MA, 1948)

John Haygood, *Encyclopedia of the Vikings*, (Thames and Hudson, Inc. New York, NY, 2000).

NATIVE TERMS

Algonquin, Algonquian – a reference to both the largest Indian language group in North America and any member tribe of that group, e.g. – Cree, Ojibwe, Chippewa, Potawatomi, Ottawa, etc. The range of Algonquin speaking people includes almost all of eastern Canada and much of the north central United States. They are the most numerous of all North American Indians.

Anishinabeg (pl.), Anishinabe – loosely translated as the 'original people or original human beings' or 'the people.' The pre-historical ancestors of the Algonquin speaking Ojibwe and Chippewa Indians. Bands of these native people occupied the lands around and to the north of Lake Superior. Today, they still refer to themselves by these names, often shortening them to 'Shinabeg or Shinabe.'

Beothuk – means "people" in their language. Pre-historical natives of Newfoundland and Labrador, Canada. Known also as the "red ocher people," for their practice of smearing red ocher over themselves and all their possessions.

Chippewa, Chippewa - members of the Algonquin speakers of Indians. The word Chippewa is considered synonymous with Ojibwa, i.e. – they are the same people. Usually referred to as Ojibwa in Canada and Chippewa in the US.

Haudeno – is the author's diminutive pseudonym of Haudenosaunee.

Haudenosaunee – "the people" or "people of the longhouses"; the pre-historical ancestors of the Iroquois Indians.

Kitchi Gami – literally, 'big water,' the Anishinabeg word for Lake Superior.

Longhouse – the large oval, timber framed, multi-family, birch bark covered house of the Haudenosaunee villages. A similar house was also used by the village dwelling Naskapi.

Naskapi – Algonquin speakers, the pre-historical ancestors of the Cree. Also known as Inyu or Innu. Numerous bands occupied all the lands north of the St. Lawrence River throughout the province of Quebec, Canada from Hudson Bay to the Atlantic coast.

Ojibwa, Ojibwe –members of the Algonquin speakers of Indians. The word Ojibwa is considered synonymous with Chippewa, i.e. – they are the same people. Usually referred to as Ojibwa in Canada and Chippewa in the US.

Orenda – the supreme, or Great Spirit of the Haudenosaunee; their principle god from whom all others are derived.

Otchipwa – this Algonquin word means "to pucker" and is a reference to the distinctive puckered seams of the moccasins worn by the pre-historical ancestors of the Ojibwa and Chippewa Indian tribes. Both of these contemporary tribal names are probably derivatives of this word.

Thalmiut – a pseudonym derived from Ihalmiut, "people from beyond" or "people of the deer." Native people of the Canadian Barrens who subsisted almost exclusively on the vast herds of barren ground caribou.

Tornit - pronounced *Dornit*. Also referred to as Tuniit (Tiniq-singular)Pre-historical people of the Dorset culture, a native people of Greenland and the Canadian Arctic islands. The Greenlanders encountered these people in the early years of both Greenland settlements before the arrival of the Inuit from the west sometime in the twelfth century.

Wigwam – a dome shaped, birch bark covered, timber framed house structure of indeterminate size used by several pre-historical Indian tribes.

Research Sources:

[1] *Wikipedia*, (Wikimedia Foundation, Inc. 2001)

Webster's New International Dictionary, (G & C Merriman Co. Springfield, MA, 1948)

Johann Georg Kohl, *Kitschi-Gami,* (Chapman and Hall, London, UK, 1860). Reprint with new material, *Kitchi-Gami* (Minnesota Historical Society Press, St. Paul, MN, 1985)